Barren Fields, Fruitful Gardens
Book 3

Roses at Sunset

Rachel Miller

ISBN: 1987529944

ISBN-13: 978-1987529944

All Scripture taken from the King James Version of the Bible.

In Loving Memory Of

My Dad –
You taught me to love, to lead, to learn, and to listen.
You believed in me when I didn't.
You held my hand, wiped my tears,
and rescued me countless times.
You were my first hero and the first man to give me flowers.
You caught me when I fell and forgave when I didn't deserve it.
I'm honored to be your daughter.

Dedicated To

The God Who heals the brokenhearted,
Whose timing is perfect,
Who is faithful to keep His promises,
Who has overcome the grave,
Who never leaves us comfortless,
and Who is *always* the same.

Acknowledgements

Special thanks to Jerry Hanley for letting three strangers crash his party so we could learn about the ghost town he loves — Maiden, MT. Thank you, Jerry, for your time, your tour, for answering our questions, and for a day we'll never forget.

I'm amazed so many people can read the same manuscript and still find unique typos, errors, and concerns. To each of you who has given your time to beta read, counsel, correct, and keep me on track — Thank you!

Anna, Cindy, Jessica, Marta,
Naomi, Sherri, and Sonia

Prologue

Red. There amidst the charred, brittle remains of prairie, almost hidden by the tangle of scarred, ancient sage, flashed a tiny glint of color. Wesley Close swung down from his saddle, squinting through the early morning fog. Maybe he hadn't seen it. Maybe he was imagining it. Maybe... No, it was there.

He dropped his mount's reins and moved forward, surveying the ground. Someone else had been here. He could see the impression of their horse's hooves. The tall rancher stooped, fingering the prints in the cold earth. With a grunt of confusion, he moved to examine the clump of sagebrush that had grabbed his attention.

"What do we have here?" he said, almost in a whisper, as he pried a torn scrap of leather from the branches and inspected it.

On one side, the leather was smooth, dyed a brilliant red, and polished. Like the rest of the fog-dampened world around him, soot covered the scrap and smeared as he ran his thumb across the red surface. One edge of the leather had torn away, presumably from something much larger.

Wesley's brown eyes rose to the western horizon. As far as he could see, the world mixed together in a blend of blackened earth and misty sky. The undulating earth hid the charred foundation of the school that had been lost in the fire. He thought perhaps, at the edge of the mist, he could make out the line of trees along the river that ran through the plains below him. Chewing at the corner of his mouth, he let out a soft, wondering sigh and turned his attention back to the ground.

The fire had started here, of that he was sure. But why? Why would someone want to harm the Edelman's ranch? And why had he never seen this scrap before? He'd been past it a dozen times if not more. Perhaps it was the fog. Maybe with the rest of the world gray, the red had been easier to see. Whatever the case, he'd found it now, and he must consider it part of the puzzle. Still, something bothered him about the whole scene, something about those tracks. Had he missed them too? He stepped back, examining them once more from a distance. He moved to another position. Something wasn't right. He'd have to give it thought. Other responsibilities were calling.

Wesley moaned, slipping the scrap of leather into his pocket and returning to his horse. He'd only seen leather that color in one other place, and the thought of it made his stomach churn.

Chapter 1

"There now, Miss, step lightly." Tom Dresden, worn from his journey and the wind that whipped about him, reached out a hand to steady
his only passenger as she moved about the stagecoach, gathering her belongings. "Be careful gettin' down. This wind'll knock you over if you're
not careful."

Jessica Bennett smiled down at the weary man. "Thank you, Tom. I
hope you boys'll get some rest before heading out again."

"Not today. We've got another three hours to go."

"I'm sorry to hear that."

Tom grinned, a twinkle climbing up in his blue eyes. "It's okay.
Takes me past home. I'll only have an hour to come back in the mornin'.
…Someone's here to meet you. He looks pretty excited."

Jess leaned forward to glance through the window. As her eyes
caught sight of the tall, dusty man standing on the boardwalk, her face lit
up with an exuberant smile. She waved, and the man stepped forward.

"Much better greeting than the last time you came to Grassdale,"
Tom said, his voice warbling with laughter. "I can *guarantee* that man
hasn't been drinkin'." Tom helped her down and stepped aside.

"Mr. Close! It's so good to see you!"

"Welcome home, Jess," the man beamed. "How was your trip?"

"Oh, I was well taken care of, as always," she said, smiling in Tom's
direction. Her gaze floated back to Wesley, and she paused, her face
scrunching into an expression of concern. "How are you, Wes? You
look…tired."

Wesley allowed a wry smile to creep across his face. He slapped the
stage master's shoulder. "About like my friend here. It's this wind. Beats
a man up, doesn't it, Tom?"

"It does at that! I'll be glad to get out of it."

"See you at church on Sunday?" Wes asked, shifting to put the wind
at his back.

"No. I'll be somewhere between here and Judith Basin. Tried to get out of it, but it can't be helped."

"Well, we'll miss you."

"I'll be back in a couple of weeks. You two have a good evening."

"You too, Tom." Wesley shook the man's hand and watched as he headed toward the livery, but then he started, spinning toward Jess. "What about your things? He didn't unload anything."

"This is it," she said lifting a limp carpetbag. "I brought home less than I took. Gave all my little gifts away."

Wesley sighed, his shoulders relaxing. Then his brown eyes twinkled with teasing. "Glad to know there won't be any more trunks to fit in that loft at home."

"You're safe there — for now. Did you come alone?"

"No. Travis is here somewhere. He's excited to see you, but the Tiedemanns got here first. He saw one of the boys as we were coming out of the General Store. I haven't seen him since."

The ever-present wind gusted and whipped between them, swirling dust up into their eyes. Both turned away from the wind for a brief moment.

"Let's get out of this wind, Jess. I need to stop by the bank and talk with Cale. Do you mind comin' along?"

"I'd be glad to."

"This Sunday's church services will be the first held in the new room at the ranch. We thought we'd have a few people join us for dinner. I already invited the preacher. Thought we'd ask Cale and Susan to stay as well."

Jessica's eyes brightened at the suggestion. Happiness flitted through her stomach. She hadn't come back to the strange, unfamiliar world that Grassdale had been three months earlier. Now, she had a place in this world. A place she had come to love.

❊ ❊ ❊

"What's this?" Cale Bennett sat behind the large desk in his office at the Grassdale Bank. He studied the piece of leather Wesley had just tossed onto his desk. Sunlight streamed through the windows around him, glinting in his blond hair. He held the leather up to the light, waiting for his friend's reply.

"I found it at Edelman's place about five feet from where the fire started," Wes said, stepping back from the desk.

"Just layin' there?"

"No, caught in the sagebrush."

Cale's eyes narrowed as he studied the find. "What do you make of it?"

Wes glanced at Jess, who stood nearby. "I have some thoughts, but I'm not sure I'm ready to voice them."

Cale considered his friend's cautious answer. None of this had been part of his plan. He wanted nothing to do with the fire, nothing to do with finding out how it had started, who had done it, or why. He wanted to put the whole affair behind them. But the parents of the children who no longer had a school, and the church members who had no church, and the town as a whole, which now realized how close they had come to losing everything—wanted answers. Situations like this had a way of digressing into strife and vigilante groups. He'd only agreed to get to the bottom of the issue to keep things from exploding. He'd insisted on choosing the men that would help him for the same reason.

"When did you find it?"

"That's what bothers me. I found it yesterday morning. I've been out on that hillside half a dozen times now. Why didn't I see this before?"

"Maybe an animal came through and brushed it into a place where it could be seen. Maybe it was too deep in the branches before."

Wesley swung his head back and forth. "No. Cale, I've been trackin' since I was a boy. The only signs of critters I saw out there were from horses."

"So you think whoever started the fire rode by and this caught in the sage."

"Seems logical enough. It's just...well, I've only seen that color leather in one place."

Cale's gaze jerked away from his friend to Jess. He eyed his cousin for a moment. He trusted Jess, but it never hurt to be cautious about how much people knew. "I think I know what red leather you're talking about, Wes. I'm not sure we want to go there yet."

"I don't want to go there at all. It could get ugly."

"Exactly. Have you mentioned it to any of the others?"

"I showed it to Dunn this morning, but he's a bit distracted right now. Things have been...*rough* at the ranch this week."

Confusion and concern drew Cale's eyebrows tight. "Everything all right?"

"We're handlin' it."

"Well, if we can help, let me know." He paused studying the scrap once more. "I'll put this in the safe with the rest of the evidence."

At this, Jessica's gaze shot up to her cousin's face, but she stopped herself before blurting out a flood of questions. She knew there had been conjecture, even before she'd gone home to see her family in Twin Pines, that the fire had been set on purpose. Now, they had evidence?

"I don't like it, Cale. Something isn't right about it." Wes was saying.

"Well, keep thinkin' about it. When you figure out what it is, let me know. I'll let the preacher and Henry Tiedemann know about it next time I see them. And I'll get back out there and have another look as soon as I can. Do you want to go with me?"

"Not necessarily. We've all been over it so many times..." Wesley's voice trailed off, and he ran a hand across his neck. "But then we have stuff like this. It just doesn't make sense. Have you found out anything new?"

"No. No one seems to have seen anything suspicious the day it started. I've talked with most of Edelman's crew."

"Who haven't you talked to?" Wes asked, crossing his arms and slouching into a comfortable position.

"That new foreman and two of Edelman's cowboys. They've all three been out with the herd every time I've tried to talk to them."

"Hmm. I've never met that foreman. Kind of keeps to himself from what I hear. What's his name?"

"Banton."

"And the other two? I'll talk with them if I meet up with them."

"Bishop and Cantrell. But, as I understand it, Cantrell wasn't even hired until after the fire."

Wes nodded. He gnawed on his lower lip as he considered the situation. "I've never met Cantrell either. ...I hate this business, Cale. I understand people are upset, but my gut says we're going to stir up more trouble than we're going to resolve."

"I know. I'd drop it in a heartbeat but for two things."

"What's that?"

"For one, the evidence. Someone started that fire. We know that for a fact. Someone cost the Edelmans their grazing land. They destroyed the school and your mother's home. Someone put men in the line of danger. Someone's actions injured some of those men and nearly *killed* you.

"If we didn't have evidence that it was intentional, I would drop it. But we do. I doubt they intended it to go as far as it did, but someone set that fire."

Cale stopped, trying to regain his composure and realizing for the first time how angry the situation made him.

Wes studied his friend, waiting for the other man to continue on to his second reason. When he didn't, the tall rancher shifted his weight from one foot to the other, his eyebrows rising expectantly. Still, Cale didn't go on.

"So, what's the other thing?"

Cale took a deep breath, frustration creeping across his face. He rose from the desk and started around it, his voice taking on a tone of annoyance. "I don't want this to turn into a brouhaha." He crossed the room, inspected the lobby of the bank, and then turned back to Wes. "Someone I've been waiting for just came in. We'll have to finish this later."

Wes shrugged. "I think we're done anyway."

Cale sighed, but then his bearing changed and he turned to his cousin with a smile. "It's good to have you back, Jess. Susan will be sorry she didn't get to see you, but we'll see you on Sunday."

Jessica's brown eyes lit up. "It's wonderful to be back, Cale. Give Susan my love."

"I will."

Chapter 2

"Wes," Jess said, stepping into the dusty street and whipping wind, "what's going on at the ranch?"

The rancher groaned. His eyes narrowed as he glanced around the street, dropping his voice to a near whisper. "Gray's been drinkin' again. Someone has been slippin' it to him when no one's lookin'."

"What? One of the other men?"

"Maybe. If so, that makes it ten times harder to deal with. They know — all of them — that we don't allow it on the ranch. It's the one thing—" he paused, shaking his head in disgust. "We've never allowed it. They all know it could cost them their jobs. Gray knew that when we hired him, and he just keeps going on. Should've let him go when—" Wes cut himself short, not wanting to have that discussion on the street.

"What are you going to do?"

"I don't know. He's the best man we've got when he's sober. I don't want to let him go. ...Let's go find Travis. I've had about enough of this wind. The sooner we get home the better." Hearing the discouragement in his own voice, he stopped mid-stride and turned toward his friend. "I'm sorry, Jess. I haven't given you a very happy homecoming. All this business with the fire and Gray, and now I'm moaning about the wind. Forgive me.

"The men are excited to have you home. They can't wait to show you what they've done in the schoolroom. To be honest, I'm so excited about it I got butterflies in my stomach when I saw the stage come around the corner. I think you'll like it."

A light had come into his eyes as he spoke. Jess laughed, finding it hard to imagine the tall, brawny cowboy with butterflies.

"I'm sure I'll love it. And, frankly, I'm just as tired of this wind as you are. It tore through the stagecoach something fierce all day. Where do you think we'll find your brother?"

"Ha! In the general vicinity of a peppermint stick."

Even with the wind roaring at their backs, the trip home was pleasant. Travis, as usual, peppered Jess with questions. But even he tired of yelling over the wind. At last, he burrowed down between the pile of lumber in the back of the wagon and a large sack of flour and went to sleep. Jess couldn't help but smile at the sleeping boy. He and her youngest brother, Danny, would be quite the pair.

"I'm glad you brought Travis along," she said as she turned back to the road. "I've missed him. I've missed you all."

Wes smiled, surprised to feel the butterflies again. He flicked the reins. "We've missed you too." He studied her for a moment. The wind had driven color to her cheeks and tears to her eyes, even so, her eyes shone. "Were you pleased with the outcome of your trip, Jess? Did it go as you hoped?"

She leaned back, blinking at the sudden change in the conversation, but her smile didn't wane. Instead, it dissolved into complete contentment.

"Yes. Thank you for suggesting it. Some moments were difficult, but I believe what needed to be made right was made right."

"I'm glad to hear that. How are your parents?"

"Papa's not doing well. He's still his usual loving, joyful self. Still prays as he always has—makes the same pathetic jokes he always has—but he's very weak. Marc was right. Papa probably won't survive the winter. I don't know how he could. I'm glad I went to see him now, when my heart is where it should be. I can't imagine what it would have been like to lose him and have all that horrible past hanging between us." She paused, meeting his eyes with sincere gratitude. "Thank you, Wes."

He smiled, but Jess could see the praise made him uncomfortable and hurried on.

"Ma tires easily. Marianne has been a big help. The preacher's daughter, Millicent, helps too."

"Good. I'm glad to hear they have help. How are your brothers?"

"Jon and Hannah are good. They're so excited to be having another little one in the spring. Jon insists it will be a boy, but Ma takes every opportunity to remind him that it could be a girl. She's convinced he'll be wrapped around that girl's little finger."

Wes chuckled. "Was your pa that way with you and your sisters?"

"I don't know. Maybe. I was so small when the war began and Papa went away. Mary wasn't even born until a month or two after he left. I was seven when he came home for good. Marc was five. He followed Papa everywhere. He would literally walk in Papa's shadow so that he wouldn't get too far away. Sometimes Papa would stop and let Marc run into him, just to remind him to watch where he was going."

She chuckled at the memory, but Wes saw a shadow fall over her eyes.

"How is Marc? He made quite an impression when we met at that auction a few years ago. I tried to see him again a couple years later."

"You did?"

"Yes. I was in the area, buyin' cattle from a few other men. But I couldn't, well…this is embarrassing."

"You couldn't remember his name, could you?"

"That, and I got lost."

"Lost? How did you get lost? It's a straight shot from town to our place."

"Well, it didn't help that I couldn't remember his name to ask directions. Besides, I wasn't coming from town. Anyway, when we met at the auction, he impressed me. I couldn't believe someone so young was starting off on such a venture as he was proposin'."

"You're not that much older, Wes."

"True. But I had the experience of workin' with my Pa and buyin' cattle alongside of him for years. Marc didn't have that. We had some good conversations in the evenings. So how is he?"

"He's all right."

"Is he?"

Jess looked down at her lap. She flicked an insignificant piece of lint from her gray skirt, noticing the thin layer of dust, which the wind had driven into the fabric. She sighed. "He's just… I'm worried about him. He's always been so close to my Pa. He's doing his best to be strong for the family, but I can see he's a mess inside. As long as the rest of us were around, he was himself—helpful, cheerful, encouraging. But so many times, when he thought no one was paying attention, I caught him sitting at the table, staring at Papa's bedroom door."

"Are you sure he wasn't thinkin' about something else?"

"I'm sure. I just wish I could do something to help him."

"You can pray. In fact, you may be in a better place to pray for him here than you would be there?"

"How do you figure that?"

"Sometimes when we're not in the middle of things, it's easier to pray because our strength isn't eaten up by the situation. I'll pray for him too."

Jess brightened at the thought. She was ever so glad that she'd met this man and his family. They always found a way to give hope, even when it required something of themselves.

"How's your Ma?" she said, "I was surprised she didn't come with you."

Disgust shadowed Wesley's eyes. "I didn't want to go into all the details when we were in town. Don't want people gossipin' about it. But, this mess with Gray has her exhausted."

"How so?"

"After the initial hubbub Gray caused, we talked. I told him I didn't want to let him go, and I gave him two options. He could either stay and quit drinkin'—completely—or he could go."

"What did he say?"

"He said, 'Boss, I don't wanna work for nobody else, but I don't think I can quit. Not on my own.' He said he was afraid to try, but if we'd help him, he'd like to stay. And that's where we are."

"He said that?"

"Yep. I was surprised, but he meant it. We told the other men what was goin' on and that if anyone sneaks anything into him, they're gone."

"How's he doing?"

"He's been a pretty sick man. I can't imagine how he was drinkin' so much that it would make him this sick to quit. ...But maybe it was what he was drinkin'. I don't know. At one point last night, it took three of us to hold him down."

"Was he better this morning?"

"Well, he wasn't flailin' around like he was last night, but I don't think he was any better. It'll still be a while before he gets back to whoever he was before this started—if he ever gets that far. I'm proud of Ma. She's done well. Especially considerin' how much she distrusted him in the past." He paused, studying his friend for a moment. "After you left, Ma and Dunn told me about what happened while I was sick. Ma said Gray went after both you and Travis. I'm sorry about that, Jess. Really sorry."

Jess waved the comment off. "God used it. If that man hadn't scared me half out of my skin, I might not have been so ready to let God back into my life when the time came."

"Just the same. Shouldn't have happened. You were at the ranch to be taken out of harm's way, not put back into it. Maybe we should've let him go then. I don't know. I'm not sure why Dunn didn't, except he was busy and needed Gray to take care of the livestock while the rest of them fought the fire."

"It's over and done with, Wes. No harm done. I'm just glad he's headed in the right direction now."

"Me too. ...I just hope he survives."

Chapter 3

Duncan Roe stepped out of the barn and waved in Jessica's direction as the wagon reached the space between the house and the barn. He turned, hollering something back into the barn's interior and then started across the yard with long, excited strides. Behind him, half a dozen men pranced out of the barn, waving, grinning, and speaking to one another in hushed, animated conversation.

"Jess! Welcome home!" Dunn called as he rounded the wagon to where she sat and reached to help her down. "It's great to have you back. Come inside. *We* have something to show you."

By now, the other men surrounded them, nodding and grinning.

"Well," she said, taking Dunn's hand, "we'd better get inside then."

Jumping down from the wagon, she followed Dunn up the front steps and into the house. Jess smiled at the men's nervous glances. They half-stepped around one another, attempting to see their resident teacher's reaction to the transformation of the storeroom and small bedroom behind it into a classroom. They were a happy lot of men, most of them big, burly, and ready to take on just about anything. And yet, all of them were somehow tamed by the quiet contentedness of the family that kept them in their employ.

"Oh, it's wonderful!" Jess exclaimed as she crossed the threshold of the new classroom. She clasped her hands together, and brought them to her lips, fighting back tears. "I don't even know what to say."

The room was far smaller than the one they'd been accustomed to in the school building, but it was cozy. The men had constructed new desks, which were positioned closer together than they had been in the old room, but not so much that they would be uncomfortable either for wiggling children or for the grown men that would squeeze into them on Sundays for church.

The two windows allowed in wonderful, southern light. The chalkboard that had been ripped from the wall in the panic the night of the fire, now hung prominently behind Jessica's bulky desk. The wind played with the light blue curtains at the open windows, bringing in the pleasant smell of blooming sage.

"Where did these pictures come from?" she asked, moving to a large picture that hung opposite one of the windows, "Paris, London, New York, and this map. What an amazing map!"

Wesley blushed. "They were Emily's. Didn't get here in time for her last school year teaching. I thought they should be put to use."

Jess beamed. "Thank you. All of you. The children will love it. *I* love it! And it will be ready for use on Sunday. That is only right. *That* should be its first use."

"I agree completely," Wes said, shoving his hands into his pockets.

The other men grinned at her pleasure, elbowing one another, and chattering to one another with satisfied delight. Wes and Dunn laughed at their antics. The Crescent Creek Ranch hadn't seen this much excitement in months. The men were nearly intoxicated with it.

When the men had gone, Wes glanced around the house, disappointment furrowing his brow.

"Dunn," he said at last, "where's Ma? I figured she'd want to show Jess what you two did upstairs."

Dunn's grin dropped into a frown. "She's down at the bunkhouse with Gray. It's been a long, bad afternoon."

"What's going on?"

Dunn strode to the kitchen table. He pulled out a chair and sank down into it, stretching his long legs out into the room and crossing them at the ankles. "More of the same." He sighed and glanced around the room. "Where's Travis?"

"I'm here." The boy emerged from the schoolroom, holding one of the many new books, which, to his delight, would now be residing in his own home.

"Go down to the bunkhouse and ask Ma to come up here," Dunn said. "Stop by the barn on your way and ask Carlson to spell her for a bit."

"Yes, sir. Then can I come back and look at the books?"

Dunn chuckled, knowing the books were no different now than they had been in the school building and that his brother had been through them a hundred times before. "Yes, you can come back and look at them, but if we need your help with something, we'll expect to get it."

"I know, Dunn. I just want to look."

"All right then, go on."

Wes watched as the boy ran out the front door and into the dwindling sunlight. Then he turned back to Dunn, his eyes leaving no doubt that he expected further explanation of what had been going on while he'd been gone.

Dunn sat forward, leaning his arm on the corner of the table. "Gray's been feverish all afternoon — chills, nightmares, convulsions. It's been bad. I'm glad Doc has been here. I don't think Ma could've handled it herself."

"Has she had any other help?"

Something in Wesley's voice struck Jess as odd, as if he thought his brother might have slacked off in this area. But if an accusation hid behind the words, Dunn didn't seem to notice.

He nodded. "We've all tried to help. The men had to put up with my cookin' for lunch. It was none too pleasin', I can tell you that."

"Well, that's a given."

Dunn shot an annoyed glower in his brother's direction, but then it broke into laughter. "They didn't complain."

"Of course not. They knew what they were in for before they even sat down."

"Wesley!" Jess exclaimed, trying not to laugh through her rebuke. "You shouldn't say such things."

"It's all right, Jess. I'm not one to fool myself into thinking I have any talent in the kitchen. Although, I have kept *him* alive a time or two. Still, breakfast is about the only meal I manage with any success."

Wesley guffawed. "Even that's questionable." The tall rancher turned away and went to the window. His eyes shadowed with concern. "Here she comes."

The room fell silent until an exhausted Anna Close stepped through the front door.

"Did you want something, Dunn? ...OH! Jess! I didn't realize you were back! How was your trip? How is your family? It's so good to have you back, so good!" The older woman hugged her friend and held her tight, her voice dropping to a whisper. "I have missed you so much, dear."

Wesley stepped toward them. "I thought you and Dunn might want to show Jess what wonders you've worked up in the loft."

"Of course we would," Anna replied, wiping tears from her cheeks. "Let's go."

Dunn led the others up the steep ladder to the small landing outside the loft room. "It's not an attic anymore, Jess, that's for sure."

Jess stepped into the room that would be her home for the rest of the school year and gasped. "It's beautiful!"

A set of lace sheers and the heavy, dark blue curtains she had used at the school graced the window. A small, well-built bed stood in one corner and beside it a rocking chair. A narrow wardrobe had been positioned on the opposite wall. To each piece of furniture some handmade item added a feminine touch.

"How did you do it? I've never had such a pleasant, homey room all to myself. It's wonderful. The curtains fit the window. The sheets and blankets fit the bed. I won't be tripping over them like I did at the school. There's even a wardrobe. I won't have to hang my clothes on a rope or keep them shoved in a trunk. Oh, thank you!"

"We wanted you to feel at home, Jess." Anna said, her eyes full of love and compassion. "You've been through so much upheaval over the past year, and we wanted to be sure that in this mess of men you had some corner to resort to for peace and rest."

"Anna, you have accomplished it. I never could have done so well myself."

"Well, with more than one woman's things to choose from, we had a broad selection."

"Abby and Tabby haven't used these things in years," Dunn added, "I think they'd want you to put them to use."

"It's perfect. And now, because of your hard work, I will have much less to do before the children come for classes on Monday. Thank you, all of you."

Dunn grinned from ear to ear. Wes watched with equal joy. Both men had sacrificed to make the little sanctuary. Dunn had given his time and energy. Wes had moved out of the house so the schoolroom could be built. He had also opened Emily's trunks to be sure their new schoolteacher had everything she needed. That had been the hardest part. Seeing his late wife's belongings had whipped up a storm of emotion, but he would have it no other way. If anyone was going to put Emily's things to use, Wes felt it should be Jess. Both men were happy. Their family was no longer spread across the prairie as it had been before the fire, and now that Jess had returned, their circle seemed complete.

Chapter 4

Marcus Bennett strode contentedly up the hill that led from the barn to the house. The lantern he carried cast a soft circle of light around him. The yard and house were quiet. The chores were done, supper and devotions were over, and by now, he imagined, all the children would either be in bed or seated around the table finishing their studies for the next day's classes. He sighed and smiled as he neared the front door. His heart was light. The day was ending, and it had gone well. He stepped over the threshold and inside their tiny home, bringing the smell of autumn with him.

"Markey!" Gretel leaped up from her seat at the table and hurried to his side, throwing her arms around his waist.

"Little Bit, why are you still up?"

"Mama said I could wait and tell you goodnight before I go to bed."

"She did?" he said, setting the lantern aside and stooping to look the girl in the eyes. "Well, I guess it's a good thing I wasn't gone long. Are you ready for bed?"

The girl nodded and looped her arms around his neck. She leaned her forehead against his, lining up their eyes so she could study her big brother's gaze.

"I love you," she whispered.

"And I love you," he returned. "Is your dolly ready for bed?"

She nodded.

"Have you said goodnight to everyone else?"

Again, the girl nodded.

"All right then, Puss, it's time."

She smiled, kissed the tip of his nose, and giggled as she scurried to the ladder.

"Goodnight, Puss," he called as she climbed the ladder's rungs.

"Goodnight, Markey!"

He grinned after her, watching as her pudgy, little legs carried her across the landing. She pulled open the bedroom door and disappeared behind it. Marc's gaze dropped to the table. Danny, Joy, and Marianne sat watching him, each with a book laid out in front of them.

"You're all lookin' very studious," he teased. "Are you about finished, Danny?"

"Yes. I just have one more page to read."

"Good. It's late. Hurry on to bed when you've finished."

"Yes, sir."

"Where's Ma?"

"She's in with Papa," Mary replied. "Did you need something?"

"I just wanted to talk with the two of them. You all seem content as you are. B'lieve I'll go see if they mind a little company."

Mary's blue eyes twinkled. "You know they won't mind."

Marc grinned his response. He tousled his brother's hair as he walked past, barely dodging the subsequent jab to the ribs from the boy.

"You're gettin' pretty quick at that, Danny. I'm going to have to be more careful."

Danny's brown eyes lit up at the thought that someday soon he might just get the better of his older brother.

Marc stepped up to his father's bedroom door and knocked. At his mother's invitation, he pushed the door open and slipped into the room.

"Evenin'," he said, almost as if they hadn't seen each other for days.

Cynthia Bennett chuckled, "Good evening, son. What brings you our way?"

"Oh, I just wanted to talk."

He strode across the room to the red armchair, which had once been his father's favorite place to sit. He sank into it and sighed, studying the older man as he did so. The man had regained little strength since the stroke he'd suffered two months earlier. His eyesight had never returned, nor the use of his right side. His right eye and cheek sagged, though not as much as in those first few weeks. Still, there was a peace about the man.

"How are you feelin' tonight, Pa?"

Jonathan turned his face toward his son, a lopsided smile pushing up the left side of his mouth. As he spoke, his words slid out in a clumsy manner. Marc rarely noticed the slur in his father's speech these days, but tonight it was especially pronounced.

"I'm a'ways glad fo' you to sit fo' a spell. A'ways."

"And I'm always glad to come sit. I've wanted to talk to you about something for a while, but it hasn't seemed to be the time. But…I think now is the time."

"Are you wantin' to get married?" Jonathan made the statement without a hint of teasing in his voice, but his wife saw the corner of his mouth twitch just the tiniest bit.

Marcus, on the other hand, missed it. "What!" the young farmer's voice cracked with surprise. "Where did that question come from? That thought never crossed my mind."

"It should."

"What?"

"Marc, you're not gettin' any younger. I don' want you marryin' yourself to this farm and wakin' up some day to find it's too late to start a family of your own."

"Pa, that's not—"

"I know. Tha's not wha's on your mind. But I wan' you to pray 'bout it, son."

"But, Pa, things here need tendin' to, and—"

"Marcus." The rebuke in Cynthia's voice almost startled her son. "I've told you time and again. We don't want things here holding you back from your own life."

"But, Ma, that's not—" he groaned in frustration, running a hand through his dark hair. This was *not* how he'd envisioned this conversation going.

"Marc," Jonathan resumed, "if you're waitin' for the right time here at the farm, it will never come. There will a'ways be somethin'. If you're waitin' for the little ones to grow up, you're a fool."

"What!"

"Sorry to be blunt, son, but think about it. This little one comin' in the spring…why, you'll be forty by the time he or she is grown. By then, you'll be so attached to this land…you won' know wha' to do with a wife, let alone how to find one. …Marcus, I'm not tryin' to scold. I wan' wha's best for you. I can' see you growin' old without a family of your own. …It would break you."

"Pa, I'm not waitin' for the little ones to grow up. I'm just…I'm content. God hasn't laid marriage on my heart, but He *has* put something else on my heart. And *that* is what I came in here to talk about."

Jonathan and Cynthia both sobered at that statement. Both had assumed that he'd come to talk about the harvest or the herd or something of that nature. Neither had expected this.

"I'm sorry, Marc. We've frustrated you. We... Your mother an' I love you. We wan' wha's best for you. Fo' today and fo' the future."

"I know, Pa."

Cynthia repositioned herself in her rocking chair, pulling her shawl tight. "What did you want to talk about, Marc?"

"Well," he said, finding that he needed to calm himself, collect his thoughts, and re-summon his courage before he could go any further. "Something's been on my mind for a while. Do you remember that preacher who came through a couple years back? The one who up and left without tellin' anyone where he was going or why?"

"Yes," the others responded together.

"Well, I saw all that he'd left behind and realized someone needed to finish what he'd started. I kept looking around for someone, waiting for someone to come, but nothing ever happened. Then I heard Preacher Nausbaum was coming. I thought once he came the conviction in my heart would go away because the need would be filled." He paused, letting his mind wander back over the previous months since the preacher and his daughter had arrived in Twin Pines.

"But?" Jonathan prompted.

"But it hasn't gone away. I know God wants me to do something about the needs I see around me, Pa. I think...that is...I've prayed about it and...I think He wants me to preach."

Cynthia gasped and tears pooled in her eyes. "Is this what you were praying about this summer?"

"Yes, ma'am. After we talked that day along the creek, the Lord made it very clear to me that this is the direction He's leading. I've wanted to talk to you both on several occasions since then, but it never seemed like the right time. Jess made me promise I'd talk to you as soon as I could. And, well, so did the preacher.

"Papa, I know I need to be taught by a man like the preacher before I can even attempt to preach or...or lead a church. I talked to him about it the night after Jess went back to Grassdale. He's willin' to train me, but we both know—we *all* know—that addin' something like that is going to take time and energy. I don't have much of either of those to spare. So, we're prayin' God will bring along someone to help out on the farm. Until then, we'll use whatever time the Lord gives us. ...I hope you don't mind that I talked to him first. I wanted to make sure he was willin' to do it."

"Mind? Son, your mother an' I have been prayin' 'bout this since before you were Gretel's age. We knew this day would come sooner or later. We've been waitin' on you."

"You have?" Marc's gaze darted to his mother who confirmed her husband's words with a teary nod.

"It's true, Marc. We've sensed the Lord had something like this for you from the time you were very small. But, if it's been on your heart for so long, what has held you back?"

Shame colored the young man's cheeks. His gaze dropped. "I didn't know how to go about it without leavin' the farm, and I *knew* God didn't want me to do that. I know you're going to think I was lettin' the family hold me back, Ma, but that's not it at all. That's why I didn't say anything. I didn't want you to feel that way. I know God wants me to take care of things here. I have no doubt in my heart about that. I just didn't know how to do both. When the preacher came, and I saw what a good man he was, I realized maybe I wouldn't have to leave to learn. ...I guess in the end, it's all a matter of timing."

Jonathan chuckled. "Usually is, my boy, usually is."

"So, you're not concerned about going in this direction?"

"Concerned? Marc, I'd be concerned if you weren't goin' this direction. No, the concern is the Lord's. ...We'll pray with you. The Lord will send help fo' the work on the farm. Someone who fits the family. ...Someone who needs us as much as we need him."

Marc smiled. Papa was always seeking ways to serve others. Even now, when he couldn't move past his bed, his heart wasn't on himself.

"Thank you, Pa."

They chatted until the moon had risen outside the room's large windows, the younger children had all gone to bed, and Marc could barely keep his eyes open.

"I think I'm done, you two," he said at last. "If I stay up any later, I won't be able to get up to milk in the morning. The kids will be late to school. I won't make it to town — the whole day will be a mess."

"Why do you need to go to town?" Cynthia asked, surprised that the young man would make a third trip in less than a week.

"Two reasons. I need to see if Tom brought any tack to repair when the stage came through today. And Jess made me promise I would send a telegram as soon as I had talked with you."

Cynthia laughed. "That girl has a way of getting you to follow through, Marcus Bennett."

"I know. I can't say no. I have a feelin', if they pushed, all of my sisters would discover my weakness. Then I'd really be in trouble."

"Your weakness?" Jonathan said, incredulous. "Wha' weakness?"

"Them! Every single one of them. I'd walk a thousand miles for them if they needed me to. If I thought it would help them in some way, or if I knew what they were asking me to do was the right thing. Like this. I knew. Jess didn't have to push hard. Jonah had already done that. Jess just found a way to bump me into action, that's all." His eyes brightened at the thought. "I'm glad she did."

Chapter 5

Jessica heaved a large stack of dirty plates from the table and started for the counter. Supper had been a merry affair. The men had been eager to hear about her trip and family. They'd pumped Wes for news from town and especially news regarding the fire, on which point he said almost nothing. They'd also filled Jess in on the happenings around the ranch, but she noticed they avoided one topic. The topic that came rushing back to her mind as her gaze rose from the plates and landed on her weary friend.

Anna sat quietly in her seat at the far end of the table, warming her hands around a cup of tea. She stared at some stain on the tablecloth, saying nothing. The woman raised the cup to her lips and sipped the hot liquid. Then she returned it to the table and rubbed her bloodshot eyes.

"Anna, you look so worn. Are you all right? Maybe you should go to bed. I can clean things up here."

A faint smile climbed in Anna's eyes. "Thank you, dear, but I'm fine. A bit weary, perhaps, but I'll be fine. I have to admit, I'm glad you're back. I'm not sure how much longer I could keep this up. I keep thinking tomorrow will be better, but I guess, we haven't reached that point yet. That poor man. He seems to have such awful visions—nightmares. It breaks my heart to listen to him. Muttering. Whimpering. Screaming. What drives a man to such a life, Jess? What does it? I'm certain he's not the sort of man that dives headlong into a life of debauchery. Something...something drove him to this." She sighed. "I'm not sure I want to know what it was, but I'm afraid we'll never truly help him until we know his past."

Jess set the stack of dishes back on the table and came to her friend's side. She admired the older woman. In the past, Anna had expressed her cautions about Ronald Gray. During the fire, they'd seen how deplorable he could be when he'd been drinking. But now, Anna sat exhausted, full of concern and compassion for the man.

"I wish I knew how to love the way you do, Anna. I know how you distrusted him in the past, but now that he is in need, that has melted away into love."

Anna shook her head, "It isn't me. I still don't trust him. It's grace, Jess, pure and simple. I know this is what the Lord wants us to do, so I'm doing my best. I just hope it's enough. He's in terrible shape."

Jess saw tears in her friend's eyes, but she wasn't sure if they were from compassion or weariness.

"It's been a long week, hasn't it? When did this all start?"

Anna leaned back in her chair and sighed, looking at the ceiling and calculating the time that had passed. "What day is it? Thursday? Yes. So, that means it started Monday afternoon, but it didn't get bad until last night. Doc's been out here since then."

"Doc! He wasn't at supper. Did anyone take food to him?"

"Yes. I saw Zane carry a plate down. ...Wait! That's it!" Anna's face brightened and she straightened in her seat. "That's it!"

"What's it? What do you mean?"

"That's how Gray got the liquor. Dunn was right. It wasn't from one of our men."

"What do you mean? Who was it?"

"Scotch."

"Scotch! You can't be serious. Why? *How* would Scotch do that?"

"It makes perfect sense. And it's a good thing we figured it out. Wes thought maybe one of our men was making that horrible homebrew right here on our land somewhere. But, no, this makes perfect sense."

"What?" Jessica's voice cracked with curiosity. "What makes perfect sense?"

Anna leaned forward, her weary eyes growing intense. "After you left for Twin Pines, Wes and Dunn moved the cattle to a different part of the ranch. They're further from the house but closer to water. Since they're further from the house, the men have been taking turns sitting with the herd. You never know when rustlers might strike, and they figured they needed to have someone watching round the clock.

"Monday afternoon, Zane relieved Gray. About two hours later, Gray came back to the house so drunk that he fell off of his horse when he tried to dismount. He had the bottle right out in the open where everyone could see it like he didn't care a whit what happened. ...Come to think of it, maybe he didn't care.

"Dunn, not realizing what had happened, ran over and helped him to his feet. I think he thought Gray was ill. When he got Gray up and realized he was drunk— Oh, Jess, Dunn does *not* tolerate drinking. He took the bottle, handed it to Amos, and walked a few steps away to gather his thoughts. I was proud of him. He remained calm, even though I know inside he was boiling over."

The woman shook her head at the memory. She drew in a deep breath. "Wes came out of the barn just then, and it's a good thing. Dunn turned back around and said, 'Ronald, this has to stop. Go sleep it off,' and we'll talk in the morning.' But Gray wanted the bottle. He growled at Dunn like some kind of animal. Then he took off in a full run, right after Dunn."

"He attacked him?" Jessica's eyes widened with horror.

"Yes. Charged at him full force, just like a bull. Knocked Dunn to the ground before he realized what was happening. Then he sat on him, pummeling Dunn for all he was worth. He was so drunk he couldn't see what he was doing, so he only got in one or two good blows—"

"That's where that bruise came from," Jess interrupted. "I noticed it as we were looking at the room upstairs, but I didn't want to say anything. In just the right light, Dunn has a bruise on the side of his face. ...How did they get Gray calmed down?"

"At first, Wes tried to catch hold of his arms, but Gray was flailing so much he couldn't get at him. Finally, he gave up and used Gray's own tactics. Knocked him clean to the ground, sat on him, and then drug him up here to the house by the collar. I think Wes thought he could sit Gray down and find out what had gotten into him. But what had gotten into him knocked him out before they got two sentences out of him. He passed out! Right there on the sofa."

"Oh, Anna..." Jess slid into a chair and stared back at her friend, "I think I'm glad I missed that. ...But, what does any of this have to do with Scotch Jorgenson?"

"Well, at the time, I didn't realize it was Gray's watch, so it didn't mean much to me. But about an hour before his watch ended, I saw a horse and rider passing by, out along the road."

"From here?"

"No, I was along the creek, gathering kindling. At first, I didn't pay him much attention; but then I realized it was Scotch, and I watched him go, wondering what he was up to."

"How did you know it was him? Even from the creek, it's still quite a distance to the road?"

Anna raised an eyebrow at her friend. "Come now, Jess, there aren't many men in this area Scotch's shape or size. Short and, well, round. Come to think of it though, he normally uses the most ridiculous, red saddle. He won it in a poker game somewhere. You can't miss it. But, I don't remember seeing that saddle."

"But, Anna, how does that prove Scotch slipped the liquor to Gray. It could just be a coincidence. He may have been out surveying the damage the fire caused to his property—the fire! Did you say his saddle is red?"

"Yes."

"Oh. Oh, dear."

"What is it, Jess? You're absolutely white."

Jess sank back in her chair and stared at the woman in front of her. "I think I know what Wes didn't want to voice to Cale today when they were talking about the fire. Oh, Anna, I know Scotch has his problems, but surely...surely he wouldn't stoop so low."

"Wouldn't be the first time something like this happened. Maybe not here. Maybe not with Scotch, but it happens, Jess. Why do you think the boys are so strict about that rule? Because they've seen up close what that awful drink can do."

Confusion drew the teacher's eyebrows together. She struggled to understand what the other woman was alluding to, but nothing from their stories of the past seemed to fit with this.

Anna glanced toward the front of the house. Seeing the front door was latched and that no one else was nearby, she turned back to her friend. Her voice dropped to a whisper as she leaned forward, resting her arm on the table.

"The men don't know this, and there's no reason why they ever should, but I think you should know. It'll give you a better understanding of our family. You'll be living in our house and, sooner or later, you're bound to wonder about things."

Jess leaned in close, curiosity fixing her gaze on the little woman before her. This was unusual for Anna. She didn't go around telling secrets, and yet here she was about to pull a skeleton right out of her own family's closet.

Anna leaned back in her chair and groaned. "Ah, Jess, it pains me to tell it."

"Then perhaps you shouldn't," Jess said, leaning back in her own seat and feeling a ripple of guilt wash over her at the thought of her eager curiosity. "I don't want to know something that will cause you pain either to tell or to have me know. Sometimes, it's best to leave the past in the past."

"Yes, sometimes it is. But this...this doesn't stay in the past. It lingers, always just below the surface, always on the verge of influencing decisions and changing plans and... It drives my sons to the sort of compassion that you see with Gray, while at the same time stirring a passionate hatred for vice and depravity deep within them. No, Jess, you need to know. ...How much has Dunn told you about his past?"

"Dunn?" Jess didn't know what she had expected, but this topic and the gentle, kindhearted man she had come to respect and admire didn't fit one another. She faltered before finally managing to say, "He... Well, he told me his last name isn't Close, that his family name is Roe. Which, of course, is common knowledge around here. He said his parents died when he was about Travis' age, and that you and your husband took him in as one of your own. He said he wonders sometimes if he was wrong not to take your name."

This didn't surprise Anna. She had known he would wonder about that, but she had also known that if he'd chosen to take their name he would have wondered later if that had been right as well.

"He's a good boy...a good man, Jess, a *good* man. But his father...his father was a different story."

The front door swung open, scraping lightly across the wooden floor. The women looked up to see Dunn entering the room and letting his gaze pan around until it rested on them. He smiled and came toward the table. Anna tipped her head toward Jess in disappointed resignation and then returned her son's smile. Her story would have to wait.

Chapter 6

Marcus slipped beneath the covers and sighed as his head sank deep into the soft, downy pillow. One step left. All he had to do was get to town, wire Jess, and his course would be set. For two years, he'd carried his secret burden. But now it was out, and it was wonderful. He and the preacher could begin. They could all pray together for the help they needed on the farm. They could work together to go where the Lord was leading—as they always had.

He sighed once more and rolled over, fixing his eyes on the ceiling. In the morning, he'd go to town straight from the school, stop by the livery, wire Jess, and talk to Jonah. Jonah needed to know. After all, he'd badgered him about this at every opportunity for at least six months. Marc chuckled at the thought. It would be good for that strain to be gone from their relationship. They always challenged one another, but this one had gone on too long. Now they could put it to bed. He wondered if he'd be able to put his mind to bed.

A soft tinkling sound caught his ear. It was the bell his mother had given Papa in case he needed something. Hoping to spare his mother, Marc tossed the blankets back and got up. He crept out of the room, through the common area, and into his father's bedroom.

"Did you need something, Papa?" he whispered.

"Did I wake you?"

"No, no. I was wide awake. My mind is spinnin' like a top."

"Oh, good. I didn' wan' to wake anyone, but I'm terr'ble thirsty, an' I'm out of water."

"Well, we'll just have to take care of that." Marc went to the small table that had been set up within reach of his father's good hand. He retrieved a cup from the table and went to fill it with fresh water. Then he returned with both the cup and a pitcher in hand.

"Here you go, Pa. Drink as much as you need, and I'll fill it back up."

Marc helped his father take hold of the cup and watched through the darkness as the man sipped the refreshing water. Jonathan's hand trembled, and Marc reached out to steady it. When the man had finished, Marc refilled the cup, setting it back on the table.

"Was there anything else, Pa?"

Jonathan hesitated. He cleared his throat and took a deep breath. "Marcus, I was wrong."

"Wrong? What are you talkin' about?"

"Sit down for a minute."

"Okay." Marc set the pitcher aside and dropped into his mother's rocker.

"I shouldn't have pushed the way I did earlier. I'm sorry 'bout that. God will lead you in His time — is a'ready leadin' you in His time — not mine. I wan' the best for you, but it's not my job to decide wha' tha' is. Tha's between you and God. ...You're a man, not a boy. God has given you discernment..an' wisdom. I need to keep my nose out of things."

"Pa. You didn't have your nose where it didn't belong. If I'd told you sooner what's been on my heart, you wouldn't have had to guess how God was leadin'."

"Jus' the same, it's between you and God. You know my heart in the matter. I hope you'll stay open to the idea of marriage, but I won't push any further. ...But... Why was it so upsettin' to you?"

"It shouldn't have been, and I know it."

"Then why was it?"

"I guess...well...two reasons. One, I had come to talk about something else, and that was so far from what I wanted to talk about. It's taken me months to get up the courage to voice what's been on my heart. When I finally did, the train fell off the tracks before it got out of the station."

"I'm sorry."

"It's all right, Pa. I've said it now, and I think we're all happy with where things were left."

"Yes. Very happy. ...Wha' was the second reason?"

Marc sighed. "You were the third person this week to ask me if I'm gettin' married. The other two assumed I was gettin' married and leavin' the farm."

"So I wasn't the first person to derail your train."

"Exactly. But it... I don't know, it sets me on edge."

"What does?"

"People suggestin' that I should be married by now and pushin' for it to happen."

"They were pushin'?"

"Not exactly, but they were making strong suggestions. Especially Mary. She was hopin' I had plans and, at the same time, scared to death that I was leavin' the farm. That in itself is reason enough for me to wait."

"Wait? Wha' do you mean?"

"I can't go off and leave everyone, Pa. This is where I'm needed. If I leave— It wouldn't work."

"Who said you had to leave the farm so you could get married? I'm sure tha's not the only option, Marc. Did you know—" a chuckle cut the man's question short. "Did you know your mother an' I lived in a lean-to at the back of my father's barn?"

Marc laughed. "Yes, I do remember you talkin' about that."

"Her father wasn't happy with me, bu' we made do until I finished buildin' our house. None of you children ever suffered fo' our six months of barn livin'. Jesus was born in a stable, so…"

"So you're saying I should find some sweet, little gal and move her into the barn?" Marc said, barely managing to keep his voice under control.

The older man joined in his son's laughter. "No, no. I'm sayin' we have 'nough land fo' you to build your own home, or expan' this one—or both fo' tha' matter. …I don' want you to be so fixed on the way things are…tha' you forget to consider the way things could be. …Use your imagination. …Look how things can grow, no' just the farm an' the herd but also you an' this family. …You're a good farmer, but you'll be a good husband and father too."

Marc sobered. He wished he shared the confidence his father expressed. He swallowed hard and cleared his throat.

"Pa, all this talk about marriage…am I missin' something? Is something goin' on that I should be seein'?"

"Wha' do you mean?"

"I don't know. That's why I'm askin'. I'm not aware of any reason— why now, of all times—this should be so important to everyone. Did I do something, or say something? Did I miss something?"

"I don't think so. I think your sisters—I'm guessing Jess was the other one—they probably sensed you were uneasy 'bout something.

They sensed you were leanin' toward making a change, a big one. ...Women a'ways think of marriage first. Marriage and babies."

"Babies! We've already got enough going on there in this family."

Jonathan laughed. "Your sisters love you, Marc. I love you. We want you to be happy. ...None of us want you to be so consumed with carin' fo' us tha' you forget 'bout your own life. ...I would never tell you whom to marry, Marcus, never. But I will tell you this. ...Good choices are rare in these parts. Women are rare in these parts. ...Righ' now, I can think of at least two very good choices...right here in Twin Pines, but they may no' a'ways be there. ...If you wait too long, someone else will see their value. You'll miss your chance."

Marc wasn't sure how to respond. He fidgeted with a bit of dry skin on his knuckle, and then looked up at his father. He couldn't voice what he was actually feeling. He knew he couldn't take that step as long as their world balanced so precariously on the older man's failing health. His heart couldn't open itself to love when it was bracing itself for loss.

"Jus' be open to the Lord's leadin', Marc. I know you have other things on your mind and in your plans, but don' close the door on havin' your own family unless God shows you tha's what He wants you to do."

"I won't. I promise."

"Tha's all I needed to hear, son. I trust you to do the right thing when the time comes."

"Thanks, Pa."

"I suppose I haven't calmed your thoughts any."

"No, but I'm glad we talked. I'm glad we understand each other. Pa, I'm sorry I didn't tell you sooner what I've been prayin' about. I thought it would cause everyone concern, but now...now I'm happy we're all prayin' and movin' in the same direction."

"I've been prayin' tha' way for eighteen or nineteen years. You jus' didn' know."

Marc stared through the darkness, considering the other man. "Pa, how did you know? How did you know to pray that way?"

"I don' know, Marc. We saw somethin' different in you than we saw in the other children. You all have unique ways 'bout you. ...Take Jon, for instance, tha' boy was a'ways fixin' things an' tryin' to figure out how things worked. One day, Jess got somethin' in her eye. ...They were both very young. I remember Jon watchin' as I tried to help your sister. He inspected her eyelid an' her eyelashes. He asked me questions 'bout the color of her eyes an' the pupils an' tears. 'Where do the tears come from?' he kept askin'. …It was a moment of awakenin' for him. From tha' moment on, he kept learnin' all he could 'bout how our bodies work an' how to heal them when we're hurtin'. …We weren't surprised when he told us he wanted to be a doctor."

"What do you see in the others? I want to encourage them and pray for them in the best way possible. What do you see in each of them?"

Jonathan pondered the question. "Maybe I should ask you tha' question. You're the one who's with them day in an' day out. Do you watch fo' their strengths an' interests?"

"I try to."

"Well then, wha' do you see?"

Marc squirmed. He cleared his throat. "Well… Jess… I've always seen Jess as perfectly suited for her work as a teacher, but after this visit…" his voice trailed off with uncertainty.

"Yes?"

"After this visit, I saw for the first time what a strength she could be to a family of her own. There's something in her of the strength I see in Ma. When she isn't focused on herself, she has a way of liftin' a man right out of whatever mud he's wallowin' in. I don't know how or where, but I believe God can use that."

"I agree. I've thought fo' a long time tha' she would make a fine wife fo' a man whose purpose reaches beyond the day-to-day."

"What do you mean?"

"Some men get up each mornin', do their work, enjoy their family, and go to bed. They start over the next day with no thought tha' there could be somethin' more. Other men get up and go to their work with the purpose of changin' lives. Maybe their own, maybe their family's, maybe their neighbor's, maybe even a stranger's. Tha's the kind of man your sister would support well. …What about Mary?"

"Ah, Merry Girl. You know I've always thought she was incredibly cheerful. She sees beauty in almost everything, but especially in people. Especially in the people others disdain. She loves them, makes them feel special. I've never seen her reject anyone. She is loyal, faithful, diligent. She loves children. She loves the Lord. She wants to do what He wants her to do, Pa. He has something special for her and all those traits will somehow be a part of it. …And I'm afraid."

"Afraid? Afraid of what?"

"Afraid that whatever it is will take her away from here…from us. …Huh. …I sound like her now. She was afraid I was leavin'. Now, I'm sittin' here confessin' that I'm afraid she'll leave. I don't know what I'd do without her, what any of us would do without her. But I'd never hold her back. Not from what God has for her." He sighed. "Maybe this is why I never consider marriage. I don't want to say goodbye to anyone."

Jonathan laughed at the sudden melancholy in his son's voice. "I think you better go to bed b'fore you star' gettin' sappy."

Marc chuckled. "But what about the others? We still have four more to go."

"We can have that conversation another time. For now, you need to go to bed."

"Promise me?"

"Promise you what?"

"That we'll finish the conversation another time."

"I promise. ...Marc, I know you doubt yourself where the family is concerned. Don'. God will lead you. Just as He led you to the decision we talked 'bout today He'll lead you in the decisions you make with the children. Don' be afraid. ...Now, go get some sleep so you can get up in the morning, take the children to school, and get started with Preacher."

Marc grinned. "I like the sounds of that. Goodnight, Pa."

"Goodnight, son."

Marc crept back through the common area and into the bedroom he shared with Danny. He sighed as he crawled into bed. His heart was singing again.

Chapter 7

Jess pulled back the quilts on her plain, sturdy bed and smiled. After three days on the stage, she was ready to crawl beneath the covers and find out just how comfortable the new bed was. *Home.* The word flitted through her mind and warmed her heart.

She listened for a moment. The house had quieted, but the wind still gusted around the eaves outside the window. Its moaning made her the more anxious to sink into the warmth of that wonderful bed. A soft, rapping sound reached her. She wondered if a board had worked itself loose in the wind. The sound came again. Someone was knocking. She rounded the bed and opened the door a crack.

"Anna! Is everything okay?"

"Of course, dear. I hope I'm not disturbing you. I thought we might finish our conversation before I head back down to the bunkhouse."

"You're going back down?"

"I think I should. I'm sure Doc could use a break."

"Can't the other men help since they're already down there?"

Anna shook her head. "They've bedded down in the haymow most of the week. It's quieter there, and they all have a day's work ahead of them tomorrow."

"But, Anna, you're exhausted. Maybe I should go—"

"No. Now, Jess, you've been on the road for three days. You need your rest. You'll realize by morning how tired you are, even if you don't realize it now. ...May I come in?"

"Of course! I'm sorry."

"Not a problem, dear. I am tired though, now that you mention it." Anna crossed the room to the rocker and motioned Jess toward the bed. "Sit down, won't you? You know, the boys need to fix one more thing for this room to be right."

"What's that?"

"They need to replace the ladder with stairs. Otherwise, we'll never get a tray of tea up here. How will we ever take tea together? Uninterrupted, I mean."

Jessica's tired eyes brightened. "I hadn't thought of that. That would warrant a set of stairs."

"Yes, it would. Ah, Jess, I'm so glad you're home. I won't keep you long, but you need to know the rest of the story. Dunn is a precious boy, but things like this stir something deep inside of him. He hides it most times, but this thing with Gray has been unsettling."

"Why, Anna?"

The small woman leaned forward, rubbing her hands over her knees. "Where to begin? I guess I haven't told you much about our life before we left England. My Charles grew up on a farm not far from London. He always imagined that would be his life. Growing the same crops. Raising the same herds. Bringing the family up on that farm, just as his father had. But shortly after we married, everything changed. A season of flooding hit the entire area, followed by a parasite that killed off much of the cattle. The farm couldn't support both his parents and us. Charles was forced to find other work. He hired on at a lumber mill and found he enjoyed the work. I don't think he had any intention of staying more than a year, but then Wesley came along.

"He'd been at the mill about five years when he met Ashton Roe. Ash, we called him. They were about the same age and were in the same position, both having lost the hope of their farms prospering. Neither of them knew where life was taking them, but both were unwilling to settle for anything less than the best course for their families. During those days, Charles and Ash started talking about coming to the territories in the American West. By then, we had two children and were expecting our third. The Roes were expecting their second."

Anna paused, shaking her head at the memory. "The Roes' child only lived a week. In the previous months, the two men had often talked about getting our boys together. Dunn was just a few months younger than Wes, and the men thought the boys would play well together. It never worked out, but they kept hoping for another opportunity. After the baby died, something changed. Ashton always declined the invitation outright. It confused Charles, but he kept trying.

"Ashton's parents never had much use for spiritual things. As a result, Ash generally ran from anything or anyone that smelled of religion—except for Charles. For some reason, he would talk to Charles. They'd been working together about two years when Charles told me he suspected Ashton was drinking. I was surprised at first. But then I remembered the stories of Ashton being late, missing work, or making dangerous mistakes at the mill. Things started to make sense. Charles tried to talk to him about it, but Ash always managed to get out of the conversation.

"One night, the sound of someone pounding on the front door woke us. It was pouring rain, but even with the noise from the storm, we could hear a woman crying out for help. Charles rushed downstairs to answer the door. I wasn't so quick, but I got there in time to see him hurrying a woman into the kitchen. The woman carried a child, a boy. He hung limp in her arms, just like a rag doll. The rain had drenched them both.

"Charles helped the woman lay the boy out on the kitchen table and began looking over his broken little body. I'm ashamed to say I couldn't take myself past the kitchen door. The boy was about the same age as Wes, and the thought that somehow, someday that could be my boy terrified me. I stood in that doorway with tears streaming down my cheeks.

"The woman was hysterical. Charles had to shake her by the shoulders to calm her. Finally, she pulled herself together and said, 'Mr. Close, please, my husband has told me over and over how kind you are. Please, help us. Help my little boy. Ashton didn't mean to hurt him. He didn't mean it.'

"Never before and never since did I see my husband go pale as he did at those words. This was Ashton Roe's wife and child. Ashton had done this to his own boy.

"Henrietta—Etta we came to call her—told us that Ash had come home drunk and angry. Etta said something that upset him, and he'd begun hitting her. It wasn't the first time.

"Even at that young age, Dunn had a heart of courage, a sense that he was here in this world to protect those around him. He climbed up on their kitchen table and jumped onto his father's back, trying to get the man to stop. Ashton became enraged. He jerked Dunn off of his back and threw him across the room."

"Oh, Anna! How could he?"

"It was terrible, Jess. How Etta and Dunn escaped alive, I never did figure out. How a man could be in such a rage to throw his own child with such force—"

Anna stopped herself, taking a deep breath to calm the angry trembling in her chest.

"Charles went for a doctor. When they came back, the two of them sat with Dunn all night. I sat with Etta. None of us could do a thing more than that. We simply had to wait and pray. My poor husband was exhausted by morning. And how would he face Ashton? For the first time, he asked me go to the mill and tell them he wouldn't be working that day. I wasn't surprised to learn that Ash wasn't working either.

"By the time I got home, Dunn was awake and improving. Charles went to bed for a couple hours. Then, when no one was looking, he slipped out to see Ash. I've always wondered what was said in that conversation. We'll never know now. Regardless, Ashton began to change for the better. I guess realizing he'd nearly killed his own boy humbled him. It took time. He failed often, but he never gave up. Not only did he stop drinking but he also came to follow the Lord with all his heart.

"Dunn didn't trust his father again for a long time, such a dreadful thing to see in a child so small. We left England the month before the Roes. Dunn told me years later that, on the ship to America, he finally realized his father had no intention of drinking again. The crew drank heavily on deck, but Ash did his best to steer the family away from it. Whenever it started, the family went below. Dunn came to trust Ashton then, but the time they had left together was so short. Both of his parents died on that ship. He arrived in New York alone. He's been ours ever since."

Jess stared at the other woman, tears trickling down her cheeks. She could say nothing. Never in her wildest imaginations would she have pictured that life for Dunn. She wiped her tears away but still couldn't speak.

Anna sighed. "Dunn has no tolerance for liquor. He's such a gentle, quiet creature most of the time, but when it comes to liquor he has no patience. Even the smell of it puts him on edge. It's no wonder. He spent so many years in a home controlled by its effects.

"Before we left for New York, Etta told me Dunn was still having nightmares about that night. It had been four years by then! When he came to live with us, he had nightmares of a different sort. He would wake up screaming, calling for his father."

Anna paused, wiping away her own tears.

"Dunn watched as his parents were buried at sea, just days apart. The thought of arriving alone in that enormous city terrified him. I still remember the fear in his eyes as he came down that gangplank. He was so little and so very, very alone. We knew immediately what had happened. The area around the ship was busy and crowded with people disembarking, selling wares, meeting family or friends. We left our children with a kind woman who was there to help the new arrivals and moved as close to the ramp as we could. Dunn didn't see us until he was right in front of us. When he did, he dropped his bag and burst into tears. My heart broke.

"For weeks, he woke up terrified, dreaming his parents were being put to sea and finding himself in that city alone. Strange how, in those moments, he longed for safety in the arms of the man he'd feared most of his life.

"Some of it will haunt him for the rest of his life. He never mentions it. There's no need to. But it affects his perspective on many situations, whether he realizes it or not. I think this week has been harder on him than on me. Working on the schoolroom and loft helped keep him occupied." Her voice trailed off for a moment as her thoughts drifted back over the week. "He slept on a bedroll up here one night."

"Here? In the loft?"

"Yes. He said he needed a quiet place to sleep. He was too tired to be kept up all night by what was going on down there, and he didn't want to sleep in the barn. I'm pretty sure he just didn't want to see it. Didn't want the reminder of what his father went through all those years ago."

"Oh, Anna, I'm so sorry. I'm sorry Dunn ever had to go through any of that. I'm sorry this week has been so awful for all of you. And I'm sorry I wasn't here to help. It's no wonder you're all so exhausted."

"Jess, you were where you needed to be. Don't apologize for that." A sudden smile brightened the little woman's face. "I do confess, however, that I am very glad you're back."

Jess started to speak, then stopped at the sound of the front door sliding open. She stood and stepped out onto the landing to see Wes and Doctor Schwarz tiptoeing toward the table.

"There's no sense in sneaking in," she said with a hint of scolding in her voice, "you've already been caught."

Wes looked up. A sheepish expression tightened the lines around his eyes, but at the twinkle in his friend's gaze, he laughed.

"Good!" he said. "Maybe someone will find us something to eat."

"I'm coming," Anna called from Jessica's room.

Concern swept the smile from Wesley's face. "I thought she'd gone to bed," he whispered.

Jess shook her head. "No, but she needs to. She's exhausted."

"I can hear you, you two." Anna stepped around Jessica and made her way to the ladder.

"Mrs. Close, it's time to rest," the doctor encouraged. "Gray has calmed. I've left Carlson and Amos in charge. I mean to get a bite and head back to the spare bed in Travis' room as soon as I can. You should get some rest too."

"You're sure things will be all right?"

The broad-shouldered doctor nodded. "I'm sure. And if it isn't, they know where to find us."

"Go get some rest, Ma. We can find our own snack."

"Didn't you get any supper, Doc? I thought I saw Zane carry a plate down."

Wesley's eyes narrowed in an expression of forbearance. "Gray got to flailing around and knocked it off the bed stand. We'll find something, Ma. Go on to bed."

The woman sighed. Her heart broke once more for the man in the bunkhouse, but she was too exhausted to express it. "I'm not going to argue hard. If you need anything, let me know." She turned and started toward her room, but as she reached the table she stopped and faced her son.

"Wes, when this is over and things have quieted, we need to do one more thing to make that room perfect."

"We do?"

"Yes."

Wes scratched his head, confused. "What?"

"Replace that ladder with stairs. It's the only way Jess and I will ever be able to take tea together without interruption."

The tall rancher burst into laughter. "Tea! How could we have overlooked tea! We'll get right on that, I'm sure."

Anna chuckled as her son came to her side and kissed her cheek. Then she disappeared down the hall.

Chapter 8

Cale Bennett swung down from his horse, pulling his heavy, leather coat tight as he stepped toward the blackened earth. The pungent smell of wet soot and grass blended in the cold, damp air. He squinted toward the west and the clouds gathering there. A soft breeze tickled across his neck, and he shivered. Winter would come early if this continued.

He let his gaze drop to the strange pattern that marked the fire's starting point. He could see from the burn pattern where someone had poured kerosene on the grass. The smell had disappeared in the weeks since the fire, but it had been strong the first time he and the other men visited this place.

Reaching into his pocket, the banker pulled out a small, brown package. He untied the string that held it together and unfolded the thick paper. Four items lay inside: a brass matchbox, a clump of wax, a scrap of leather, and a coin. By themselves, the items meant nothing, but together they were beginning to tell a story.

He picked up the matchbox and fingered its stamped surface. He'd never seen anything quite like it. On the front, the box bore the image of a small flower surrounded by tall grasses. The initials *ABJ* graced the back in an elegant script. Several matches remained in the box. Henry Tiedemann had found it ten feet from the place where Cale stood. Ten feet, he now realized, in the direction of the ranch buildings.

He replaced the brass box, laying it next to the lump of white wax. They'd found the wax by following the char pattern in the grass to the fire's origin. The wax had surrounded a perfectly round indentation in the ground. That in itself was suspicious. Now, he held the wax up against the backdrop of the surrounding landscape, making mental note of where it had been in relation to the matchbox.

He plunked the wax back into the package and picked up the piece of red leather. He wished now that he'd brought Wes along. Wes would have been able to show him exactly where he'd found the leather. They also might have found some clue to ease the concerns the scrap had caused the other man.

The last item in the package confused Cale. So far, he had no way to connect it to the fire. Since they'd found it outside of the burn area, he couldn't tell if it had been there before the fire or not. It certainly wasn't something you normally found lying around grazing land. And, it couldn't have been there more than a few months at most. He lifted the coin from where it nestled in the crevices of the paper and rolled it over in his fingers.

It was a nickel, one of the new ones that had come out earlier in the year. He was sure of it. He'd seen several come through his bank over the previous months. The face bore the liberty head, surrounded by a ribbon of thirteen stars. The back boasted a large Roman numeral V, seated in a wreath. But this coin was different from the others he had seen. This one was gold, and *that* confused him more than any of the other evidence.

He fingered the coin a moment longer, and then placed it beside the other three items. He folded the package once more, tied its strings, and slid it back into his coat pocket. Then he went to his horse and retrieved a pencil and leather portfolio from his saddlebag.

He sketched out the black landscape around him, noting where they'd found the wax and the coin. He calculated the approximate distance from the wax to where they'd found the brass box. But, before he could add it to the sketch, something stopped him. He froze in place, listening. There it was again, the soft padding of hooves through thick grass and the huffing of a horse that had recently been run.

"Can I help you with somethin'?" a gruff voice broke into the stillness. "This here's private land, and we don' take kindly to trespassers."

Cale didn't have to look to know the other man was armed. He'd punctuated his warning with the sounds of a rifle being prepared for action. Slowly, Cale raised his hands and turned to face the newcomer.

The voice belonged to a sloppy, soft-bellied, middle-aged man atop a spindle-legged gray.

"Well?" the man demanded, glaring down at Cale from behind the rifle.

"Not trespassing," Cale said. "I'm supposed to be here. Mr. Edelman knows I'm here."

"Who are you?"

"Cale Bennett. Mr. Edelman and several others asked me to look into what started this fire. I'm just doing my job."

The other man's eyebrows sank deep over his gray eyes. "I heard there was folks pokin' around out here, but how do I know yor one of 'em? How do I know yor not jes wantin' to stir up more trouble? Maybe you was the one what started it?"

Cale shrugged. "I suppose you just have to trust me. ...Or you could ask Edelman since he knows I'm here."

The man drew a grubby hand across his mouth, scrutinizing Cale until at last, he grunted out, "Where d'you work?"

"I own the bank."

"A banker? How's a banker s'posed to figure out who done this?"

Cale tipped his head to one side, considering the impertinent man. He wasn't gaining any points this way, whoever he was. But then, he shrugged off the insult. "Maybe I won't be able to, but at least we have a safe place to keep the evidence."

"Evidence!" the man screeched, lurching forward with surprise and nearly falling from his horse. "You—" He stopped, disengaging the rifle and laying it across the pommel of his saddle. A ravenous curiosity rose in his eyes as he returned his attention to the banker. His voice lowered. "You got evidence?"

"Maybe. But why would I tell you when you haven't told me who you are?"

The man leaned back in his saddle. "S'pose you wouldn't. I'm Corey Banton, Edelman's foreman. I seen you ride over that ridge and thought trouble was a brewin'. Seems yor all right though. We're all a bit jumpy these days."

"I suppose you would be. Were you here the day the fire started?"

"What?"

"The day the fire started, were you here at the ranch?"

"Sure. I was the one what spotted the smoke. Come out here to check on it. By the time I got here, the fire had done burnt five hundred feet out an' 'bout three hundred feet across. I rode back and called the others. We thought we was gonna manage it, but that wind come up, and it was off like a horse with its tail on fire. Reckon it woulda gone all the way to town if those boys hadn't used their heads when it jumped the river."

"I'm sure it would have. A lot of people would have lost their homes, maybe even their lives. Did you see anything strange that day, anything out of the ordinary that might have led to the fire starting?"

"The day it started? No. Well, I don' know. The whole week was strange."

"What do you mean?"

"I don' know. Seemed somethin' was afoot. Boss was real antsy…wound tight as a clock. I don' know what was under his skin, but he was on edge. I even seen him yell at his kids. He don' do that too often. The day of the fire… Is that right? …Yes, I think it was the day of the fire, Scotch Jorgenson showed up. He and the boss went to the shed back of the house and had words. Don' know what they said, but I'm guessin' Scotch was layin' it to Boss 'cause Boss took out a loan and ain't made his payments."

Cale's eyes widened at this bit of information. No one had mentioned this before. None of the other ranch hands had said a word about Scotch let alone Edelman's debts. Come to think of it, Edelman had never mentioned it either.

"How many payments is he behind?"

The foreman shrugged. "Don' know. Ain't none of my business, I reckon. All I know is Boss was more on edge after Scotch left than he was b'fore he come."

"How long after Scotch left did you find the fire?"

Banton tipped his face to the sky and the sun. "Maybe a couple hours. If I remember right, Scotch was here b'fore noon, an' I didn't find the fire until mid-afternoon."

"Hmm," Cale said, stopping to write the times down on the corner of the map he'd been sketching. "And no one saw anything suspicious?"

Banton shrugged and, for the first time, Cale noticed a slight shift in the man's gray gaze. He seemed nervous as if he were covering for someone.

"I can't speak for the others," the foreman said at last, "but I didn't see nothin'. We was all busy puttin' up straw for the winter."

Cale nodded. That was what the other men had told him as well. He sighed, feeling strangely tired of the conversation. "I still haven't talked with two of your men—Cantrell and Bishop—would either of them be around right now?"

"Cantrell's gone to town for supplies. I sent him just before I saw you ride over the ridge. But Bishop should be around. Cantrell won't be of no help. He got here the week after the fire was out. I don' rightly know why the boss hired him. With as much pressure as Scotch was puttin' on him, and now… Now the pasture's burned. I don' know as we're gonna have enough feed to carry us through the winter. Bad enough we're buyin' food for the cattle without adding one more man's mouth to fill too. B'sides, I 'magine Scotch'll be along to collect this place b'fore too long. Wants what's his."

Cale contemplated the man's words. Banton seemed rather loose with information most folks would consider private. A quick glance over the man's shoddy appearance, however, stopped that thought. Anyone as lazy as this man appeared to be in dress and personal cleanliness would be lazy in just about everything else—especially his speech.

Regardless, he had to consider what the man had said. The very name Cale and the others had been loath to mention had dropped from this man's mouth no less than a half dozen times. Cale groaned inwardly. This wasn't the direction he'd hoped this conversation would go. Not that he was sure which direction he'd hoped it would go, but this was not it.

* * *

Cale stepped into Edelman's barn, letting his eyes adjust as he peered through the long, dark room. A bustling at his elbow caught his attention, and he turned as Banton pushed past him.

"Bishop!" the foreman yelled. "Where you hidin'?"

"I'm not hiding, Boss. I'm right here." A tall, wiry man stepped out into the center of the room, dusting dirt and straw from his gloved hands. "Did you need somethin'?"

"This here is Mr. Bennett from town. He's the one lookin' into how the fire started. He's got some questions for ya. I'm headin' to see how the others is doin' mendin' that corral."

Bishop grinned and stepped toward the two men. Unlike Banton, he wasn't new to the area, and Cale's was a familiar face. He stretched out a hand to greet him. "How can I help, Mr. Bennett?"

Cale shook the man's hand, but delayed his answer. He watched over his shoulder until he saw Banton's shadow pass over the cracks in the walls and disappear.

"Bishop, were you here the day the fire started?"

"Sure was," he chuckled to himself. "I'm here most days."

"Where were you? What part of the ranch?"

"I was out with the others, gatherin' straw."

"Did you notice anything out of the ordinary?"

The smile left Bishop's eyes and his gaze dropped. He kicked at something on the floor. "Well, there was a lot goin' on that week. Some was stuff between the guys, some was stuff with Mr. Edelman and Scotch Jorgenson, some was just the heat."

"That sounds like a lot of 'stuff', Bish."

"I suppose."

"Can you be more specific?"

The man's gaze dropped once more. Cale stepped closer, lowering his voice.

"Brandon, this is important."

"My job is important, Cale. Winter's almost here. I can't be without work."

"True. But the church is gone. Anna Close's house is gone. Your boss lost his grazin' land. Men were injured. Wes Close just about died. If you saw something, we need to know."

Shame colored the other man's cheeks. Cale knew he was a good man, an honest man, young but upstanding. He hated putting him in a situation that made him feel compelled to jeopardize his own livelihood, but it must be done. He watched as Bishop leaned out around him to see if anyone was in earshot.

"It's not that I saw something. I just... I don't know. This place is a mess. It has been all summer. Things didn't go well at roundup time. I'm thinkin' Mr. Edelman lost money when it came time to sell. He took out a loan from Scotch last fall and couldn't pay him back this spring — or this summer. Scotch had been comin' out here about once a week, puttin' pressure on Edelman to pay up. Every time he came things got tense."

"Was he here that day?"

Bishop shifted his weight nervously. "I don't remember if he was here *that* day, but he was here that week for sure. And things got worse around here. We were all walkin' on eggshells. Edelman was rough on everyone, his wife, his kids, Banton. I tried to mind my own business and stay as far from it as I could."

"So you don't remember if Scotch was here that day?"

"No. To me, it seems he was here earlier in the week, but once the fire started we were in such a panic. Most of that week just blurs together."

"I'm sure it does. Anything else you remember that seemed out of the ordinary?"

"Not off hand, but if I remember anything, I'll let you know."

"Sounds good. Like you, I'm in the same place most days. Not hard to find." Cale laughed at his own joke, knowing it wasn't funny and appreciative of the smile he got from the other man. "Tiedeman, the preacher, and Wes and Dunn are helping out as well. If you can't make it all the way to town you could sure talk to any of them. Thanks, Bish. You've been a big help."

"Cale, you really think someone set that fire?"

"I do. Now we've just got to figure out who and why."

❁ ❁ ❁

"I thought this might help." Cale spread his sketch of the fire scene out on the table and leaned over it. Wes and Dunn joined him, curious to see what he had brought.

"See, here is where the fire started," he continued, "and where we found the wax —"

"Wax?" Jess said as she left the schoolroom. "You found wax at the fire?"

The three men looked up at her and then cast nervous, sidelong glances at one another.

"Did I say something I shouldn't have?"

"No, no," Wes said. "We all responded with the same surprise. It's just that...well..."

"It's okay, Wes." Cale straightened and faced his cousin. "Jess, it's going to be hard for you and Anna to be in this house and not know what's going on. I'm not going to try to hide things from you, but I do ask that you keep everything you hear to yourself. People are already talkin' and makin' assumptions — some pretty wild assumptions. We just want to get this right."

"I understand. I can go upstairs if you want."

"No, there's no need for that."

Jess considered going anyway, but she was much too curious. She took a step toward the loft and then stopped, a grin brightening her face. "So," she drew the word out slowly, "you found wax at the fire?"

Cale laughed. "Come over here, so you can see what we're talkin' about."

Jess all but skipped to the table. She set down the pile of papers she was preparing to grade and stepped up close to Wesley. She smiled at the others, signaling she was ready and ignoring the rolling of the eyes from both Cale and Dunn.

"So, as I was sayin', this is the overall scene. Here is where we found the wax, at the front of this pattern left by the kerosene —"

"You think they used a candle to start it?" Jess interrupted.

"They did more than that," he replied, his voice rising in an indignant tone. "They used it to give themselves time to get away before it started. They pressed the candle into the ground and left it to burn down. As long as the wind was still, whoever started it would have had plenty of time to ride off without being seen. Or, if someone did see them, they would have thought nothin' of it."

"But don't you think they would have waited to make sure the fire took?" Dunn said.

"Not necessarily," Wes replied. "Anyone who knows Edelman knows that's his winter pasture. They hadn't moved the cattle yet, and weren't plannin' on moving them for a couple more weeks, just like we hadn't moved ours yet —"

"You mean *haven't* moved ours yet," Dunn said, annoyance clear in his voice.

"Well, we've moved them, just not to where we want them for the winter. But that's beside the point. The thing is, since that land wasn't being used there wouldn't have been any rush. If they set it and it failed, they could just come back and try again. Whoever started it was depending' on that to give them time to get away. The kerosene would get the fire going good, but there was hardly a whisper of wind to push it. Edelman and his boys kept up with it for a day and a half before that wind started drivin' it."

"True," Dunn conceded.

"So, really," Jess said, "anyone could have set it and gotten away without anyone thinking a thing."

Cale shook his head, absolute conviction crossing his face. "No. When you add together everything Wes just said, it can only be someone who wanted to hurt the Edelmans. Nothing more. They weren't aimin' for it to spread as far as it did. It wasn't angst toward the whole community. Someone was out to cause the Edelmans trouble."

"But why?"

"That's exactly what we've got to figure out, Jess," Wes said. "We could throw out names all day, but whoever did this had a reason, and when we find that reason it will confirm who did it."

"*Confirm* who did it?" Her eyes widened as she spoke. "You mean you already know who it was?"

Wesley shrugged. "We have some ideas."

Cale leaned back in his seat, crossing his arms over his chest. "We found three other things out there, Jess. Two of them point to one man. I was hoping it was just our imagination or coincidence. But, Banton and Bishop both brought him up this mornin' without me askin' about him."

"Who?"

The three men glanced at each other, hesitating. No one had actually said it yet. Once they did, they'd have to pursue it.

Cale sighed and groaned out the words, "Scotch Jorgenson."

"What?" Jessica's voice rose with incredulity. "You don't really think…I mean… He can be horrible. I know that first hand. But this? Scotch? Do you really think he would go that far?"

Wes ran a hand across his neck. He agreed with her, but that didn't change things. "With the way Scotch has behaved himself over the last few months, I don't know what to expect from him anymore."

"It was Scotch slippin' that whiskey to Gray," Dunn added. "And it wasn't the good stuff either. It was some home-brewed coffin varnish. Doc said it was a miracle it didn't kill Gray."

The others sensed Dunn's frustration building as he spoke. Cale's gaze grew intense. He drummed his fingers on the table, and for a moment Jess was stunned. She had seen the expression and mannerism in her brother, Marc. She wondered where, from which distant relative, the two men had acquired the trait.

Cale drew a deep breath. "How's Gray doing?"

The tension lines in Dunn's face melted away. "Better. He's not out of the woods yet, but at least he's gettin' a little nourishment and keepin' it down."

Cale nodded. "We'll keep praying for him."

"So what is it that makes you think it could have been Scotch?" Jess said. "You said there was evidence."

Cale reached into his pocket. He pulled out the paper package, opened it, and laid it out on the table for Jess to see. "Two things," he began. "There's this matchbox. I never would have seen a link between it and Scotch if it wasn't for the initials on the back."

Jess took the brass box and examined it, turning it over and studying every line. "It isn't very masculine, is it? I don't understand. Just because the initials end in *J* doesn't mean it belongs to Scotch Jorgenson. There must be a hundred other family names that start with that letter."

"True, but how many of them had a wife named Alma?"

Jessica stared at Wesley. "He had a wife?"

"A very long time ago. No one knows what happened. No one knows whether she is dead or just couldn't take life with Scotch anymore. When Scotch first came to Grassdale, he'd start drinkin' and Alma was all he could talk about. Then he went away for a while. Couple of years, actually. No one knows where he went or how he came into money, but he did. That's when he built his businesses. In the months and years before you came, he actually managed to be a tolerable character. The Scotch you've seen over the last few months is more like the Scotch we knew the first couple years he was back. Something set him off again, and I don't think it was your arrival, Jess. I think it started a while before that."

Jess considered what Wes had said, finding the story brought more pity for her former employer than it did suspicion. She reached into the paper package and lifted the scrap of red leather from its folds. It was familiar to her since she had been there the day Wes gave it to Cale. Now it pierced her heart a little.

Cale sighed. "There's only one place I've ever seen leather that color, Jess."

The young woman nodded. "Scotch's saddle. Anna mentioned it the other day when we were discussing the whiskey Scotch gave Gray. As soon as she did, I knew that was where this had come from."

She dropped the leather back into the package and groaned in disgust. Then she spotted the gold coin and plucked it up with curiosity. "What's this? I've never seen anything like it before."

"That," Cale said with great emphasis, "is a fake."

"What?"

All eyes were on the banker now, and he was none too worried about hiding his pleasure at the surprise the announcement had brought them.

"It's a fake. I don't know where it came from or how it made its way to Grassdale, but it is most definitely a fake. It appears to be gold, but in reality, there's only a thin layer of gold covering one of the new nickels. It's as fake a gold coin as ever there was."

"Well, I never." Wes took the coin from Jess and examined it. He pulled out the knife that he wore at his belt and cut into the soft gold. His eyes widened as the shiny metal flaked away. "Would you look at that!" He held the coin out to Dunn, who inspected the mark Wes had made.

Dunn gave a low whistle. "Someone was bold. Something tells me Scotch either has himself in over his head, or he's about to."

Chapter 9

Cynthia Bennett stretched and yawned as she stepped out of her pantry bedroom into the tiny kitchen. A second yawn shifted to an expression of confusion as she realized she wasn't alone. Marcus sat in his usual seat at the far end of the table. His Bible, several sheets of paper, and a thick book spread out in front of him. Cynthia glanced at the clock on the mantel. But, even without looking at the clock, she knew it was early. Marc had been there long enough for his candle to burn low. He yawned, rubbed his eyes, and then set his gaze on her.

"Still asleep?" he asked.

"What?"

"You've just been standing there for a couple minutes."

The woman chuckled. "I didn't think you realized I was here. You surprised me. Getting a little study in before you do the chores?"

"No. I've already done most of the chores. I'll have Danny milk when it's time."

Cynthia glanced at the clock once more. "Marc, why are you already so far into your day? What time did you get up?"

"I don't know. I just got up. I have an assignment to finish for the preacher before I head into town."

"Head into town?"

"Stage is comin' through this afternoon. I have some items for Tom to take with him, and I imagine he'll have a few to drop off."

Cynthia considered her son. Her mouth scrunched off to one side in displeasure, causing her cheek to dimple. Marc's decision to accept Tom Dresden and Shamus O'Leery's offer to help him build up his tack repair business had relieved the immediate pressure from the rest of the family after Jonathan's stroke. In the long run, however, Cynthia had known it would add pressure to her son. The extra trips to town, the deadlines—all of it. And now he'd begun studying with the preacher at his father's urging. Very many mornings like this, and he'd be struggling to get air at all.

"Do you need anything from town?"

"No." Cynthia shuffled to the table and sat down. "You bought everything we needed the last time you went. Well, the immediate needs. We still need to do our big trip to get ready for winter."

The farmer nodded. "I know. I've been thinkin' about that. I have a list of things I need around the farm, but I think it will be different this year."

The woman's brow pulled together in confusion. "How do you mean?"

"Well, as long as the road is passable, I'll be making trips into town. If the stagecoach is runnin', then I'll be runnin'."

Again, Cynthia's brow knotted. "Marcus, I don't like it. I don't like that any more than your idea of hauling freight for Mr. Judd at the mercantile. When Joe got caught out in that blizzard he was just comin' home from town. Just like you'll be doing."

"But, Ma—and I don't mean to slight Joe when I say this—Joe had been warned, and he didn't heed it. You know I'll be careful, and I'll be sure to travel with the right gear. That way if a storm does come up, I'll be able to hunker down. It'll be all right, Ma. The Lord will take care of things."

Cynthia sighed. "Why you children haven't made me completely gray by now, I don't know. Between you and Jess and Danny... My prayer life has certainly grown with each of you."

"If only three of us make you gray, I'd say you're doing pretty good."

"Ha! Believe me, it's not just the three of you. Did you know your brother went out on his rounds, was gone for nearly three weeks, left his family in town, and never said a thing?"

Marc shrugged. "I knew he was gone. I checked in on Hannah every time I went to town."

"Why didn't he say anything? Why didn't *you* say anything?"

Marc's eyes twinkled with the smile that spread across his face. "We didn't want you to go gray."

❈ ❈ ❈

Three hours later, Marc and his wagon rattled down the lane to the Nausbaums' home. It was a pleasant morning. A soft rain had moistened the earth overnight. Now, the damp fragrance of autumn hung sweet in the air. Marc breathed the fresh air deeply as he threw the brake and climbed down from his seat. He grabbed the saddlebag that had ridden at his feet and strode across the lawn to the front door.

He knocked, noticing how the door gave way and rattled in its frame. He'd intended the door to be a temporary affair. Then Papa had gotten sick, and the door slipped to the back of his mind until moments like this.

"Marcus!"

Marc spun toward the voice and the loud clattering that accompanied it. Millicent Nausbaum stood at the corner of the house. A washbasin and pile of dishes still rattled at her feet as she clapped her hands over her chest. She stared wide-eyed.

"Millie? Are you all right?"

"What are you doing here? You scared me half to death!" The pretty, dark-haired girl stooped and began gathering up the basin. "I'll probably have to wash these dishes over again."

A compassionate smile touched Marc's lips. He set his saddlebag down near the door and joined his friend and her pile of dishes. "I'm sorry. I didn't mean to startle you."

"I know you didn't. What are you doing here so early?"

"I have to get to town before the stage comes, but I needed to drop something off for your pa first." He paused, curiosity climbing in his eyes. "Are you still washing dishes out by the well?"

"Yes. That's why I didn't see you coming down the lane."

"I thought your pa was going to build a counter for you."

Millicent blushed. "He tried."

"Tried? What happened?"

"One end fell off with the first heavy load of dishes."

"*With* the dishes?"

"And two full basins of water."

"It flooded the house, didn't it?" Marc said, reaching for the last dish and placing it in the basin.

"Not the whole house. Just everything from the front door to Papa's bed." Millicent laughed at the memory. She rose, grateful that Marc had already lifted the heavy basin of dishes. "I confess, I screamed as loud then as I did when I saw you standing there. I need to work on this being easily startled thing. Come on inside. Papa's in the barn, but we'll get those dishes out of your hands."

Marc followed her inside the tiny cabin. He set the basin of dishes on the table, which all but filled the small space between the two curtained-off bedrooms. He brushed dirt from his hands, realizing Millie was right about rewashing the dishes. "The evenings are gettin' pretty cool. Has the cabin been warm enough?"

"For the most part, but Papa says we're going to have to work on tightening things up a bit."

"I was noticing the door—before I ruined your mornin's work. ...I'd intended to replace it with something that fits better, but then—"

"You've got enough on you without worrying about our door, Marcus Bennett. If you take on one more thing, your mother will be beside herself."

Marc tilted his head to one side. "Has she said something?"

"Not straight out." Millicent pushed a stray lock of black hair away from her face and moved to set the kettle on the stove. "It's all the little things she says."

"Like what?"

"Well, whenever you mention doing this or that, or planning this or that, she makes a comment."

"Like?"

"Like, 'I don't know when he thinks he's going to do that.' Or 'that'll take longer than he thinks it will.' Or 'He'll never get that done. Not with everything else.' You do keep yourself rather busy."

"I do, but I didn't realize it was botherin' her."

"I don't know that it's bothering her. She just... We all wonder how things work in that brain of yours. You're constantly adding more to your days."

Marcus chuckled. "And lately to my nights. ...Would you like me to rewash these dishes for you?"

Millicent stared at him for a moment, then tossed her head back in laughter. "NO! That's exactly what we were just talking about."

"But I feel bad that I made you drop them like that."

"I appreciate that, Marc, I do, but no. You came to see Papa, and you're on a schedule. You'd better go see him before you make yourself late."

"All right. But we *do* need to fix that door before winter sets in, or you'll both freeze."

"We'll be fine. You just worry about what you've already got. Go on."

For a moment, her gentle rebuke stung, but then he saw the sincerity in her kind eyes. He grinned, tipping his hat as he left his friend and her muddy dishes behind.

The barn was every bit as rough and inadequate as the house, but Adolph and Marc both felt it would do for the time being. By all appearances, it would collapse at the first heavy snow, but it was solid.

"Preacher?" Marc called as he drew close to the building. "Are you down here?"

The short man stepped out of the building, clapping dust from his hands. "Marcus? What brings you so early?"

"I brought my assignment over. I need to get into town, but I thought I should drop it off on my way. In case it gets late, and I can't stop on my way home."

The preacher nodded. "Is it up at the house?"

"It's in my saddlebag, which I think I left at your door when I startled Millie. Made her drop the dishes she'd just washed."

"Is that what that racket was? I wondered what she was doing up there."

Marc grinned. "From what I hear, she was tryin' to avoid a flood."

The preacher rolled his eyes. "Very funny. I don't know what I did wrong, but that counter did not work. Did you finish the assignment?" he asked, as he motioned Marc to lead the way to the house.

"Yes. Just this mornin'."

"Good. I'm looking forward to going over it. I have another one for you."

"Already?" Over the previous weeks, the preacher had reviewed Marc's assignments before moving on. He'd never given a new assignment at the same time as receiving the completed one. Marc had come to expect the break. He needed the break.

Adolph, seeing the surprise on his young friend's face, laughed. "Yes. Already. If you're going to be a preacher, you'll need something prepared to share with others every week... a few times every week. This will help you get in the habit."

Marc worked a kink out of his neck as he walked, Millicent's comments about his schedule haunting him. He knew the preacher was right, but they still didn't have extra help at the farm. He pushed the concern aside and glanced at the other man. "So what's the assignment?"

"It's similar to the last one. I have a few specifics written down for you. I'd like you to outline chapter three of the Gospel of John. Then organize your thoughts into something you can share with your family...or mine...or both. Whatever works."

Marc gulped as the two men stepped up to the front door. He scooped up his bag and followed the preacher inside.

Two cups of steaming coffee waited on the table. Between them, sat a plate of buttery, skillet-toasted bread and a jar of chokecherry sauce. Marc's eyes brightened at the sight, and he caught himself licking his lips as he sat down.

"I'd like you to have this done by Tuesday, Marc," the preacher said.

But, Marc's attention was on the chokecherry sauce. The younger man tossed a grateful grin in Millicent's direction and reached for the jar. It wasn't until his stomach rumbled with loud anticipation that the preacher realized he'd lost his student.

* * *

Noon had come and gone before Marc reached the livery. But he was happy. His new assignment would be more work than any so far, but after talking it over with the preacher he was eager to begin.

"What are ya smilin' at, lad? Look like you've just found a pot of gold."

Marcus laughed and turned toward O'Leery, who stood in the door between the livery and the blacksmith's shop. "I just came from the preacher's. I was thinkin' about the assignment he gave me. It's a good one."

The livery owner raised an eyebrow. "I reckon there's more to it than that if yer comin' from the preacher's."

"What do you mean?"

"Nothin', lad. I've just seen how well ya fit in with 'em. I know you've found a kindred hearth in their home. I'm happy for ya. Especially with their place being so close to yer own folk. Did ya bring yer wares?"

"I'm not sure I'd call them my wares, but I brought what I have repaired. Everything due today is here, and a few that weren't needed until next week."

"Good 'cause I'm 'spectin' you'll need the extra time this week."

"Oh?" Marc's grin faded as he watched O'Leery walk from the doorway to his workbench.

"A man came through yesterday who'd been in a bit of an accident. He'll be back by Tuesday, and he'll need his saddle by then." O'Leery reached below the bench and pulled out a mangled saddle. He set the saddle down on the workbench, followed by its horn.

Marc's eyes widened. He stepped close, fingering a billet strap that had nearly detached itself from the saddle. "What kind of accident caused all this?"

"I didn't ask. Angry he was. Whatever happened, he wasn't about to talk about it. He walked through those doors, dropped all this down in front of me, and said, 'I need a saddle. I'll come back on Tuesday, and I'll need this then'. Then he just stood there, waitin'."

Marc inspected the saddle. "He needs a new saddle."

"Can you fix it by Tuesday?"

"Fix it? The horn is broken off!" Marc swept his hat from his head and ran his hand through his dark hair. "Did you give him a price?"

"No. He didn't care to hear the price."

"Good. I'll do my best with what I have, but I can't have a new saddle from start to finish by Tuesday. The only thing I have is…" he stopped and glanced over his shoulder. Through the open door, he could see the corner of his brother's house one street over. "The only thing I have is a saddle I was makin' as a gift for my brother. Jon needs something better for when he's out visitin' his patients in other places. The saddles are close enough in size to make it work. I'll do my best to finish it by Tuesday, but it'll be twice the usual cost."

"Twice?"

"Twice. I'm going to have to put in late hours, and I'll have to start all over for Jon. I already missed his rounds this month. I wanted to have it ready for the next time he goes out. Now, I'll miss that as well. I might be able to use a few things off this saddle, but not much. …I haven't missed the stage, have I?"

"No. Should be here in about an hour. Maybe you should start workin' on the saddle while you wait."

Marcus grinned. "I just might do that." He sighed and examined the mangled specimen once more. "On the other hand, I may need to pick up a few items to make sure this is done on time." He shook his head in disbelief, wondering how the saddle had met its sad demise.

"Tom said he'd be bringin' a lot this week if he has room."

"He did say that, didn't he?" Marc's gaze grew intense. He leaned forward against the workbench, drumming his fingers on its surface.

"You've lost yer smile since ya came in here. Sorry about that, lad."

"Ah," Marc waved the comment away. "It'll be back."

His eyes twinkled with the remark, but O'Leery was shaking his head.

"No, lad, yer smile's been missin' most of the time for weeks. And that's okay. The missus and I understand."

Marc's countenance fell.

"It's all right, Marc. I know you thought you were hidin' it, but we know you. We know what's goin' on. ...How's your pa?"

Marc shrugged, finding the sudden change in the conversation unsettling. "About the same. Not much changes. When it does, it doesn't seem to be for the better."

"And the family?"

"Everyone's fine."

"Marcus. I've known you and yer family for a long time. I can see by the way you walk that things are not fine." The man laid a compassionate hand on his friend's shoulder. "If this saddle is too much, lad, then don't do it."

"It's okay. There's just a lot happening between now and Tuesday."

"Be sure it doesn't take you from them that need you. Your family's far more important."

"Thank you, Mr. O'Leery. I know they are."

"If there's anything we can do, you tell us. We'll be there."

"Thank you. ...I'm going to hunt up the wood I'll need to start a new saddletree. I'll be listenin' for the stage." Marc paused, grinning. "Just don't take in any more saddles like that one while I'm gone."

He turned and left the building, groaning as he stepped into the street. How was he ever going to finish everything by Tuesday? He glanced toward his brother's house, regretting that he wouldn't have the saddle ready as soon as he'd hoped. "Lord, we're trusting you to bring someone to help on the farm. Please, bring them soon."

Chapter 10

"Hi, Mr. Gray!"

"Hello, Mr. Gray!"

Travis and the Tiedemann boys ran through the common area of the rambling house, waving at the grizzled ranch hand as they passed.

The man smiled from his place at the table and waved in return, envying their happiness.

"Well, Mr. Gray," Jess said as she followed the boys through the house. "I didn't realize you were up here."

"Miss Bennett," he replied with a quick nod.

"How are you, Mr. Gray?"

The man nodded but said nothing.

"You're looking better these days."

Again he nodded.

"Is there more coffee? It's a bit chilly this evening."

"B'lieve so." The man watched as she made her way to the stove and checked the coffee pot at its back. She pulled a cup down from the cupboard and filled it with the dark liquid. Then, lifting it to her lips, she closed her eyes and prepared for the warm satisfaction it would bring.

"UGH! That's awful!" She spit the coffee back into the cup, "Did you make that?"

Gray's shoulders heaved with laughter, a rare light coming into his blue eyes. "Yes'm. What d'you think keeps a man goin' out on the range when it's s'cold yer nose hairs is a freezin'? Sure ain't that weak tea Mrs. Close is always makin'."

"How do you drink it? It's horrid."

"I reckon that depends on what yer used to drinkin', ma'am."

Jess, who was about to dump the remaining coffee, stopped. Compassion crept into her eyes. "How are you holding up, Mr. Gray?"

59

Gray shrugged, and Jess realized the man's situation was far too complex for such a question. She dumped the coffee and set about making a new batch. All the while, she felt his intense gaze following her. She'd just set the pot back on the stove to heat when the man finally spoke.

"There was a reason why I started drinkin', Miss Bennett. When I was drinkin', I didn't have to think about things I didn't want to think about. …But now they're back." He sighed. "It didn't fix nothin'. Just put it off till now, and I can't do no more about it now than I could then. Not a stitch more."

The man stared into the large mug of coffee before him. He turned the cup methodically, watching the liquid spin, first high on one side of the cup and then low on the other. In that moment, Jess saw Ronald Gray in a new light. A great weight had been set down upon him, one he was completely unprepared to carry.

"I was a model citizen, Miss Bennett. You probably can't imagine that, but it's true. Had me a shop, a haberdashery. Farmed the land my father farmed and his father before him. Married the prettiest little gal, and we had us a sweet daughter. Then the war come. For four years, it drug me from battlefield to battlefield. I didn't have the heart for it. Watched men die at the bullets hurled from my rifle. Saw men lyin' in their own blood, torn by my bayonet, just as I was torn by theirs."

He paused, rolling up the sleeve of his right arm and revealing a long scar along the bicep.

"I wasn't made for war, but I had no choice. We was all there. Young. Old. Rich. Poor. All of us in for somethin' we never planned on, but believed in…some more than others.

"I went dead inside. If I could just survive, that's what I aimed to do. Survive. Not for my sake. There weren't nothin' good left in me worth keepin' alive. But somebody had to provide for my Phoebe and little Ava, and that somebody shoulda been me. Shoulda been.

"We marched fer days, Miss Bennett. Did any o' yer kin fight in the war? Yer too young to remember, I suppose."

But Jess was nodding as she slipped into a seat at the table. "My pa was on the railroad lines and both of his brothers were in the infantry. Mama's brother was cavalry."

"Did they tell ya 'bout the mud and the cold and the trenches?" Disgust crimped the man's face.

Jess nodded. The man was growing more passionate about his story. Jess suppressed the fear rising in her heart at the memory of his angry outbursts during the wildfire.

"I figured if I could just survive an' get home, I could at least find a shadow of the man that I was b'fore the war. But when I got home… Everythin' was gone. Everythin'. The haberdashery failed. The farm failed. And… and Phoebe and Ava, they was sick. Bad sick. The doctor said I shouldn't see them 'cause I might get sick and die. I didn't care. If they wasn't gonna live, I didn't wanna live.

"In a week's time, they was both dead and buried, and me—I had nothing. Nothing but a couple dollars in my pocket. I went and bought a bottle o' whiskey, and then another and another. Till there was so many bottles I couldn't remember there ever not bein' a bottle. And then, I just survived. I don't know why I survived. I didn't have no one to survive for no more. …I ain't a bad man, Miss Bennett. I just ain't got much good ta make me happy like other folks."

He stopped abruptly. His eyes narrowed and he searched her face with an intense, probing gaze. "Yer a God-fearin' woman, Miss Bennett. So tell me this, why does God take things from us and make us go on livin' as if nothin' ever happened? It don't seem fair. If He's gotta rob a man of his family an' his life, why don't He just go ahead an' take the man too?"

An amused smile lifted the corner of Jessica's mouth. She looked away, first studying her hands and then rising to check the coffee. "I've asked myself that question many-a-time, Mr. Gray, many-a-time."

"D'you ever come up with an answer? 'Cause I sure ain't."

"Mrs. Close once gave me a very good answer. I certainly didn't want to hear it at the time, and I didn't fully understand it until much later. She said sometimes God takes the sweetest things in our life, so He can make something special out of them. Like berries for a pie."

"Berries! What do berries have ta do with anythin'?"

Jess chuckled. "Probably doesn't make much sense without knowing the rest of the story."

"No, ma'am, I'm sorry, but it don't."

The teacher filled her cup and raised the coffee pot in the man's direction. Gray declined with a dismissive wave and a grunt.

"You didn't see much of me before I moved here, did you?" Jess asked as she slid back into her seat at the table.

"Can't say as I *ever* saw you b'fore you moved here. …From what I'm told our first meetin' weren't too flatterin' on my part. …I'm sorry 'bout that."

Jess sobered. "No, Mr. Gray, it wasn't. But that is long ago forgiven and forgotten. …If you had met me in the weeks before the fire, you would've found me to be a much different person—a horrible person. I was angry and bitter…and mean."

"You? You were mean?"

Jess nodded, finding the truth still forced tears to her eyes. "I was so very mean. I was asking the same question you just asked me. To tell the truth, I wasn't listening for an answer. I wasn't planning on getting an answer or paying any attention if I did get an answer."

Gray's eyebrows dipped low over his blue eyes in a scowl, but he said nothing.

"I'm sure I never told you why I came to Grassdale," she continued, running a finger around the rim of her cup.

"No, ma'am. I'm sure you haven't."

"I was running away."

"Runnin' away? You? From what? You're a fine woman of good breedin'. I hear you talk 'bout your home and your family. What could you possibly have to run from?"

"God. My family. Myself."

Gray stared in disbelief, his mouth hanging open the tiniest bit.

"Oh, Mr. Gray, I was foolish. I was so busy lookin' at all the things God had taken from me that I didn't have time to see all the things He'd given me."

"Like what?" he retorted, his disbelief morphing into disdain.

"What had He taken, or what had He given?"

The man hesitated. His cheeks colored and a sheepish expression came into his eyes. He'd addressed her more emphatically than he'd intended. He cleared his throat. "Both."

"God had given me so very, very much. But all I saw was that He'd taken the man I was to marry. Joe was caught out in a blizzard and couldn't get to safety. He suffered in the cold for four days. By the time they found him, it was too late. …But my problems started long before that, and they continued after it."

The man listened intently as Jess told her story, from the day she received the news her father was sick, to the night she'd knelt along Crescent Creek, pouring her heart out in surrender to God. In some moments, Gray's face softened and tears rose in his eyes, though he never let them fall. But as she came to the end of her story, she saw his face harden. He looked away, realizing he wasn't ready to entertain the response her story required.

"That's all fine for you, Miss Bennett. But I want to know two things before I can ever make peace with God. Why did he take Phoebe and Ava? They was all I had left. And why didn't he take me with them? I don't wanna live if I have to live without them. I don't understand why He don't just take me. It's been nearly twenty years, an' still He makes me go on. Why don' He just take me? Why didn't He take me with that brew Scotch was feedin' me? Came close enough as it was. Why didn't He just finish the job? I don't wanna be here anyway."

The man's pain drove tears to Jessica's eyes. She looked away for a moment, considering her answer. She prayed silently, taking a deep breath before meeting his gaze once more.

"Perhaps, Mr. Gray, it's His mercy."

"Mercy!" the man leaned forward passionately, his face reddening. "Have you lost yer mind? Mercy?"

"Yes, Mr. Gray, mercy."

"Forgive me, Miss Bennett, but I don't think you understand what I been sayin'. He took *everything* from me. Every last thing. How can you say that's a mercy?"

"I'm not saying the loss is a mercy. I'm saying that not taking *you* is a mercy."

"What! It ain't no mercy—it's misery. Pure and simple. I'd rather be back in those muddy trenches than live with the misery of the last twenty years. Mercy..." The burly ranch hand's voice trailed off. He shook his head, glaring in disgust. He pushed the cup away and moved to leave his chair, but her quiet voice stopped him.

"Are you ready to face Him?"

Gray turned toward her, anger burning in every line of his face. "What?"

"Are you ready to stand before God? It might just be He's given you this time for that purpose."

Gray's eyes narrowed. He picked up the empty mug and slammed it against the table. "I don't want to stand b'fore no God what's as unjust as all this. And I ain't plannin' on answerin' nothin' b'fore Him neither."

He rose, his chair toppling behind him, and stomped toward the door.

"Mr. Gray," Jess said with determination.

The man glared over his shoulder. "What?"

"You won't have a choice."

Disgust and conviction mixed with the anger in the man's face. He muttered something under his breath and stormed through the front door.

"Seems you found the crux of it all."

Jess spun in her seat to see Wesley standing in the hallway. "Where did you come from?"

The rancher shrugged as he stepped into the room. " I came in the back door a while ago and heard you two talking. I was cold and wanted some coffee, but I didn't want to interrupt. I figured I'd just wait out the conversation. You think he's all right?"

Jess shook her head. "You'd be wise to keep a close watch on that man. I wouldn't put it past him to put a gun to his head...or to get someone else to."

A shadow crept across Wesley's gaze. He went to the front window in time to see Gray and his barebacked horse tear out of the barn and into the hills beyond the ranch buildings.

"He's still in pretty bad shape, isn't he?"

"He's lost a lot, Wes, and now we've taken the only thing he knew to help him hide from it all. He's in desperate shape. He's running from the only One who'll be able to help him now. Just like I was."

Wesley didn't respond. He went to the stove, poured a cup of coffee, and joined her at the table. "Doesn't seem very willing to listen," he said at last.

"No more than I was before the fire."

"Well, I hope we don't have to have another fire to fix things. I've had enough of that for one season."

Jess smiled, her cheeks coloring. She knew she'd walked right into his teasing. "I hope so too. But I have to admit, I'm grateful for that fire now."

Wesley's eyes brightened. "Me too."

He studied her for a moment and then let his gaze fall away as he sipped the coffee. He had waited in the hallway for a long time and had heard most of the conversation. He was proud of Jess. She'd handled the conversation far better than he would have. He couldn't help the faint smile that twitched at the corner of his mouth. God was doing a beautiful work in his friend, and he was pleased — privileged — to watch it unfold. He shot a glance in her direction and realized she was growing uncomfortable in the silence. He took another swig of the coffee, and then set it down with an indignant curl of his lip.

"Who made this coffee? It's so weak I can taste the water through it, and our water doesn't even have any taste."

Chapter 11

"Evenin'." The door through which Ronald Gray had so recently exited swung open and the tall, lean Carlson strode through. "I hear there's a pinch of supper left on a plate for me somewhere."

"There was," Wes said evenly, "But I'm pretty sure it went the way of Zane's stomach about an hour ago."

Carlson's bright expression dropped into disappointment. Then, at Jessica's laughter, it shifted to confusion.

"Don't listen to him, Mr. Carlson. We have plenty."

Jess rose, went to the counter, and began pulling together the remnants of the evening meal. She listened as the man tossed his hat on the sofa and came to the table to sit with Wes.

"I saw Gray headed up into the hills like a wild man as I was coming under the gate. Everything all right?"

"No. We need to keep an eye on him. He's a mess."

"Reckon I would be too after what he's been through. I ain't never seen a man suffer like that from lettin' go of drink. I didn't know it was possible. Don't ever want to see it again." Carlson repositioned his chair, scraping it across the wooden floor, and propping his feet on the seat of the chair next to him. "Things is pretty stirred up in town. People are talkin' about the fire. Wantin' answers."

"Who's talking?"

"Everyone I guess. Maybe seein' me and knowin' you and Dunn is helpin' Cale figure things out stirred 'em up. Everywhere I went I heard people whisperin' about it."

"Let them whisper. We'll figure things out in time. It's more important to get it right than to rush in and put the blame in the wrong place."

"That's what I said to them what asked, but there weren't too many of those. I bumped into Cale on my way to the General Store. He wants you two to come into town tomorrow to talk about it. Said Tiedemann'll be there and the preacher."

Wesley sighed. "We were going to move the herd tomorrow."

"We can handle it, Boss. Nothin' to worry 'bout there."

"Well, we'll see what frame of mind Gray is in. I don't want him stayin' back here alone, which means someone will have to nanny if he doesn't go along. That's two men you're short. If Dunn and I go to town, that's four."

"Hadn't thought of it that way. Whatever you wanna do, Boss, we'll do it."

Jess brought a plate of food to the table and set it before the eager Carlson. He dropped his feet to the floor, pulled the chair forward, and dove in as if he hadn't seen food in days.

"Slow down, man. You're not in a barn." Wesley's voice cracked at the man's lack of manners.

Carlson's attention darted up from the plate, surprise and hurt on his face. "I didn't get no lunch. I'm starvin'," he said through a lump of biscuit, which he'd barely managed to tuck into his cheek. "Oh, I almost forgot. You made me think of it, Miss Bennett. You and this wonderful plate of food. I brought the mail. There's about three letters for you, Jess."

"Really?"

"Yep. Let me go get it. I left my saddlebag hangin' over the rail." The man sprang from his seat, rushed out the door and returned with saddlebag in hand. He opened the bag and pulled out an assortment of tools, tack, and apples.

"Apples!" Wes said, "You had apples in your bag, and you let yourself starve?"

But Carlson was grinning and shaking his head. "No. I had a *pie* in my bag—it just ain't been made yet. Them are for your ma."

Wesley's face brightened with delight. "Now there's the kind of thing I like to see coming out of a man's saddlebags. Apple pie." He licked his lips and leaned forward, curious about what else would appear on the table. In the end, the apples proved to be of most interest to the man, but the large stack of mail also intrigued him.

"I can't believe how much mail came this time," Carlson said. "Seems almost everyone on the place got something. Everyone but Gray and Zane."

"Well," Wes said, reaching for the stack, "we'll make up for that with apple pie." He sorted the mail into piles, occasionally stopping to take in an advertisement or examine an address. When he finished, he scooped up a pile with three thick envelopes and handed it to Jess. "You're going to be readin' for a while, I'd say."

Jess smiled, taking the stack and flipping through it. "Thank you. If you gentlemen don't mind, I think I'll just go do that right now."

"Of course, we don't mind," Wes said, "Go right ahead."

Normally, Jess would have taken the letters to her room in the loft, but she knew her day was far from done. Carlson and Wes were just the first to come for their evening cup of coffee. The others would be coming soon, and they were likely to want something to eat as well. Realizing her window of opportunity was small, Jess went to the sofa in the common area and sank into its soft seat. She longed to pull the quilt down from the sofa's spine and wrap it around her shoulders, but once again, she resisted. She would have time to get warm and comfortable later.

She examined the three letters. One was from Kate Hightower, another from her sister-in-law Hannah, and the third from Marcus. This would be almost as good as going home. She smiled as she tore open the letter from Kate.

"*Dearest Jess,*

"*Oh, how good it was to see you, and how it makes me miss you all the more. Life was quite busy in the days after you left, everyone getting ready for winter and a few still buying things for their children for school. But now, it seems we've all settled back into our autumn routines, and life has taken on a slower pace.*

"*Jonah has been away much of the last few weeks. It bothers me at times that he travels so far with only Mr. Alder knowing where he has gone. It has always concerned me. If a man does not pay his debts, how can he be counted upon to receive the debt collector with any degree of respect? Jonah would never tell me such things, but I overheard him telling Marcus that, on his last trip, one man pulled a rifle on him and another shot at his horse.*"

Jess couldn't help the tiny gasp that escaped her. She'd never imagined this side of Jonah's work. It made sense though, and she determined to pray for her friend more diligently.

The gasp caught Wesley's attention, and he glanced in her direction. He watched for a moment, but when Jess continued reading he was convinced all was well.

"I went with Jonah last week to visit your family. I hadn't been to see them since you left. It's wonderful that we see one another at church each week these days, but there's nothing quite like spending an entire day at the farm with everyone. The Nausbaums were there for the evening. I'm so glad they have come here. Millicent is such a sweet girl. She does well with the children, and I believe they truly love her.

"Your family seems to be doing well. Your papa is about the same as when you were here. Your ma always encourages me. Marianne is her usual cheerful self. She tells me she has started working with Millicent to finish up her schooling. She seems excited. Finding the time to get her studies in proves difficult, I think, but she's enjoying it. The younger children are well. Joy was a little quieter than normal, but Mary said she was working on an assignment for school that had her worried.

"Marcus seemed good, but somehow tired and distracted. I've seen him in town often of late, usually just through the window as he's going about his business. Jonah says he's been busy with extra work from the livery and studies of his own. Something in his bearing has changed, Jess. The spring is gone from his step. It concerns me. Jonah says Marc is just trying to adjust to his new work. But I think there's more to it. Pray for him. Maybe I'm reading too much into what I see, but I thought you should know he needs encouragement."

The letter went on, but Jess found the report of Marcus distracted her. As she returned it to the envelope, she sighed, once again drawing Wesley's attention.

This time Wesley saw a shadow fall over her eyes. His stomach knotted, but when she picked up the next letter and smiled, he relaxed.

A small piece of paper fell out of Hannah's letter. The scribbling of little hands adorned the scrap. Without reading the letter, she knew the art was the work of her small nephew, Samuel. She fingered it lovingly, and then laid it aside and unfolded the letter.

"*Jessica,*

"*This will have to be short. Jon is visiting a patient outside of town, and I am running both the clinic and the house until he returns. I wanted to drop you a line or two. You've been on my mind so often since you left. Mary told me about your conversation as you were getting on the stagecoach. She told me you were worried about Marc, and how he's dealing with your papa's health. I wanted you to know, Jess, that we've seen it too. We've been just as concerned. It was better for a while after you were here, but something is weighing on him again in recent days. He doesn't talk about it, doesn't even allude to anything bothering him. But it's there.*

"*Jon is hoping to meet someone in his travels who would be a good fit at the farm. He's been looking for months. God will bring someone in His timing. I know He will. I just wanted you to know that we will do our best to help Marc and the rest of the family. Jon will be home soon, and we'll be seeing more of them.*

"*I saw Mrs. Vass at the mercantile on Saturday. She said to tell you hello with my next letter, and to let you know that she'll be writing soon.*"

Again, Jess found it difficult to concentrate on the remainder of the letter. Without finishing, she laid it aside. She picked up Marc's letter and tore into it, all but holding her breath. She unfolded the pages and bit the corner of her lip as she began to read.

"*Jess,*

"*By now, you should have received my telegram. Since then, I have started trying to spend one morning a week with the preacher, and he has given me assignments to complete. Tom has been bringing more tack to repair than I can keep up with between his trips. O'Leery took in a saddle that was destroyed in some kind of accident. My only recourse was to use the saddletree I'd prepared for Jon's saddle, and try to get something done in time. In the end, it was worth the rush. He paid what I required—twice my usual rate—and added a little extra because he liked the work. The money will go a long way toward the winter's expenses and starting over on Jon's saddle, which he still doesn't know I'm making.*

"*I regret that it took so much time away from the family. O'Leery warned me that it would. My studies too are requiring a lot of time. I know this is the path the Lord wants me to take, but I feel as though the last precious days with Pa are being squandered on other things. Good things, yes, but still I would rather be with the family than in the barn with a pile of leather.*

"The children are doing well. Joy concerns me. Since Papa's stroke, I've seen her pull inside herself. We've never had the open relationship that I have with you and Marianne. I'm not sure Joy shares that with anyone. Please pray for her.

"I'm afraid you won't find this an encouraging letter. Please, know that we are all well. The preacher is a joy to learn from, the children are doing well in school. We have new challenges to work through, but we are not despairing. We all love and miss you. Papa sends his love as always. Write when you can.

"Much love, Marcus."

Jess drew in a deep breath and then read the letter once more. This wasn't the sort of letter she was accustomed to from her brother. It lacked energy. It lacked hope. He had always been the one to give her hope, but now she sensed he was clinging to but a fine thread. His heart was as broken now, as it had been the day he'd sat with her in the wagon and wept at the thought of losing their father.

Heavy footsteps sounded on the front porch, and Jess realized the men had come for their coffee. She also realized tears had risen in her eyes. She wiped the tears away and began gathering up the letters as hastily as she could. She hurried to the schoolroom, tucked the letters in a desk drawer, and then stopped to gather her composure. She straightened her skirts and returned to the common area as the crew of rowdy men filtered through the front door.

Wesley still sat at the table with Carlson, but he stared at Jess. He said nothing, but his gaze followed her around the room as she went to the stove and started another pot of coffee.

Feeling his gaze but afraid to meet it, Jess kept her back to the man. She closed her eyes for the briefest moment and prayed silently, "Lord, please help me trust. That's all I need to do at this moment. ...And please, comfort my brother."

"Everything all right?" Wesley, on the pretense of getting mugs for the other men, had come to her side and now reached into a cupboard over her head.

Jess nodded and wiped her eyes once more.

"Is your pa all right?"

Jess nodded again, busying herself with the task she had set about.

"Then why are you crying?" he whispered.

"Please, Wes, not now. Not in front of everyone else."

"Okay. Later?"

"Yes."

"I'll hold you to it."

Jess smiled. "Thank you, Wes."

"Where's my mother?"

"She went for a walk."

"Oh. ...Gray's back. Seems to have pulled himself together. Looks like we're going to town tomorrow. Do you want to come along? Give you a chance to get out of the house for a bit."

"I'd like that. I need a few things for the classroom. I should probably write some letters tonight as well."

"I should do the same. My sisters haven't heard from me in months."

"Months?"

"Months. Dunn's the correspondent in our family. There's no excuse for it. I just don't like to sit that long."

Jessica laughed. "Somehow, I don't have any trouble believing that." She paused, finally daring to look up at him. "Everything is all right, Wes. It's just Marc. He's discouraged and hurting and, I think, overwhelmed. I've always depended on him to help me. Now, I need to help him, and I'm not sure how."

"The Lord will show you, Jess."

"I know. ...Would you read the letters? Tell me what you think."

"Sure. I'd love to."

"I'll go get them."

As Wesley set out plates to load with the day's leftover biscuits, Jess went to the schoolroom and retrieved the letters. When she returned, she laid them on the counter next to the plate he was filling.

He smiled, scooping up the letters and sliding them into his jacket pocket. "The Lord will work things out, Jess."

Jess nodded. "I know. I just need to trust Him. ...I just need to trust Him."

Chapter 12

"Well, if it isn't Tom Dresden. How ya been, ol' friend?"

"Wesley Close! What brings you to the livery this time of day?"

Wes shook the other man's hand and then leaned against the stall nearest his friend. He pushed his hat back and grinned. "Truth be told, I was huntin' for you."

"Me?" Tom's voice cracked and then lowered with the scowl that crossed his face. "What did I do now?"

"Do?" Wes laughed. "Do you always assume you've done something when someone comes lookin' for you?"

"No, I always assume that *they* assume I've done something. Stage masters make good scapegoats. We're never in town for long, nobody sees our comin's and goin's, 'cept when we ride in and ride out. Makes for a lot of blamin' and assumin'. Truth usually comes out though, so I make as light of it as possible."

"Well, you can rest easy. This has nothing to do with anything you've done...or maybe it does. Have you been to Twin Pines lately?"

"Sure. I was there last week."

"Have you seen Marcus Bennett?"

"Of course. He meets the stage every time I come to town if possible. I've been haulin' all sorts of tack for him to repair. Why?"

"Does he...I mean...have you noticed...I mean —"

"He's changed over the last couple of months if that's what you're gettin' at. Yeah, I've seen it. There's something kinda hidin' in his eyes. Doesn't seem as free to be hisself as he used to."

"What do you think it is?"

The stage master shrugged. "I reckon it's his pa. I hear they're pretty close, and his pa's in pretty bad shape. Marc'll be okay. He's not the type what goes over the edge, as they say."

"No, no. I didn't think so. Listen, I wondered if you could help me."

"I can try."

"Can you keep an eye on things? Miss Bennett got several letters from home last night, and they left her in tears. I've read them, and I can see why she's concerned. I just..." Wes paused glancing around the livery to be sure no one else was listening. "If she needs to go, I'd like to know as soon as possible. I don't want her gettin' there too late, if you know what I mean."

"I'll tell you what, if ever I see things changin' in a concernin' way, I'll leave a note with your mail. If anything serious ever comes up, I'll get word to you however I can as fast as I can."

"I'd appreciate that, Tom. I really would."

Tom nodded, "It's the least I can do."

Ten minutes later, Wesley settled himself in a large, comfortable chair in Cale Bennett's office. Dunn found a similar seat and the men waited for the arrival of the rest of their group.

"Did you talk to Tom?" Dunn whispered.

Wes nodded.

"What'd he say?"

"He's going to keep us posted as best he can."

"Do you think we should say anything to Cale? They're family after all."

Wes tipped his head to one side. "Guess I hadn't thought of it. Maybe we should leave that up to Jess."

Dunn shrugged. "I think Cale would want to know."

"Know what?" Cale said, gliding through the doorway and across the room. "What's up?"

Dunn cast an apologetic glance in his brother's direction.

"Something about the fire?" Cale pressed, his attention fully fixed on the two brothers.

"No," Wes replied, groaning as he spoke.

"Something about Scotch?"

Dunn shook his head. "Something about Jessica's family."

"Then you're right. I'd like to know. I had a letter from Marcus last week, and it seemed...different. Like there was something he wasn't telling me, something serious."

"He's on a lot of people's minds these days." Wes straightened in his seat, wishing Dunn had kept his questions to himself. "Jess is concerned for him. Even Tom has sensed a change. I asked Tom to keep an eye on things for me. If Jess needs to go back to Twin Pines, I want to know about it."

Cale studied his friend for a moment. The action didn't surprise him. He'd always known Wes to be protective of his family, and he knew the Closes had taken Jess in as just that—part of the family. He'd seen the same in their response to the situation with Ronald Gray. Both men had been furious with Scotch when they'd realized what was happening, but they'd dealt with it circumspectly. Wesley's request of Tom gave Cale hope. It bolstered his respect for the man. He knew he could trust the two brothers to approach the situation surrounding the fire objectively.

"I appreciate that, Wes. I wish I could do more for them. Marc mentioned he's lookin' for help on the farm. I've been keeping an ear out for someone needin' work, but haven't come across anyone yet. My guess is he's just plain overwhelmed."

Wes nodded and turned his gaze toward a movement behind Dunn. Henry Tiedemann stood just inside the doorway. A moment later, Jason French stepped in behind him.

"Come on in and find a seat," Cale said, waving the men toward various chairs around the room. "We've got quite a bit to discuss. Dunn, do you mind pushing that door shut?"

Dunn obeyed and the room fell quiet. No one wanted to be there. No one wanted to discuss what they were about to discuss, but it had to be done.

"Well, gentlemen," Cale began, "we've had some developments since the last time we were together." The banker presented everything he'd shared with Wes and Dunn a few days earlier, this time in greater detail. Twenty minutes later, all five men leaned back in their seats, groaning in unison.

"We've got to talk to him, Cale. That's all there is to it," the preacher said. "I'm willing to go with you if you want a witness. I think it should be Henry or one of us for sure. There's too much history with Wes and Dunn—too much recent history. Scotch and I have had our run-ins, but it's been a few months."

"I agree. I imagine he'll be pretty easy to find this time of day. How about if we all meet back here in an hour?"

The others nodded their consent. Then the five men stood and filtered out of the room without a word.

✻ ✻ ✻

"Are you asking me if I set that fire?" Scotch bellowed from behind his desk. "That's what you're asking me, isn't it?"

"No," Cale said in a measured tone. "We're asking where you were the day the fire started."

"Which means you think I did it."

Cale and the preacher exchanged glances. Cale sighed. "No. We're just followin' the evidence wherever it takes us."

"Well, what 'evidence' led you to me? I had nothin' to do with that fire."

"Some of the men at the ranch said you were out there that week and had words with Edelman."

Scotch hesitated. "We've talked several times over the last couple of months."

"What about?" the preacher asked.

"He owes me money, and he hasn't been makin' his payments."

"When was the last time you were out there?"

"The week of the fire, but I didn't have anything to do with the fire startin'. I told him he had until the circuit judge and marshal come through to catch up. If he hasn't caught up by then, I'll be takin' it to the authorities. That's all."

"How did he respond?" Cale said.

"Well, he wasn't happy about it."

The preacher leaned forward, resting his forearm on the desk and squaring his steady gaze up to Scotch's shifting eyes. "What did you say you'd be asking the authorities to do?"

"I told him I'd foreclose on the property. Take the land. But I ain't goin' into a mess like that without the law behind me. I ain't the fool you people think I am."

"So where were you the day the fire started? Were you out there?" Cale persisted.

"No. I was out there earlier in the week, but I left town straight from his lane. That is, I had to come back through town to get where I was goin', but I didn't stop nowhere. I left here and was gone for the next week. By the time I got back, it was all over and done with."

"Did anyone see you go?" Jason asked.

"I don't know. Maybe. What you fellas are askin' me don't make sense. Look, Preacher, you and I had our arguments in the spring about that church building. Cale, I know I done wrong by your cousin, meetin' her at the stage like that and bein' such an idiot about the repairs at the school. I know I upset Dunn Roe with that liquor I was slippin' to Ronald Gray, but why…what would possess a man to set a fire that would destroy his own property? My land is worthless now. The entire section. Every bit of it. Even without the school and church there, I could've at least put cattle on it. Now, I can't even do that until the land recovers. Why would I do that?"

"We don't think the person who set the fire ever intended it to leave Edelman's property," Cale said.

Scotch glowered. "So, against all common sense, you're still assumin' it was me."

"We're not assumin' anything. We're just trying to get to the bottom of things."

"Scotch," Jason added. "We've put this conversation off for a couple of weeks. We didn't want to think you had anything to do with it. But we have to follow the evidence we've found."

"Well, what have you found that points to me? …Other than the fact that I was out there talkin' to Edelman."

Jason sighed. "A piece of leather —"

"A piece of leather! How does that link anyone in particular to anything? Any man in this prairie rut could've lost a piece of leather."

"It's the same color as your red saddle." Cale's even voice quieted the room.

Scotch leaned back in his seat, stunned. The brightly colored saddle was a rare specimen, he knew. "But that saddle is in good shape. It's not missin' any pieces. Nothin' torn."

"Could we look at it?"

Scotch blanched at the preacher's question. He swallowed hard. "I don't have it."

"What do you mean, you don't have it?" Cale asked, struggling to keep the frustration out of his voice.

"I sold it."

"Sold it! Why did you sell it? I didn't think you'd ever sell that thing. I thought it was your prized possession."

Scotch shrugged. "Sometimes somethin' more important than our prized possession comes along, and it makes sense to give it up."

"Who did you sell it to?"

"The livery in Maiden."

"Maiden!" Jason said. "What were you doin' in Maiden?"

"That's none of your business. The point is I sold it. The man who runs the livery there, he could vouch for me. But I'm sure that saddle is long gone."

Cale and Jason, who had both moved to the edge of their seats, glanced at one another, wondering what their next step should be. Both had a thousand questions running through their minds, none of which they could voice. Cale turned his attention back to the miserable man across the desk from them.

"You realize this is just going to make you look that much more guilty. Scotch, I don't want to make mistakes in this. I don't want to say anyone is guilty if they aren't, but you're not givin' us much to go on. Is there anything you can tell us that would help you out?"

Scotch shrugged. "I suppose you could ask around town and see if anyone saw me leavin' town. I didn't tell nobody I was goin'. I just went. I had business to tend to, personal business that don't make no matter to nobody else."

"Business so important you'd go to prison for it?"

Scotch squirmed in his seat. He'd never been keen on the idea of prison. Who would be? But he wasn't sure he was willing to let his secret out. Not yet.

"Maybe. …You could always ride to Maiden and talk to the man at the livery. I'm telling you, he'll vouch for me and for the saddle. It was that week I sold it. That trip."

"That trip? Have there been others?" Jason said.

"Sure. I go every few weeks if I can. Most folks don't miss me. My workers all know I'm gone from time to time. They don't know where I go, but they know I go. I'm usually gone about a week."

"You'd have to be. It's a three-day ride over there." Jason said, his face reflecting the exhaustion he felt at the thought of the trip.

Scotch shrugged. He leaned back, weaving his pudgy fingers behind his head. "Two, if you ride hard. …It's worth it."

Once again, Cale and Jason shot glances in each other's direction. This had gotten them almost nowhere. Cale groaned inwardly. He regarded the saloon owner across from him, his gaze growing intense. "Well, Scotch, for now, we'll see if we can find someone who saw you leavin' town. If we can't, you'd better come up with something that will help us out."

Scotch's face reddened. "Did it ever occur to you that Edelman might have set his own fire to spite me?"

"Now why would he do that?" Cale said. "How would that get him anywhere?"

"Where would it get me if I set the fire? How does it make any more sense for me to set it than if he set his own fire? Maybe he set it with the intent of makin' it look like I set it, so he could get out of his loan. Did you ever think of that?"

Cale *had* thought of that, on more than one occasion. But there was no proof to back it up. "Scotch, we're just following the evidence we have. If you have evidence to prove it was him, you'd better produce it. Otherwise, we have to go with what we've got."

Scotch slammed his fist down, rattling the massive desk. "In other words, you're going to assume it was me until you prove differently. Get out. This conversation is over."

"No. We're just—"

"I don't care what you're doing. Get out! Don't come back until you've done your job right!"

Cale and Jason stood. Both men attempted to speak, to somehow relieve the tension in the room. But Scotch waved them away, his face still red with anger. The men sighed as they turned to leave. If Scotch was innocent, they had no way of proving it. Not today.

Chapter 13

Marc plopped down onto the sofa in the Hightower's parlor and groaned. If he had to wait more than five minutes for Jonah to join him, he'd be asleep. He was sure of it. The stagecoach was late. Jon and Hannah weren't home. His errands were done. So Marc had resorted to spending the next hour waiting at his best friend's house — but Jonah wasn't home either. Kate, however, had taken pity on him. She'd ushered Marc into the parlor and then made her way across the short distance from her home to the bank where her brother was still finishing up the morning's work.

The house was quiet. Only the vigorous ticking of the small, porcelain clock on the coffee table broke the silence. The faintest hint of biscuits and simmering stew hung in the air. He knew that meant Kate had been preparing their noon meal. For a moment, he regretted that he'd interrupted her preparations, but then he dared to hope that he'd get to sample her work. A contented smile spread across his face. He slid down into the sofa, leaning his head into its corner. He stared into the fire on the hearth across the room. His eyelids grew heavy as he sighed and relaxed.

"OH, no you don't!"

Marc jerked awake and spun toward the voice.

"You go to sleep now, and we'll be hours waking you up."

Marc stared wide-eyed at his best friend, his heart racing. "Why do you do that?" he gasped.

But Jonah was laughing. "Because *you* always do *that*. I can't help myself. Every single time you come straight off that sofa with the look of a wild man in your eyes. It's the only time I can pull anything over on you. You always hear me coming when you're awake."

"You're horrid. I need to find a new friend. Someone who won't scare the life out of me every time I dare to take a nap."

Jonah laughed again. "Yeah, but who would bail you out every time you got in trouble with your ma or one of your sisters...or *my* sister for that matter?"

"True. Was I actually asleep?"

"You were snoring. Kate and I both heard you as soon as we came in the door. Didn't we, Kate?"

The pretty young woman, who had just come through the parlor door behind her brother, lifted her hands innocently. "What can I say, Marc? It's true. You were pretty well on your way to a full night's sleep. ...Why don't you two come to the kitchen, and I'll have lunch on the table in no time."

Marc stood groggily. "Wow, I must have been out. Feel like I'm going to fall over. Probably a good thing you woke me up."

"Of course, it's a good thing. You can always count on me to watch out for you."

Marc snorted. "And to shorten my life by several years every time I see you."

They were soon seated around the table and well engrossed both in their meal and their conversation. Jonah kept them in stitches, which Marc had needed for days. Jonah knew this, of course, and took pleasure in providing the relief. But he knew something was hanging over Marc. To ask outright would get him nowhere. So, as their laughter subsided and Marc reached for a drink of coffee, Jonah stepped out cautiously.

"I haven't been out to the farm for a while. How's everyone doing?"

"They're good," Marc said, setting his cup down and wiping his mouth with a napkin.

"How are the girls?" Kate asked.

"Good. Ma is doing well. Seems to be feeling better than she did at first. She still has to be careful, but she hasn't had as many headaches the last couple of weeks."

"How's your pa?" Jonah said.

Marc shrugged. "He's about the same. He's seemed to tire more easily over the last couple of days, but overall I'd say he's about the same. He..." but his voice trailed off.

The others waited, but when Marc didn't go on they knew they'd found what had been troubling their friend over the previous weeks. His gaze dropped to his cup of coffee. He sloshed the dark liquid around in the cup, and then lifted it to his mouth, taking a long drink.

"It's going to be a long, hard winter," he said at last. He returned the cup to the table, but still didn't meet their eyes. "I don't even want to—I can't—think about it. I think I'll fall apart if I think about it."

Kate bit her lip at the realization that her friend had taken that long drink of coffee in an effort to force back his emotions.

Jonah leaned forward on his elbow, resting his chin in his hand. He drummed the fingers of his other hand on the table until his silence forced Marc to look up. Then, he squared his gaze up to his friend's, determined to get the full picture.

"You think he's going downhill? Maybe faster than Jon thought he would?"

"No. I think it's going to be slow and uncomfortable. I think he's going to have ups and really low downs. I think he's going to fight for all he's worth because he loves us, and I think it's going to hurt to watch it. ...And I think I'm wasting precious time on work I never really intended to have."

"You mean the tack repair?"

Marc nodded. "Between that, the regular chores, and the study I'm doin' with Preacher, I rarely see him even a complete hour out of the whole day. Ten minutes here, ten minutes there. All broken up. I never intended things to get to that point, but I don't know what to do about it. We've all been prayin' God would bring us someone to help. We've all been lookin' for help. I just...I thought it would happen sooner than this."

Jonah studied his friend. For the first time, since he'd jerked the other man out of his sleep, the loan collector's face expressed the depth of concern he bore for Marc. He remembered far too well the pain of arriving home from St. Paul only to discover that his own father had already passed away. For weeks, he'd been haunted by the fact that he'd missed his father's final hours by so little. He didn't want that for his friend. Somehow, he wanted to protect Marc from that, give him a solution, but his mind was blank.

A knock at the front door broke the silence. Kate started to rise.

"I'll get it, Kate," Jonah said, jumping up and hoping his sister would have an answer for his friend.

The others watched him go, and then let their eyes fall to the table in front of them. An awkward silence threatened to settle around them, but then Kate plucked up her courage.

"Marc, forgive me if I'm speaking out of turn, or if this idea is completely ludicrous, but..." she hesitated, looking away in embarrassment.

"Go on, Kate. I've never known you to have outlandish ideas. I usually feel pretty safe when you start making suggestions."

Kate laughed. "As opposed to?"

"Your brother. I never know what I'm getting into with him."

"Neither do I. Every day, I wonder what harebrained idea he's going to bring home with him."

Marc grinned. "See, having you around is probably the only thing that has kept him alive! Go on. What were you thinking?"

"Well, I might know how you can spend more time with your pa and still get everything else done."

When Jonah returned a moment later, the entire atmosphere in the room had changed. Marc smiled. Hope had climbed in his eyes. Jonah couldn't help the swelling of pleasure he felt at the scene. Kate hadn't failed him. He cleared his throat.

"I've got to go. They need me over at the bank."

Marc stood, knowing he should head back to the livery as well. He picked up his dishes and carried them to the counter and then turned back toward his friends. He beamed a smile at Kate and then did something he hadn't done in a very long time. He stepped forward and hugged her with a hearty, strong, grateful hug.

"Thank you," he said. Then he stepped past Jonah and headed out the front door.

❈ ❈ ❈

Marcus strode into his father's bedroom, Bible and textbooks in one hand, cup of coffee in the other. He stared out the large windows, noticing how low the sun had sunk in the sky. It would be setting soon, much sooner than he'd realized.

"Are you goin' to tell me your reason fo' comin', or jus' stan' there torturing me with the smell of tha' coffee?"

Marc chuckled. "Would you like a sip?"

"I'd like a whole cup."

"I doubt Jon would look too highly on that."

"Is Jon here?"

"Well, no—"

"Then he'll never know."

"Pa, you're going to get me in trouble."

"Not if we both keep our peace."

Marc chuckled. "Here, you have this one. I'll go make another."

Marc stepped up to the bed and placed the cup in his father's hand. He watched for a moment, making sure the cup wasn't too heavy. The coffee was fresh and very hot. The young farmer cringed at the thought of the other man spilling and burning himself.

"I thought you were goin' to get another cup."

"I will," Marc said. "I just wanted to make sure it wasn't too hot."

Jonathan lifted the cup to his mouth, blowing on the drink for a moment, and then sipping it cautiously. He sighed with delight. "It's perfect, son, perfect."

Marc grinned. "Good. Then I'll be right back.

He set his books down in the chair next to his father's bed and hurried out of the room, avoiding eye contact with his mother as he went about his task. Still, he could feel her gaze following him the entire time.

"I think Ma knows we're up to something," he whispered as he came back to the room and seated himself.

"Ah, she'll be fine. She's snuck a cup or two of her own in here."

Marcus laughed. "So you've got everyone hidin' from Jon."

"Hannah was the only one with the gumption to say no."

"That's because she has to live with him."

"True. Wha' brings you my way, son? It's been a while since we had coffee together."

"It has. That very thing has been bothering me. But Kate gave me an idea today, and I thought we should try it."

"Oh, wha's tha'?"

"What would you think of studying with me?"

Surprise flashed across Jonathan's face. "Wha'? How would tha' work? I can' exac'ly read these days, you know."

"No, but I can. I can sit here and tell you what I'm studyin' and read parts of it to you. I can tell you what I'm findin' in the books the preacher lends me. I'm sure we won't do all of it together, but maybe...maybe a little each day. What do you think?"

The older man was smiling now. Tears had become a common part of Jonathan's life since the stroke, but the tears sliding down his cheeks now were truly tears of happiness.

"Son, I would like tha' very much."

"Good. Because I brought everything with me." He set his coffee aside and flipped open his Bible. He couldn't squelch the smile that spread wide across his face. His heart was about to burst. He and Papa would study together, just as they had when he'd been a boy. Tears of joy climbed into his own eyes as he turned to the passage he'd been studying that morning. He shook his head. Kate and her safe suggestions, how would he ever repay her?

Chapter 14

"He did it again, Cale. That's the third time this week."

Wesley tossed his hat into a chair in Cale's sitting room and let both hands come to a rest on his hips. His pale face and red ears told the story of a man who'd spent hour upon frustrating hour out in the cold. Mud spattered his pants halfway to his knees. His dark hair stood on end in a ridiculous manner, and a thin line of mud ran along one cheekbone.

"I've about had it. If he didn't start that fire, then why on earth does he insist on makin' life miserable for the rest of us? It's not helping his case any."

Cale sat at his fireplace, legs crossed comfortably, hot drink in one hand, book in the other, eyes fixed on his frustrated friend in a stupefied manner. "Where did you come from, and *what* are you talkin' about?"

"Your wife let me in, and I'm talkin' about Scotch. Something has to be done about that man."

Cale's brow furrowed. "What did he do? I haven't heard any complaints from anyone."

"Well, you're about to hear one from me. If I see him close to my cattle again…"

Cale waited, but when Wesley didn't continue, he underscored his friend's dilemma with a raised eyebrow and a tilt of his head. "You'll what?"

Wes sighed and turned away, running a hand across the back of his neck. "I don't know. That's what frustrates me so much. I don't know what to do, or if I can even do anything."

"Wesley," Susan Bennett's soft voice broke into their conversation. "Would you like something hot to drink? It's a terribly raw afternoon."

He smiled at the gentle redhead who stood in the doorway, grateful for the offer. "That would be wonderful, Susan. It's downright miserable out there."

"I'll bring it right away."

"Thank you." Wes watched the woman go, and then returned to the chair where he'd tossed his hat. He scooped up the hat and sank into the soft seat.

"I don't know how many more times I can chase my cattle down without havin' a mutiny on my hands, Cale."

Cale set his cup down on an end table and leaned forward. "What do you mean? What's going on?"

"When we moved the cattle, we found we had a few that were either sick or injured. There were too many of them to bring into the main corral by the barn, so we set up a holding pen on the edge of the winter pasture. Just so we could keep an eye on them. Three times this week, the cattle in that pen have been let out and chased off. We spent two days regathering them the first time. Today, I just happened to ride up to the corral in time to see them disappear over the horizon. Who do I see riding after them? Scotch. Big as life. I tried to go after him, but he had too much distance on me. He disappeared into the trees and up the mountainside somewhere.

"Fortunately, Dunn and the others weren't far behind me. We managed to get the cattle back to the corral in about two hours, but we can't keep eatin' up our days with chasin' them down. More importantly, runnin' them off like that could do a few of them in. I can't afford to start losin' cattle over this."

Susan returned to the room just then, bearing a large mug and a plate of cookies. Wes could see steam rising out of the cup and realized he was eager for the warmth of the drink. Susan had been right. The weather was reminding them all that November was about to become December.

"Here you are," she said happily. "I hope you enjoy it."

Wes received the plate of cookies, noticing that a similar plate sat on the end table near Cale's chair. He took the mug Susan offered him and looked at the hot liquid inside it.

"Is this — ?"

"Hot cocoa," Susan beamed. "My sister sent cocoa powder last week. I had just made this and thought since you were so cold and seemed frustrated maybe you'd enjoy something special instead of old coffee."

Wesley's brown eyes brightened as he blew on the hot drink and then sipped at it. "It's delicious! Thank you! Hits the spot."

"You're welcome. I'll let you two talk. But don't think for a minute, Wes, that you're going to get out of here without a full on attack from our children. They're waiting for you outside the sitting room door."

"So there's no chance of me sneaking up on them."

"Not a chance in the world." The woman laughed and left the men to their conversation.

"Wes," Cale began, "why do you think Scotch is so determined to make life miserable for you? He's done nothing to anyone else as far as I know. I would've thought he'd go after Edelman or even me if he felt the need to retaliate. Why you and your cattle?"

"I don't know. I'm wonderin' if he thinks we're makin' accusations about him and the fire. That's the only thing I can come up with."

Cale nodded. "Well, I doubt he'll run your cattle off again now that he knows you've seen him. But if I were you, I'd set men to guardin' things. We should let the others know this is going on. If he feels like he can't do anymore at your place, he may move to someone else."

Wes nodded and took another long sip of the delightful chocolate. "I think you're right."

The two men sat in silence for a while, then Cale stirred and cleared his voice. "I still haven't found anyone who saw, or who'll admit to seeing, him leave town the week of the fire. It's going to be hard to prove this, one way or another. People have formed opinions about him over the years, and most of those opinions aren't good. Somehow, he seems to be at the top of everyone's list of suspects. People are losin' their objectivity."

"Anyone who knows he was *gone* during the fire?"

"Madam Fulbright said she thought he was gone. Her exact words were, 'So what if he was gone? Says he's shuttin' us down, so as far as I'm concerned he can be gone all he wants.' Then she said, 'Sure he was gone. A coward like him wouldn't find a place on those fire lines.' Needless to say, she doesn't have much respect for him at the moment."

"Shutting them down? Do you really think he's shuttin' down the brothel?"

Cale shrugged. "I hope so. This town would be a lot better off without it."

"I agree with you there, but why would he close it down? That doesn't make sense. I've never known Scotch to close or quit anything that was makin' money, except when he left all those years ago. And it seems the more disagreeable the means of makin' the money, the better. So why would he close it?"

"That's a good question. Maybe there's more afoot than we realize with that man."

Wes guffawed. "There's always more afoot with Scotch Jorgenson than anyone realizes."

"True."

"You don't think he'll leave town do you?"

"You mean for good?" a tone of surprise rang in Cale's voice. "Why would he do that?"

"To get away from our questions, and maybe to get away from the truth."

"Wes, I'm not sure he did it, even though all the evidence points in that direction. The problem is, I don't know where else to look."

"I know. I'm still not convinced everything was as it seemed the last time I was out at the fire site. I keep going over every inch of that spot in my mind, but I can't put my finger on the problem."

Cale sighed. "I've been prayin' God will show us what we're missin'. We're definitely missin' something. ...Are you in town for long or just for this?"

Wes sighed. "I had to do something to put my men at ease, Cale. I knew you couldn't do anything about it, but I felt you should know what's been going on. I'll pick up the mail and a few other things while I'm here, but this is why I'm in town. I headed here straight from the corral, so I didn't have much of a plan."

"Is that why you're such a mess? It's not like you to come to town with mud on your face."

"What?" Wes wiped at his face with the back of his hand.

But Cale was laughing. "I'm messin' with you. It's not that bad."

Wesley rolled his eyes, groaning and then sighing. "Guess I should hurry so I can get on out to the Tiedemann's and Edelman's before going home. Now that I've got that cocoa in me though, I just want to take a nap."

"That makes two of us." The banker leaned back in his comfortable chair and closed his eyes. Then as if highly amused, he chuckled and a sly grin slid up one side of his face.

"What's so funny?"

"I was thinkin' about how I'm going to lean back and nap, and how you're going to walk out that door and get piled on by my wild, little tribe."

A lazy smile slipped across Wesley's face. He chuckled, his own eyes closing as he slid down in the chair. "Maybe I'll go out the window."

Chapter 15

"I'll have that man's red saddle and his own hide to boot next time I see him! Who does he think he is? The gall! I oughta—"

"Afternoon."

Corey Banton, the soft-bellied, gray-eyed foreman of the Edelman Ranch, spun to face the voice that stopped his tirade, shovel in hand.

"Who are you?" he demanded.

"Name's Wesley Close. My place is a couple miles west of here. Is Mr. Edelman around?"

"No. He went to town to buy lumber to fix the mess Scotch Jorgenson left us."

"Oh? What mess?"

Banton jabbed the shovel into a wheelbarrow mounding with manure and pointed beyond where the other man still sat his horse. Then, following his own finger, he said, "Follow me. I'll show ya."

Wes turned his horse, following the angry man away from the barn toward a corral that stood off in the distance. He had to wonder why anyone would build a corral in that spot. The nearby stream had flooded the entire pen.

"There, you see," Banton said, "he left us a hog wallow instead of a horse pen. That's the mess I'm talkin' about. And worst of all, he don't care we know it was him what did it."

"Scotch caused this? How?"

"See that stream of water flowin' in there? That only comes this way 'cause the boss redirected it from the creek. Makes it easier for waterin'. It don't usually come in here though. Scotch broke down the ditch so it come pourin' all across the yard, the pen, and the chicken yard. Next time I see that man, I'm liable to ring his neck, just like a worthless ol' hen. I've had about all—"

"What was your name?" Wes interrupted, sensing the man's protests would go on at length.

"What?" Banton shot back at him, confusion clear in his eyes.

"I don't know your name."

"Name's Banton. I'm Edelman's foreman."

"I see. And you saw Scotch do this?"

"Course, I seen it. I was up on the hill bringing the horses down to drink. We'd been out all morning. We all needed a break. An' just as I get within seein' distance, there he is, hauling away at that ditch with the biggest ax a man like Scotch ever did wield."

"And you're sure it was him?"

"Course, I'm sure. Ain't nobody else in these parts what rides a tall, skinny horse just to make up for that he's so small and round. Course, it was him."

"Hmm," Wesley didn't doubt the man had seen Scotch. But something wasn't right about what Banton had said earlier when Wesley had first arrived. Now, his gaze swept from the man to the distant hillside and back to the man again. His eyes narrowed as he spoke, "You saw his saddle from over there on that hillside?"

"What?" Banton spat indignantly.

"In the barn, when I first arrived, you were saying, 'I'll have that man's red saddle and his own hide to boot,' so you saw his saddle?"

Banton's eyebrows drew together, pulling his broad brimmed hat forward on his head. "I guess. I mean, maybe."

"So you're not sure?"

"Well, no. Is that important? Why is that important?"

"Maybe it's not." Wes studied the man before taking the conversation any further. He didn't appear to be the sort of man one would normally bring on as foreman. He was sloppy in his dress, his speech, and his general appearance. In fact, his general appearance gave Wesley the sense that Banton was spiteful, willful, and lazy. Why would such a man be kept on as foreman? He grunted, dismissing the thought. He was becoming too suspicious with all this fire business.

"So what brings you here anyway, Close?"

A humorless smile pushed up one side of Wesley's mouth. He let out a soft chortle. "I came to warn you something like this might happen."

"What?"

Wesley cringed, struggling not to roll his eyes and wondering again at Edelman's choice of foreman.

"I came to tell Edelman that Scotch has been causin' trouble at my place and that he'd be wise to keep a close watch on things here. But I guess I'm too late."

"You guess right. What'd he do over there?"

"Drove the cattle out of the holding pen — three times this week."

Banton shook his head in disgust and spat into the mire at his feet. "What's got into that man? Somebody needs to do somethin' about him b'fore he goes and hurts someone. I'll bet it was him what set that fire. Spiteful. Vengeful. Couldn't get the money from the boss, so decided to force him into even worse straights. Then he can take the land when the boss can't pay. That's what I think he done."

"Well," Wes said calmly, "we're not speculatin' on any of that. We're gonna follow the evidence where it leads us, and so far the proof we have isn't enough to say for sure it was him or anybody else. ...I reckon I'm done here. Tell Edelman and the family I said hello. It was nice to meet you, Banton. I'm sure we'll be seein' you around. Have a good evening."

With that, and not waiting for the other man to respond, Wes turned his horse. He nodded at Brandon Bishop and a tall blonde man as they passed him on their way to the barn. Then he rode back down the lane. He sighed as the horse stepped onto the road home. The further things went, the more confused they made him.

The sun was sinking low on the horizon just to the south of the road as Wes rounded the bend marking the last quarter-mile to home. He'd been distracted by the situation with Scotch as he'd ridden the first mile from the Edelman ranch; but as the sun lowered itself in the sky, he'd become more vigilant. Now, in the light of its last brilliant rays, he saw a strange movement on the road ahead of him. He leaned forward in his saddle, squinting into the light.

Dust billowed up from a strange cluster of large, moving shadows. Wes reined in, slowing his horse enough to steady his gaze. He stared into the distance and then blinked in confusion. What he was seeing made no sense. Just beyond the gate of the Crescent Creek, he could make out a rider and a frantic string of horses. The animals tossed their heads wildly and pulled against the lead lines. At first, Wes wasn't sure he was seeing right. The light was too uncertain. But as he drew nearer the gate to the ranch, he could only shake his head in baffled wonderment.

"Jason, *what* are you doing?" he called, urging his horse toward the other man.

The preacher, whose attention had been fully upon the rowdy string of horses behind him, spun in his saddle, nearly losing his grip on the lead lines. He gasped. "Don't sneak up on a man like that, Wes. You just about had us chasin' after these beasts all over again."

"Us?" Wes laughed. "I'm done chasin' beasts for the day. You would've been on your own. What's got them all stirred up? And why are you clear out here?"

Jason, feeling the pull on his lines, looked back at the wild-eyed animals behind him. "Easy," he said softly, "We're done runnin'. Easy."

"You've got them all lathered up."

"No. Scotch has got them all lathered up. I don't know what he did to frighten them, but they ran and ran and ran. Took me all afternoon to catch up with them, and another hour to get hold of them. We just got back on the road, and, as you can see, I haven't gotten them calmed down yet."

Wes nudged his horse forward, coming alongside a sidestepping mare and placing a gentle hand on her neck. She flinched at his touch, but then at the calming tone of his voice began to quiet. "Easy girl, you're safe. Easy. ...Why don't you bring them up to the ranch? We've got an empty holding pen at the moment. Put them in there overnight, and they'll be good to go in the morning."

"I'd appreciate that, Wes. We all would. I'll pay you for whatever they eat."

"No need. We're all in this together. Scotch has hit us all today from the sounds of it. Got Edelman too."

Jason shook his head, exhaustion filling his green eyes. "This is exactly why I never wanted to question him about the fire. I don't know why he responds this way, but he always does."

"I don't understand it either, Jase, but it's where we are. Come on. I'll help you get them to the corral, and by then it'll be just about time for supper."

The two men split the line of horses, each taking three of the frenzied beasts and leading them up the lane past the house to a small corral at the far end of the ranch's structures. They went to the barn and cared for their own mounts before returning to the holding pen to tend to the horses that had escaped the preacher's corrals.

By the time they were finished, supper was not only on the table but nearly half-eaten.

"Did you save any for us?" Wes asked as he came to his usual seat at the table.

"Just the bones," his mother replied with a twinkle in her eyes. "Here's a clean rag for each of you since I can see you're in no hurry to wash up. The rules don't change. No dirty hands or faces at my table."

Jason laughed, receiving the wet cloth and wiping his face and hands. "We certainly need it, Mrs. Close," he said, noticing that the white cloth had turned a gritty brown.

"Speak for yourself, Preacher. I'm hungrier than I am in need of a bath." But as he laid his own dirty cloth down on the table, Wes had to admit that maybe his mother was on to something. "Well," he amended, "I guess a little tidying up might be in order."

"Just a little." Anna scooped up the two rags, kissed her son's cheek, and made her way back to the kitchen. "Everything should be on the table, so help yourselves."

"Thanks, Ma." Wes motioned for Travis to pass a less than mounding bowl of mashed potatoes. He glanced at the preacher, wondering if there'd be enough for both of them and preparing to let the other man have his portion. Then he saw Jason reaching for a second, much fuller bowl. He smiled. It was good to be home and good to be eating.

The remainder of the meal was spent in discussion of Scotch's ill behavior. No one understood, and no one could offer any solutions. At last, Wes gave up the topic and pulled out the mail. There wasn't much this time. At the very bottom of the stack was a letter to Jess from Jon.

The letter surprised Jess, for, like Wes, Jon wasn't the correspondent in the family. She was pleased that he would write to her, and at the same time afraid of what the letter might say. The others took their letters and opened them immediately. But Jess slid hers into her apron pocket and waited until everyone was engrossed in the news they were reading. Then she slipped to the counter and began cleaning things up for the night.

Zane noticed it first. He saw Jess glance over her shoulder at the rest of them and pull the envelope out of her pocket. She studied it, took a deep breath, and opened the letter with trembling fingers. She let her eyes run over the page, biting her lip as she read. When she wiped her eyes, Zane gave a meaningful kick to Wes' foot under the table.

Wes looked up in confusion, but Zane only pointed toward their friend. They watched as Jess read the letter once more. She wiped her eyes again, and then with a brave, settling breath returned the letter to her pocket. Wes glanced around the table, realizing everyone was watching. They'd all seen her tears, and they were all worried.

"Everything okay, Jess?"

She nodded and smiled at him over her shoulder, but everyone saw she was blinking back tears again.

"Is your family all right?" Anna said.

"Yes, they're fine. Papa's struggling again. That's all. Nothing has changed really. I mean…I mean we all knew he probably wouldn't survive the winter. …And I suppose we all knew that meant he'd have bad times." She paused, trying desperately to regain control of her emotions. "Everything's fine."

But everyone at the table knew nothing was fine. They looked at each other, concern drawing out the fatigue most of them felt from the day's labors. Wes was no exception. As he had passed out the mail, he'd also discreetly slid a note from Tom into his pocket unread. Now, seeing the others so concerned and Jess so obviously upset, he rose from the table, clearing his voice.

"Anyone want more coffee?"

He took in the faces that nodded back at him and filled their cups. He refilled his own cup and went to Jessica's side. "I need some air," he said softly, "If anyone needs me, I'll be outside."

"All right."

He smiled at her, patted her shoulder, and then went to the front porch. He checked to see that no one was following him and then lit the lantern that hung in the middle of the porch. Part of him had hoped Jess would follow him outside, but she didn't. He reached into his pocket for the note from Tom, once more glancing toward the shadows shifting behind the curtains at the front window.

"*Wes,*

"*Stopped in Twin Pines on my way home. Saw Jon Bennett. His pa is not doing well. Thinks he'll come out of it, but further convinced he won't survive the winter. I asked if Jess should come home. He said not now. But his wife didn't seem so sure. Does Jess have plans to go at Christmas? I think it might be wise. Good for them all.*

"*Tom.*"

Wesley sighed. He hadn't thought of that. Christmas was just around the corner. Most likely, it would be the last Christmas Jessica's family would have with her father. And here she was, all these miles away, still trying to heal and grow, and missing them something terrible. He kicked himself inwardly. How could he have missed such an important thing? Of course, she needed to go, but she had said nothing about it. Then he remembered her pay. He knew most of her savings had gone toward the previous trip. Maybe she had no way of getting there.

The front door opened, and Ronald Gray stepped out into the cold night air. He shut the door and turned toward Wes.

"That girl needs her family, boss. She needs her family. That's all I'm gonna say." And with that, he disappeared into the night.

Chapter 16

Cynthia stepped out of her tiny bedroom and into the common area of the house. She rubbed her growing belly and glanced toward the light that glowed on the other side of the room.

"Why are you still up, son?" she said, catching a glimpse of Marc at the table.

Marc looked up with a tired smile. "Just reading."

"What time is it?"

"I don't know."

The woman moved to the kitchen and poured a glass of water from a pitcher that stood on the counter. "Couldn't you sleep?"

"I didn't even try."

Cynthia joined her son at the table. She took a long drink of the water, and then set the glass down, twisting it in her fingers thoughtfully. "Aren't you tired?"

"Sure I am. I guess I'm a little restless. Got a lot on my mind."

"Like what?"

He shrugged. "Like you and the baby and Pa and the girls and Danny and Preacher and Millie and Mrs. Vass and Jon and Hannah and the tack repair and the studies and the herd and—"

"Stop. Marc, why are you worryin'? That's not like you."

"I don't know. I feel like I'm always on the verge of forgettin' something—if not already beyond the verge."

"You've taken on too much."

He studied her face. She was a beautiful woman. Of course, he'd always thought so because she was his mother, but in this moment he saw it anew: her compassion, her strength of character, and the kindness, humility, and joy in her eyes. Before he could speak, she took hold of his arm.

"This, for instance, Marc. This is the only time we talk, either very early or very late because you're never around otherwise. Every moment of every day is full, son, and it's wearing on you. Marcus, you told me the other day that you're concerned about Joy. You said she seems to have pulled inside herself, but you're doing the same thing. I know you're carrying the load as best you can, but we're here to help you. And we can't help if we don't know what's going on."

The young farmer let his gaze drop to the book before him. She'd said something similar just before the barn fell in on top of him. He hadn't wanted things to ever be at that point again, and here they were just a few short months later. He sighed.

"What's discouraging you?"

His head swung back and forth slowly. "I don't know. I think...I thought our prayer would be answered sooner than this. I thought once I'd stepped out and started working with the preacher God would answer right away, and send us help. But that help hasn't come."

"Does that make this any less God's will?"

Marc's gaze jerked up from his hands to his mother's face, surprised by the question. "No."

"God didn't promise you it would be easy. In fact, I don't remember you saying He promised you anything in return. He simply said to do it. So, do it. But do it wisely. Maybe you need to change something."

"I've been praying about that."

"And?"

"I think Danny can handle more than I've been givin' him, and I think he'll do well once he's used to it."

"Do you think that will lessen your load or add more to it?"

He shrugged. "I'm sure there will be moments. But I can give him little tasks, especially at first. That's how I learned."

"I like the idea, Marc. But don't be surprised if your brother resists."

"You never know about Danny. He's got a mind of his own."

"Yes, he does. A lot like Jon, but stubborn...more stubborn than any of the rest of you have ever been."

"I've noticed."

Cynthia laughed, knowing Marc had endured more than one clash with his younger brother's will. "But, Marc, if we can help him learn to turn that stubbornness into purpose and tenacity, your brother will do well. Stubbornness for stubbornness' sake never did anyone any good, but determination is another matter."

Marc smiled, his mind running back to his conversation with his father and the things he saw in each of the children. The two men had revisited the subject several times, but for the first time Marc realized his mother was as much a part of that as his father. They'd seen it together. The thought lifted his spirits. He wouldn't have to see it all. She would be there. They were in this together.

"I love you," he blurted out. "I don't know what I would do if you weren't here. Please take care of yourself and the baby. I know you do. I know I don't have to say it, but there's so much more going on this time around. So much extra on you than there has been in the past. Don't push too hard."

The woman reached out and smoothed his hair. "Don't let your mind dwell on things we have no control over, Marc. *The morrow shall take thought for the things of itself.*' Don't worry about me or the baby. I think the distress you're feeling is coming from your own heart. Give it to the Lord, just like you did with Jess before she went to Grassdale. Just give it to Him."

The young man nodded and looked away. Cynthia took another long drink of water, contemplating her son and the lines of concern that had returned to his face. "What else is bothering you?"

He fiddled with the corner of his Bible, flipping through its pages with his thumb. His cheeks reddened. "There's no sense in talkin' about that. We both know what it is. Talkin' about it doesn't change it."

"You're only saying that because you don't want to upset me."

Marc hesitated. She was right, of course. He didn't want to upset her, but he knew if he didn't talk it would upset her every bit as much. He sighed.

"I just want to make him better, but there's nothing we can do."

"I know." Cynthia felt the same pain every moment of every day. Watching her husband with the greatest of care. Wanting him there, wanting him in her arms, wanting his conversation, his wisdom, his laughter, and his teasing. She lived every day, wishing with all her might that she could relieve the suffering and discomfort, wishing she could make it better...for all of them.

"I'm sorry, Ma," he said, noticing the tears that had come up in her eyes. "I shouldn't let it get to me. I didn't want to upset you, and now I have. Forgive me."

"Hush. This is where we are. Both of us. All of us. Marc, you love your papa. Of course, it hurts to watch him suffer. It hurts all of us. We just have to go one day at a time, moment by moment if necessary. Keep loving him the way you always have. Keep loving the little ones the way you always have. Keep your eyes on the Lord. That's where you'll find your peace."

"I know. ...I don't know how you do it, Ma. You never seem to lose perspective."

"Oh, I do. Believe me. But, I've learned—from your papa—that as long as we keep the Lord in the center of our gaze our perspective won't wander far from where it should be. Just keep your eyes on Him, love."

"I'm tryin'. I really am."

"I know you are. Now, put your studies up and get to bed. Tomorrow comes early. You'll be exhausted if you don't get some sleep." She kissed his cheek and stood to return to her room. "I love you, son."

"I love you too, Ma."

Marcus watched his mother go. He gathered his books and set them on a shelf under the loft. He put out the lamp and slipped through the darkness to his father's open door. Gone were the days when the older man knelt for hours near his bed. Gone their long discussions about crops and cattle and news from town. But they still had moments, every one of them a precious gift. He leaned against the doorframe and stared into the dark room. All seemed well.

"Goodnight, Papa," he whispered. "I love you."

Chapter 17

Something had been lying just under the surface for days. Jess wasn't sure what it was, but it was there. Every time she came into a room the men—all of them—avoided eye contact. They seemed nervous around her. Even Wes and Dunn approached her with caution. She thought perhaps it had something to do with her response to Jon's letter and had scolded herself more than once on that account. She shouldn't have read it around the others, and she'd known it. Now, she had everyone on edge. This strange world of men was new to her. She wasn't quite sure how to keep from knocking it out of balance. She needed to fix things, but she didn't know how.

Still, she felt there was something more. She'd seen Dunn and Wes step off into a corner the night before. They spoke in low voices and kept glancing around the room to make sure no one else was listening. Then they'd called Anna over and the conversation had gone on. Now Dunn sat at the foot of the table, bowl held out to his mother, having just announced that he was going to town.

"What's got you all stirred up that you have to go to town this morning? It's cold out there," Anna said, bringing a large pot from the stove to the table.

"I've got some business to tend to, and I'm quite sure you know what it is, so there's no sense in pretendin' you don't."

Jess chuckled at the interaction between the two. Dunn grinned in his mother's direction as Anna slapped a generous spoonful of oatmeal into his bowl.

"Well," the woman said, "eat up, so you'll stay warm."

Dunn left for town as soon as the meal was over. The day was cold but clear. His trip should take no longer than usual. Two hours in, a couple of hours around town, and two hours back should put him home in time for supper. But as suppertime came and went, there was no sign of him. Jess was beginning to worry when, finally, after the dishes had been done, the evening chores were finished, and they had all settled into the sitting area for the evening, Dunn stepped through the front door. He nodded at them all, went to the kitchen, found the plate of food Anna had set aside for him and filled a mug with coffee. Then he sat down to pray over his food — all without uttering a word.

Jess watched as the man prayed. He cupped the mug of coffee in both hands, trying to warm them. When he had finished, he looked up and caught Wesley's eye. He raised his chin meaningfully, but the meaning was lost on Jess. She waited for them to say something, but they didn't. She waited for Anna to ask about the trip, but she didn't. She watched for a moment more and then, noticing a receipt from the bank sticking out of Dunn's coat pocket, she groaned inwardly.

If he'd been at the bank, he'd seen Cale. And if he'd seen Cale, then maybe he'd been there to discuss the fire. She knew all the evidence they'd found so far pointed to Scotch, but she couldn't believe it was true. Even with all he'd done since the men had questioned him. She still didn't see him as the sort of man that would do such a thing. Although there was that time he'd tried to strangle the preacher. Even that, however, didn't convince her. Scotch had been drunk at the time and had lashed out in anger. The fire, on the other hand, had been thought out and intentional. Scotch was good at making things complicated but not at plotting.

The evening wore on without a hint of what was going on. In the end, Jess didn't mind. It was a quiet evening. She caught up on a few things that had been falling behind and started planning lessons for after the Christmas break. The break would be coming soon, and she'd rather not spend the entire time planning lessons.

Morning offered no answers about Dunn's mysterious trip to town. The busyness of the day soon pressed all thoughts of it from Jessica's mind. Her students were restless, knowing their school week was at its end and having little desire to spend its last day in diligent study. She'd managed to keep their attention, but, as they hurried toward home, she wondered if they would retain any of their lessons.

Jess completed her usual routine of cleaning the room and putting everything in order for the Sunday services. She corrected the work the advanced students had turned in at the end of the day. She spent a moment straightening the bookshelves before finally stepping up to the window and looking out toward the road. She hadn't been there long, though perhaps it was longer than she realized, when she heard the shuffling of men climbing the front stairs and the scraping of the front door across the floor.

She sighed, her routine must have taken longer than she realized. The men had come for supper, and she had done nothing to help Anna with the preparations. She leaned in toward the window, straining to see as far as she could see.

"There you are."

Jess spun around to see Dunn standing in the doorway.

"Ma's lookin' for you. She thought maybe you'd stepped out somewhere, gone out with the children or something."

Jess laughed. "No. No, I'm here. At least in body. I'm not sure about the rest of me though."

The man's eyes twinkled. "And where might the rest of you be?"

"Oh, Mr. Roe, I'm in another part of the territory altogether."

"Wouldn't happen to be in the Twin Pines area would you?"

"Oh, about ten miles east of there. You caught me."

"I've been wondering about that. We all have actually."

"About what?"

"Christmas. You haven't said anything about going home for Christmas. It's only two weeks away."

"I hadn't really planned on going."

"Don't you want to?"

Jess glanced back toward the window and sighed. Then she met his gaze with sad eyes. "Of course I do, Dunn. But—"

"But what?" His voice rose in a friendly dare to find sufficient reason. A dare she didn't quite understand.

She hesitated. "I— I can't—"

"You need to go home, Jess. I know you do. *You* know you do. I think even Travis knows you do. Come out here."

Jess tilted her head in confusion.

"Come on," he urged, his voice once again rising with a cheerful lilt.

He was up to something. Jess was sure of it. She came cautiously to the door and, as Dunn stepped aside, saw the entire crew and the rest of the family gathered at the end of the table, waiting for her appearance.

"Dunn, what's going on?" she whispered.

Sensing she was nervous, the man placed a hand on her shoulder and smiled down at her with the kind, gentle smile that so matched his personality. "You need to be with your family, Jess. You need to be with your pa."

Jess bit her lip, tears stinging in her eyes. "But, Dunn, I can't. I don't have the money to go. I can't—"

"Yes, you can," he said. The smile widened into a broad grin as he reached into his pocket and pulled out a slip of paper. "I've already paid the fare. All you have to do is pack."

Jessica gasped, covering her mouth with her hands. Tears spilled down her cheeks. "What? When did you do this?"

"Yesterday."

"But, but I thought you'd gone to talk with Cale about the fire."

"I did that too. Didn't find out anything new. But *this* was the main reason I went."

"We decided last week, Jess," Wesley said, stepping forward. His eyes danced with excitement. "We all want you to go. We all pitched in, all of us. Even Travis. In fact, even the preacher and some of the parents joined in."

Jess looked down at the ticket Dunn was holding out to her. She took it from his hand, almost afraid that if she wasn't careful, it would disappear. She studied it. Her name was there, written in the same beautiful script that she'd seen on her ticket home three months earlier. Then she saw the dates, and her heart sank.

"But this says I leave on Monday. I can't leave on Monday. We still have classes next week."

"No, you don't," Wes triumphed. "We canceled next week. Everyone agreed that with the weather this time of year the journey could take longer. We wanted to make sure you had plenty of time not just to get there and back but also to be there with your family."

"But—"

"My dear girl," Anna interrupted happily, "if you haven't learned it already, you will soon learn that once my boys set their minds to something they are rarely swayed. You'll never move them on this one. Just go!"

Jess burst into a brilliant, teary smile. She threw her arm around Dunn's middle and gave him a squeeze. "Thank you. Thank you all!"

She rushed to Anna and wrapped her arms around the little woman. "Thank you. Thank you so much."

She said it over and over, moving on to Zane and Carlson and Wes, and then everyone else, including Ronald Gray who blushed a deep shade of crimson and turned away to hide his happy tears.

Chapter 18

Jess was happy to be home. She found this time, more than when she had visited in the fall, that she had to guard against the old attitudes of discontent and anger that had ruled her heart after Joseph's death. Her family, especially those toward whom she had behaved the worst, recognized the struggle. She sensed the caution in their approach to conversations, especially if those conversations involved the difficulties of their day-to-day reality. She saw things, many things, which they had left out of their letters. It frustrated her at first, but then she realized they had omitted those things to protect her.

Wes had told her she might be better equipped to pray for her family away from the situation. Now, she understood why. Had she been there, she would have been overwhelmed, just as they were.

The challenges of the situation and her family's care for her humbled her. She found herself running to the Lord in prayer numerous times each day. At first, the desperation and frequency of her prayers frightened her. Then she realized that a year earlier her prayers wouldn't have been for God's help. Her prayers a year earlier had been full of anger and blame. With that realization, she determined to continue as she was. She'd been down the path of sorrow without the grace of God's comfort before, and she had no desire to do it again. Yes, the battle in her heart was hard, but it was worth winning.

She noticed differences in each of her family members, but especially in the three siblings just younger than her. Joy had grown distant. She had never been vocal and had always tended to go off alone, but the tendency had grown. Jess could see that it concerned her mother and brothers, but no one seemed to have an answer.

Marianne had matured in a becoming manner. She was no longer the free-spirited girl she had been even the previous winter. But the joy that set her apart from others was still there, channeled into her many responsibilities around the home.

Marc had changed the most. As expected, he had moved into the roles his father was no longer able to fill. Just as he had in the past. They no longer shared the responsibility of family devotions. Marc led these brief times of teaching and worship morning and evening. He helped Mary and Ma whenever he could when the children were struggling with their studies. And, though Jess sensed it made him uncomfortable, he stepped in to correct and discipline when necessary. He carried out the tasks well with the same love and care his father had always displayed. He laughed and smiled with the rest of them, but Jess often saw a distance in his eyes. The tension there betrayed him. He wasn't allowing himself to enjoy any moment to the fullest. Something held him back. He kept things running smoothly. The household never missed a beat in the transition from father to son, but Marcus was disappearing.

Christmas Eve, after the little ones had gone to bed, Marc slipped out of the house and down to the barn to retrieve the tree he'd been hiding there. Jess followed, hoping for a few moments alone with her younger brother.

"Where did you find the tree, Marc?" she asked as she stepped up behind him.

The farmer spun around. "Jess!"

Jess laughed. "Sorry. I assumed you heard me leave the house behind you."

"Not so much as a footstep."

"So where did you find it?"

"In the coulee on the back side of the east field. Might be the last decent tree between here and the trading post."

Jess chuckled, knowing the trading post was more than a day's ride away. "I'm sure it's better than the sagebrush we used the first year we were here."

"I don't know. It's pretty scraggly. See for yourself." He pulled the tree out of the stall where he'd hidden it, shaking the branches back into place and sending the pungent fragrance of pine whirling around them.

"Hmm. Well. It isn't...well—"

"Pretty scraggly, huh? The little ones won't know. They don't have anything to compare it to. That's not what's important anyway."

A smile lit Jessica's eyes as she reached out and stroked the prickly needles. "You did good, Marc. The children will love it. ...You're doing a good job with the little ones, Poke."

Marc's gaze shot up at the unexpected remark and the use of his childhood nickname. But then he let his eyes drop back to the tree between them.

"I'm sure it hasn't been easy the past few months, but you're doing a good job."

"I don't know about that. ...Here, hold this." He handed the tree off to her and disappeared into the tack room. When he returned, he carried a stand, which he had built for the small tree.

"Sometimes..." he began, "Sometimes it feels so wrong. It's Papa's job. Not mine. It's always been his job."

"How is it any different than things in the past? You've stepped into his shoes before. You've been stepping up and filling in for years."

"Not with the children. Not in this way. The farm and the crops...that's just work. I've always been careful to leave the child rearin' to Ma and Pa. Sure when they weren't around or when we were out in the fields, I've done my share of correctin' and instructin' and even scoldin' if need be. But he's their father. I'm just their brother. I don't have the wisdom or experience he has. I don't have—" He cut himself off and looked away. "I'm not sure I have what it takes. I'm worried about the baby. What do I know about raisin' a child from birth? I know nothing. I just...I don't know, Jess. It doesn't seem right."

Jess was quiet, praying the Lord would beat down the ire rising within her. It wasn't toward Marc but rather the whole situation. She loved him and wanted the best for him. She didn't want him to hurt in this way. She wanted him to be at peace.

Marc, noticing her silence, looked up and realized the struggle she was facing. "I'm sorry, Jess. You didn't need to hear all that. No one does. Forgive me. I was wrong—"

"No, Marc. Stop. I've got to face it just like you. I'm done running. I'm sure the last few months have been the hardest of your life. The truth is I've worried about you."

Jess paused to contemplate her brother.

"What?" Marc said, surprised to see an amused smile come up in her eyes.

"I'm sorry, but if you told Jon what you just told me, he'd probably break out laughing."

Marc's eyebrows came together. "Why do you say that?"

"Because, Marc, I had the same conversation with him before Samuel was born. Do you really think any first-time father has a clue about what they're doing?"

Marc shrugged, his head bobbing to one side. "I guess I hadn't thought of it that way."

"You've had more practice than most, and Ma—Ma's an expert. You have nothing to worry about there."

"What if something happens to Ma? I can't do this on my own, Jess. I can't."

"Marcus Alan, don't let yourself think such things. Why would you ever think such a horrible thing?"

Marc dropped his gaze. He didn't expect Jess to understand. She wasn't the one facing the decisions he faced every day. She didn't have to consider the possibilities down the road.

"Marc," she said, drawing his attention back, "remember what you've been telling me throughout this long, dreadful year. This isn't what we imagined would be, but it is what is. Trust, Marc, trust. Trust that the Lord will be true to His promises. He said He'll never leave us or forsake us. Don't you believe that's still true? I know you do. The Lord will be faithful. Don't doubt His grace in your life. Don't doubt His ability to lead. He will guide you. And, please, don't give up. Please. ...We need you."

"I know," he whispered.

"Marc, don't let things get you down. Don't forget who you are, and what God has given you to do. He'll use you in the lives of the little ones, just as He's used you in my life. I wouldn't be standing here if it wasn't for you. Don't forget that." She allowed the tree to fall against the wall and took hold of both his arms, her piercing gaze searching his eyes. "Please, Marc, don't get so tied up in making up for Papa, that *you* disappear. We need you, not a shadow of you."

The young man turned away once more, uncomfortable with the conversation. How would he manage to do what she was asking of him? If he even understood what she was asking of him.

"Marc, I wish I could put into words how much I love and respect you. You may be my little brother, but you've already far outdone me in the way you have spent your life. ...And you're just beginning. Don't give up."

"I'll do my best," he said, at last, managing a weak smile and willingly receiving her embrace. "We'd better get this tree up to the house. Ma's waitin'." He handed her the tree stand and grabbed hold of the tree. Then he turned and led the way to the house.

Jess started to follow but then stopped at the barn's door. She watched him for a moment. A light snow had begun to fall. It dusted down around them, leaving a soft sprinkling of white across Marc's shoulders as he trudged toward the house.

Jess sighed. *Trudged* was the only way to describe that gait. Her heart sank and tears rose in her eyes. Her words had only added more mire to the pit of helplessness in which he found himself. How had her brave brother come to this point? It was so unlike him. So uncharacteristic for the young man who had stepped up and come to their rescue time and again. She watched as he neared the house. This had nothing to do with the children, nothing to do with the concerns he had voiced. She sighed, but didn't have time to formulate her thoughts before, as he reached for the door, he turned in search of her.

"Are you coming?" he called.

"Yes. I'm sorry," she said, taking off in a run, "I got distracted."

He laughed. "Of course you did. Wouldn't be you otherwise."

Chapter 19

Christmas was as Christmas should be. A fresh dusting of snow covered the ground, and a sapphire sky gleamed above. Inside, the hearth was warm and the love of each heart was warmer still. Jon and Hannah arrived with Samuel shortly after the others had finished their morning chores and were putting the finishing touches on breakfast. Jon and Marc moved Papa from his bed to the red chair and carried him to the sitting area so he could join the family for the day. As Marc tucked a quilt over his father's legs, a knock at the front door signaled the Nausbuam's arrival, and their circle was complete. Soon, they were crowding into their places in the sitting area.

"Uh oh," Jon said, dropping onto the floor near the Christmas tree, "he's thinking it again, Ma. I can see it in his eyes."

"What are you talking about?" the woman replied as she made her way to her rocker.

"Marc. He's sitting here thinking he should build another sofa, and then reminding himself that he'd have to build another house to put it in."

Marcus laughed. "It's true. That's exactly what I was thinking." The young man glanced around the room, taking in the happy faces of each member of his family. "Well, Jon, since we've all managed to squeeze in here, would you like to read the Christmas story this year?"

"I'll pass. I can't compete with your reading."

"There's no competition."

Jon shook his head. "I don't even like to hear myself read aloud. I don't want to subject anyone else to that misery."

"It's not that bad, love," Hannah encouraged.

The doctor grunted. "Not *that* bad, but not *that* good either. I'll tell you what, Marc, I'll practice with my boys. When Christmas rolls around next year, I'll be ready to take my turn."

"Your boys?" Cynthia said indignantly. "You're still convinced the baby will be a boy. I'm telling you, son, it could be a girl."

"There's no convincing him of that, Cynthia. I try every day, but he's determined we'll have two boys in our house come March."

Jon shrugged. "You'll see."

"And what about you, Cynthia?" Hannah continued. "Are you making any predictions about your little one?"

Cynthia shook her head emphatically, her eyes wide. "Absolutely not. Every time I've guessed, I've been wrong. I stopped guessing after Mary—who was Martin until the day she was born. No, I'm not making any guesses."

Marc cleared his throat, trying to retake the conversation before it descended into the realm of cradles, blankets, and lace. "Well," he said, repositioning his Bible in his lap, "we know for sure that Mary and Joseph didn't have to do any guessing in that area. Let's get started."

Cynthia couldn't help but chuckle as her son picked up his Bible and began to read. She reached for her husband's hand and listened to the familiar story, watching the faces of her children, and occasionally snapping a finger to remind her youngest son to pay attention. She had to admit, on more than one occasion she had looked at the boy, or at his sister Gretel, and wondered which of them was about to lose their claim as the youngest brother or sister. She smiled at the thought and squeezed her husband's hand. How she loved him. How she loved them all.

The circle of family and friends was so cozy and the spirit so sweet that, when Marc had finished reading and had prayed over their waiting breakfast, no one wanted to move. No one, that is, but Danny.

"Come on," he urged from his new place at the table. "Aren't you hungry? I'm starvin', and it smells so good!"

"Daniel, we're not going to let you starve. We never have."

"But, Ma, it smells so good!"

"Well then," Cynthia said, sliding to the edge of the rocking chair and pulling herself up, "I guess we'd better get you fed."

Danny's eyes danced as an enormous grin spread across his face. He licked his lips, sending the rest of the room into soft chuckles.

After breakfast, they made their way back to the sitting area and Marianne distributed the meager pile of gifts that had appeared under the tree throughout the morning. Most of their gifts were small and of very little expense but made with love and a great deal of thought. One gift, however, was quite large. It had been wrapped in a tattered, woolen blanket, tied together with a rope, and set at the very back of the tree against the wall. Mary hadn't seen it come into the house, and no one seemed to know for whom it had been prepared. Every other gift had been delivered, opened, and admired before Gretel's curiosity got the better of her.

"Markey, what about that gift?"

Marc turned toward her absentmindedly, distracted by the conversation he'd been having with Jess. But then he saw where she was pointing, and his eyes lit up. "That, Little Bit, is for Jon."

The doctor looked up from his seat on the floor where he was wrangling his son and his unending energy. "For me?"

Marc nodded. He rose from the sofa and moved to the tree, lifting the wool swathed gift from the floor and carrying it to his brother. Jon handed Samuel off to Hannah. He took the heavy gift from his brother, noticing that Marc had been very careful to hand it to him just so.

"What is it?"

"Unwrap it and find out." Marc stepped back and sat down on the edge of the sofa, his face bright with anticipation.

Jon untied the rope and folded the blanket back just enough that he could see inside. Then he stopped, eyes wide and disbelieving. He stared up at his younger brother, astounded.

"What is it?" Gretel said in a tone of misery as if the suspense was nothing short of torture.

But her answer was to be delayed. Jon still sat wide-eyed, looking back and forth between his brother and the contents of the blanket. "Marc, I don't believe it. Did you...I mean...you did. You made this, didn't you?"

Marc nodded, the excitement on his face somehow finding a way to flip-flop in his stomach. "Do you like it?"

"Like it? It's beautiful."

"What is it?" Cynthia asked with as much excitement as the children.

"I know," Jess replied.

Jon glanced at her and then at the gift in his lap. He pushed the blanket back, so the others could see.

Hannah gasped.

"It's a saddle!" Gretel squealed.

Jon inspected the saddle, running his hand over the smooth surface and examining every part. "Marc, this is one of the most beautiful saddles I've ever seen."

"I'm glad you like the way it looks, but I hope you like the way it rides. I made it with your rounds in mind. That saddle you've been using isn't worth more than a couple-hour ride."

"You're telling me. Marc, thank you. I can't imagine how much time this must have taken."

Marc shrugged. "It was worth the expression on your face. Besides, that's what Christmas gifts are all about. If there's no sacrifice of ourselves in our gifts, how does it reflect what we've been given?"

At that remark, Cynthia saw a faint, approving smile twitch at the corner of her husband's mouth. It pleased her every bit as much as their son's comment had pleased his father.

Gretel, Elizabeth, and Daniel stood around their eldest brother, admiring the saddle. Gretel stooped down and stroked it. She fingered the mountain scenes Marc had carved into the seat and stirrup straps. Then she jumped up and hurried to Marc.

"Will you make one for me?" the girl asked, sending the others into laughter.

"When you're older and have a horse of your own, then I'll make one for you."

The girl's face lit up and she threw her arms around her brother's neck. Then she ran back to Jon. "Did you hear that, Jon? Marc's going to make one for me when I have a horse!"

"That's wonderful, Gretel." Jon laughed, and at the same time he scooped up his son and set him in the saddle. Instantly, the boy squealed with delight and grabbed onto the horn with both hands. Again, Jon was laughing. "You may have a few more of these in your future, Marc."

They spent the rest of the day in pleasant conversation, laughter, games, and song. The happy chatter was music to Jonathan's ears. He listened to Jessica's conversations especially. Her words and responses still reflected the changes he had seen in her in the fall. Instead of anger and resentment, he heard genuine joy in her voice. He was pleased to join the others in conversation, to laugh with them, and to listen to the concerns on their hearts. He noticed Marc was especially quiet during the latter type of conversation, but he wondered if, like him, his son was merely listening. Jonathan enjoyed the stories Jess told of the children in Grassdale and of the men on the ranch. He sensed she was concerned about the events surrounding the fire and the search for the man who had started it and purposed to pray more specifically. He tired long before he let on, but he wasn't about to leave the others' company until he had to.

All through Twin Pines, there was much happiness. The Hightowers took their Christmas to Mrs. Vass, where they spent a cozy afternoon. The Phillips' house was a bit more subdued. Their son's absence was sorely felt.

Jess thought of them often throughout the day. They had all been together the year before. They'd held the hope of many Christmases together with the families permanently linked by the expected marriage — but that would never be.

Late in the afternoon, the thought of Joseph and the emotion that came with it nearly overpowered her. When no one was looking, she grabbed her mother's woolen shawl from a peg near the door and stepped out into the cold air. The sky was still clear, but she could smell snow on the breeze. She pulled the shawl tight and stepped away from the house, letting her feet take her toward a low knoll near the west field. From the knoll, she could see both her family's farm and the Phillips' ranch.

She had come here with Joseph often. Sometimes they chatted while they watched the little homes. At other times, they simply enjoyed each other's company. Now, she realized for the hundredth time that, although she had made things right with her family and his, she could never make things right with Joe. She could see the tree where they had gathered for his funeral. The thought of it sent chills down her spine.

"Oh, Joe, I was so wrong. How I wish I could tell you that in person. Thank you. Thank you for making sure I knew you'd forgiven me for the awful way I behaved toward you and God and everyone else. I don't know what I would've done if I'd had to carry that burden for the rest of my life. Thank you for loving me, even when I didn't love you as I should have. Thank you for showing me God's love, even though I didn't see it for what it was until much later. Thank you. ...I will always love you."

Jess bit her lip as tears coursed her cheeks. She drew the shawl tighter and sighed heavily. As she did so, she heard Jon's familiar footsteps behind her.

"Are you all right?"

She nodded as he stepped through the thin layer of crunching snow to her side. He wrapped his arm around her shoulders and drew her close.

"I thought there might be some difficult moments for you today."

She nodded again.

"It's okay, Jess. Missing him is healthy. You need to let your heart grieve...the right way."

"Thank you, Jon. I know you miss him too."

The tall, broad-shouldered doctor said nothing. Instead, he tightened his embrace. They stood there for half an hour, not speaking, just being together, remembering Joe and all he had meant to them, and allowing any differences that remained between them to simply melt away.

When they returned to the house, the others greeted them warmly and sat them down to Cynthia's special Christmas cake. Jess studied her mother as she ate. She saw her joy at being surrounded by the ones she loved. She saw the sorrow in her eyes as her husband bid them good-night and their last Christmas together came to a close. She saw the love the woman already carried for the child growing within her. She saw the beauty of her mother's quiet spirit, the peace that made the home a haven even in the darkest storms.

Gratefulness swelled in Jessica's heart. She had felt a longing for home, but the Closes had seen the true depth of her need to be here. It gave her new appreciation for their wisdom and foresight. She had to smile at the thought of them gathered in the sitting area and kitchen with all those men. It would be a happy occasion full of laughter, singing, and stories. She sighed wistfully as she climbed the ladder to the loft and the sea of mattresses that awaited her there. As she crawled under her blankets, she found herself wishing she could be in two places at once.

Chapter 20

Anna Close wiped the last of the crumbs from the counter, rinsed her rag, and draped it over the edge of the washbasin. She looked around the kitchen and then at her three sons as they milled about the common area of the house. A satisfied smile spread across her face.

"What a wonderful Christmas we've had," she said. "I only wish your sisters could have been here."

"And Miss Bennett," Travis whined.

"You aren't still sore that we sent Miss Bennett home for Christmas, are you?" As he spoke, Dunn plucked a cookie from the basket his mother had left on the table and headed for the sofa.

"Not sore. It's just not the same when she's gone."

Wes watched his brothers from the ottoman, which he'd pulled over by the fireplace. Dunn dropped comfortably onto the sofa, but Travis stood in the middle of the room, arms crossed over his chest and lower lip protruding into a pout.

"We laugh when Miss Bennett is here…and sing." The boy moaned.

"We've been laughing all day!" Dunn said, unmoved by the boy's petulance.

"But we haven't been singing. We could've sung if she was here, but she's not."

"Travis, we've already talked about this. We all thought you wanted her to go. You even pitched in with the stagecoach fare. Don't you want her to be with her family?"

The boy shrugged, a twinge of guilt pricking at his heart. "I suppose. But I sure do miss her. I didn't know I would miss her this much."

"Well," Dunn said, his voice light and encouraging. "That just shows how much you like her, and how special she is."

The room fell silent. Travis trudged to the mantel and took down a book he'd been reading over the break. He moved in the direction of the sofa, but then, remembering Dunn was there, he turned and went to a chair opposite the sofa. Anna watched from her own seat, a new over-stuffed chair, which her sons had given her for Christmas.

Wes returned to the book he'd been reading before the conversation began, but he didn't read. He thought about what his brothers had been saying. Travis wasn't the only one regretting their decision. He'd never been so homesick for someone. Was that strange? Could a person *be* homesick for another person? Of course, he never would've made any other decision, but Jessica's absence left an enormous hole in things. He found it strange that a person could become such an integral part of life in such a short time. One minute, you could be arguing and squabbling and the next— He had to stop and think about that next minute. *What* was happening?

"What are you thinking about so serious-like over there, Wes?"

"Huh?" the man looked up at his mother, surprised.

"You're a hundred miles away. What are you thinking about?"

"I-I guess my mind was just wanderin'," he said, his cheeks coloring slightly. "I certainly wasn't thinking about this book."

Wesley snapped the book shut and set it aside. He leaned forward, resting his forearms on his knees and shifting his gaze to his youngest brother.

"Travis, I'm with you. I think we should finish the day with some music. Run down and see if the boys want to join us. See if Carlson'll bring his harmonica. At least we could have that much accompaniment."

Travis' eyes lit up. "All right!" he said, leaping up from his chair and running toward the door. The rest of the evening promised to be much more to his liking.

❁ ❁ ❁

As the days passed, Wesley often found his thoughts wandering across the territory to Twin Pines. He'd been there once before, but he'd only met the men from whom he'd been buying cattle. He wondered where the Bennetts' farm was and if he'd passed it during his time there. He wondered about the family and how their Christmas celebration had gone. And he wondered about Jess. More than once, he caught himself counting the days until her return. And more than once, he found himself wishing they weren't so many.

When at last the day came, however, he found he didn't trust himself to meet her at the stage with the others. All morning, his stomach went from a flutter of butterflies to a tangled mass of knots. Part of him wanted to herd the others out the door as quickly as possible. But another part of him wanted to hide in the hayloft and watch in secret as they pulled away. He couldn't understand why, on the one hand, he was so nervous for her return, nor why, on the other hand, he was so anxious for it. Was he too anxious?

"Wesley Close, move out of the way."

"What?" Wes turned toward his mother, surprise evident in his face.

"What is the matter with you? I've caught you staring off at nothing more times in the last week than over the last five years. Your brother is trying to move that bench so he can finish sweeping, and you're standing right in the way. Now, move."

Wesley's face turned a deep, embarrassed red. He winced at his mother's reproof.

"Sorry, Ma. Sorry, Travis. I'm movin'." He sidestepped into the sitting area and found himself face to face with Dunn, who was carrying a stack of crates out of their newly built pantry under the loft.

"Now you're in my way," Dunn said, not bothering to hide his annoyance.

"Sorry. I'm sorry." The words tumbled out as Wes stepped to the side once more.

"What has gotten into you this mornin'? You're a mess."

Dunn made the statement in jest, but Wes realized his brother was right. He *was* a mess, and the others were starting to notice. "I'm not goin' to town with you," he blurted out before he could stop himself. "I'm… I'm going to stay here and work on some things."

"What?" Anna's voice rang with disbelief and disappointment. "Don't you want to come with us? We've all missed Jess, and it's one of our few opportunities to spend the day in town together. I was hoping we could eat at the hotel for a change. Come with us."

"No," Wes replied with an adamant shake of his head. "I need to stay behind. You go on, Ma. I'm sure you'll have a wonderful time together, but I need to stay here."

Dunn studied his brother with great curiosity. Wes had been skittish all morning like he was up to something or hiding something. This, however, was completely out of character. He never passed up an opportunity to go to town with the whole family.

"Is something wrong?" Dunn queried.

"No. No, I just feel it would be better if I stayed to tend to things here."

"Are you worried about Gray?"

"Gray? No. He seems to be doing good these days. I just feel I need to finish some things. You know, before the snows begin in earnest."

But Dunn was raising an eyebrow at him. He couldn't imagine what needed to be done in such a hurry before the snows came.

"Jess will be disappointed," Anna said. "Her telegram said she was looking forward to seeing us *all*."

"Ma, she's still going to see me. She's going to see me every day."

"But you won't get to sit with us and hear about her trip."

"I'm sure she'll be glad to tell it again." As he spoke, he realized the idea of walking with her to the creek and listening to every detail was appealing to him. Maybe too appealing. That strengthened his determination. He was a mess inside, and he'd make a mess of everything else if he tried to go with them. "No. I'm not going. I have things to do." In three long steps, he reached the door, pulled his hat and coat down, and was outside before he'd even donned them.

Twenty minutes later, Wes stood awkwardly in the yard as his family loaded into the wagon. Dunn organized the crates he'd collected for the supplies he intended to pick up in town. Then he stepped over the back of the seat and sat down next to his mother.

"Are you sure you won't come, Wes?" Anna pressed once more. "We'll miss having you along."

"No. It's okay, Ma. I'm up for a quiet day here at home. I don't have any business to tend to in town, and there's plenty to keep me busy here."

"Like what?" Dunn snorted. "I've been tryin' to figure it out for the last twenty minutes. What do you have to do that's so important? The cattle are safe in the winter pasture. The tack is all mended except for what I just loaded into the wagon to take to town. The house and barn repairs are all caught up. We even managed to build that pantry. What can you possibly have to do that is so important? Aren't you itchin' to get away for a couple of hours? The snow'll be here soon, and we'll all be stuck, one right on top of the other, like a bunch of uncooked biscuits in a bowl."

Wes laughed. Carlson was wearing off on his brother. He had him speaking in similes, but he hadn't driven the grammar out of him yet. When the word *ain't* started creeping in, they'd all be in trouble.

"I'll be fine, Dunn. There will be other chances to go to town."

"Not with all of us, and not on such a special occasion."

Wes cringed at the disappointment in his mother's voice, but he stayed his course. "I'm sorry, Ma. I just don't feel like goin' to town today."

"Are you feeling poorly?"

"No, I'm fine. I just don't want to go to town."

"Well, I'm sure Jess will be just as disappointed as I am, but if you feel you need to stay, then I suppose you need to stay."

Anna's mouth twisted to one side in frustration and disappointment, but a light was dawning on Dunn's face. He'd been watching his brother as the conversation progressed. He'd seen the tiniest flinch around the other man's eyes when their mother mentioned Jess.

"Oh, ho!" he cheered. "I see what the problem is. You might as well give up, Ma. He's not going to budge. Not with things like that on his mind."

"Things like what?"

"Don't worry, he's not sick. Nope, that's not the trouble. It'd be best to leave him be, or he's liable to get testy."

"Dunn, *what* are you talking about?"

"Oh, I reckon we'll find out soon enough. Won't we, Wes?"

"Hold your tongue, Dunn, and get a move on before you're late."

Dunn leaned toward his brother, lowering his voice. "Don't worry, your secret's safe with me." Then he winked and broke into full-bellied laughter. His blue eyes twinkled as he turned toward the horses and slapped the reins across their backs. "Walk on!" he called to the animals, still laughing as they started down the lane.

Wes watched until the others were out of sight. He couldn't help but wonder if he'd made the wrong choice. Now, not only wasn't he sure about himself but Dunn was also onto him. Dunn never let these things go, not with him. Half a dozen of their men had fallen in love, gotten married, and moved away over the years. Dunn had rarely said a word to any of them about any of it. Wesley knew, however, that *he* was a different story. He wouldn't hear the end of it until Dunn had gotten him to say whatever Dunn wanted to hear. He sighed, dragging his feet through the brittle winter grass and scuffing up the wooden steps to the house.

His dog, a scruffy, somewhat emotional, Border collie lay on the porch near the door. Her head rested on her paws, and she gazed up at him with pitiful, brown eyes. As Wes reached for the door, she whimpered, slapping her tail against the floor.

"You know I'll get in trouble, don't you?" Wes said. "Things aren't the same since Ma came to live here."

The dog patted her tail against the floor again, tilting her head as if to say, "But she's not here now."

Wes looked down the lane. From the porch, he could see the wagon had turned onto the road. He grinned down at the dog.

"Come on. Might as well enjoy the fire while you can."

As he opened the door, the dog jumped up and scurried past him. He laughed at the small black and white animal. "Spoiled," he said. "I've spoiled you since you were a pup."

The dog made her way to the fireplace and curled up on the floor near the hearth. Wes, on the other hand, went to the kitchen and poured a cup of coffee. Then he turned to survey his home.

Months had passed since he'd been alone in the house. Things had changed. He chuckled at the thought. Everything looked the same, but it was different. It was clean—clean and neat and alive. The piano, in particular, had come to life since the women had moved to the house. Jess had played it lovingly, hour after hour. He wondered what Emily would have thought of the changes. Then his stomach churned. What *would* Emily have thought of the changes? What would she have thought of the schoolroom and the new pantry and—Jess?

He crossed the sitting area to the mantel and picked up the photograph of his much-missed bride. He fingered it gently, once again confused by the direction of his thoughts. One thing he knew for certain, if Emily had been there, she would've known how to untangle his thoughts. But then, if Emily had been there, those thoughts never would've been entertained. He sighed, his confusion growing.

"You know she wanted you to remarry, don't you?"

Wesley's gaze shot up from the photograph. "What are you doing back?" he said, surprised to see his brother standing in the open door.

"Ma forgot the package she wanted to mail to Abigail, so we had to come back. ...You do know Emily wanted you to marry again, don't you? She told me so. She wanted you to be happy, wanted you to have a family. We all do, Wes."

Wes considered his brother for a moment, but then he looked back at the photograph in his hands. He set it up on the mantel but didn't turn away. "It's too soon."

"Too soon? Wes, it's been more than two years. I know three or four men who remarried within months just so they wouldn't starve!"

Wes chuckled, but the smile that flitted through his brown eyes was gone almost as soon as it came. He sighed. "I'm not talking about me, Dunn."

"Who then? None of us would shame you for pursuin' someone else after two years. Are you concerned about Jason? He's been concerned about *you*. Worried you'd be afraid to take a chance if someone came along."

Wes snorted. "Like Jason should talk. I don't see him gettin' married, or *you* for that matter. ...It's not Jason."

"Then who?" With every question, the tone of Dunn's voice rose a note or two until it finally cracked. "I don't understand who it's too soon for. Ma? Travis?"

Wes shook his head in frustration. He faced his brother with a gaze so penetrating that Dunn nearly took a step back. "No. It has nothing to do with any of us. It's Jess. It's too soon for Jess. For *her*, it's barely a year."

Dunn stared. The determination in his brother's eyes had dissolved into personal defeat at the hand of his own compassion. "So," he ventured in a low, serious voice, "I was right?"

"I don't know." Wes stepped away from the mantel and began pacing the floor in front of the fireplace. "I truly don't know."

"Well, take your time and figure it out, but don't take too much time, or she'll be grievin' all over again."

At that, Wes spun toward his brother, horrified at the thought.

"Wes, it's going to happen. We all know it. She knows it. That's why we sent her home for Christmas. And when it does happen, she's going to need a family until she can get to hers. You need to figure out where you stand before then."

"I know. You're right. I don't even want to think about that, but I know you're right."

"I haven't helped you much, have I?" Dunn said, noticing the discouragement in his brother's voice. "I just... I wanted you to know about

Emily. I know you loved her, and that love will always be there. But I also know she wanted you to go on with life and, frankly, I think she would like Jess. The rest of us sure do."

Wes blushed a little at his brother's teasing smile. He couldn't help the grin that lifted one corner of his mouth. "Thanks, Dunn."

"Come with us. You'll be fine. I think you'll be glad you did."

"All right. Just kick me or something if I start doin' anything dumb."

"Oh, you know I will. Now, where is that package?"

"I saw Ma set it on the counter earlier. There it is, by the bread."

Dunn scurried across the room, picked up the package, and hurried back across the room. Then he noticed his brother hadn't budged. "Are you comin'?"

"Yeah. I'll be out in a minute."

"Okay. We'll wait, but don't be long. Don't want to be late for the stagecoach."

Wes nodded and watched his brother run down the front steps. He studied the photo of Emily one last time and smiled. "Dunn's right, Em. I do still love you...and I think you *would* like our Jess."

A whimper at his feet caught his attention. He looked down to see the dog, blinking up at him, tail wagging. "You!" he said, "Why didn't you warn me he was coming! Traitor."

Chapter 21

"We missed it?" Anna said, looking around Main Street in search of Jessica. "We missed the stage?"

"I'm sorry, Ma. I know that's my fault." Wes apologized from where he stood in the street, having just left the stable and brought the news that Tom and the stagecoach were already gone.

Anna shook her head. "No, if I hadn't forgotten that package, we would have made it."

"But *I* wouldn't be here, and I'm glad I am. We'll find her. She probably went over to Cale and Susan's house. I'll tell you what, I'll go see if she's there. You three head over to the hotel, and we'll join you for lunch as soon as I find her."

"That sounds like a plan," Dunn said from his seat beside his mother.

Wesley waved to the others as Dunn pulled away and started down the street. He'd gone about three steps when something stopped him. He listened for a moment, heard nothing, and went on.

"Wait! Wes! Anna!"

This time, hearing joyful laughter behind him, Wes turned toward the voice and found himself engulfed in an enormous hug.

"Jess," he gasped, trying to regain his breath. "I was looking for you. Welcome home."

Jess stepped back and beamed up at him. "It's wonderful to see you, all of you."

"It's good to see you too. Where were you?"

"I was sending a telegram back to my family. I saw the others driving away as I came outside."

Anna stepped up beside the pair, smiling.

"Anna! Oh, I'm so happy to see you!"

The two women embraced. Wes was surprised to see tears on his mother's cheeks. He knew she had missed Jess, but he hadn't realized how much the young woman had come to mean to his mother. He felt tears rise in his own eyes and turned away before anyone could notice.

Anna stepped back and wiped the tears from her cheeks, smiling at her friend. "We were thinking we could get some lunch at the hotel before we head back to the ranch. Was there anything else you needed to do first? Where are your things?"

"I left them in Cale's office. He didn't see any reason for me to carry them all over town. Oh, and, Wes, he said that if I saw you and Dunn before he did to tell you he needs to talk with both of you. I think it's about the fire."

"Hmm," Wes mused. "Do you think we should go there first, or could it wait until after lunch?"

"Wesley!"

Wes looked away from Jess to see Cale standing on the front steps of the bank. He waved, but, instead of returning the wave, Cale motioned him toward the bank.

"Grab your brother and get over here."

"Well, I guess that answers our question," Wes muttered. He turned toward the wagon in time to see Dunn jump down with Travis close behind. "Ma, how about if you and Jess head over to the hotel with Travis. We'll be right behind you."

"Do you mind if we stop by and see Susan first?" Jess asked.

"Not at all. I'm sure she'll be glad to see you made it home safe. Take your time and enjoy yourselves. Let's go, Dunn."

The two men headed for the bank, Dunn managing a quick hug and a "welcome home" as he passed Jess.

Cale waited on the steps, his face expressing dissatisfaction and frustration to everyone who passed on the street.

"Well, you two," he said as they reached the steps, "Scotch is on the loose again. Come on inside."

The brothers exchanged wary glances and followed their friend through the bank to his office.

"Have a seat. Shut the door." Cale crossed the room to his desk and dropped into his chair. "I'm glad you're here. I'm starting to wish you lived in town."

"What's going on?" Wes asked as he sank into a comfortable chair.

"Ever since that business with your cattle and everything else, Scotch has been causing all kinds of havoc, mostly for the preacher. And now, he's disappeared."

"Disappeared?" Dunn's voice cracked with surprise. "What do you mean?"

"I went to talk to him one night, but he wasn't home. I tried every day for almost a week. Finally, I bumped into Madam Fulbright on the street. She said he's been gone since three or four days before Christmas. No one knows where he's gone or when — or if — he'll be back.

"I'm not sure what to do. People are startin' to notice that he's gone. Some of them are convinced he ran because he realized we had evidence provin' he started the fire. I don't know how they even know we have that kind of evidence. They want me to go after him. I'm not a sheriff. We sure need one though. I don't even know where to start looking for him. And more than that, I can't leave my family and the bank to chase that man all over the territory." He paused, groaning. "I don't know what to do."

"Does Jason know he's gone?" Wes asked.

"Yes, and he's the one who first let me know people were talkin'. They've since gotten bolder and started givin' me their opinions themselves."

"What does Jase think you should do?" Dunn said.

"He thinks I should wait a few days."

"I agree. Scotch told you that he makes trips to Maiden. If he left three or four days before Christmas, that would have gotten him there Christmas day. Maybe Christmas Eve. Let's say he stayed there three or four days. Three days back doesn't put him here until tomorrow, any more than three days put Jess back here today. Who knows what the weather is like up in those mountains."

"True." Cale conceded. Dunn always seemed to keep his head about him. Cale appreciated that. "So for now we wait, but what if he doesn't come back? I can't leave town, but I'm concerned if we don't do something, everything will be in an uproar. Then we'll have the same brouhaha on our hands that we were tryin' to avoid in the first place."

"Then let one of us go, or Jason, if it comes to that," Wes said. "That's why we're working together, so it doesn't all weigh on one person."

"I agree, Cale. One of us can go if the need should arise."

Cale sighed and leaned back in his chair, relief evident in every line of his face. "Thank you."

"We're going to have to start movin' faster though, I'm afraid," Dunn added. "The longer this drags out the more frustrated people are going to get. That's just the way of things. We need to pull the pieces together and figure out what we're missing."

"I know," Cale moaned. "Wes, have you had any new thoughts on what you saw out there?"

Wes shook his head. "How about you? Have you had any more of those five dollar coins come through?"

Cale laughed. "You mean the golden nickels? No. Not a one."

"With all the carousing that goes on in Maiden, it seems like a mighty fine place to pick up a golden nickel," Dunn said.

"Could be," Cale responded, leaning forward in his seat and resting his forearms on the desk. "But don't forget it wasn't that long before the fire that we had a whole herd of cattle and cowboys camped outside of town. There was a lot of poker going on. I even heard some of your boys were in on that. Truth is, any one of those cowboys could have brought in a coin like that, and just about any man in this town could've won it at a game. I think that coin may be more of a distraction than a clue."

"Maybe," Wes said, "but it got to Edelman's somehow on someone's person, and it's our job to find out who and how. If you think some of our men were in on the gamblin', then let us do some askin'. Maybe one of them saw something. Maybe they heard someone braggin'."

Cale nodded. "I think that's a good place to start."

"Did you talk to Scotch about the matchbox?"

"No. He hasn't spoken to me in real sentences since that day Jason and I went to talk to him. All I get out of him is a glare, a slur, and if I'm lucky, he spits the butt of his cigar at my feet instead of my face."

The brothers groaned simultaneously.

"I'm sorry for all of this, Cale," Wes said. "I know you didn't want it any more than any of the rest of us, and you've ended up with the brunt of it."

Cale shrugged. "We'll survive. ...I'm keeping you from Jess and your family. I should let you go. Thanks for stopping in."

Dunn guffawed. "You didn't give us much choice! I mean, when a wild man stands on the steps of the bank, waving you down in the street and his customers are starting to wonder about the wisdom of bankin' there, well...what else could we do?"

Cale rolled his eyes. "I have been a bit mad with all this. My poor wife is ready to move to a new town."

Wes frowned. "That's too much. Is it Scotch that's got her so upset or people in town?"

"Both. She's worried Scotch will do something. She can't go about her business without someone giving her their opinion — which they strongly imply should be my opinion — about the whole affair."

"If the five of you don't mind sleeping in one room, you're welcome to come to the ranch for a few days to get away from it all."

Dunn nodded his agreement. "We'd find a way to make it work. There's no sense in this mess adding that kind of pressure to your family."

A weary smile reached Cale's eyes. "Thank you, both. I'll talk to Susan. Don't be surprised if we show up tomorrow morning."

Dunn grinned. "We'll be ready."

❆ ❆ ❆

Lunch at the hotel was a rare treat. Jess, of course, had enjoyed her fair share of hotel and even saloon food on her trips back and forth to Twin Pines. Most of it had been little more than slop. The hotel in Grassdale was different. The cook prided herself on her cooking. She made every effort to please not only her guests but also customers from around town and the surrounding areas. She may well have been the best thing Scotch Jorgenson ever brought to Grassdale. Even so, the wonderful meal wasn't what held the family's attention.

Jess shared story after story about her journey and her family and their Christmas together. Then Anna told Jess about everything she had missed at the ranch. Travis all but exploded with the excitement of rehearsing his favorite parts of the holidays to his teacher. Dunn was always ready with a comment or a joke or a story of his own.

Wes was content to watch and listen. A happy smile perched unwavering on his face. His gaze rarely shifted away from Jess. He watched her with great care. He could see she was glad to be back, but something was missing. Something that had been in her when she'd come back in the fall was now gone. Or was it? One minute, she seemed like the same bright, cheerful woman God had brought back to them after the fire. The next minute she seemed weighed down by some secret sorrow. Perhaps she was just tired from the journey, but perhaps it was something more.

Part of him regretted their invitation to the Bennetts, or rather he regretted the suggestion that they come the following morning. He didn't want to share Jessica yet. He wanted to know what was going on in that mind of hers. He wanted to know what was causing the shadows in her eyes. He wasn't going to find out with five extra people in the house.

He sighed, not realizing he'd done it.

"Is something wrong, Wes?" Jess asked.

"What?"

"You sighed a very heavy sigh. I thought maybe something was troubling you."

"Don't mind him, Jess," Anna said, waving the teacher's concern away. "He's been like this since Christmas. No one knows why. He's got something churning in that brain of his, and he's not about to let it out."

"Actually," he said in a very measured tone, "I was thinkin' about the fact that we invited Cale and Susan to spend some time at the ranch. Cale said they might come as soon as tomorrow. I don't want to give up our time with Jess, but I think maybe we should head toward home. We'll need to rearrange a few things if we're going to have guests."

"They can sleep in my room," Anna offered. "I'll go back with Travis."

"That's kind of what I had in mind if you're up for it."

"It's fine. Travis and I slept in front of the same fireplace for years. We're used to one another's snoring."

Dunn laughed. "You *have* to be used to that boy's snorin' if you're going to sleep through the night in the same room."

"Hey!" Travis protested, an expression of hurt crossing his face.

But Dunn didn't give the boy any more chance to fuss. He pushed his chair back and grinned at the rest of them. "Let's get a move on then."

"You know," Anna said, "we've been having such a pleasant time, but we forgot about our shopping. Jess, I know you're tired from your journey. Maybe the rest of you should stay here, and I'll go as quick as I can."

"I'll come with you, Ma," Dunn said. "I'm sure some of it will be heavy."

"Thank you. I'd love the help."

"I'll come! I want to see what's new at the store."

Anna frowned. "Travis, we're trying to make this quick. I know how you get when you discover new things at the store. You examine every detail and read every label. We don't have time for that today."

"I won't, Ma. I promise. I'll just follow you around and look."

"All right, but I will hold you to it. Do you two mind staying here then?"

Dunn snorted at the comment but said nothing.

Wesley shook his head, shooting his brother a warning with his eyes. "I'm the one who didn't want to come to town in the first place."

"True. What about you, Jess?"

"I don't mind. It's nice to sit still for a while before getting back on the road."

"Very well. We'll be off then, and we'll meet you back here as soon as we're done."

Anna spun around, motioning for Dunn and Travis to follow.

"You didn't want to come to town?" Jess questioned when the others had gone. "That's strange for you. Is something bothering you, Wes? You've hardly said a word the entire meal."

"No. I'm just takin' everything in. And I'm noticing something different about you. How are you really? Something doesn't seem right."

She sighed and looked away. "You noticed."

"I noticed you're not tellin' us something. Something pretty weighty. Is it your pa?"

She shrugged. "I don't know. Papa isn't doing well, but he's still as much a part of the family as he can be. He has good days and he has really bad days. I feel like those bad days are killing them all."

"How is your ma?"

"She's worn. At first, I thought she was all right, but the longer I was there, the more I saw how tired she is. Marc and Marianne are doing a good job of picking up the slack for her, but it's still a lot. Marc worries about her. I think Marc is worrying about a lot of things. I think he's doubting himself. I've never seen that in him before. It scares me, Wes. The family needs him now more than ever. What if he buckles under the load?"

Wes considered her for a moment. His mouth twisted to one side, indicating he didn't know how to answer. She started to apologize, but he held up a hand before she could speak.

"This is where faith comes in on your part, Jess. Not faith in Marc and his ability to lead your family, but faith that God will take care of it all. Marc probably is doubting himself. He can't do anything to stop what's happening, and that tends to make a man feel helpless. From what I've seen of your brother, he'll step up when the time comes. And if he doesn't have the strength or courage to do so on his own—well, he knows where to go to find it. And that's just what he'll do."

Jess nodded, but tears glistened in her eyes.

"What is it?"

"I'm scared for him, Wes. He's trying so hard to be who everyone wants and needs him to be, but *he* is disappearing. I talked to him about it, but I think he saw it as one more thing to keep up with—probably the one of least importance. I want the best for him. That's all I've ever wanted for him. I wish I knew what that was."

Wes grinned. "Don't we all. You may not know what is best for him, Jess, but I can guarantee you the Lord does. As long as Marc keeps his eyes on the Lord, he'll be okay. God won't let any of you down. He won't leave your brother and He won't leave you."

Jess nodded, wiping her tears. "You're right. I know you are. Thank you."

"Anytime." He sighed, patted her arm, and leaned back in his chair, stretching his long legs out in front of him. "I haven't sat so much in one day since the fire. My legs aren't sure what to do about it. ...Travis really missed you. He pouted for two hours Christmas day. ...Truth is, we all missed you."

"I missed you all too...so much. I felt guilty sometimes."

"Guilty? Why?"

Jess blushed. "I was having such a wonderful time with my family, but part of me wanted to be here with you. I lay in bed Christmas night wondering how you'd spent the day and how each of you was doing. I was surprised to find that I was homesick. I suppose I'm blessed to have two places I want to be at once."

Jess stopped, feeling she'd begun to ramble, but the kindness in Wesley's eyes told her that he was more than happy to listen. She blushed under his attentive gaze, and shifted the conversation. "It sounds like you had a nice Christmas."

"We did. Did you know that Ronald Gray plays the fiddle?"

"What?"

"Yes. He doesn't have one at present. He's chiding himself rather vehemently these days over the various things he sold so he could buy just one more drink. But he's saving up. He informed us that as soon as he gets a new one, we'll be the first to benefit from his playing. I think he was trying to console Travis. He was very upset that you weren't around to provide music on Christmas Day."

Jess laughed, happy to be back with the cheerful family. Glancing toward the floor and noticing the small suitcase Wes and Dunn had brought from Cale's office, her thoughts shifted. "Has anything new come to light about the fire?"

Wes rose from his seat and scooped up his cup. "Not really. I think I want more coffee. It'll be nice to have a little warmth in me before we leave. Would you like anything more?"

"No. I'm fine. Thank you."

He began to step away, but then he stopped and squared his gaze up to hers. "I'm glad you're home, Jess. It wasn't the same with you gone." He patted her shoulder as he stepped around the table and went to find more coffee.

She watched as he went. Something was different in him too. He seemed happy, but he also seemed to be hiding something. Something was making him nervous.

"We have a surprise for you at the house," he said as he returned to the table.

"You do? What is it?"

"Not tellin'. If I tell, it won't be a surprise. I think it'll make life easier for you though."

"What? Now, I'm curious. And you're going to make me wait until we get home, aren't you?"

"Of course I am."

"Is that what you've been hiding?"

"Hiding?" he exclaimed.

"You're distracted. You didn't want to come to town. But you won't talk about the fire. It's the fire, isn't it?"

"You really are curious, aren't you?"

"Almost as curious as Travis. I get it from my mother."

Wesley laughed. "*No one* is as curious as Travis." He paused, considering his answer. He could hardly tell her that he didn't know how to behave around her because he was pretty sure he was falling in love with her. That was out of the question. But he didn't think he should say much more about the fire either.

"It's all right if you can't tell me, Wes. I could tell Cale was upset by the fire business."

"There's nothing new to tell about the fire. I think that's upsetting Cale as much as anything. One of us may end up takin' a little trip to check into some things, but that hasn't been decided yet. I imagine we'll be talkin' with our men in the mornin' too, to see if— How did you do that?"

"Do what?"

"Get me to start talkin' about it?"

Jessica laughed. "I don't know. By telling you, you didn't have to, I guess. Go on. What are you going to talk to the men about tomorrow?"

Wes rolled his eyes. "Nice try. Now you'll just have to wait until mornin'."

Chapter 22

Wesley's surprise greeted Jess as soon as she walked in the front door. While she'd been away, the boys had closed in the area under the loft, creating a large pantry. A beautiful set of stairs wound up the outside wall to her landing. Upon seeing it, Jess clasped her hands together, looked at Anna with a beaming smile and said, "Tea! Oh, Anna, now you'll be able to come to my room for peace and quiet and tea."

Jess fell easily back into her routine. She was happy to be back with her students. She loved them all. She also loved spending the evenings with the family. Wes offered to move the writing table to her room since the stairs made it easier to carry her work to the loft, but Jess chose to leave it where it was. Although she spent most evenings with her back to the room, she enjoyed listening to the family's conversation and even joined in from time to time.

She enjoyed her time with Anna, fixing meals, scrubbing floors, doing laundry and more laundry and more laundry. The time they spent together was sweet. Through her steady example, Anna taught Jess much about love and forgiveness. She helped Jess find ways to comfort her mother even from so far away. As the days passed, Jess realized she had come to love Anna as a second mother.

Unlike Cynthia's quiet, rarely fluctuating temperament, Anna was prone to express exactly what she felt, the way she felt it, and as soon as she felt it. She wasn't rash. Wisdom tempered that. But she never left any doubt about her position on things, especially if it involved her children.

One frigid afternoon in late January, Jess heard the front door slam shut and Anna stomping her way across the sitting area. A moment later, the schoolroom door swung open, and Anna marched into the classroom.

"That son of mine must have a death wish!" Every muscle of the woman's body was tight with frustration. She huffed loudly and looked at Jess as if expecting her to offer some solution to the problem. Whatever the problem was.

"Which son?" Jess asked somewhat cautiously from her desk.

"Which one do you think? Dunn would never be so foolish."

"What happened?"

"It hasn't yet." Anna paused, crossing her arms across her chest. "Wesley's got it in his head that he has business in another part of the territory and that he must take care of it now."

"Where? What does he need to do?"

"He won't say. He's leaving in the morning and taking Zane with him. That's all he'll say."

"Leaving! But, Anna, it's been just above zero for days. They'll freeze."

"My point exactly. But would he listen to me? No. No matter how hard I tried to talk him out of it. He's made up his mind. He says it can't wait. If he puts it off any longer, there'll be too much to do with round-ups and calving and then it will be too late. He's going. That's it. No more discussion."

Jess said nothing. Wesley wasn't a man prone to make rash decisions. She couldn't believe this was some random, overnight decision based on a whim. No. Something had happened to provoke his decision. Or he'd been praying about something and had finally reached a decision. She thought back over the previous days. "Do you suppose it has anything to do with the letter Carlson brought back from town last night?"

"Letter? What letter?"

"I don't know. I never saw the envelope. I don't know who it was from. Carlson came home and handed Wes the stack of mail. Wes pulled out a particular letter and read it several times. Then he left the house. Later, when he was pretending to read that book he's been pretending to read since October, I saw him reading the letter again."

Anna shook her head. "I don't know, Jess. Maybe you're right. …You're definitely right about that book. I don't know why he doesn't put it away and read something else. He obviously doesn't like it. Stubborn. Just as stubborn as —" she sighed. "Just as stubborn as his mother."

Compassion drew a smile across Jessica's face. "What did Dunn have to say about it?"

"Wes wouldn't even let Dunn open his mouth. I don't understand. They always do everything together, but Dunn doesn't seem to have any idea what this is about. Maybe he'll find a way to talk some sense into his brother before morning. I don't know. Wes sure wouldn't listen to me."

Anna moved to the front of the room and sat down at one of the desks. "What can I do, Jess? He's a man. He's going to do what he feels he needs to do. There's no stopping him unless God does it."

"Did you ask him if he had prayed about it?"

The woman nodded, defeat rising in her eyes. "Yes, I did."

"And?"

"He has."

"And?"

"He feels he should go. I just wish I had that confidence."

"Anna, as angry as it used to make me when my brother would tell me this, I guess this is where trust comes in. Trust in both Wesley and the Lord."

"I know. I know the Lord will take care of them. I just hope Wes heard the Lord right."

"I suppose that's between him and the Lord."

Anna eyed her young friend for a moment. She had pluck. Few women would have dared to put her in her place like that, especially with regard to her sons. The woman ran a hand over her gray hair and let out a deep sigh. "You're right. I know you are. Come on. Let's start dinner."

Saying they should trust was much easier than doing it. Jess was just as afraid as Anna. Since she'd been home, not a single day had been above freezing. She knew all too well what could happen to a man stranded in that cold. The thought of losing two more friends to its ruthless grip terrified her. She thought she might do her part to dissuade Wes from making the trip, but, as they sat down to the evening meal, she knew it would be pointless.

Wes took full control of the conversation. He gave directions concerning the work he expected the men to complete while he was gone. He told Zane how to pack for the trip. He asked Anna and Jess to prepare food for their journey.

Jess watched and listened, but added nothing to the conversation. Wes managed little more than the occasional furtive glance in her direction. If, by chance, he caught her looking at him, his gaze darted away.

It made no sense. He had never behaved this way toward her. In fact, for most of their friendship, he had been the one trying to get more out of her. She, at least initially, had been the one who tried to close him out. As she watched him, she realized he must be afraid she would find out what he was up to. Or perhaps, he was aware of the uneasiness his trip would cause her. Either way, his strange behavior unnerved her all the more.

As the meal came to a close and the others had begun to talk among themselves, Wesley finally settled down to the food on his own plate. He jabbed his fork into a mound of mashed potatoes and deposited a large helping into his mouth with a great sigh. The buttery goodness brought a deep sense of calm and satisfaction. As he looked up from his plate, he saw Jess watching from the other end of the table. Her eyes shot questions, which he couldn't answer.

"Why are you doing this?" they seemed to say. "Don't you know what could happen to you out there?"

Guilt swept over him. He went back to his meal, unable to hold her gaze.

Somehow, in the short time since she had come home, he'd found a way to balance the feelings in his heart with the peculiarity of their situation. He couldn't court her, not yet. Not only was she living in their home but she was also their teacher. Her position forbade suitors. He wouldn't jeopardize her job, nor her reputation. Unless something in their situation changed drastically, he felt it unwise to make his intentions known until school was out. But there was no longer any doubt in his mind. He loved her.

Now, however, he felt ashamed. Her fiancée had died in the face of a much smaller risk. And yet, Wes was asking her to trust him with no information or explanation to give her hope. Even he was upset with himself. It seemed cruel. And yet, it had to be done, and it had to be done now.

The others cleared their places and went about their evening chores, but Wes lingered at the table. He savored every bite of what could be his last hot meal for days to come. He watched his mother and Jess clean up the mess from the meal. They both sighed from time to time, but neither spoke as they worked. They were anxious, and *he* was the cause of it.

He had just laid his fork down next to his empty plate and was reaching for his cup of coffee when he saw Jess pick up the compost pail.

"Anna, do you have anything else to go in this? It needs to go out."

Anna turned to see what the young woman had and then shook her head. "No, I'm going to fold those towels and rags and put them away. Then I'll be finished."

"All right. I'll take it out then. It's smells something awful."

"I'll go with you."

Both women spun toward Wes in surprise. He rose from his seat, picked up the steaming mug of coffee, and motioned Jess toward the door.

"We need to talk."

The man's voice left no room for questions. Jess glanced at Anna, shrugged, and then made her way out of the house with Wesley at her heels.

The rancher said nothing as they made their way down the stairs into the dark yard. They went around the corner of the house, and across a wide, flat expanse to the compost heap at the end of the garden. He sipped his coffee and watched her toss the contents of the pail onto the pile. Then he took a deep breath of the frigid night air.

"Jess, I know this trip makes you nervous. You have every reason to feel that way, more so than any person in there tonight. ...But I need you to trust me."

Jess didn't respond. Wes wished they'd chosen a night with a full moon to have this conversation. Then at least he might have been able to read the expression on her face. With that thought came another. He and Zane would be traveling by this light for much of their journey. Their days were still among the shortest of the year. They wouldn't be able to wait until sunrise each morning or stop when it was dark. They had to travel as far as possible every day. With no moon, keeping watch at night would be difficult. His stomach churned. Then he realized Jess was shivering and hurried on.

"I wouldn't do it if it weren't so important, Jess. Please, don't worry about us. Just trust the Lord to keep us safe."

"Why does it have to be such a secret, Wesley?" She said, pulling her shawl tight. "Why can't you at least tell us where you're going? If something happens to you two, we won't even know where to look for you."

He shook his head. "If I tell you where I'm going, it will raise even more questions than my not telling you. Questions I can't answer. ...Two weeks, Jess. I promise we'll do our best to be back in two weeks. Maybe even less, but that would only be if things don't go well—" He ran a hand through his hair in frustration. "I know this is bad timing, Jess. I know it is. I don't want to ride in this cold, but it has to be done, and it has to be done now."

Jess took a deep breath, feeling the bite of the cold air in her lungs. She cleared her throat. "Anna said you've prayed about it."

"Yes. I have. I've been praying about it for a while and then...then I got a letter last night —"

"I thought that had something to do with this."

"You saw it?" Wes panicked. No one was to see that letter. No one.

"No, no," She replied. "I didn't see it so much as I saw you reading it — several times. It seemed to cause you concern."

"It did. Jess, I wouldn't be going anywhere this time of year if I wasn't sure this was where the Lord was leadin'. I wish I could tell you. I do. But I can't."

"Well, I guess all I can do then is trust that you're letting the Lord lead you, and that He'll keep you safe, both of you."

"You mean that?"

"Yes. I mean it. I'm not saying it's going to be easy, but I mean it."

"Thank you, Jess. Thank you. We'll be careful. I promise."

"I know you will be. Please, Wes, please don't take unnecessary risks."

"I won't. I promise."

Wesley let out an enormous sigh. He offered her his arm and led her back through the dark night to the house.

Jess climbed the steps and went to the front door, but then she stopped, watching him stride across the yard to the bunkhouse. An uneasiness rose in her stomach. She drew her shawl tight again, hoping to drive away the cold and the fear building in her heart.

Her thoughts wandered back over the months that lay behind them. Of all the people upon whom she had poured out her disdain after Joseph's death, Wes had been the least deserving. And yet, he had loved her patiently, firmly, and kindly. He had welcomed her into his home even when the gulf still lay between them. He had comforted her in the face of loss even though his own family had lost so much more. He had encouraged her back to the Lord when she had felt so unable to return. He had rescued her, whether he knew it or not. Tears rose in her eyes as she realized once more how much he had come to mean to her. The thought of losing him terrified her.

She watched until he was out of sight. Then she stood silently, listening to the sound of his boots on the frozen earth. She heard the cold wood of the bunkhouse steps groan beneath him. The door scraped open and then clicked shut.

She bit her lower lip and tears spilled down her cheeks. Morning would come, and they would say goodbye. Would she ever see him again? She wiped her eyes, pushing the thought away. She would trust. She had promised him that she would, and she intended to keep that promise...but it wasn't going to be easy.

Chapter 23

Cale Bennett sat quietly at his desk as he did every day, going over accounts and ledgers, making sure everything was in order both for his bank and for his customers. He sipped at a cup of coffee, wishing something—anything—would take the chill off of the day. He sighed, took another drink of the coffee, and went back to his work.

"I heard you was lookin' for me."

Cale's head jerked up. "Scotch!"

"Yep. It's me. I heard you was lookin' for me."

"I was. Come in and have a seat."

The short, heavy man stepped into the room and dropped down across from Cale. He said nothing.

"A lot of people have noticed you haven't been around, Scotch. Some people thought you'd left town for good."

Scotch shrugged. "People will think what people will think."

"I suppose you were in Maiden."

"Suppose whatever you want to suppose."

Cale studied the man across from him, his eyes growing intense and his fingers drumming the desk lightly. "Scotch, we need to...I don't know...come to some kind of agreement. I don't like this business any more than you do, but this is where we are."

"Yeah, except you are the one doin' the accusin', and I'm the one being accused. There's a difference, Bennett. A big difference."

Cale was tempted to defend himself, but he stopped before the words fell out of his mouth. "You're right, Scotch. There's a big difference. I wasn't lookin' for you so I could make accusations. In fact, I never wanted to make accusations. I was just tryin' to figure things out."

"I didn't do what people think I did."

"Then help me prove it."

Scotch considered Cale for a moment, his eyes narrowing. "How are we supposed to do that?"

"Well, we can start by cuttin' out things like drivin' off livestock and floodin' Edelman's corral. We *know* you did those things. Wes and Dunn and the preacher have no intention of takin' the matter up with the law. I'm pretty sure I can convince Edelman to agree to the same if you'll agree to stop."

Scotch shifted in his seat. "That was too much. I agree. I talked to—" He stopped as if realizing he was about to say too much. "I was thinkin' about it while I was gone. I was angry at you an' the others for your accusations and lashed out. Somebody coulda been hurt. I shouldn't have done it. I'll stop, but you've got to promise to look for the truth."

"I promise, Scotch. That's what I've been after all along. I asked you the questions I asked because I had to. ...And I need to ask you some other questions too."

"Questions or accusations?"

"Questions."

"All right. Shoot."

"Have you—" but a movement outside the door caught Cale's attention, and he cut the question short. Corey Banton stood in the lobby of the bank, staring at the two men in the office. Cale cleared his throat and lowered his voice. "I think perhaps we should finish this conversation later."

"Later? What for? I have businesses to run, Bennett. I don't have time for games."

"Someone has been listenin', Scotch, someone I don't know much about. I promised you the truth, and I'm not going to hunt for it while I know someone is eavesdropping."

Scotch turned in his seat, catching a glimpse of Banton just as the other man realized he'd been caught and turned away. "Was that Banton?"

"Yes. He doesn't like you very much, Scotch. He's the one who had to clean up the mess you made in the corral. I doubt he'll look highly on the two of us sittin' here together. I'll tell you what. I'll meet you tonight at your house."

"I sold my house."

"What!"

Scotch shrugged. "Sometimes you just need somethin' different. I sold my house, and I'm stayin' at the hotel until I get a new place built. I don't want to live in town anymore. Too many people watchin' and whisperin' all the time."

"I'm sorry, Scotch. I'm sorry things have come to that."

Scotch shrugged. "It's my own fault, and I know it." He lowered his voice, not wanting the world outside the office to hear and yet finding release in the confession. "I've behaved the part of the fool for the better part of my life. Now, I'm reapin' the consequences...just when I thought things was turnin' around for the better, for the happier. ...I'm closin' the brothel as well, but don't go spreadin' that 'round town. I'm tryin' to find good work for the girls, not...you know...this kind of work. That's part of the reason I've been away. I'm sending Madam Beast back to where she come from. She's been a thorn in my side since I met her."

Cale stared. He couldn't believe what he was hearing. This wasn't the Scotch Jorgenson he had known since coming to Grassdale. He was humble, meek even.

Scotch pressed on. "I'll answer whatever questions you have, but if you're not wantin' to be seen, I don't think you should come to the hotel. There's an abandoned cabin about a mile west of town. It's a good three quarters of a mile from the road, but you can see it from the road. Meet me there tomorrow mornin', say, around ten. We can finish our conversation then."

"All right. I'll be there."

"Good." Scotch stood and, for a moment, appeared as if he were about to extend a hand to Cale. Then the expression on his face changed. "Tell the other men I'm sorry for what I done to their livestock and pens. It won't happen again. I'll pay for whatever damages I caused. Just have them stop by my office. I'll see you in the mornin', Bennett."

Cale watched as the man shoved his hat on his head and turned away, leaving the bank without another word.

※ ※ ※

Dunn pulled his coat tight as he tied his horse outside of the bank and turned toward the tall wooden structure. The ride to town had been miserable. Cold wind and tiny ice pellets bit at his face the entire way. He was eager to get inside, and even more eager to find a stove and, with any luck, a cup of coffee. He climbed the wooden steps and pulled open the heavy door. The lobby of the bank was quiet. And no wonder, who in their right mind would venture out on such a day?

"Mr. Roe," came a cheerful greeting from behind the counter, "how can we help you?"

Dunn managed a sincere, if somewhat frozen, smile at the man behind the bars. "A cup of coffee would be nice. Wouldn't happen to have any would you?" he shivered.

"Is that Duncan Roe out there?" came a voice from the corner office.

"Yes, sir. It is," said the man behind the counter.

"Send him in here, Mitch, and get him some coffee."

"Yes, sir. ...You heard the man, Mr. Roe. I'll have your coffee in just a minute."

Dunn drug himself across the room, his limbs stiff and aching with cold.

"*What* are you doing here?" Cale said as Dunn entered his office. "It's freezing out there. Sit down."

"I'll admit," Dunn said, lowering himself into a chair, "I'll be glad to have that coffee in my hands."

"Dunn, your lips are blue. Why did you come to town on such a horrible day?"

"I've got a sick horse. Needed to pick up a few things at the General Store to make sure we don't lose her. More than that, I wanted to talk to you. But we need to talk with no one else around."

"That can be arranged. Do you want to go over to the house?"

Dunn grunted happily. "I don't want to move past this chair now that I'm in it."

The man from behind the counter stepped into the room with a large mug of steaming coffee. Dunn received it gratefully.

"Mitch, make sure there's enough for another cup if he wants it. If not, put another pot on, and then you can go for the day. Make sure you close things up properly."

"Thank you, Mr. Bennett."

"Enjoy your evening. Close the door behind you, please."

Dunn smiled as the man left and the door closed. "Well, that works."

"I'm finished for the day. My head is spinnin'. I've had too many surprises. Are you here about the fire?"

Dunn hesitated, "Well...in a manner of speaking...yes. ...I suppose you could say that. ...No. Not really. ...I'm here about my brother, but if you need to talk about the fire first go ahead. I'm all ears."

"Your brother? Which one?"

"Wes."

"Is something wrong?"

"Not exactly. ...I mean...I don't know. I was hoping you could tell me."

Cale raised an eyebrow. "What could I possibly tell you about your brother that you don't already know?"

Disappointment crept into Dunn's face. Maybe this had been a dumb idea.

"What's going on, Dunn?"

"Did you send Wes to Maiden?"

"Wait. Wes is in Maiden?"

"Then I take it your answer is no." The kind-featured man removed his fur hat and plunked it down on his knee. He ran a hand through his sandy hair and let out a long, frustrated groan. "Did Wes come in here to make a withdrawal a couple days ago?"

"Yes. Zane was with him."

"Did he mention going anywhere?"

"No. Now that you mention it, he was pretty tight-lipped. What's going on?"

"Wes told us three days ago that he had business to tend to in another part of the territory. He wouldn't tell us what the business was or where he was going. Two days ago, he and Zane left. He promised they'd do their best to be back in two weeks, but no one knows where they're going or what they're doing.

"After they left, Jess told me that she'd seen Wes reading a letter he'd taken out of the pile of mail Carlson brought from town. She saw him read it several times. Wes admitted to her that the note had influenced his decision, but he didn't tell her who it was from or what it was about. I thought maybe you'd decided to take him up on his offer to go check out Scotch's story. I thought maybe he'd gone to Maiden to find Scotch."

"Scotch is back. He just left my office an hour ago. I didn't send Wes anywhere, Dunn. ...This is the wrong time of year to be makin' trips like that."

"You're tellin' me! My mother was beside herself when she found out his plan. I don't know what's gotten into him. I can't figure for the life of me what business needs to be taken care of on such short notice in such terrible conditions. I only rode two hours in here, and I thought I wasn't going to make it. I can't imagine going all day and then tryin' to find shelter for the night."

"He didn't give *any* indication of where he was going?"

"None. It's not like him. That's why I thought it had something to do with the fire."

"Maybe it does. Maybe he found something out and went to check into it before he told the rest of us. Maybe he's like me, tired of people jumpin' on every tiny move we make."

Dunn sighed. "I suppose that's possible. ...I'll tell you what, if he doesn't get back here in two weeks' time, he's going to have at least one angry woman to reckon with when he does show up."

"Your mother?"

"Yes. She goes around mutterin' about it every time she thinks she's the only one in the room. It's rather comical actually, but I know she's worried."

Cale considered his friend as the other man paused to take a long drink of the hot coffee. "How's Jess doing with it?" he asked at last. "I'd think with her experience with her fiancée this could set her on edge as well."

Dunn nodded. "She's been a bit subdued, but I think she's doin' all right. I've been keepin' an eye on her as best I can. I don't know how Wes could pull a stunt like this with her right now."

"What do you mean?"

"It's a year this month since her fiancée passed. I don't know the exact date. We're probably already past it. But why would he put her through the torment of wonderin' every day for two weeks if they're safe? I thought he was fallin' in love with her. He'll never win her this way."

Dunn gasped at his own words and covered his mouth, sending laughter into Cale's blue eyes.

"Well, that's an interestin' bit of news. Does my cousin know about this?"

"Which one?"

"Jess, of course. Who did you think I meant?"

Dunn laughed. "Any one of her brothers comes to mind. Don't say anything to anyone, Cale. I don't think Wes feels he can pursue her so long as school is in session. He's been careful not to let on about anything to anyone. I just happened to figure him out."

"I won't say a word, not even to my wife. Although, that may prove difficult. Do you think Jess has any idea of his feelings?"

"I don't know, but I'm pretty sure her feelings for him are similar. She's never said or done anything to make it obvious, but I saw the concern on her face as he rode down the lane. For two people who started out at each other's throats, they sure have come to greatly appreciate one another...at the very least."

Cale was grinning. Wes and Dunn had been some of his closest friends since the day he and his family arrived in Grassdale. He respected and admired both of them. He couldn't think of a better choice for his cousin than either of them.

"I'd be glad to see that go somewhere, Dunn. I think they have common ground to build on. I think they'd make a good couple."

"I agree. Jess has brought life back to Wes in a way he didn't even know he was missin' it. And Wes, well, I think Wes helped Jess more than any of us will ever fully know. ...We talked to our men."

A small furrow appeared in Cale's brow at the sudden change in conversation. "About?"

"Gamblin' with the cowboys from that cattle drive that came through last summer. We were going to talk to them about it the day after we talked with you, but then we decided to wait until you and your family had come back to town. Thought it might make the conversation more natural without guests around. Anyway, a few of them admitted they'd been in on the gamblin'. That was no surprise. But none of them had seen or heard anything about golden nickels. Or gold coins in general for that matter. I know our men pretty well. I didn't see anything that made me think any of them were being dishonest."

Cale nodded, disappointment clear in his eyes. "I was afraid they wouldn't know anything. Well, no matter. It is what it is. I'm supposed to meet with Scotch tomorrow morning in an abandoned cabin west of town. I'm going to ask him about both the nickel and the matchbox then."

Concern washed over Dunn's face. "I don't like the sound of that, Cale. It could be a trap."

"I don't think so. Something's different about that man."

"Just the same, take someone with you. Take Jason. ...And take a gun."

Chapter 24

A fresh layer of snow crunched under the horses' hooves as Cale Bennett and Jason French rode through the sage and tall grasses toward the small, wooden house. The men rode in silence, studying the dark structure. The roof was caving in on the back corner. Torn, faded curtains hung over windowless window frames, moving in and out with the breeze as if the house were breathing. A chill ran up the preacher's spine at the sight.

"I don't see any sign of Scotch," he whispered. "Do you want me to circle around back, make sure no one's hiding?"

Cale nodded, his blue eyes fixed on the house. "Go slowly."

Jason nudged his horse forward. A knot tightened in his stomach, and he found himself reaching back to touch the butt of his rifle. As he started the wide circle around the back of the building, he realized he'd gone the wrong way. The sun would work to the aid of anyone hiding behind the house, pushing their shadows away from him and his own shadow out in front of him.

He stopped the horse before breaking the line of visibility around the house. He listened. The only sound was the faint dripping of snow melting in the morning sun. He waited a moment more and then moved forward. A broken down barrel and an odd assortment of rakes and shovels leaned against the wall near the back door. A rabbit scampered away from the barrel. Then everything was still again. He urged his horse forward and completed the circle, peering through the eerie house as he went.

"Nothing back there," he said as he returned to Cale's side, "and you can see clean through the house as you go. Do you want to wait out here, or see if the door's open?"

"Let's wait inside, but let's leave the horses where Scotch can see them."

The men dismounted and led their horses to the front of the house.

"You ever been to this house before?" Jason said as he tied his horse to a porch rail.

"No. I don't even know who lived here. Must not have been here long. Doesn't look like much was established on the land. Something must have happened to make them leave."

Cale checked the door and found it unlatched. He pushed the door open and stepped cautiously inside. The building was cold and drafty. Ice clung to the walls in places. The single room was even more haunting from inside. Life here had just stopped with all of the trappings still in place.

"Not sure it's going to be any better in here than it would be waiting outside," Cale said, "Might actually be warmer out in the sun. Looks like they up and left everything. They even left dishes in the washbasin."

The preacher nodded his agreement and began circling the room. Again, chills danced up and down his spine. "I don't like this place. I have a feelin' something bad—sorrowful—happened here."

"I agree."

The men stood in silence, feeling the weight of the strange house creeping in around them. Jason was about to suggest they go back outside when he heard a noise through the window. He brushed a wind-shredded curtain away from the gaping hole in the wall and peered outside.

"He's here. ...The saddle on his horse is as plain as yours or mine."

"I never doubted that he sold the saddle. I only wanted to verify *why* he sold the saddle."

The two men fell silent again, waiting for Scotch to join them. When at last the round man stepped into the doorway, it was with a lopsided grin.

"You boys actually trust this house to stay standin' long enough for us to have our little chat?"

Cale grinned. "I don't know about the preacher, but I was about to move back outside when we saw you comin'. Whose place is this?"

"Family named Porter. Left here about three years ago."

"Porter?" Cale said. "I remember them. They had a baby."

"Baby died," Scotch said, pulling a cigar from one pocket and fishing a match out of another.

"I remember now too," Jason said, "What happened to them? They just disappeared."

Scotch lit the cigar, tossing the match into the washbasin on the counter. He took a long draw on the cigar and then blew smoke out toward the other men. "Woman couldn't take it here. With the baby gone and being so far from home and no friends nearby. She pert near went crazy. I'd loaned them money to build. When they decided to leave they turned the deed over to me."

"So it's yours?" the preacher said.

Scotch shrugged. "Sure. A lot of things are mine. That don't mean I have any particular affection for them."

"Is this where you're going to build your new house?" Cale asked, nudging the conversation in the direction it had been going the previous day.

Scotch rolled the cigar between his fingers as if the matter were of great concern. "Hadn't thought of it really. Wouldn't be a bad place to build, but I reckon I'll be further to the west."

Cale raised an eyebrow. Maiden was to the west, a long way to the west. "How far?"

"Don't know. But further than this. …What were you wanting to ask me, Bennett?"

"I had a couple of questions for you actually. Have you seen any five dollar, gold coins around town?"

"Seen a fake one."

Cale's eyes widened. "Where?"

"One of the girls from the saloon. She come flyin' into my office one day, all excited. Said she'd got a tip from some cowboy who was passin' through and then laid this gold coin down on my desk. She wasn't happy when I told her it was nothin' more than a nickel covered with a thin layer of gold."

Cale reached into his coat pocket and pulled out the coin they'd found near the fire. "Did it look like this?"

Scotch glanced at the coin. "Pretty much, except no one had tampered with it. That one's had the gold flaked off on that one edge."

"Did the girl tell you anything specific about the man she got it from?"

"No. Not a word. She called him a few names. Can't say as I blame her. …Where'd you get that coin?"

"Near the point where the fire started."

"So you've found where it started?"

"It was pretty obvious."

"How so?"

Cale squirmed, not wanting the conversation to grow tense as it had in weeks gone by. "That's not something we're talkin' about at this point."

"Don't want everyone in town to know how it started. That makes sense. It'd be hard to spot someone who has firsthand information that way."

"Exactly." Cale watched the other man for a moment.

Scotch seemed at ease. He reached into the pocket from which he'd taken the match earlier and fidgeted with the remaining matches absentmindedly.

"Do you always carry your matches loose like that?"

"Sure. Always have."

"So you never use a matchbox."

"I wouldn't say *never*. I have one at ho— Well, when I had a home, I had one on my end table in the parlor. Now, I suppose it's in a crate somewhere."

"Is it something like this?" Cale pulled the brass matchbox from his pocket and held it out to the other man.

"No. No, it's nothing like that. That's a beaut. I've never seen anything quite like that. May I?"

"Of course."

Scotch took the matchbox from Cale's hand and fingered it. "The design is quite feminine, don't you think? Not sure why a lady would have a need for such a thing, but then maybe it didn't belong to a *lady*." He flipped the box over, seeing for the first time the initials etched in the smooth surface. "Hmm. I see now why you felt it necessary to question me. You thought perhaps this had belonged to my wife, and maybe I lost it there where the fire started. I don't blame you for that suspicion. In your shoes, I would've thought the same way."

"But?" Cale prompted.

"My wife's middle name don't begin with the letter *b*. Her initials are *AGJ*. Alma Gene Jorgenson. And in case you're wondering, her maiden name was Smith."

Cale nodded, accepting the man's answers and returning the brass box to his pocket.

"Anything else you'd like to ask me?"

"There's still the matter of confirming you were out of town when the fire happened."

"I've told you where I was. It's up to you to confirm it. Same with the saddle. I've told you where I sold it. It's up to you to confirm it, *and* to confirm that it was in fine condition when I sold it."

"I reckon you're right, Scotch, that part is our job. Thanks for meeting us here. Is there...I'm not sure how to go about this."

"What?"

"Well, I think we might need to talk with...well..."

"He means we need to talk with the woman who had the gold coin."

"The fake gold coin," Scotch corrected the preacher with a hint of pleasure in his eyes. "I can arrange for her to come by your office, Bennett. I imagine that's a conversation you'll want to have in a public place."

Cale did not miss the scoffing tone in Scotch's voice. His face went red. "What you do to those girls is abominable."

Scotch shrugged. "As I said yesterday, I'm working to find them good work. You meeting with one of them in public could help restore her reputation. Whatever's left to restore. ...Besides, this girl is different."

The preacher, hearing of Scotch's plan for the first time, started to speak but then stuttered to a stop.

"What?" Scotch demanded.

"You're findin' them different work?"

"Not in Grassdale. There will probably never be a place for them in Grassdale. People know too much. But I'm findin' what I can in other places."

"So it's true then? You're shuttin' down?"

"Yes. I'm done with that place. *I*, gentlemen, am done with a lot of things, including this conversation. Have a good day. Enjoy the ride back to town."

He turned and left with no pomp, no ceremony, not even a wave.

The preacher stared after him, as did Cale, for a long moment. At last, he turned to his friend, shock still written in the lines of his face. "Something has happened to that man. This isn't the Scotch Jorgenson I'm used to dealin' with. I don't understand him. One minute, he's drivin' my horses off, and the next he's closing the most godless institution in town?"

"I don't know what's going on, Jase, but I think the answer lies in Maiden."

The preacher sighed. "I was afraid you were going to say that."

Chapter 25

"How much further?" Zane shivered, casting a sidelong glance at Wesley and hunkering deeper into his heavy coat.

It was the first comment to pass between the two men in more than an hour. They had traveled at a quick, though not exhausting pace since leaving Grassdale. For the most part, Zane had found Wes ready for conversation, eager even. But on the point of the purpose of their journey, he refused any information. Now, two and a half days into their trip, both men were exhausted. They were tired of the cold, the wind, and the biting sting of ice against their faces. Zane had grown weary of waiting. It seemed ludicrous that Wes would drag him this far without the slightest hint of where they were going or what they were doing. This time, he decided, he was going to get an answer.

"Wes?"

Wesley drew in a deep breath. He stretched his stiff back and then let his eyes take in the vast horizon. "Shouldn't be much further now."

"It'll be dark soon."

Wes shrugged. "We'll go all the way tonight."

"And that will take us where?"

"You'll know soon enough."

"Come on, Wes," Zane moaned. "We've been riding hard almost three days. There's nobody around. Can't you tell me where we're going?"

"I'll tell you when it's time."

"Why'd you drag me along if you didn't want me to know anything about what we're doing?"

"You'll know soon enough. Just hold your horses."

"My *horse* is tired...and so am I. Why am I here, wherever here is?"

"I brought you along because I couldn't bring Dunn or Travis, and because I know Ma would've been more upset if I'd gone out alone. I felt

I could trust you to keep what goes on here to yourself. ...Don't make me regret that decision."

"Wes, if you can trust me not to talk about it when we get home, why can't you trust me now?"

Wes considered the question for a moment, and it appeared to Zane that he might finally get an answer. Then Wes shook his head, and, raising his hand apologetically, said, "If I tell you, I'll just have a hundred more questions to answer. The truth of the matter is when we get where we're going, I won't need to explain anything. Just hang on an hour or two."

Zane scowled at his boss, spun in his saddle to face the road, and huffed. He wasn't satisfied with the answer, not in the least, but he could see Wes wasn't going to budge. The two men rode in silence. Zane was tempted on several occasions to ask again how much further they had to go. Each time, however, he'd glance at Wes, see the determination in his boss' face, and realize asking was pointless. Then he'd let out an enormous, dissatisfied sigh.

After the fifth or sixth such sigh, Wes spun toward him, sitting nearly sideways in his saddle.

"Would you quit with the sighing already? Look, up there, not more than two miles. That's where we're going."

Zane squinted through the fading light toward the horizon. A cluster of small, wooden structures rose up out of the prairie. He watched as they drew closer. The further they went the more structures he saw until, at last, he realized they were approaching a town. Not a large town, but a town. He sighed once more, this time contentedly. Beds. They were sure to have beds.

Wes, sensing the change in the younger man's sigh, glanced in Zane's direction. He rolled his eyes at the expression of absolute bliss that had come over his companion.

The two men rode silently into town, passing a livery, a bank, and a mercantile, all of which appeared to be closed up for the day. Light spilled out onto the dusty street from the front windows of a saloon and the hotel next to it. Without hesitation, Wesley passed the first and went straight to the hitching rail of the second.

Zane, noticing the gnawing hunger in his belly, swung one leg over his horse, eager to dismount.

"Where are you going?" Wes said.

"What do you mean?" Zane stared back at Wes, still standing in one stirrup. "I'm going inside with you."

"We're not stayin' here tonight."

"What? But you said this is where we're going."

"This is the town we're going to, but I just stopped here to get directions to the spread we're looking for."

"Well, how much further is that going to be?"

"I don't know. That's what I aim to find out. I'll be right back."

"No. I'm coming with you. I'm half off my horse anyway."

Zane dropped to the ground and fell in stride with his boss.

Wesley shrugged. "Suit yourself."

The two men lumbered through the front door of the hotel, their limbs stiff with cold and the hours in their saddles. They stopped just inside the door and let their eyes take in the bright room.

"Evenin', gentlemen. How may I help you?" A friendly man greeted them from the large, ornate counter that stood off to the left.

"Evenin'. I was hoping you could give me directions."

"Directions? Where to?"

Wes stepped up to the counter, pulling a small sheet of paper from his pocket and laying it down on the counter. "I'm looking for these two men. Can you tell me how to find them?"

The man behind the counter picked up the sheet of paper and smiled. "You aimin' to find them tonight?"

"That would be best."

"Well, you'd best go here then, to the second one. He's just on the edge of town. The other'n, he's way out—at least ten miles. But here, I'll write down directions for both, and you can make up your own mind."

The young man found a pencil and began writing out the directions, his curiosity anything but satisfied. "You new to these parts?"

"Just tendin' to some business. Won't be here long."

"Well, those two are good men. They'll do good by you, no worries there."

The man handed the paper back, and Wes glanced over the directions. Both sets of instructions were clear, but he disagreed with the man. Even though the home of the second man on the sheet was closer, he was drawn to the first. Somehow, it seemed safer.

"Thank you kindly," he said. "Have a good night."

Wes turned and rejoined Zane, who still stood near the door.

"Did you get directions?" the younger man asked as Wes pulled the door open and stepped back out into the cold.

"Right here."

"Is it far?"

"It's a ways, but I think we can be there by nine."

"Nine! But, Wes, that's got to be at least another hour."

"More like two."

"Wes, come on." Zane stopped on the steps and watched as Wesley went to his horse and mounted. "Do we have to go all that way tonight? Can't we stop here, sleep in a warm bed, and head out early in the morning?"

"We won't have to pay for a room there. And I imagine there'll be plenty of good home-cooked food, too."

"You imagine? Are these people expecting you?"

"Nope."

"What if they turn us away?"

"They won't. Get on your horse. You're causin' a scene."

"But what if they do?"

"When they realize who we are, they won't."

"When they *realize* who we are! Do you even know these people?"

"Well," Wesley's voice rose in pitch with the embarrassment of what he was about to admit. "I met them once. One of them. I met one of them once, but I think he'll recognize me."

"You think! You drug me all this way to do business with someone you met once, who doesn't know you're coming, who you *think* will recognize you, and who you *imagine* will put us up and feed us! Have you lost your mind?"

"Look, Zane, it's not as bad as all that. I'm just as tired as you are, and I'd like to be done with this day — with this cold — as soon as we can. If you've got the extra money and want to stay here that's fine with me. You can stay. In the morning, ask the man at the desk to give you directions to the Bennett place."

Zane's eyes widened. "The Ben — *The* Bennett place? As in Miss Bennett?"

"Keep your voice down. Are you comin' or not?"

"Oh, I'm comin'." Zane's face brightened with excitement. He rushed to his horse and swung up into the saddle. "Does she know you're here?"

"Did anyone know?"

"Ha-ha! I'm speechless. I don't even know what to think!"

"Keep your voice down. Let's go."

Chapter 26

Marcus left his father's bedroom and joined his mother and Marianne at the table. He set his Bible and several sheets of paper down and stretched before sliding into his usual seat.

"What a day," he said with a sigh.

"It has been a long one, hasn't it, son? Is Papa asleep?"

Marc nodded. "He's been asleep for at least an hour. Didn't have much in him tonight, I guess."

"There's a fresh pot of coffee on the stove," the woman said, hoping to ease the discouragement she sensed in her son.

"Oh, that sounds wonderful." He stood with renewed energy and made his way to the stove. "Are the little ones in bed?"

"Well, they're supposed to be. Time will tell. Joy took the girls up, so I don't expect much nonsense."

"I think I might head over to Pete Savage's place tomorrow. See how he's holding up."

Marianne stared at her brother for a brief moment. Then she blurted out, "Really? Do you think he'll let you in the door?"

"I don't know, but I do know he didn't fare well at harvest. He did so much to help us when the barn collapsed last year. I just...I think it would be the right thing to do. You know, just to check and make sure things are okay at his place. If he chases me off, he chases me off. Doesn't hurt to try."

"I think it's the right thing to do, Marc. Pete's prickly, but he's our neighbor and we're still supposed to—" Cynthia cut herself short, turning toward the front of the house. She listened for a moment and then turned back to the others, lowering her voice. "Did you hear that?"

"Hear what?" Marc said, setting his untouched coffee down on the counter that separated the kitchen from the rest of the common area.

"Shuffling. Just outside the door."

"Are you sure?" he said, his voice now equally as low. "I didn't hear anything."

The room fell silent as the three listened. A moment later, they heard the soft, unmistakable sound of hooves padding across the yard.

"There it is again," Mary whispered. "Maybe — "

Thud! Thud. Thud.

All three jumped at the powerful knock that rattled the door.

"Who would be here at this time of day?" Cynthia whispered with wide eyes.

"Stay back," Marc replied, moving quickly through the common area, around the table, and up to the window under the loft. "Looks like two men, but it's too dark to recognize them. Just stay there."

Another knock came as Marc went to the door and took down the rifle that hung above it. He lifted his finger to his lips, indicating that the others should be silent. He unlocked the door and pulled it open a couple of inches, keeping it secured with his foot.

"Can I help you?" Marc said, peering through the small opening at the two large forms on his front step.

"Marcus Bennett?" the man closest to the door said through chattering teeth.

"Yes."

"I'm Wesley Close from — "

"Wesley?" Marc opened the door a little wider, letting the light from the common area fall on the other man's face. "Well, what do you know? It is you. Get in here before you freeze!"

"Thank you," Wes chattered. "It's terrible tonight."

Marc stepped aside and let the two men pass, securing the door behind them. He recognized Wesley, of course, but the younger man was new to him. Marc eyed him cautiously.

"This is Zane," Wes offered. "He's one of the best hands we've ever had at the ranch."

Zane's gaze jerked away from the pretty girl he'd just spotted at the table. He'd never heard his boss speak about him to strangers before. A slight smile lifted the corner of his mouth at the other man's praise.

"Well," Marc was saying, "I imagine you're both cold and exhausted. Mary, that cup of coffee I just poured is on the counter, can you fix another?"

"Of course, and I'll put another pot on as well." Mary jumped up from her seat and went to the kitchen, bringing a smile to the faces of all the men standing near the door.

"Ma, Mary, this is Wesley Close from Grassdale."

"Mr. Close?" Cynthia gasped. "Jessica's Mr. Close?"

Wes laughed. "Yes, Mrs. Bennett. That Wesley Close. But most folks just call me Wes."

Cynthia was on her feet and moving toward the men before Wes had even finished, her eyes bright with excitement. "It's so good to meet you, Mr. Close. This is my daughter, well one of them. This is Marianne. Please come in and get warm. Have you had anything to eat?"

"No, ma'am, we haven't. But we should tend to our horses before we settle down too much ourselves."

"Marc, is the extra room ready?"

"Sure is. Why don't we go on down to the barn, Wes? By the time we get back up here, there'll be hot food and coffee ready for both of you."

Marc stepped around the other two men, hung the rifle back over the door, and grabbed up his hat and coat.

"How's Jess?" he asked as he led the other men down the slope to the barn.

"She's doing well," Wes replied.

Marc could hear the weariness in the other man's voice. He wondered if the two men would actually make it through a meal. Cold like they'd ridden through all day had a way of sapping every last drop of energy. For a moment, he considered keeping conversation to a minimum, but then Wes was speaking again.

"She does a wonderful job with the children. My youngest brother, Travis, moped around for hours Christmas day because she was gone."

Marc chuckled. "From what Jess said, I thought he helped get her here."

"He did, but once Jess was gone, he missed her. ...We all missed her."

"Well, be sure to tell Travis that we're grateful he was willing to share her with us for a few days. Here, you can put your horses in these two stalls. Help yourself to whatever provisions you need. I'll go get the stove in the extra room ready for you, so it'll be warm by the time you're ready to bunk down."

Marc slipped into the guest room and built a fire in the potbellied stove. He checked the cots that stood on either side of the stove, making sure there were blankets enough to keep the two men warm through the night. He found himself excited to have the men visiting. He wasn't sure if it was the connection to his sister or the thought of renewing the acquaintance with Wesley. Maybe he just enjoyed having company. Whatever the reason, he was glad they had come.

By the time they returned to the house, Mary and Cynthia had two plates mounding with hot food on the table. Fresh, steaming coffee also awaited their arrival. Fatigued as they were, Wes and Zane were soon devouring the meal with enthusiasm.

"What brings you this way, Mr. Close?" Cynthia asked.

Wes hesitated, hoping the food in his mouth would provide ample chewing time to formulate an answer.

"Wes has some business in the area," Zane responded for him.

"What sort of business?" the woman replied.

Zane shrugged, laughing. "I'm just along for the ride."

Cynthia turned back to Wes, who responded with a shrug of his own. "Something came up, and I felt I should come take care of my part in it before too much time went by."

Cynthia, ever curious, wasn't satisfied with the answer, but Mary spoke before she'd had a chance to push any further.

"How long will you be in the area?"

"I don't know. We'll see how things go. The way I feel right now, it may all depend on when we wake up again. Might just fall asleep and sleep through the rest of the winter."

Cynthia chuckled. "I'm sure you're both exhausted. We won't keep you up. I'm pretty well beat myself. Mary, why don't we let the men finish their meal in peace? We'll find out the whole story in the morning."

The woman stood, running her hand over her large belly and groaning slightly as she made her way to the kitchen with her empty cup. She came back and kissed her son's cheek and hugged her daughter. She stopped by her husband's door to check on him once more and then went to her own room.

"It's so nice to meet both of you," Mary said, gathering up her cup and the men's plates. "Would anyone like anything more before I go?"

All three men nodded, each reaching for his cup. Marc pushed his seat back and stood. "I'll get it, Merry Girl. You go on to bed. I know you're tired."

Mary smiled. "I won't argue there. Thanks, Marc." She wrapped an arm around his waist and gave him a squeeze. "Good night, everyone."

Marc watched as she climbed the ladder to the loft and then disappeared into her room. He retrieved the pot of coffee and brought it to the table, but as he reached the table Zane stood.

"I'll let you fill my cup, but if you don't mind, I think I'll take it with me to the barn. I'm beat."

"No problem. Here you go." Marc filled the cup and watched as the younger man left the house. He filled Wesley's cup and his own, and then took his seat. He could feel his own eyelids growing heavy, and took a drink of the coffee, hoping it would get him just a little bit further.

"So what really brings you here, Wes?"

Wesley shifted nervously in his seat. He looked down at the cup and turned it in his hands. "I didn't want to say anything with everyone around, not yet. But, um, the business I have here in Twin Pines is...well, I came to talk to your Pa."

Confusion twisted Marc's features. "My Pa?"

"About Jess."

"Jess? Is something wrong?" Marc leaned forward in his seat, resting his forearms on the table and squaring his gaze up to Wesley's. "You said she was fine. Is something wrong?"

"No. Absolutely not. Nothing's wrong. She is fine. In fact..." he hesitated again, but this time a hint of color crept into his cheeks.

"Oh..." Marc said, leaning back. "Oh, I see where this is going."

"Marc, your sister, completely unwittingly and without even trying, has captured my heart. I was as bad as Travis while she was away. I'm just grown up enough not to let on. I love her, and I couldn't stand not being able to tell her or anyone else anymore. And...well, I know your pa hasn't been doing well. It was important to me to talk with him, to get his approval."

"Does Jess know you're here?"

"No. And if your Pa's answer is no, then I'd just as soon keep it that way. We eat at the same table, sit by the same fire, day after day. If nothing comes of this, it would make life very awkward if she knew I'd been here and why. I don't want that. I'm sorry to come in so unexpected like this. Maybe I should've written first, but I was afraid if I waited any longer it'd be too late. Calvin' season is right around the corner, and I won't be able to get away then."

Marc nodded, understanding the man's reasoning. He had his own concerns about calving season. He ran his hand over his tired eyes and took a drink of the coffee once more. Then he sighed.

"Well, I reckon we'd better plan on talking with Pa first thing in the morning then. Of course, first thing in the morning tends to be around ten or eleven for Pa these days. Don't feel like you have to be up at daybreak. ...Pa will want time to think things through, I'm sure."

Marc paused, studying the other man. Wesley's eyes were full of nervousness. Marc didn't blame him. It took courage to ride three days in the bitter cold to ask a man he'd never met for permission to court his daughter. But Jonathan Bennett, Sr. wasn't going to be Wesley's greatest obstacle, and Marc knew it.

"I wouldn't be too nervous about Pa if I were you. The one you're going to have to work hardest at is my older brother, Jon. He's always been protective of our sisters. If he'd seen the look Zane gave Mary when you first arrived, Zane would be sleeping in the corral. My sister's fiancée was Jon's best friend. Jess and Jon clashed something fierce after Joe died. Jess wouldn't even speak to Jon for months. But they've made up. To tell you the truth, I think it's made them closer than they ever were before. Joe and Jon were very close. It was a huge loss for Jon. He might not be ready for someone to step into his friend's shoes in that way. It may be too soon for him."

"I understand, and I know it might be too soon for Jess as well. That's the other reason I didn't tell her where I was going. I love her, Marc, I truly do. I don't want to hurt her or anyone in your family."

"I appreciate that." Marc smiled and then yawned. "I've got to go to bed. Do you need anything?"

"No. Thank you. I'm pretty worn myself. Got myself all worked up now though. Don't know if I'll be able to sleep."

Marc laughed. "You're on your own on that one. You'll be fine, Wes. Pa doesn't bite."

Wesley got to his feet, tapping his cup thoughtfully on the table. "I'm not worried about your pa, not anymore. But I'm glad I made Zane ride all the way out here instead of stopping at Jon's for the night. I might not have gotten to meet the rest of the family."

Marc was laughing again. "Well," he said, "you would've made it here, but Jon might've drug you by your ear. ...It'll be fine, Wes. You'll be fine."

Wes considered Marc for a moment. He'd kind of hoped their previous acquaintance would help him, but now he wasn't sure.

"What about you, Marc? Do I have a chance with you?"

Marc, a little surprised by the question, looked the other man over. He wasn't ready to give a definitive answer, but he didn't think Wes was asking for that. From what he remembered of the man, he liked Wesley. He respected him. But he wasn't sure he should give him quite that much yet. He grinned, his eyes lighting up with a sparkle of mischief. "Maybe. I'll let you know."

Chapter 27

Snow swirled in the wind that whipped around the ranch house. Dunn's cheeks were red with cold as he pulled open the front door and stepped inside with Ronald Gray close on his heels. His blue eyes danced with the story Gray had just told him. He was about to repeat it to his mother when he came to a dead halt. His mother wasn't in the common area of the house, but Jess was.

The young woman hadn't noticed their noisy entrance. She stood silently at one of the two south facing windows, her eyes fixed on the storm that raged beyond the windowpanes.

For a moment, Dunn thought to tell Gray's story anyway. It would break the tension the storm had caused and ease the concern it brought for Wes and Zane. But then he saw tears trickling down her cheeks. He motioned for Gray to go to the table and tiptoed to his friend's side.

"They'll be all right," he whispered. "The Lord will take care of them."

Jess nodded, biting her lip but not looking up at him. "I know."

He stepped closer. "Are *you* all right?"

She nodded again, but this time her gaze dropped from the window and she stepped forward. She reached out and touched the frost that had built up at the corners of the glass. Four days had passed since the men had left, four days. She'd stood at a similar window a year earlier, watching, waiting, dreading what she knew in her heart to be true and cursing God for it. She determined she would not respond that way this time, but the very thought drove new tears to her eyes.

Dunn laid a gentle hand on her shoulder and leaned in, speaking softly. "Jess, what is it? What's wrong?"

She shook her head, not sure she could speak the words, not even sure she knew how to verbalize the ache in her heart.

Dunn waited, worry creeping up in his heart.

Sensing his uneasiness, Jess wiped at her tears, trying to regain her composure. But as she glanced up into his eyes, the concern and compassion there brought the tears anew.

"I'm sorry, Dunn. I thought I'd be okay. I thought...but the storm... Why did they go? Why did any of them go?"

The question confused Dunn. *Any of them?* But as he studied the broken woman beside him, things became clear.

"It's not just Wes and Zane, is it?"

She shook her head. "I'm sorry, Dunn. I thought I'd be okay. I thought..." She sighed. It was useless to avoid the truth that hung over her. It would be better for them all if she just said it. "It's a year, Dunn."

"Today?"

Jess nodded. "I thought I'd be okay, but then I saw the storm, and...and I thought of them out there. And I thought of Joe...and it all...I'm sorry."

"Ah, Jess." The man drew his friend into an embrace and motioned for Gray to find Anna. "Jess, why didn't you tell us? We don't want you carryin' that alone. I'm so sorry."

Jess broke into heart-wrenching sobs. She clung to the man's heavy coat, the pain of loss crushing down on her as it had a year earlier. "Why did they go, Dunn? Don't they know what could happen?"

"I'm so sorry," he said, making mental note to have a serious discussion with his brother when he returned. "Wes didn't know, Jess. He didn't know it was today. I'm sure he didn't know. He'll be careful. You know he will, and he took Zane with him. They'll help each other if they run into trouble. God will take care of them."

"I know. Oh, Dunn, I'm so sorry."

"Don't apologize. There's no need. We should be apologizin' for not realizin' what was going on."

A motion caught Dunn's eye, and he looked up to see his mother emerging from the hallway, still tying her apron strings behind her. He sent a pathetic smile in her direction, his eyes pleading for help. Anna hurried across the room, coming to her friend's side and smoothing the younger woman's hair back from her face.

"Oh, Jess, what is it? Come here, child."

Dunn released Jess and allowed Anna to step into his place. He watched for a moment and then laid a hand on his mother's shoulder.

"Why don't you take her upstairs? I'll put the teapot on. I'll send the children home when they get here."

"No," Jess said, stepping back from Anna and wiping her eyes. "No, I'll be fine. Please, Dunn, don't make them come all that way for nothing."

"Jess, Dunn's right. You need to rest, at least for a while. Spend some time with the Lord. Let Him comfort your heart. I doubt many of them will come in this weather anyway. I'll cover for you this morning, and we'll send them home at lunch. All right?"

Seeing the wisdom in the little woman's suggestion, Jess nodded.

"Come on, let's go upstairs. I want you to be up there before the children start arriving."

Anna took her friend by the hand and led her toward the stairs and the room that had become Jessica's haven. The teacher sat down on the bed, exhausted by the emotion that tore at her heart. Anna studied her, compassion filling her eyes.

"It's the storm and Wes and your Joe, isn't it?"

Jess nodded.

"I thought so. Mr. Gray said something about it being a year. Is that it, Jess?"

Again Jess nodded.

"Oh, dear girl. I'm so sorry. I know that is a hard day, and my son has gone and made it that much worse. I'm so sorry. Is there anything I can do?"

Jess sat still, considering the question. For a moment, Anna thought she would say nothing, but then the young woman nodded once more.

"Will you pray with me?"

"Of course, dear, of course. I would like nothing better."

The gray-haired woman sat down next to her friend. She took the younger woman's hands in her own and bowed her head. She was surprised to find that she couldn't speak at first. Her own chest had tightened with emotion. She knew the pain her friend was experiencing, the agony. Her heart ached for her. It yearned for her own lost husband and for her son and Zane. She took a deep breath and let it out slowly, steadying herself.

"Dear Father, we are so very weak. Our hearts are fragile, but we know You are the God of all comfort. Father, help my dear friend. Comfort her. Oh, Lord, help us all. You know we're all nervous. We're all concerned for Wes and Zane. Help us to trust You. Help me to trust You. Give each of us the grace to wait patiently for their return and to trust that You will keep them along the way. Provide shelter and warmth for them. Protect them along the road. Keep them safe when they have to travel at night. Lord, we commit them into Your hand. We trust You to keep them safe in Your powerful grasp. We ask for Your peace and for surrendered hearts. Oh, how we love You."

* * *

When Anna returned to the kitchen, she found Dunn standing at the counter, vigorously chopping carrots and onions.

"When that brother of mine gets back, he's going to get an earful," he said. "What was he thinking? It's bad enough, he's got us all on pins and needles, but this... This is inexcusable."

"He didn't know, Dunn. You know that. None of us knew."

"He knew it was this month, and he knew how it happened. He, of all people, should know better than to add that kind of worry to such a time."

"Duncan, get a hold of yourself. It wasn't intentional, and you know it."

Dunn drew in a deep, measured breath and set his knife aside with equal care. "I hate to see her that way, Ma. She's so far from home, and I'm sure she worries about things there. She's been doing so well. This isn't helpful."

"That may not be true, son."

He stared at her, confusion swimming in his eyes. "What do you mean?"

"Dunn, faith is proven in the storm, not in the calm. Jess has surrendered to the Lord. She's committed to let Him guide and lead her life and to accept what He allows in her life. But the true test of her surrender will come when she faces things out of her control, things she doesn't understand and cannot change. That will reveal the depth of her surrender. That is where she'll grow.

"Now, I don't like it any more than you do. You know I didn't want them to go. But your brother said he'd prayed about this. He said he felt strongly that this was when he needed to go. If the Lord is leading Wes, then we need to trust that He has a plan to strengthen Jess through this."

Dunn sighed, resting his hands on his hips and relaxing a little. "You're right."

Anna patted her son's arm and then examined the pile of carrots and onions. "What are you doing?"

"I figured if you were going to be teaching that left me to fix lunch. Figured I'd better get started."

Anna nodded. "Well, you've got a good start on something. I've never seen you cut that fast." She took a step back and looked toward the classroom. Then she giggled and swung her twinkling gaze back to her son. "Do you think I can handle all those children?"

Dunn laughed. "You're about to find out. ...You'll be fine. All of you."

Anna chuckled, but her smile slid quickly away. "You really don't know why Wes left, do you?"

"No. I even asked Cale if it had anything to do with the fire. He didn't know anything about Wes leavin', let alone where he'd gone. It doesn't make sense to me, Ma. He's never done anything like this before. Why is he all fired up to head to some other part of the territory this time of year? I don't understand."

"It would be nice if he'd at least let us know when he gets wherever he's going, but I know that may not be possible."

"I don't think he'd do that. That would mean a postmark, and that would give away where he's gone. We're just going to have to wait, Ma. For whatever reason, that's what he expects us to do."

"Well, he's never given us a reason not to trust him, so there's no reason to doubt him now. We just have to put him in the Lord's hands and trust. ....Could be the Lord is using this to prove our faith every bit as much as He's using it to prove Jessica's. I'd say neither of us is doing a very good job of trusting at the moment. ...Where'd Mr. Gray go?"

"Outside. Seemed kind of shook up. I think he's got a soft spot for Jess."

"I think most of the men have soft spots for Jess. I think some of them are afraid she'll leave at the end of the school year."

Dunn shrugged. "The thought has crossed my mind and not in a happy way. I don't want her to go. She belongs here."

"Of course she does. She's family whether she knows it or not. ...Oh, I see someone coming up the lane. I'd better get this tea up to Jess and then get busy being a teacher."

Chapter 28

The sounds of Marc talking to the livestock, cleaning up messes, milking the cow, and occasionally dropping things drifted into the spare room, pulling Wes from that sweet place of deep sleep. He stretched, finding his muscles were none too happy with his three days in the saddle followed by a night in a drafty barn. With a groan, he rolled off of his cot, pulled his scarf, coat, gloves, and hat back on, and made his way to the main part of the building.

"Mornin', Marc," he said through a yawn.

"Mornin'. You still look beat."

Wesley ran his hands over his tired eyes and then rubbed his cold arms. "Just woke up. Anything I can do to help?"

"I probably woke you up. Sorry about that. My hands are so cold this morning. I keep dropping things. You boys hungry?"

"I am. Zane's still asleep."

"Well, breakfast will be ready by the time I head up to the house. You can come up and meet our little people before I take them off to school."

Wesley yawned again, nodding.

"After I drop the children off at school, I'll head on into town and bring Jon out here. Then we can all talk. I need to stop by the preacher's at some point and another neighbor's place as well. I may just tell Jon to come out this afternoon."

"That sounds like a plan. I'd happily ride along."

"Are you sure? You've been on a horse for three days. Figured you might want to rest a little this morning."

Wes shrugged. "I don't think I'll be at ease until we've got things out in the open. Might as well keep myself busy and be of use wherever I can."

Marc grinned. "Suit yourself. We got enough snow last night that I'll be takin' the sledge. Won't be enough room for everyone. You'll have to ride alongside."

"No matter. I'll be less likely to fall asleep that way. I'll go wake Zane."

"I'm awake," came a disgruntled, pillow-muffled voice from the other room. "How can I not be awake with you two jabberin' on out there."

Marcus laughed, lowering his voice. "Somethin' tells me he's kept your trip interesting."

A smile climbed into Wesley's eyes. "I seem to be very good at annoyin' him."

The aroma of coffee, fresh eggs, and salt pork hit the three men as soon as they opened the cabin door. All of them, as if on cue, took in a deep breath, letting it out noisily with great satisfaction.

"It smells wonderful in here, Ma," Marc said, stepping through the door and finding himself face to face with a roomful of staring children. Gretel, seeing the two strangers behind her older brother, squealed and jumped up from her seat, running to her mother who stood near the stove.

Marcus laughed, motioning the other men further inside and closing the door against the January cold. "It's all right, Little Bit, these are Jess' friends."

The girl said nothing. She stared at the two cowboys, taking in every inch of their frames.

"They're good men. They won't hurt you."

But Puss didn't move from behind her mother.

"You must be Gretel," Wesley said, striding across the room and stooping down to the girl's level.

Her eyes widened, but still, she was silent.

"No?" he said, with an exaggerated look of confusion on his face. "Not Gretel? Let me see...Ah! I know who you are. You're Puss. Your sister has told me a lot about you. She talks about you every day and prays for you too."

The girl bit her lip, studying the man a little closer, less wary but still cautious.

"I brought something for you, Puss." Wes reached inside his coat and pulled out a brown paper package. He folded one edge of the package back and slid out a perfect peppermint stick. He held it out to the girl, smiling and waiting for her to take it.

Gretel looked up at her mother, who nodded her consent. She reached out and took the candy with great care as if afraid she might break either the peppermint stick or the man himself.

"But you have to ask your mama when it's okay to eat it. Right before breakfast probably isn't the best time."

Gretel nodded. Wesley began to stand, but the girl stopped him.

"You know my Jess?"

He smiled at the possessive connotations of her question. "Yes. She lives with my family."

"You're Mr. Close!" came a voice behind him.

Wes stood up and turned to see the speaker. A slender, pretty girl of fifteen eyed him with excitement as she finished plaiting her long, red locks into a single braid.

"Yes," he replied, "and this is Zane. He works for us. You must be...let me think...you must be Joy. And then we have—well, Danny is easy. This must be Elizabeth, and we've already met Marianne."

"Have you met Jon?" Gretel asked, touching her tongue to the peppermint stick.

"No. Not yet."

"Have you met Papa?"

"No, Papa was asleep when we got here last night."

"Oh. Like us. ...But you'll meet them later."

"Yes. I hope so."

Cynthia cleared her voice, confiscating the candy and nudging the girl toward the table. "All right. Now we're all acquainted, and we're all going to be late if we don't get set down to the table. Joy, put the plates on please. Make sure to set enough for our guests. Mary, go ahead and pour the coffee. Danny, why aren't you dressed? How did you get this far into the morning without your shirt?"

"I spilled water on it when I was washing up. It's hangin' by the fire. I'll put it on when we're done."

Cynthia rolled her eyes in exasperation. "Very well. Sit down then. Let's go, everyone."

Children scurried in every direction. Then, just as suddenly as the action had begun, the house had grown quiet. The seats at the table were full, and the children waited expectantly.

"Well, now," Zane said, "that was impressive."

Marc grinned. "There are too many of us around here not to know what we're supposed to be doing."

Zane watched in amazement, not registering the fact that Marc was praying over the meal until the other man had finished.

Cynthia, directing her children to pass the food to their guests first, looked up at Wes and smiled. "We've got hot water on the stove. The washtub is set up in my bedroom if you two want to get cleaned up after breakfast, Mr. Close."

Wes glanced at Marc. "Well, I told Marc I'd ride into town with him."

Marc dismissed the comment. "Unless you plan on soakin' till you're wrinkled up, you'll have time. By the time the children are ready—and Danny is dressed—and the team is hitched up, you'll be good to go."

"We eat earlier than we really have to because some of our little ones are also a little slow." Cynthia glanced meaningfully at her youngest daughter.

Wes grinned. "I'll do my best not to follow suit."

❊ ❊ ❊

Three hours later, Marc and Wes stepped into the preacher's barn. The children had been safely deposited at the school. Jonah had been there and had promised to send Jon out to the farm when he got back to town. From the school, Marc and Wes rode to Pete Savage's place. But either no one was home or Pete was unwilling to come to the door. They'd crossed the short distance from Pete's to the preacher's house. No one was home there either, but Marc knew the milk cow had been sick and had promised the preacher he'd keep an eye on her as best he could.

"I think she'll be all right," Marc said after a few moments examining the cow.

"She's a beautiful animal."

"Preacher brought her with him from the east. I'd say she's got pretty good blood. He doesn't seem to know much about her though. Someone gave her to him as I understand it. Seems he didn't have much need for livestock in Philadelphia."

Wes grunted. "I suppose you might not. ...I hate to bring this up, Marc, but...is this barn going to make it through the winter?"

Marc straightened to his full height, breaking into full-bellied laughter. "You noticed it's a little on the flimsy side, did you?" He laughed again, stepping out of the stall and into the open space in the center of the well-ventilated structure. "Was it the cracks between the wall boards or the groan with every breath of wind that gave you concern?"

"The hole in the back wall."

Marcus laughed. "Don't worry, Wes. After havin' a barn collapse on me, I wasn't about to let the preacher have a barn that won't survive the winter. It's rough, but it's sturdy. As to the hole, well, that cow we've been babyin' for the last twenty minutes kicked that out. I thought the preacher was going to patch it up. Probably hasn't had time. Maybe we should just fix it for him while we're here."

Marc went to the preacher's workbench and scrounged around until he'd found a handful of nails. The hammer was easier to locate. The board, he realized, might be the problem. He spotted a flour sack, scooped it up, and moved toward the back of the barn.

"This'll do for a temporary fix. At least it will stop the wind. I don't see any scrap boards around, but we can fold this in half and seal the hole up tight enough to keep out any critters."

Wes took the sack and leaned down, stretching the fabric over the hole, adjusting it, refolding it, and measuring it again until he had it just right. Marc watched as the other man worked. The rancher was careful and accurate at every step. Always double-checking. Making sure the nails were secure. Marc smiled, pleased by the diligence the other man displayed.

"So," he said, "you're here on account of my sister."

The sudden turn in the conversation surprised Wesley. "Yes."

"Does she return your...affections?"

Wes studied him for a moment and then grinned. "I sure hope so."

Marc couldn't help but laugh. "Especially after ridin' this far."

"Exactly. ...I've tried to be very careful. People are watchin' all the time. My brother guessed it about a month ago, but he knows me pretty well. It's almost frightening how well he knows me. Anyway, I don't know if she has sensed anything or not. I've seen things that have caused me to hope, but maybe it's my hope seein' them. It's a delicate situation. Dunn and I sleep down at the bunkhouse with the other men, but Jess and I are around each other all day, every day. I try to be very careful."

Marc gnawed at the corner of his mouth. "You've, uh, you've been married before, right?"

Wesley blinked back at Marc, not surprised that he knew about Emily but surprised that he would go there so soon. He let his gaze return to the flour sack, checked it one last time, and then stood up to face Marc.

"Yes. I have. Her name was Emily. She was our preacher's sister. A very special lady. She's been gone two years now. Well, a little more than that actually."

Marc shoved his hands into his coat pockets. "I'll be honest with you. I wouldn't want Jess livin' in another woman's shadow, constantly being compared to someone she can never be, never replace. At the same time, I wouldn't want Jess doing that to whomever she marries — comparin' him with Joe, I mean."

"I see what you're sayin'. It makes sense." Wesley paused, searching for a response. "Marc, Emily was a good woman. She was a wonderful woman. I've never met anyone like her. Ever. But the Lord saw fit to take her home. I know there'll never be anyone like her, and, honestly, I don't think I'd ever like to meet anyone like her. I like knowin' that she…she was Emily, and there's no one else like her in the whole world.

"Jess isn't like Emily. She's very different — in a good way. I'm not sure how to put it exactly, but she's different. I…I feel safe around Jess. Other women make me feel like turnin' and runnin'.'"

Marc's eyes widened with an expression of understanding. "I know a few of those."

"Your sister's not like that. Even before the fire…well, she was pretty angry with me for a while. Even when she'd made things right it was like she couldn't get past the guilt…but she still just seemed to fit. Not only for me but for my whole family. That's important to me. She and my mother are almost inseparable. Both of my brothers would give their lives for her."

Wes stopped, not sure how to continue.

"I'm glad to hear how your family feels about her, Wes. I'm glad she fits, but I want to know how *you* feel."

"I love her, Marc. Jess is an amazing woman. She's strong, and yet there's a gentleness about her. It makes a man want to do whatever he can to see that she doesn't have to exercise that strength. I want to protect her and provide for her and…and to just…walk through life with her. I can't offer her life in a palace. That's for sure. It'll be full of work and probably a few difficulties just like every other place in this part of the world. But I'll do my best to make sure it's also filled with joy and family and love. That may be all I can promise her, but I'll make that promise with all my heart. And I know she has the strength to stick it out, and the grace to accept what comes our way."

"Are you sure about that?"

Wes blinked and stepped back as if the other man had slapped him.

"You know as well as I do, Wes, that when you met my sister she was angry and runnin' from God because of her *lack* of ability to accept the things that had come her way."

Wes sobered. "I know. But the change in her since the fire is astounding. It's real. She knows she has to be careful and guard against the old responses, but when she's strugglin' she asks for help. A couple weeks ago, you sent a letter about your pa not doing so well. The first thing Jess did was go to my mother and ask her to pray with her."

"You're sure you aren't choosin' to overlook something that could cause a world of trouble later? Don't get me wrong. I love my sister. I'm only suggestin' she might not be ready in that one area yet."

"I understand. I've considered it, often. But every time I question it, she goes and proves she's headed in the right direction. I don't plan on going back and demandin' a weddin' first thing. That's not what I'm lookin' for. I don't want to do anything until it's God's time and she's ready. I came because...well...for two reasons. Most importantly because I love your sister, and I felt God wanted me to do it now. But also because havin' your Pa's approval was important to me, and I know it'll be important to Jess as well. I was afraid if I waited any longer, I would miss the chance."

Marc nodded, a shadow darkening his gray eyes. He sighed and turned away from the other man, running a hand across his neck as he did so. "You're probably not too far off on that one. Time is runnin' out. ...Let's close things up and head home. Lunch'll be ready soon."

Chapter 29

Jessica sat quietly, her back against the wall and her feet dangling over the edge of the bed. Her Bible spread across her lap, open to the book of Isaiah. She took a deep breath and let it out slowly, smiling at the sound of the children leaving for the day. She considered going down to bid them goodbye, but she knew she was where she belonged.

She wondered for a moment what would have happened if she had taken this approach a year ago. What would have happened if she had listened to Marc and stayed home that day? What if she had listened when he offered to spend the day at the school with her and had talked things over as he'd asked? What if she'd ridden home with him, made a long, slow ride of it, and told him her struggles? How would things have been different? How much heartache would she have spared herself and her family and Anna and Wes?

Wes. She sighed at the thought of him. Why had he gone? What could be so important that he would risk not only his life but also Zane's?

She leaned forward, stroking back the pages of her Bible. Entertaining questions like that would get her nowhere. She couldn't change the past. She knew that, even if she had gone with Marc that day, she never would have listened. Her heart had been too hard. If she had stayed home, she would have sat in her room brooding. Nothing would have been different. As much as the thought hurt, she knew the fire and all that surrounded it was the only thing dreadful enough to break the stone in her heart. She couldn't go back and change things, so it made no sense to dwell on them. She could do nothing about Wesley's decision either. As much as it troubled her, as much as she wished he hadn't gone, she couldn't change it.

She let her fingers run across the lines of the verses that had arrested her attention more than an hour earlier. She breathed the words in as she read them silently, *"Thou wilt keep him in perfect peace, whose mind is stayed on thee: because he trusteth in thee. Trust ye in the Lord for ever: for in the Lord Jehovah is everlasting strength."*

"Lord," she whispered, "You know I'm afraid for them. You know I feel like my heart would crumble away if anything happened to them. You know how much I fear the pain of losing them in that way...of losing anyone in that way ever again. Lord, I choose to trust You. Please, drive out my fear with Your perfect peace. Help my unbelief. Give me the strength to wait and trust and pray."

A soft knock at the door drew her attention away from the passage. Less than five minutes had passed since the children had left for the day. Jess was surprised that Anna would be at her door so soon, but she was certain it was the little woman's knock.

"Come in."

The door squeaked open, and Anna stepped awkwardly into the room balancing a full tray of food in one hand and managing the door with the other. "Hello, dear. Were you able to rest?"

"Yes. Thank you. Anna, what is all this?"

"This is Dunn's way of helping. He, horrible cook that he may be, always resorts to meeting the most basic of needs when someone he cares about is hurting. And so, you and I get stew. I have no idea what it will taste like, but it was made with love."

Jess chuckled, her eyes brightened by her friend's act of kindness. "It smells good."

"It does, doesn't it? Perhaps he's improving." Anna set the tray down on the bed next to Jess. "How are you really, dear?"

"I'm fine, Anna. Really, I am. ...I miss him. I regret so many things that happened both before and after he died. I wish I could tell him. That is the one relationship I will never be able to make right—the one that meant so much to me. The one I used when I should have been cherishing it. That weighs heavy on my heart. I can't change anything...but I do miss him."

"Of course you do." Anna joined the girl on the bed, sitting down beside her and taking her hand in her own. "You'll always miss him. It may not always be as sharp as it is right now, but you'll always miss him. He was a precious part of you."

Jess leaned her head on the woman's shoulder and snuggled up against her. "You miss Charles too, don't you?"

"Yes. Every day. I think I've missed him more since coming here to the ranch. Not only is our cabin gone but seeing this place thrive, seeing the dreams we talked about together coming true—without him—makes his absence more noticeable."

Jess squeezed the little woman's hand. Then she took a deep breath. "Oh, Anna, I don't want my mother to know this pain. I can't imagine what it will be like for her after so many years with Papa. They…" but her voice tapered off.

"They love each other deeply?"

"Yes. But you loved your husband deeply too."

"Of course. I still do. I understand what you're saying, dear. You don't have to be afraid of hurting my feelings. I don't want your mother to know that pain either, and I've never even met her."

"I wish you could. I wish somehow you could be there to comfort her when the time comes. She'll be strong and brave for everyone else, but I know her heart will be so broken."

It was Anna's turn to silently squeeze the younger woman's hand. Tears had filled her eyes, and she couldn't speak.

"When we first came to Montana," Jess resumed, "my papa worked long hours every day, from first light to the tiniest glimmer at the edge of dusk. Mama was often alone all day with us children. It was hard. We had no well for quite some time. Papa had to try several different places until he finally found water. That meant we had to carry water from the creek. It was a long haul, especially if we were doing it by hand and not with the wagon. We lived in a sod house that seemed always full of bugs and mice… I even remember a snake getting into the walls once. It was horrible. It tried to make its nest right in our home.

"But one night, just as the sun was setting, Papa came home from wherever he'd been working in the fields. Mama was in the yard finishing a tub of washing. I remember watching as Pa strode up that hill in long, gliding steps, almost as if he were floating. He stepped up to her and presented her with a handful of the most beautiful, delicate roses I had ever seen. They were wild roses and pink, of course, but the sunset turned their edges gold. Tears came to Mama's eyes. She didn't say anything. She just took the roses from him and admired them.

"I remember him saying to her, 'Cynthia, my love, I know this land is hard, and it may grow harder still, but it's burstin' with beauty if we just look for it. And you, you are its most beautiful flower.'

"I'll never forget how she placed her hand on his cheek and kissed him. Then she stepped back and looked at the flowers once more and said, 'Jonathan, we're going to be all right. Keep bringing me roses at sunset, and we'll be just fine.'

"And he did—often. Even after his health began to fail. Whenever he could, he'd slip down by the creek or out along the pasture, cut a stem of roses, and bring them home right before sunset.

"How do you lose that and still keep on breathing, Anna?"

"Oh, child. …You take one breath at a time and with every breath a prayer. You breathe out your commitment to trust, and you breathe in the peace that only comes from our Savior's hand. You cling to Him because if you cling to what you've lost, to the pain, the anguish of it all…that's when you'll stop breathing. It will overwhelm you."

"That was my mistake, Anna. I clung to loss after loss after loss."

"But now you have let them go, Jess, and that is where you must stay."

Jess nodded. "I know. I want that peace, and I know it only comes from keeping my thoughts on who He is and all that He has promised. It isn't easy, Anna, but that's what I want more than anything else."

"That's exactly what I want too. We'll help one another. When the worry and the hurt come, we'll help one another." Anna was quiet for a moment, but then she giggled. "How 'bout if we help one another taste Dunn's stew. The smell is driving me mad. I think he's finally learned to make it."

Jess joined in her laughter. "It does smell wonderful."

* * *

Anna had just left Jessica's room and stepped into the kitchen to finish putting lunch on the table, when the front door swung open and Ronald Gray stepped inside.

"Oh, hello, Mr. Gray. How can I help you?"

"I finished up a bit early. I know lunch ain't ready yet, but I'm miserable cold. Can't seem to get warm today, no matter what I do."

"Well, there's hot coffee on the stove, and Dunn has stew simmering. I'm finishing up some cornbread, and we'll be all ready for a nice hot lunch. Shall I get you some coffee?"

"I'd like that." The man watched as Anna busied herself about the task. He went to the table and pulled out a chair, seating himself with a groan. "My bones are gettin' too old for this kind of weather."

Anna laughed. "Mine have always been too old for this weather. Winter has never been my favorite. I'm fond of spring and summer, but winter…well, I suppose it's a necessary part of life."

"I imagine Miss Bennett feels the same way. How's she holdin' up, Mrs. Close? She seemed awful tore up this mornin'."

"Ah, Mr. Gray. It's a difficult day. It's been a year, you know, a year to the day since she lost her fiancée. But I think she'll be all right. She had her Bible out when I went up a while ago. Sounds like she's decided to simply trust."

"Seems a hard thing to do when a person you love goes out into a situation that took another person you loved."

Anna turned away from the coffee and stared at the man. "A person you love, Mr. Gray? What do you mean?"

"I ain't blind, Mrs. Close. I see the way those two look at each other. Funny thing is, they neither one look at the other that way when they think the other is lookin'. It's like they're afraid the other will figure them out. But I see it. I know she loves him, and why not? To hear her tell it, he's done a lot to help her."

"And you think *he* loves her in return?"

Gray waved the comment off almost scoffingly. "Of course he does. Why do you think he was so morose over Christmas? Cause she wasn't here. I've watched him ever since. He's got it bad, Mrs. Close, real bad."

"Hmm. Wouldn't be the first time such a thing happened."

"I imagine she's worried for him, 'specially with this storm a-brewing."

"Yes. And I confess, I am too. But there's always the chance that the weather is clear wherever those two have gotten themselves. We just have to put them in God's hands, and let Him take care of them."

"Is that the way Miss Bennett sees it?"

"Yes. It's not easy. It takes courage, if you ask me, to trust in a situation like this with her past. But she seems committed to do just that."

The man shook his head. "I ain't never had that kind of courage."

Anna stepped close to the table, mug of coffee in hand. "It doesn't come from within her, Mr. Gray. I think she'd be the first to tell you that. It comes from Christ."

"I'd expect you to say that. But I'll have to see it to believe it. I'll be watchin'. Maybe what you're sayin' is true, maybe it ain't. But I need to see it with my own eyes."

Anna's gaze grew serious as she locked eyes with him, but then she saw he wasn't defiant. He was determined. Whether he was determined to see Jess succeed or to see her fail, Anna couldn't tell, but he was determined.

"The Lord won't fail her, Mr. Gray. That doesn't mean she won't struggle or falter or even fail herself. It simply means the Lord won't fail her."

Gray shrugged, taking the cup of coffee she offered him and sipping long and hard at the hot liquid. Then he set the cup down. "Time will tell, Mrs. Close. Time will tell."

Chapter 30

"What is that amazing smell?" Wes said as he hung his hat on a peg near the door of the Bennetts' cabin.

"That is chicken and dumplings, Mr. Close," Marianne said with a twinkle in her blue eyes.

"You didn't do that special for us did you?"

Mary smiled. "Perhaps. But chicken and dumplings are always just an ask away in this house as long as we have a chicken available."

"You haven't eaten until you've tried Mary's dumplings, Wes," Marc said.

The rich fragrance of the broth reached Wesley's nose once more and his stomach growled.

Marcus laughed. "I hope you made a lot, Mary. I think we're going to need it." The wiry farmer stepped over to the window beneath the loft and peered outside. "That's what I thought. I heard something as we were coming inside. Jon and Hannah are here."

"Hannah?" Cynthia said as she emerged from her husband's room. "Why would that girl come out here so close to her time?"

Marc shrugged as he dropped the curtain. "Maybe she wants to have the baby sooner rather than later. Have a seat, Wes. Looks like we'll be ready to eat as soon as they get inside."

But the announcement of Jon's arrival had driven away Wesley's appetite. He felt the color drain from his face at the thought of facing the doctor. "Where's Zane?" he asked, hoping to mask his nervous response.

Mary pointed toward the sitting area, but when Wes turned in that direction he saw no one.

"On the sofa," she said softly.

The man looked down to see his friend rolled tightly in a blanket and sound asleep on the makeshift sofa. He chuckled. "Don't guess he'll be joinin' us for lunch."

"He's been there for two hours. I can't believe he didn't wake up when you two came in."

"Zane could sleep through a stampede. I'm sure he needs it. I pushed pretty hard to get here."

Mary smiled. She liked what she saw in this man so far. She didn't know why he'd come, but, knowing the difference he'd made in her sister's life, she hoped above all things that Jess was his reason for coming.

The front door opened and Hannah tottered inside. She smiled as she caught sight of her sister-in-law in the kitchen.

"Marianne, you've been making dumplings, haven't you? I could smell them before I even opened the door."

Mary nodded. "I have. We have company, and that calls for something special."

"What smells so good?" Jon pushed the door open and stepped in behind his wife, taking in a deep whiff of the simmering meal and letting it out with great satisfaction. "Wow, Mary. If you ever cook outside this house, we'll be fightin' suitors off left and right."

Hannah, horrified by her husband's comment, elbowed the doctor in the ribs. "Jon, mind your manners."

"What! It's true. There's not a man in this territory that wouldn't want to walk into a house that smells like this every night."

"Well, I can guarantee this house does not smell like this every night," Mary said, blushing. "We have company. That's all."

"Company?" Jon said, glancing around the room for the first time.

"Yes. Marc, why don't you make the introductions while I start setting the food on the table."

"Of course. You got here sooner than I expected, Jon."

"Jonah said you wanted us to come right away. I thought something was wrong."

"No, we just wanted you to join us. …Where's Samuel?" Marc searched for the toddler, wondering how he'd missed his entrance.

"Like I said, we thought something was wrong, so we left him with Kate."

"I'm sorry, Jon. I didn't mean to concern you."

"Well, it may have had more to do with your messenger than with your message."

Marc chuckled. "That's possible. Jonah does tend to get a bit passionate at times. So let me introduce you. Jon, Hannah, this is Wesley

Close from Grassdale. The fella asleep on the sofa is Zane, but I don't think we'll be meeting him just yet. Wes, this is my brother Jon and his wife, Hannah."

Wes held out a hand to the big doctor, but Jon didn't take it. He looked the rancher over suspiciously. "What brings you this way, Mr. Close? Business?"

Wes glanced nervously at Marc, and then back at Jon. "You could say that, I suppose."

Sensing the growing tension, Mary cleared her throat. "The meal is just about on the table. Why don't you all get settled?"

Jon, forgetting his interview with Wes for a moment, turned to help his wife with her wraps. Then, removing his own hat and coat, he hung all of it on one of the many pegs along the front wall. The small group gathered around the table, each finding a seat and taking it with little conversation. Mary brought the last of the food to the table and took a seat next to Wes while her mother finished pouring a round of coffee.

"I'm sure you're all cold. It's certainly bitter out there today." The woman set the pot down and raised an eyebrow at Marc, who at once bowed and prayed over their meal. When the prayer ended, Marc set about dishing up platefuls of the steaming chicken and dumplings. He smiled, noticing more than one lick of the lips as he served the others.

Jon, by nature of where he was seated, received his food first. He set it down before him and then waited as Marc continued to ladle out the fragrant dish. At last, his brother finished and seated himself. Jon lifted a spoonful of broth to his mouth and sipped it contentedly.

"This is wonderful, Mary." He scooped another bite up and then laid his spoon to rest across his plate. "This is a pretty bad time of year to be so far from home, Mr. Close. You going to be travelin' long?"

"I don't really know for sure. It depends on how things go."

Jon nodded, scooping another bite of dumplings into his mouth and watching the man as he chewed. "So what brings you over here?"

Wes took a long sip of coffee followed by a deep breath. "Well, I came to meet your family."

"To meet our family?" Jon raised an eyebrow at that, his suspicions about the man growing by the moment. "You rode three days in the middle of winter to meet our family? Seems strange. You should've brought...that is... I can't believe Jess didn't... I mean... Why are you here?" Jon's voice dropped to a serious, challenging tone as he lobbed the question in Wesley's direction.

Rachel Miller

To his own surprise, Wesley didn't flinch. "I think you've already guessed it. Dr. Bennett, over the last six or seven months, I've come to see what a precious, beautiful woman your sister is. I've prayed much about it, and—"

"No."

Wesley's mouth dropped open, his eyes widening in the same moment.

"Jon," Marc said with a hint of rebuke in his voice, "let the man finish."

"No. The answer is no. To think you would have the audacity, Mr. Close—you who have yourself lost a wife—to think that you would have the audacity to consider such a thing so soon, and especially now. No."

"Jon," Hannah said in a soft, measured tone, "You haven't even heard what he has to say. Give him a chance to speak."

"I don't need to. It's out of his own self-interest that he's come, not her best interest. I don't aim to let it go any further than it needs to."

Cynthia leaned forward in her seat. "Jon, stop. You're not being fair. He's ridden three days. The least you can do is hear him out."

"I've heard enough. I've seen enough. It's out of the question. No."

"Jon—"

"No, Marc. How many times do I have to say it? No."

"Jon—"

But Wesley reached out and laid a hand on Mary's arm, stopping her protest. He stood to leave. "It's okay, Mary. Dr. Bennett, I came because I love your sister. The last thing I ever want to do is cause division in your family. I'll go. I'm sorry I didn't get to taste your dumplings, Mary. They smell wonderful. Marc, send Zane into town when he wakes up, will you?"

"Sit down," Marc said.

"What?"

"Sit down. No one is being driven away from this house in such a manner. Sit down."

Wes, feeling he had no option but to obey, took his seat.

"Jon, you heard the man—he loves her. He loves her enough to walk away from her in order not to hurt us. Now, I recommend you cool your heels, and let the man say his piece."

Jon glared at Marc with disdain. He pushed away from the table and stood angrily. "No. Not now, Marc. Not today." The man turned away from the family and left the cabin, rattling its walls with the slamming of the door behind him.

Hannah stared after her husband tears of both shock and sorrow rising in her eyes. She stood to follow him but felt a gentle touch on her arm. She looked down to see Marc's kind, gray eyes gazing back at her.

"Sit down, Hannah. It's not time to go home just yet. I'll go talk to him. I think I know what the problem is." The authoritative tones that had brought the conversation to its climax had melted into kindness. He went to the wall, took down his own coat along with his brother's, and stepped up to the door. "You all finish your dumplings. We'll be back in a few minutes."

Wesley watched Marc go and then turned back to the others. "I'm sorry. I never intended — "

"Wes, *I'm* sorry," Cynthia said. "After that scene, you're probably terrified at the thought of marrying into this family. First Jess lets all of her wrath out on you, and now Jon. I am sorry. If Jonathan had been out here... Well, I imagine it would've gone about the same. Jon's his own man."

"Mr. Close," Hannah said, "please understand it isn't you. My husband and Joe were very close. He's dealt with it pretty well for the most part, but this week — today to be exact — is the anniversary. Just making it down that road through all this snow set him on edge. It's not you, Mr. Close."

The color drained from Wesley's face, and he suddenly felt very sick. "I didn't know," he whispered in horror. "I knew it was in January, but from what she said...I thought it was earlier in the month...I thought...I waited, but I couldn't wait any longer, not with...Oh, I am so sorry. I should go. I'm so, so sorry. I should go." Wes stood and retrieved his wraps. "Send Zane into town when he wakes up. I'll be at the hotel. I'm so sorry."

He opened the door and stepped out into the bright winter sunlight. A glance toward the barn revealed that Jon had locked himself inside. Marc stood outside, pleading with his older brother to let him in.

Wes groaned, running a hand through his hair. "What have I done?"

Cynthia stepped up beside him. "Wesley, please come back inside."

But the man shook his head. Then he turned away. "I think I'm going to be sick."

* * *

Marc ran a hand across his neck and gave up. Jon had locked the door from inside, and he wasn't going to open it. Marc groaned. He hadn't been paying attention to the calendar, not for this reason. He'd been watching it with calving season in mind. He hadn't thought about how Wesley's visit falling on this day would affect Jon. If he had, he would have waited a day or two before letting Jon know Wes had come.

Groaning once more, he turned and went around the barn to the side door. He found his brother seated at the workbench in the tack room with arms resting on the bench and head down.

"Jon."

Jon sighed at the sound of his brother's voice, but he said nothing.

"Jon, there's no way he could've known, and...and I didn't think it through. If I had, I would have waited to ask you to come out. He's a good man, Jon. He's not tryin' to replace Joe, and he's not tryin' to find a replacement for his wife either. I've spent the last hour questioning him. He's just trying to love and protect Jess. He came now because he was afraid if he waited, he wouldn't get a chance to talk to Pa. There's something to be admired in that."

"I'm sorry, Marc. I'm sorry."

"I'm not the one you should be apologizing to."

"No, you're wrong." Jon sat back, his eyes reflecting sorrow and weariness. "You were right when you said no one should be driven from the house in such a manner. Love has always been Papa's underlying principle in the way he has sought to build this family. Now, that responsibility has fallen on you. My actions went against everything he has built into this family and everything you're trying to keep in it. I'm sorry."

"I forgive you, Jon, but I think that's an apology best made to Ma."

Jon nodded. "I'll talk with her too. I really am sorry, Marc. ...Me and my mouth."

Jon rose and reached for the coat Marc held out to him.

"I know it still hurts, Jon. I know how much Joe's friendship meant to you. I'll pray more specifically about that."

A faint light climbed in Jon's blue eyes. "Thanks for taking pity on your wreck of a brother, Marc."

Marc smiled. "That's what brothers are for—draggin' each other out from under buildings and pullin' in the reins when we get a little off course."

Jon laughed. "For the record, it was Ma and the girls who pulled you out. I just put you back together."

The two men entered the cabin, noticing the somber mood that met them. Jon looked around, one scowl after another greeting him from the women in his family.

"Where's Wesley?"

"He's outside," Cynthia said. "Lost everything he'd had to eat all day, which, thanks to you, didn't include chicken and dumplings."

"What?"

"After you left, Hannah told him why you were so upset. That was enough to have him packing up and heading to town. But when he went to get his horse, he realized you'd locked yourself in the barn. The thought of his presence here hurting this family as much as it appeared to be hurting us was too much. I tried to get him to come back in, but he was too upset. He said he'd just wait until you two came out, slip down to the barn, get his things, and be on his way."

"What! No!" Jon spun on his heels and hurried outside just in time to see Wesley walk stoop-shouldered into the barn.

"Wesley! Mr. Close! Wait!" The tall doctor ran through the snow to the barn. "Wesley, please don't go," he begged, reaching out and turning the tall rancher around. "Please, don't go. I was wrong. I behaved like a child. I'm sorry. I'm the one who was selfish, not you. I'm sorry. Please, forgive me. Please, come back up to the house, and let's talk."

"I don't want to cause any more pain, Jon. I didn't know. When Jess told me the story, well, I thought it happened closer to the New Year. She wasn't very specific about some of those details. If I had known—"

"I know. Don't second-guess yourself because of my foolish behavior. I was wrong. Please, come back up to the house. We'll get you some lunch if you're up to it. It would be a shame to sit at that table and smell that wonderful meal and have it staring back up at you from your plate never to even taste it. Come on. We'll eat, and then we'll all go talk with Pa."

Relief drew a smile into Wesley's eyes. "Thanks for giving me a second chance."

Jon smiled. "No. Thank *you* for giving *me* a second chance. I don't deserve it, but I am grateful."

The men started toward the house, but then Wes stopped, squaring his gaze up to the doctor's. "Jon, I'm sorry for your loss. I've been there. I know that pain. It rips the guts right out of a man, and it's a long time getting things put back together. I don't suppose they ever really go back together the way they were before, but eventually, the wound begins to close. Don't be too hard on yourself."

Jon smiled and motioned the rancher toward the house. They may have gotten off to a rotten beginning, but maybe there was more to Wesley Close than he'd allowed.

Chapter 31

As Wesley stepped into Jonathan Bennett's room, he knew the note he'd gotten from Tom Dresden hadn't exaggerated the man's condition. Jonathan was uncomfortable and weak. Even so, the room was bright and filled with such a peace that Wesley wished it had been his first stop in the turbulent day.

"Love, we have company," Cynthia was saying.

"Oh?" Jonathan replied, grunting with the effort of repositioning himself. "Who's here? I thought I heard a commotion while ago."

"It's Wesley Close from Grassdale."

"Wesley Close? Jessica's Wesley Close?"

"The very one, dear."

"Well, hello, son," Jonathan said, stretching out his left hand to greet the other man. "I'm glad you've come. I've been hopin' for an opportunity to thank you."

"Thank me? For what, sir?"

Jonathan chuckled. "For lettin' God love our daughter through you. ...You do know tha's wha' brought her back to Him, don' you?"

Wesley couldn't hide his surprise. He wasn't sure he'd understood properly. The family obviously had no difficulty understand the man's slurred speech, but Wes wasn't as confident. He glanced at Cynthia. "What do you mean?"

Cynthia motioned for Wesley to sit. "Wes, when Jess realized what you had been through yourself and how you had loved and cared for her spiritual wellbeing in spite of the way she'd been treating you... Well, it was your example that made her willing to trust again."

Wesley stared at the woman, unable to speak.

"Thank you, Mr. Close," Jonathan said. "Thank you. ...So why have you come to Twin Pines?"

Wesley hesitated. He cleared his throat, looking back and forth between the man, his wife, and their two eldest sons who had stepped into the room behind him.

"Well, perhaps for the very reasons you have just alluded to, sir. I have grown to love your daughter...deeply. I know it hasn't been long since she lost her fiancée, and I wouldn't wish to cause any more pain or resentment on anyone's part. It's not the best time of year to travel, but I felt I could wait no longer..." Wesley went on to share his heart, just as he had with Marc and Jon, both of which listened as attentively this time as they had before.

When Wes had finished, Jonathan sighed, but it wasn't a weary or heavy sigh. In fact, it came with a smile.

"Wesley...May I call you Wesley?"

"Of course! Most folks just call me Wes."

"Very well then, Wes, we've been expectin' you."

"What?" Wesley shot a wide-eyed glance at Marc and Jon but they were busy sending their own questioning glances at one another.

"Cynthia," Jonathan continued, "tell him."

"It's true, Wes. From the day Jess told us what had happened in Grassdale, we both sensed you might show up here someday. We've talked it over a little. If you could love Jess then—and we know how hard it was to love her at times—then you'll be able to love her through other difficult times."

"Bu' many things make a man who he is," Jonathan resumed. "How long can you stay?"

"I promised my mother and Jess I would be back in two weeks. That gives me a week here at the most."

"Then a week it is. We'll give you our answer then...after we've spent time with you. Does tha' seem fair?"

"Fair? That sounds like a good bit more than I'd ever allowed myself to hope for, Mr. Bennett. Thank you."

"We're glad you're here, son. Can you ask Marcus to come in here?"

"I'm here, Pa, so is Jon."

"Ah, okay. Wes, if you'll excuse us, I need to chat with my sons for a moment."

"Of course." Wesley stood and left the room, instinctively closing the door behind him.

"Is something wrong, Pa?" Marc asked when Wes had gone.

"I don' know," Jonathan replied. "You two tell me. I heard wha' soun'ed like an argument 'bout an hour ago, an' I heard it go all the way down to the barn."

Jon hung his head in shame. "I'm sorry, Pa. That was me. I didn't treat Wes the way I should've when I realized why he'd come."

"Did you sense somethin' wrong with him?"

"No, sir. I didn't give him that much of a chance. I...I'm sorry, Pa."

"So wha' was the issue?"

Jon sent a pleading glance in his mother's direction, but he could see she wasn't going to speak for him. He sighed. "It upset me that he came here askin' to pursue Jess today of all days."

"Today? Why should today be any different than any other day?"

Cynthia, seeing the horror and the hurt in her son's eyes, spoke up. "Joe died a year ago today, love."

Sorrow crossed Jonathan's face. "I'm sorry, Jon. I'm sorry I didn't realize wha' day it was."

Jon shrugged, but then, knowing his father couldn't see it, rushed on. "I thought I had my emotions under control, Pa. I've been bracing myself against this day for weeks, and then...then *he* shows up. I let all that emotion out on him. It was wrong of me, and I've told him so."

"So things are fixed?"

"Well, as fixed as they can be. I wouldn't blame him if he shied away from me for a couple days. I would in his place. I take full responsibility, Pa. He did nothing wrong."

"And you'll continue to make things right?"

"Yes, sir."

"You won't let it cloud your judgment?"

Jon hesitated, realizing he still bore a measure of resentment toward Wes and his purpose for being there. His chest tightened at the thought of Joe and the years of friendship that had been lost in that blizzard a year earlier.

"Jon?"

"Sir?"

"Son, you owe it to your sister to be objective. ...Tha' man has put up with a lot from her. He rode all this way...at his own peril in order to do things the right way. ...A man like tha' is rare. Unless we discover some great flaw of character this next week... Well, I've thought ever since fall tha' he's probably the one God has been preparin' fo' your sister...an' she fo' him."

The comment stung, but Jon said nothing.

"I need you boys in this, both of you. You can see things tha' I can't. And, as men, you'll notice things your mother may not. ...But you have to look with eyes wide open an' with nothin' impairin' your sight."

"I understand, Pa," Jon said. "I'll do my best. ...I want what's best for Jess. If that's Wesley Close, then I don't want to be the one who makes it impossible."

"Thank you. I know you won't be here every day. But whatever time you spend out here, I wan' you to be aware...and watchin'. But I also just wan' you to...get to know him."

"Yes, sir."

"And the same for you, Marc. I'll be expectin' your observations at least once a day."

"Yes, sir."

"When did Wes arrive?"

"Late last night."

"So you've already spent some time with him. Wha' do you think?"

"He's exactly what I remember from when I met him in Miles City a few years back. He's responsible, a hard worker, got a good head on his shoulders, and you can tell by talkin' to him that he loves the Lord." Marc went on to share the conversations he'd already had with Wes. Finally, he took a deep breath. "To be honest, Pa, I like him. I can already see why he's been so good for Jess. He seems pretty even-keeled. ...And there's Zane too."

"Sane?" Jonathan lisped.

"He came with Wes. He's one of their ranch hands. I get the feelin' he looks up to Wes like an older brother. From some of Jessica's letters, I think Wes and his brother both try to help their men in the right direction as much as they can."

"Remember that conversation we had about the kind of man she should marry? You said you always felt she'd be suited for a man who had a purpose beyond the mundane. I think he's that kind of man."

"Hmm," Jonathan mused, "*tha'* is somethin' to ponder."

Marc glanced out the window. "Pa, I hate to bring this conversation to an end, but I need to leave if I'm going to make it to the school on time."

"Ah, sorry. I didn' realize it was so late. Go on. Just both of you keep your eyes open."

"We will, Pa. You three enjoy yourselves. Jon, don't beat yourself up too much. Wes is fine. I'm sure he's tangled with worse than you over the years. Will you be here when I get back?"

Jon nodded.

"Good. I'll see you then. Don't eat all the leftover dumplings while I'm gone." Marc laughed. He slapped his brother's back and then stepped out of the room.

Chapter 32

Ronald Gray shivered on the doorstep. He was just far enough back on the step that he couldn't be seen through the window, but still close enough to hear what was going on inside. He'd been there for ten minutes and nothing had changed. She was still singing.

"What are you doing out here, Gray?" Dunn said, stepping up to the stairs and sending a confused look in Gray's direction.

Gray jumped at the man's voice. "Boss! You like to scare the snot outta me. Where'd you come from?"

"I've been watchin' you from the barn. You just keep standin' here, like you're waitin' on something. What are you doing?"

Embarrassment rose in the man's eyes. "I was…well…I was listenin' to Miss Jess sing. She's been singin' for ten minutes, hardly a break even though she's workin'."

Dunn raised an eyebrow. "You mean you're standin' here being entertained while the rest of us work?"

Gray laughed. "No. I was going in for some coffee, and then I heard her, and I stopped to listen. How does she do it, Boss? How does she sing? I saw how tore up she was the other day. I know she's still hurtin' over the man she lost and worryin' about Wes and Zane. I don't understand how she can still sing in the midst of that."

Dunn considered Gray's question. A rather pat answer sat on his tongue, but he didn't feel it would be the right thing to say. At the same time, he wasn't sure what to say.

"Probably seems dumb, me wonderin' about it."

"No. Not really. But *why* are you wonderin' about it?"

Gray shrugged. "Cause I never could've done it. After my wife died, well, I tried to find someone else. It was a few years later. I thought I'd be okay. I wasn't drinkin' as much in those days as I was by the time I come here. I met this nice little gal. Her name was Ann. She was a precious thing. Kind. Sweet. Pretty. Smart too. I was about to ask her to marry me...but I couldn't."

"Why not?"

"I was afraid."

"Afraid! You? Ron, I've never seen you afraid of anything."

"Well, I was."

"She sounds wonderful. How could you be afraid of her?"

Gray shot an indignant glare in Dunn's direction. "I wasn't afraid of *her*, you numbskull. She was one of the daintiest creatures I ever met."

"Well then what were you afraid of?"

A shadow passed over Gray's eyes, and he sighed heavily. He picked at a small tear in his coat sleeve.

"I was afraid of losin' her. I heard rumors that people was gettin' sick in the next town over, and some of 'em died. I couldn't do that again. I wouldn't. So I left. I never told her goodbye. Never told her where I went or why. I just left. I shouldn't have done it. But I did. I did it 'cause I was scared."

Gray dropped his gaze and shoved the toe of his boot up against a clump of ice that clung to the doorstep. "That's why I don't know how Miss Jess can sing. I went off and drank till I woke up in jail in a town I'd never even heard of b'fore. And I just kept runnin' after that."

"Have you asked her?"

"What?" Gray's gaze jerked up to Dunn's. "Why would I do that?"

"Because you want to know."

"Yeah, well maybe I don't want her to know that I want to know."

Dunn shrugged, turning to go inside. "Suit yourself."

"Boss, don't do that."

"Don't do what?"

"Leave me hangin' like that. You know what it is. I know you do."

"Let me ask you this. What do you think she'd say if you asked her?"

Gray leaned back against the wall and thought for a moment. "She told me a while back 'bout how she used to run from God. She said she'd stopped runnin' and given Him everything. I s'pose she'd say it had something to do with that."

"I suppose you're right. She can't change anything that has happened, and she can't prevent anything that might happen. So, she's put it in God's hand."

"What's that mean? I mean, how does a person put somethin' in God's hand? You can't see Him, and 'specially if it's another person, it's not like you can pick 'em up and put them in an invisible hand."

A soft chuckle escaped Dunn. "No, you're right. You can't see God, and you can't pick a person up and put them in an invisible hand. It's a matter of trust, Ron. It's sayin', 'God, I can't do anything about this situation, so I'm trustin' You to take care of it.'"

"But what if He don't? What if Wes and Zane never come back? What if they freeze out there?"

"That's the hardest part of trust, the part that says, 'I'll accept the outcome, no matter what it is.' That's where trust is tested."

"That's foolhardiness. There ain't no one you can trust like that. No one. Not even God...especially not God. I like to hear her sing, but I'll never be doin' the singin'. Not if that's where it comes from."

The man pushed away from the wall and flung himself down the stairs. In a few quick strides, he was halfway to the barn, and Dunn was left staring after him.

Chapter 33

"I don't know how you keep up with everything." Wesley stepped out of the tack room and moved toward the stall Marc was mucking out. "You've kept us busy the whole time we've been here, and I'm guessin' most days it's just you."

Marc grinned. "I'm takin' advantage of you is what's happenin'."

"Well, I figured that. Not to mention the need to make sure I can find my way around a barn before sendin' me back to your sister. ...Seriously though, Marc, you need to get some help around here."

Marc drew in a deep breath and leaned heavily against his pitchfork. "I know. We've been lookin'. We just haven't found anyone who fits. I've got my sisters to think about, you know. I don't want just anybody out here."

"True. That's not an element I've had to give much thought until Jess came. The men we have now are good men. No worries there, Marc."

Marc chuckled. "If they're anything like Zane, I'm not worried one bit. That kid could work circles around any man I know."

"He's a good one."

"How long has he worked for you?"

"Oh, 'bout eighteen months. ...I'm serious though, Marc. You're going to run yourself into the ground."

Marc considered his friend. He hadn't been up long, that much was evident. His brown hair stood on end and his cheek still bore the impressions of a crumpled pillowcase. Any other time, Marc might have harassed Wes about it, but not now. Even when they'd only been casual acquaintances back at the livestock auction in Miles City, he'd respected Wes. The past four days had only served to increase that respect. This concern, however, he sensed was coming from his own sister.

"Jess has been talkin' to you, hasn't she? Just like she talked to Tom Dresden." Marc grabbed the pitchfork and stepped back into the stall, frustration evident in his movements.

"Tom Dresden?"

"Tom stopped me on the street a few weeks ago. He took me to lunch and told me he's afraid I'm 'disappearing,' which are Jessica's words exactly."

"Disappearing? That does sound like a woman's way of puttin' things. I don't know anything about that. I mean, she's concerned for you, and she has talked about it. But I've been watchin' everything you've tried to do over the last four days. You're going to kill yourself at this rate. I'm used to a heavy day's work. Zane's used to a heavy day's work. But you've got both of us exhausted. If this is the way you run day in and day out, I don't know how you're even standin'. Even in this cold, you've made two trips into town dealin' with that tack repair."

"That tack repair is what puts food on the table, Wes."

"Is the wheat doing so poorly that you can't survive on it?"

"The harvest was all right, but we had to put a new roof on this barn. That doesn't come cheap. Then there's the cost of the medicines and herbs Jon's used to treat Pa...it all adds up."

"Jon charges you?"

"No, of course not. But I know he can't afford to be here all the time instead of out with payin' patients. Add to that the expense of medicine. I feel we should help. It'll be fine, Wes. I appreciate the concern, but it'll be fine."

"I don't think so, Marc. If you'd been going at this pace for a few weeks, then maybe I'd agree with you. But as best I can tell from what your mother and Marianne and Millicent tell me, this has been going on for months."

"Oh! So you've been listenin' to all the women," Marc laughed, trying to make light of the conversation and hoping to bring it to an end.

Wes, however, didn't join in his laughter. He stepped closer to the stall, his eyes narrowing into a serious gaze. "I've been talkin' to the preacher, and if you make me, I'll talk to Jon. You're going to kill yourself if you keep workin' this way. And this family...this family needs you. I know you don't want to stop and think about what's going on, but you need to. I know it doesn't come cheap, and I know it's hard to find the right fit, but you've got to find help, and you've got to find it before the calves start comin'."

Marc grimaced at the other man's rebuke. He stepped away from the stall and out into the main floor of the barn, keeping his back to Wes. "I know."

Wes sighed. He didn't enjoy this kind of conversation, but from everything he'd seen over the previous days, he knew it was necessary. He'd come to love the family as much as he loved Jess. He wanted them to be safe, just as he wanted his own family to be safe.

"Marc, you have an advantage I never had."

Marcus turned toward the other man at this, confused.

"You know what direction things are headin'. I didn't. I didn't have a chance to plan. I didn't have a chance to prepare. None of us did. Pa was standin' there strong and healthy and happy one minute and the next he was dead. Just like that. I can't begin to tell you what that feels like, and I can't begin to tell you the turmoil it unleashed at our ranch. My sisters left, Marc. They left. Sure they write, but I haven't seen either of them since they went back east. I may never see them again.

"*You* have time to prepare. Take it. I know it feels like someone's slowly tearin' your guts out every time you let it cross your mind, but you owe it to your family to slow down and be here with them.

"Marianne and Joy need you. They're both scared. I see it in their eyes. They're scared for your Pa, your Ma, for themselves, and, frankly, I think they're scared for you."

Marc looked down at his boots. "I know you're right. I figured if I could just get us through every day, we'd be okay. But I know they need more than that."

"And you're too busy to give it to them. You've got to find help, Marc, you've got to find help before calvin' begins."

"I know. I'll try —"

"No. Don't try. Do. It isn't a matter of trying. You're past that. You've either got to find help, or you've got to drop something."

Marc nodded, feeling the chastening acutely.

"Marc." Wes had calmed now, the pitch of his voice lowered, and he spoke in a near whisper as if he were afraid someone would hear. "I respect you. I've always respected you. I respect your Pa, and for all his blusterin', I've even come to respect Jon. I want the best for you and your family. We're so far away in Grassdale. Three days doesn't sound like so much, but when you make the trip the way we just made it — I realize now how truly far we are from you. I won't be able to help after I'm gone from here, but let me help now. I'll do whatever I can to help.

I'll even give you the first month's pay to hire someone if that's what you need."

Marc waved the last comment off. "We're fine there. The stage company decided they owed me for some repairs I made for Tom. Paid me five months of back wages that I never even considered due me. I put it back to hire someone for calvin' season. Truth is I just haven't met anyone who's looking for work yet."

"Is there something else I can do?"

Marc hesitated, knowing he had exhausted the other men and not wanting to add to it. "Well, there's one thing."

"What's that?"

"It'll require more work."

"Go on."

"Well, when we hire someone, we need a place for him to sleep. The guest room where you and Zane have been sleepin' gets too much use to have someone livin' in it."

"So what were you thinkin'?"

"For now, I want to build a lean-to against the back of the barn. It won't be large, but all he'll need is a place to sleep and somewhere to store his gear."

"And a way to keep warm."

"Well, that too. I've already got a stove. I just haven't had the time to build the lean-to. I'd hoped to pull Danny in on it. I don't want that boy leavin' this farm without knowing how to build. But maybe we just need to do it."

"I'd say so. It's not the best time of year for buildin', but if it's got to be done, it's got to be done."

"We don't have any room for him up at the house, and…I think my family will need more privacy than normal over the next few months."

"Have you drawn up any plans?"

"Sure. They're in the workbench. I'll show you."

Marc abandoned the pitchfork and strode toward the tack room. In a matter of moments, he had a lantern lit and was busy showing Wes his plans.

"This will work," Wes said at last, "but not until I've had my coffee. Are you about finished with your chores?"

"It'll take me about five more minutes."

"Good. I'll get Zane movin'. We'll have breakfast and set to work while you take the little ones to school."

Marcus grinned. "Thanks, Wes. For everything."

* * *

"Pa, he's right, and I'm as grateful as can be for his help puttin' that lean-to up. We'll have it done by tomorrow afternoon, maybe even sooner."

"But?" Jonathan said, sensing concern in his son's voice.

"But I'm just as committed to askin' the Lord for help as I've been since the beginning. We can look, we can even look harder than we did before, but it's got to be the Lord that brings him, whoever he is."

"I agree. So does tha' mean you need to cut back on a few things? Maybe only go to town once a week instead of two or three times."

Marc was silent, considering the matter.

"It would take some weight off your mother, Marc."

"Has she said something about it?"

"No, but I can tell it bothers her. The baby will be comin' soon. This house is going to be different. Mary won' be able to make up for you as much if she's makin' up for your Ma as well."

Marc cringed. "Mary's been makin' up for me?"

"Who do you think hauls the water and brings in the wood and checks the animals in the middle of the day when you're gone? Danny's in school, remember?"

"I'm sorry, Pa. I try to have the water and wood up here before I leave. I didn't realize it was becoming a problem."

"Pshaw. You know your sister. She doesn' complain, but I sense tha' she's weary."

"I'm sure she is."

The conversation lulled. The day had been long, as all Marc's days were, but he wasn't ready to bring it to an end. The others had all gone to bed. The house was quiet. He'd been sitting in the dark with his father for a half hour now, but it didn't seem long enough. And something else was on his mind.

"Pa, have you talked with Jon about Wes?"

"Sure. We talked this afternoon."

"What did he say?"

"He thinks we're draggin' things out too long. Thinks we should give him an answer."

I agree with Jon. I don't see any need to draw things out. Jon's still here. Let's talk to Wes in the morning."

"Wha' 'bout Hannah? She isn't here."

"I'm not lettin' Hannah go anywhere until after the baby is born," came a voice from the common area. "She'll miss it no matter when we talk to him."

Marc laughed at Jon's sudden entrance into the conversation. "I thought you were asleep."

"How? How could I possibly be asleep with you two yammerin' away in there? It's no wonder Zane gets so frustrated with you and Wes."

Marc laughed again. "Well, then it's settled. We'll talk with him at breakfast."

"After breakfast," Jonathan corrected. "You'll all come in here after breakfast. We'll have devotions together, an' then we'll talk to him."

"Sounds good," Jon agreed. "Can we go to sleep now?"

※ ※ ※

Wesley sat with his back against the bedroom wall, crowded onto a long bench with Danny on one side, Cynthia on the other, and Gretel in his lap. Jon, Marc, Mary, Joy, and Elizabeth sat on a similar bench on the other side of Jonathan's bed. Zane sat on the floor in the doorway, back against one upright and feet high above his head on the other. Try as he might, Wesley struggled to focus. He hadn't slept well. In fact, he hadn't slept well a single night since leaving Grassdale. The trip had been exhausting, but the sleeping conditions along the way had never allowed for good sleep. Once at the Bennett's, the tension and nervousness that always disappeared during the day, flooded back over him at night. Now, with Gretel's warm body in his lap, and a delicious breakfast in his belly, he was losing the battle to keep his eyes open.

"We seem to have exhausted you, Wes," Jon said, laughing.

Wes looked up, shocked to realize that at the very last sentence of their closing devotional prayer, he'd fallen asleep. He felt his cheeks color with embarrassment. "Sorry. I haven't slept much since leavin' home. Guess it finally caught up with me."

Jonathan chuckled. "Well, perhaps we can help you sleep better. Mary, let's plan to have supper earlier this evenin'. ...We could all use the extra rest. Cynth, why don't you make sure...to have a nice cup of warm milk ready for Wes come bedtime. Tha' a'ways helps me sleep. An', Marc, when we're done here, le' him take a nap...while we work on that letter."

"What letter?"

"The one telling Jess we've given Wes our blessing."

Wesley's eyes widened. He leaned forward in his seat, nearly losing both his Bible and Gretel. His mouth gaped open. "What?" he choked out at last. "Do you mean it?"

"Of course we mean it."

"But it hasn't been a week. I mean, are you sure?"

"We're sure. We wouldn't have said it otherwise."

"But, Mr. Bennett...I mean...I thought —"

"Would you like us to take it back?"

"No! I mean..."

"We could require the full week."

"No. No. I mean —" Wes paused, taking a deep breath to calm himself, and then bursting into a grin. "Thank you. All of you. Thank you for giving me a chance."

Jonathan smiled his kind, lopsided smile. "Wes, I don' know how...the process will go from here, but from wha' I know of you so far, I'll be glad to have you...as a son-in-law. Welcome to the family."

"Thank you. Oh, thank you. I don't know what else to say. Thank you."

Zane chuckled from his place on the floor. "Maybe now *I'll* get some sleep."

Chapter 34

Wesley turned in his saddle, wincing with the effort it required of his cold muscles. Wind and ice bit at his face. A long shiver ran down his spine and across his neck and arms, urging him to turn back toward the road. He resisted the temptation. Instead, he faced Zane, yelling over the wind. "Wasn't that abandoned cabin somewhere near here?"

"I thought so, but I don't see any sign of it yet."

"We'd better find it fast, or something like it, otherwise we're in trouble."

"Look, up ahead. See those trees?" Zane pointed past his employer to six gnarled cottonwood trees. "I remember that stand of trees. I think the cabin's just over the ridge behind them."

Wes nodded, too tired to shout any longer. He urged his horse into a jog, hoping to see over the ridge a little sooner. Several minutes later, he crested the hill just in front of Zane. His heart sank. There was no cabin beyond the ridge. In fact, from here, he could see more than two miles, but nothing resembled a cabin.

Zane rode up next to him, quickly making the same deduction Wesley had made. They were in trouble. "What do you want to do, Boss?"

"We don't have much choice. We keep going until we find someplace out of this wind. I'd say it's going to start snowin' in the next ten or fifteen minutes. We can't spend the night out here. Sorry to drag you through this mess, Zane."

Zane shrugged. "It's been worth it so far. Let's go."

They pushed on, drawing their coats in a little tighter and pulling their collars up around their necks to protect from the fierce wind. An hour later, the road dropped into a narrow valley, which, from their previous vantage point, had been hidden by the lay of the hills around it. They pulled the horses to a stop and squinted through the swirling snow to the landscape below them.

"Is that it?" Zane said, nodding toward a cluster of small structures a half-mile away.

"I think so."

"Are you sure it's abandoned?"

"Don't see any smoke at the chimney. On a day like this, there'd be a fire on the hearth or in the stove...or both. If it's not abandoned, I'd like to hope that whoever lives there might take pity on us. Let's go. It'll be dark soon. I don't want to be out in this when that happens."

The men pressed forward, fighting the wind and snow and their balking horses. As they approached the cabin, they slowed, taking in the forlorn structures. A modest cabin sat less than a hundred feet from the road. Behind it, stood a woodshed with a small stack of logs visible through its open door. The door of the barn was also open. They saw no sign of life, still, they moved cautiously, watching to make sure nothing—or no one—was lurking in the shadows.

"Cabin seems dark," Zane commented. "Don't see any critters or supplies around either. I think you're right. I don't think anyone lives here."

"Hello, the cabin!" Wes yelled over the storm, but no answer came. He dismounted, leaving Zane to watch as he led his horse through the snow to the front door of the house. "Hello!" he called again, knocking loudly and watching with amazement as the door swung open beneath his fist. He glanced back at Zane and then stepped cautiously into the dark house.

The floorboards groaned as he moved into the cabin's single room. From the waning light that crept in at the door and the four small windows, Wes made out a fully furnished room. Whoever had abandoned this hadn't been gone long. He stepped back outside.

"Well?" Zane said, shivering.

"Let's check out the barn. This will be a good place to sleep, but I'm not so sure it's abandoned."

"But who would leave everything standing open like this?"

"I don't know. I just think we should check everything out."

The barn was furnished with clean straw, hay, and even a small sack of oats. Everything needed was there, though it wouldn't last more than a day or two.

"Seems strange," Zane said. "The only thing missing is the livestock. Why would someone leave all this?"

"That's what bothered me about the house. I didn't see any food, but everything else was there."

"What do you want to do?"

"We don't have much choice. We stay here. If we go on, we'll freeze in this storm. I noticed a pile of wood in the shed behind the house. You get the horses put up for the night, and, if you don't mind, I'll carry our gear up there and get a fire and some grub started."

"If I don't mind? My stomach's been growlin' for two hours. Have at it!"

Wes grinned. "Sometimes you're as bad as Travis — always hungry."

An hour later, the two men sprawled across two small beds that lined one corner of the cabin. Their bellies were full, the cabin was warm, and the soft glow of several lanterns filled the room. The wind ripped outside the cabin, but they were safe and quickly on their way to sleep. Wes stared at the ceiling, his mind drifting back over the memories of the previous days. He smiled at the thought of the family they had just left behind.

"Thinkin' about Jess?"

"What?"

"You're layin' over there grinnin'. I figured you were thinkin' about Jess."

Wes laughed. "No, but I was thinkin' about her family."

"I like them. If I wasn't workin' for you, I'd go work for them."

"Good thing you're tellin' me that now. I might have left you behind."

"Yeah, right."

"I'm serious. Marc needs help."

"I noticed that. But I think we got a lot done for him. Should help some. At least for a while."

"I hope so."

The men fell silent. Wesley's thoughts turned home. They were going to be late by at least a day. The weather hadn't been in their favor since leaving Twin Pines. He knew his mother and Jess would worry, but nothing could be done.

The rancher's gaze swept slowly around the cabin's interior. He saw no personal effects, no photographs, mementos, or anything that would carry sentimental value. But the cabin was furnished as if the owner had walked out in the morning, expecting to return that night. Why would someone walk away from all this and leave it to the elements or thieves or...squatters like himself? Things were dusty, but not as dusty as he would expect of a home that had been long abandoned. Even the beds were in good shape as if they'd been waiting for the two men. No signs of bugs. The linens appeared clean. And there were no cob-webs...anywhere. Even lived-in homes in the territory had cobwebs. Something wasn't right.

"Zane," he said abruptly, "I don't think this cabin is abandoned. I think we need to leave at first light, no matter what the weather is like. I think —"

The front door flew open, crashing against the inside wall. Snow swirled in through the open door and a grizzled, snow-covered man appeared before them, pistol drawn.

Chapter 35

"Good evenin', boys. Let's see them hands. There ya go. I see ya made yerselves to home. Now, who are ya, an' why are ya sleepin' in my beds?"

Wes and Zane, who had both sat bolt upright at the man's unexpected appearance, shot startled glances from one another back to the wild-eyed man before them.

"Well, don' jes sit there. Speak up! Who are ya?"

"We're just passin' through," Wes began. "We'd been ridin' all day, and were bone tired and half froze. We needed someplace to sleep for the night. The door was open. We thought the place was abandoned."

"Oh, ya did, did ya? Well, it ain't. Where ya headed?"

"Grassdale."

"Where ya comin' from?"

"Twin Pines."

The man gave a low whistle through lips hidden by the matted beard that clung to his face. "That's a fer piece in weather like this. What's so important you gotta make that trip now?"

"*He* fell in love," Zane said, rolling his eyes in Wesley's direction and allowing a distinct tone of annoyance into his voice.

The grizzled man raised an eyebrow. He snorted and broke into a high-pitched peal of laughter. "You're ridin' through this mess because *he* fell in love?"

Zane nodded, and the man burst out laughing once more. He cackled for what seemed a very long time, pointing a finger first at Zane and then at Wes and then laughing again until he nearly doubled over.

"You..." he said, gasping for air between the word and his continued laughter, "you went along with it...Ha-ha! I don't know which is worse. ...You fer fallin' in love...or you fer lettin' him drag you into it."

The man burst out again, laughing until tears ran down his rosy cheeks and into his beard. He laughed as he swung the door shut behind him and reached for the latchstring. He managed to subdue his giggling until he'd secured the door. As soon as he turned back to them, however, the laughing began again.

"In all my days…I've seen some desperate fellas…but this…" he laughed until he could hardly stand for breathlessness. Then he pulled a chair out from the table and sank down into it, swinging his left arm over its back and resting his right hand—and the pistol—on his knee. He gasped a happy gasp and sighed contentedly, wiping tears from his eyes.

"Ya did at least make coffee, didn't ya? I thought I smelled it as I was comin' to the house. Smelled somethin' else too, but it didn't smell as good."

Wesley's mouth twisted off to one side, and he imitated the look Zane had given him a moment before. "*He* burnt the beans. I told him to watch them, but he let them scorch."

"So they're ruined? And nary a drop else in the house, I suppose."

But Wesley was shaking his head. "We've supplies to last another three or four days. You're welcome to…in fact, I'll make somethin' if you want."

The man waved the answer away. "No need. I've my own supplies."

Zane glanced at Wes, confused by the statement. The stranger had come in the door with nothing more than the clothes on his person and the pistol. He'd latched the door, so it didn't seem he'd be heading back out to his horse. Where could he possibly have supplies? But Wes didn't seem to notice the discrepancy.

"Is this your place?" Wes asked.

"As a matter of fact, it is." The man laid the pistol on the table. He stood and went to the stove, looking around the area where he knew the men would've been cooking. Other than the bowl of blackened beans that hid beneath a plate, there wasn't a trace of the meal.

"Ya cleaned things up perty nice. Must be used to havin' a woman chase after ya."

Wes chuckled at that. "My mother and the local school teacher moved in with us after their homes were destroyed in a fire. They keep us in check."

The man laughed. "Like I said, yer used to havin' a woman chase after ya. That's good since ya done fell in love. Get ya prepared." The man was chuckling again. "I s'pose ya fell in love with that teacher. Sure. That's it. I'm right, ain't I?"

Wes didn't reply, but the laugh Zane stifled behind his hand was all the answer the grizzled man required.

"I knew it. She done got ya, and now ya been had. Next thing ya know, it'll be 'yes ma'am this' and 'yes ma'am that.' Might as well make out yer will and go to yer grave. She'll have ya runnin' here an'—wait now."

The man swung around, a twinkling suspicion climbing in his eyes as he reached for the pistol once more.

"If she lives with ya, then why you makin' this trip in this awful blizzard?"

Wes shrugged, looking past the gun to the man's intense gaze. "I went to talk to her father. He's dying, and I wanted to do things right."

"And did you?"

"Talk to him? Yes."

"And?"

"And what?"

"What did he say?"

"How is that any of your business?"

The man frowned. He set the pistol back on the table. "He said no, didn't he? Shame on him. Not many men would travel that far for a thing like that. For a herd o' cattle, yes, but for a schoolteacher?" he shook his head, turning back to the stove to rebuild the fire. "Sorry to hear that, lad."

"He said yes!" Wes said, his voice rising indignantly.

The man turned toward him, eyes dancing. "Well, then! That calls for celebration. How 'bout another cup of coffee and a bit of cake?"

Not waiting for a response, the gangly man left the stove and moved to the table. He pulled out all four chairs and pushed the table back its full length. Then he stooped down and flipped back a dirty rug that lay across the floor, revealing a door. The man produced a key from his pocket. With hands still cold and fumbling, he unlocked the door, pulled it up, and leaned it against the table. Grabbing up a lantern, he held it over the gaping hole in the floor, revealing a cozy, warm apartment in what had once been a root cellar. He grinned up at his new, surprised companions and laughed.

"Bet ya didn't 'spect that now did ya? Heh, no one ever does." He stood erect and extended a hand to the other men. "My name's Fisher Smith. Most folks just call me Fish. Welcome to my home, boys."

❀ ❀ ❀

"So you live in the cellar?" Zane said, leaning back in a comfortable winged back chair and clutching a cup of hot coffee in his hands.

"I do," Fisher Smith replied. "Oh, I do my cookin' and eatin' above ground, but when I'm home I spend most of my time below. It's best that way."

The room was cozy. Large, brightly colored rugs lined the walls and floor. Several ornate lamps sat about the room on fine wooden end tables, which stood between two winged back chairs and the sofa from which Wes was taking in the whole scene.

"I've never seen such a comfortable room in all my time in the territory, but why did you put it in the cellar?" Wes said.

"Because of men like you," Fish replied, eying the other man meaningfully.

"Me? What do you mean?"

"My work takes me from home often. I built my cabin too close to the road. Seems travelers come by an', findin' no one ta home, assume it's abandoned. More times than not, I come home to find I'd been plundered. Now, I see you two would never steal, but others would—an' not jes because they was a-hungered. They'd steal b'cause it was there for the takin'. It costs a shiny penny to keep a cupboard stocked. An' *many* a shiny penny if you have ta do it every time ya turn around 'cause some pilgrim robbed ya blind. So, I worked out a plan. Look here."

The man stood and, with a creaking gait, crossed the room to the wall behind his chair. He pulled back the rug that hung there, revealing shelves stocked with every imaginable provision.

"I figured if people thought the place was abandoned, it'd be better that way. There's a room like this'n under the barn as well. Not so fancy, but thet's where I keep my feed an' the like. I leave out enough so's a wayfarer can feed his stock. But most folk who pass through never think to look below them for more. They think they've plundered the lot of it, and pass on their way without so much as a second look. They're just content to have had a bed an' a dry place ta sleep out of the wind and the snow."

"So you leave food for the horses, but not for the 'wayfarer'?" Wes said.

Rachel Miller

"Would *you* eat food left for who knows how long in an abandoned house?"

Wes shrugged. "Suppose that depends on how hungry I am."

"I suppose. Seems my wayfarers were none too hungry. I was jes' wastin' food on them. Or maybe the food was wastin' b'fore they got here. Don' rightly know. Either way, it was a waste. This way, I'm wastin' nothin' and providin' shelter for them what need it. I don' often show up at the same time as the travelers. Sometimes I see someone's here an' jes' spend another night on the range. But it were too cold fer that tonight. 'Taint many what I show this room, but I felt I could trust ya."

The man returned to his seat and reached for his mug of coffee.

"What is it you do, Fish?" Wes asked.

"Oh, some might call me a trader. Reckon with all my wayfarers I shoulda set up a tradin' post an' lodgin' right here long ago, but I like my quiet. I gather goods from places like Twin Pines or Grassdale or even sometimes Billings. Used to go as far as Miles City, but Billings is closer now. I buy up the goods most folks is needin' an' then go up into the mountains an' find my trappers. Most times, I trade their furs for goods, but sometimes I pay for the pelts. Then I take them back to Billings or some tradin' post and sell the pelts, so I can buy more goods to take back to the trappers. Saves the trappers the travel, an' makes me a comfortable livin'."

He took a long sip of his coffee, eyeing the other men over the cup's brim. He let out a contented "Aaah" and then set the cup back down.

"So now it's my turn to ask questions. You said somethin' earlier 'bout a fire. Is that the one I've heard rumors of? Burned a home an' a school and grazin' land. Heard it nearly killed a man and injured others. I also heard it mighta been set on purpose."

Wes squirmed at the question, he'd been relieved to be away from the talk of the fire on their trip, and he wasn't eager to get back to it. Zane, on the other hand, held nothing back. "That's the one. And it *was* set on purpose. There's no question about that."

"And how are the injured men?"

Zane shrugged. "I think they're all mostly healed by now."

"And the man who was nearly killed?"

"I'm fine," Wes said, a grumpy tone coming into his voice. As long as there was talk of the fire, he would be reminded of his own foolishness.

"You? It was you?"

"It was me, and it was my own dumb fault. Not anybody else's, even if they did set the fire."

"Do they know who done it?"

Wes shook his head. "No. We've got a few ideas, but nothin' to prove anything. Folks are gettin' impatient with us."

"Seems yer gettin' impatient with yerself."

"Maybe. I'm disappointed in myself. I've been trackin' and readin' signs in the dirt and the landscape since I was a kid, but there's somethin' about this one I can't figure out."

"Why not?"

"Somethin' isn't right about what I'm seein' there."

"I've done a fair bit o' trackin' in my day. Tell me what you're seein', maybe I can help ya see what yer missin'."

Wes considered the suggestion. Somehow he felt this man had done more than his fair share of tracking. He imagined Fisher Smith tracked down the trappers by sheer skill every day of his life. But they'd all guarded the information about the fire so closely. He glanced at Zane and then back at Fisher Smith.

"Neither of you can tell anyone what I'm about to tell you, not until we've gotten this mystery solved."

Chapter 36

"Wes should be home soon." Dunn strode through the front door and across the room. He tossed his hat down on the table and let his hands come to a rest on his hips. "It's been two weeks."

"And a day," Anna replied, not turning away from the pan she was washing.

"It's not like him to be late."

"No. It's not."

"Are you worried, Ma?"

Jess, who listened from the schoolroom, heard concern in Dunn's voice.

"Not really worrying, son. Just wondering what's keeping him."

"I sure wish he'd given us a little more information before he left."

"Are *you* worrying, son?" the small woman teased.

"I guess maybe I am a little."

Jess heard the scraping of a chair against the floorboards and looked up from the papers she was grading. Dunn had pulled out the chair at the foot of the table and seated himself. He pulled his hat close and fiddled with its brim.

"Temperature's dropping pretty fast out there. It's going to be downright frigid tonight. I hate to think of anyone being out in it. I'm sure they'll be all right. Wes is no fool, and I know God will protect them, but I wish I knew more."

"What good would it do, Dunn? You still wouldn't know what is keeping them. It might frustrate you more. Maybe that's why he didn't tell us."

"Maybe."

"It does seem strange that he didn't tell *you* anything. I know he doesn't tell me everything. Just like you don't tell me everything. But it seems he would have mentioned something that might give you a clue."

Dunn shook his head. "I could make some guesses, but I don't think he'd want me to mention them, and if I were wrong— No, my guesses are better left unsaid."

The conversation lulled. A gust of wind hammered the front door and rattled the windowpanes. Jess let her eyes wander to the window nearest her desk. It was nearly dark. The chances of the men reaching home tonight were shrinking.

"Did they take enough supplies to last this long?" Dunn said.

"No. Wes said they'd buy more along the way if they needed it."

Dunn sighed. "I suppose a man can only carry so much on a horse."

"This is true. Do you know how much money he took with him?"

"Not as much as I'd like to think he had along with him. I suppose he might have already had some money in hand. He only withdrew ten dollars from the bank. He wasn't plannin' on stayin' in hotels, that's for sure."

Jess had heard all she cared to hear. The thought of her two friends sitting on the frozen prairie or in the mountains with nothing in their stomachs and a wretched gathering of sage or pine branches for a fire was more than she cared to consider. She rose quietly, crossed the room, and closed the door, leaning up against it as if to keep the conversation out.

"Oh Father," she whispered, "please help us trust You to protect them, not to worry or doubt. I know You're able. I know Your plan is best. Please, Lord, help me trust. I'm afraid. I'm truly afraid. Please quiet my heart. Keep them safe. Bring them to shelter along the way. Bring them to safety tonight. Please, Lord."

Dunn didn't miss the closing of the door. He gnawed at his lower lip, considering the young woman hidden away in the other room.

"How's Jess doing, Ma?" he asked, his voice low.

"She's seemed fine. Why?"

"She closed the schoolroom door. She heard us talkin'."

"What?" Anna turned away from the counter toward the closed door. "Oh, dear. You're right. Maybe I should go talk to her."

"No. If she wanted to talk, she would've joined us."

"Your brother may find he has a lot to answer for with that girl."

"He has a lot to answer for with *me* regardin' that girl."

"You've said it yourself, Dunn, he didn't know."

"He didn't know the timin', but he knew the how."

"Dunn, don't get yourself worked up. What if something happens? How would you go through life knowing you'd spent his last days angry with him?"

"That's a rather morbid way of lookin' at it."

"Well? How would you?"

"I understand what you're sayin'. It's just that... Ma, I think he loves her, and I don't understand why he would risk — "

"You think he *loves* her?" Anna's whisper grew softer still.

Dunn shrugged. "I've been watchin' them, and, well, I think I see something there from both of them. I could be wrong. ...Do you see something there?"

"I haven't, no. But...but Mr. Gray said the same thing you just said. Maybe it's true. If it is, then I agree with you. Why would he risk his life and her affections by going off the way he has? It doesn't make sense."

Dunn sighed. "Wes has never kept anything from us before. I think we just have to trust that when the time comes, he'll tell us. ...We keep comin' back to the same conclusion, don't we?" He drummed his fingers on the table, then grabbed up his hat and shoved it on his head. "Well, as much as I'd like to sit here until bedtime, I'd better get everyone finished up for the night. How long before supper?"

"Oh, about an hour probably."

"Sounds just right. If you think Jess needs more time, just let me know. I'll be loud with the door on my way out, so she knows I'm gone."

Anna laughed. "I don't think that'll be necessary."

"That's my excuse. The wind is going to slam the door, and there's not a thing I can do about it. See you in a bit, Ma. I'm already hungry."

❈ ❈ ❈

Two days passed. The temperatures continued to drop. When it wasn't snowing, the skies were clear, letting all the warmth escape. The wind howled, driving the existing snow before it and whipping it up into ground blizzards. On the third day, Dunn braved the snow and rode to town, hoping to find a letter or even word from Tom, but there was nothing. He'd come home, told his mother and Jess his news, and then trudged back out of the house. Jess had watched him go. She stood at the window watching down the lane for a long while. Eventually, she set about preparing supper while Anna finished up a tub of washing in the back of the house. Time after time, however, she was drawn back to the window, wondering where the men could be, if they were safe, if they would ever be home.

"What are you doin', Miss Bennett?" Travis said, stepping up beside her.

"Just looking out the window. What are you doing?

"I finished up my chores. I was wonderin' if you could help me with my arithmetic. I didn't understand today's lesson."

"Of course I will, Trav. You should have said something. You get everything together, and I'll be here when you're ready. We've got venison roasting in the oven. I need to start a batch of skillet bread, but I think we can manage that and a little arithmetic." Jess glanced back out the window. The lane had nearly disappeared in the twilight.

"You're worried about Wes and Zane, aren't you, Miss Bennett?"

Jess sighed. "They *were* supposed to be home days ago."

"God will keep them safe. You'll see."

"You're right. I keep reminding myself of that."

The boy hugged her. "I'm glad you're here. I'm glad you're part of our family."

Tears welled in the young woman's eyes. "So am I, Travis."

He turned and hurried down the hall to his room.

Jess watched him go. "Oh, Lord," she whispered, "You put that boy in my life to teach me how to trust You, didn't You? Help me trust like he does."

By the evening of the fifth day, everyone had grown concerned, even Travis. No one spoke more than necessary during supper. Dunn didn't even join them at the table. He stood at the window, watching the swirling snow.

"Son, won't you come eat," Anna implored as the men began their exit for the evening. "Watching won't bring them any sooner. It'll only make you more anxious."

Dunn stepped closer to the window and peered harder through the last of the evening light. "Sure wish this snow would clear."

"I know, son, but worry won't change it. Only prayer can do that."

"They'll be all right, Dunn," Jess said. "The Lord will take care of them."

The man turned and stared at Jess who quietly went about the business of clearing the table. He watched as she carried a plate to the counter and returned to the table with a pot of coffee, humming as she refilled Ronald Gray's cup.

"If *you* can say that, then I have no excuse." The words tumbled out of Dunn's mouth before he could stop them.

Jessica's gaze jerked up to meet his. "Oh, Dunn. I wish I were always that confident. I spend as much time asking the Lord to help my unbelief as I do trusting. Maybe more. But we know we can trust Him, Dunn, we know we can."

Dunn looped his thumbs in his suspender straps and sighed. "You're right."

"Come on, boss," Gray said. "Get yourself some coffee, and we'll finish up for the night. Get your mind off things."

"I suppose that's the best thing. Can't do much else for now."

"You can pray, Dunn," Jess said.

The man nodded and smiled. "Chorin' is the best time for that."

Chapter 37

Marc rocked quietly back and forth in the rocker nearest the fireplace. He'd found months ago that it was the best seat in the sitting area. He could see everything from here. He understood now why his mother so often chose this seat. She could rest while keeping the entire house under her watchful gaze.

The house was quiet now. The children and Mary had all gone to bed, and his mother had gone shortly before them. In a few minutes, Marc would have to go back out into the cold to check on the cow he'd cut from the herd earlier in the day. Chances were he'd spend most of the night down there waiting for a new calf, but for now he was content to be in the stillness and warmth of the little house.

He wondered about Wes and Zane. More than a week and a half had passed since they'd left for Grassdale. He'd asked Wes to wire or at least to write when they got home, but so far nothing had come. It didn't surprise him really. The weather had been fierce since their departure. They'd heard nothing from Jon and Hannah in that time either. He and the preacher had moved Millicent to Mrs. Vass' attic, so she could make it to school each day. The little ones had missed the previous three days because of the wind and snow.

He heard a clank from his mother's room and realized the woman wasn't sleeping. He drummed his fingers lightly on the arm of the chair, wondering what he should do. He knew she tired easily, but she rarely said anything of it. He watched her closely in the evenings, not so much because of the baby as because of his father. Papa's strength continued to wane. More than a week had passed since the man had felt strong enough to share in Marc's studies. Marc often saw sorrow in his mother's eyes as she left his father's room at night. It plagued him, but he didn't know how to relieve it.

Cynthia spoke little of her concerns. Marc had hoped perhaps she spoke to Mary about things when he wasn't around, but Mary had dashed that hope the night before when he'd asked her about it.

"No, Marc," she'd said. "Mama is like you. She talks to the Lord...and Papa. Except I don't think she's been talking to Papa about this. Unless he's coaxed it out of her when I haven't been around." The conversation had left Marc feeling weary. But, everything left him feeling weary these days.

He leaned forward in his seat, peering around the furniture that stood between him and what had once been the pantry. The light coming from beneath the door surprised him.

The young farmer stood and made his way across the common area without a sound. A soft, sniffling came from behind the door. He knocked and waited.

"Come in."

As he pushed the door open, his heart broke. There sat his mother on the edge of the bed, robe drawn tight around her, face damp with the tears she'd tried to wipe away.

"Marcus," she said with a gasp of surprise. "I thought it would be Mary."

"No. It's me. Mary's gone to bed. May I come in?"

"Of course. Is something wrong?"

He smiled, turning to shut the door behind him and then sitting down beside her. "No. I just wanted to talk."

The woman returned his smile, tears rising in her eyes once more. "It has been a while since we've had a good chat, hasn't it? Is everything all right? Is something troubling you?"

"No. I didn't come to talk about me. I came to talk about you."

"Me?"

He paused, taking hold of her hand and squaring his gaze up to hers. "You've been so strong for us, especially for Papa, but I see the sorrow in your face when you put him to bed at night."

Cynthia squeezed her son's hand and looked away, tears spilling down her cheeks. Marc moved closer, laying an arm across her shoulders and drawing her close. He kissed her head and waited for her to speak.

"Oh, Marc. I love your Papa more than I can ever tell you. I wonder sometimes if I love him more than I should. I don't know. I can't stand to see him suffer, but the thought of losing him..." her voice trailed off.

"I know. It's unbearable."

She nodded, but then she looked up at him. "But he's not ours, son. He's God's. We have no right to keep him here if God is calling him home. No matter how badly we want to and no matter how much it hurts to think of it. He is God's and if God calls him home…your Papa will obey. And we…we will trust the Lord to comfort us, and we'll go on doing whatever the Lord gives *us* to do."

Marc smiled, though he wasn't sure he felt it in his heart. He wiped his mother's tears away. "Mrs. Bennett, you're the bravest woman I know."

"I'm not brave, son. I'm not brave at all. But I am confident. God will get us through this, Marc. Somehow, we'll survive."

"I know. Just don't feel you have to do it alone, Ma. We're here. Me and Mary and Joy and Jon, even the little ones—we're all here for you."

"I know. And pretty soon, this little one, who is very excited to meet you, will be here too." She laughed. "Every time you talk, he or she kicks me."

"What?"

"Yes! There they go again. Here, feel it." She took her son's hand and laid it on her stomach. "Say something."

"What should I say?" Instantly, he felt the tiny kick. "Well, what do you know?"

"Seems you've already got a little friend."

Marcus laughed. "I don't mind that one bit." He kissed his mother's cheek and patted her belly. "I should let you get to bed. I love you, Ma."

"And I love you, son. Don't worry. We're in God's hands. He won't let go."

"I know."

Cynthia giggled. "I think your friend knows you're leaving and isn't happy about it."

Marc grinned. He reached down and patted his mother's stomach again. "Goodnight, little friend."

He felt a happy kick in return as if someone was saying, "Don't go! It's time to play."

Marc's eyes danced with delight. "I love you, Ma. I love both of you."

Chapter 38

Cale Bennett shivered at his desk — again. He glanced around the room, trying to see where the cold air was creeping in, but nothing caught his eye. Every winter was the same. No matter how many improvements he made over the summer, he still froze. It wouldn't be so bad if winter weren't so long. He stood and crossed the room to the window that faced out over a side street.

Running his hand along the window frame, he checked for cold air seeping in around the glass and frame but felt nothing. He sighed and glanced out over the street. He didn't expect much traffic on a day like today. In fact, the bank had seen no more than three customers all day long.

A sharply dressed woman left the saloon that stood kitty-corner from the bank. Cale had never seen her before. He watched with interest as she stepped out into the street and looked in the bank's direction. She seemed unsure of how to proceed. After several moments of hesitation, she stepped forward, squaring her shoulders with determination and heading straight for the institution.

Cale leaned forward, placing a hand on the wall and watching her for as long as he could. When his face touched the glass and he could see her no more, he stepped back.

"Huh? That's odd."

He started to return to his desk, but then stopped. He touched the wall once more. It was cold. He let his eyes run along the wall toward the ceiling and noticed a faint sparkling on the wall. He pulled a chair over to the wall, stepped up into it, and then touched the shimmering wall. Ice. No wonder he was so cold.

"Mr. Bennett," came Mitch's voice from behind him.

"Yes?" Cale turned to answer, surprised to see the woman from the street peering curiously around the clerk.

"There's someone here to see you."

"Oh. Oh, all right. Please send them in." Cale jumped down from the chair. He slid it back into its place and brushed the dust—imagined or otherwise—from its seat.

"Leave the door open and throw another log on the fire, won't you, Mitch? It's freezin' in here today."

The clerk nodded and left the room.

Cale turned his attention to the woman. "Hello, ma'am. I'm Cale Bennett. How may I help you?"

"My name's Sadie—" She cut herself short, shaking her head. "That's not so. Most folks around here know me as Sadie Rose, but my name is Cassandra Parker. I've served drinks at the saloon for Mr. Jorgenson for the last three years. It isn't very pleasant work, but I work hard. A few months ago, a cowboy left me a gold coin. I thought it was my ticket out of this town, but Mr. Jorgenson said it was a fake. He said you wanted to talk with me about it. So here I am. I don't know how much longer I'll be in town, Mr. Bennett. Just until Mr. Jorgenson finds respectable work for me. Not sure where or when it'll come. But for now, I'm here. I'll tell you whatever you need to know."

As she spoke, Cale took in the woman's appearance. From the window, she had appeared to be well dressed. Now that he saw her up close, he realized she was merely dressed in bright colors. Her tailored coat was thinning at the seams. Her hat, though once fashionable, showed signs of long wear. Her torn gloves revealed calloused fingers. She was a pretty woman, but Cale saw shadows of heartache in her eyes. He wondered how long it had been since anyone had truly cared for her.

"Please, sit down, Miss Parker."

"Thank you."

Cale returned to his seat across the desk from her. "Can we get you anything? A cup of tea or coffee?"

"No. I'm fine. Just had my lunch before I came over."

"Very well. Do you still have the coin?"

"Yes. I brought it with me." Cassandra pulled a small, velvet purse from her sleeve and loosened the drawstrings. She plucked the coin out of the purse and handed it across the desk to Cale.

Scotch had been right. The coin was identical to the one they'd found at the fire. "When did you get this?"

"A few months ago?"

"Before or after the fire?"

"Before. I don't remember how long, but I know it was before."

"Was it during the time that cattle drive camped outside of town?"

"No. It was later than that. A few weeks at least."

"You're sure?"

"Absolutely."

"Can you tell me about the man who gave it to you? What he looked like? A name?"

"Of course I can. A lady remembers a man who flatters her, especially when he turns out to be as fake as that coin. I don't know his name, but he'd been in the saloon all night, causing trouble, but not enough to throw him out. He's a tall man, slender, and yellow-haired. He's got a nice looking face, but he's no gentleman. He was gambling with a few fellas. Seemed to be winning."

"Do you think that coin could have come out of his winnings?"

"No. No of that I'm sure. That coin came out of his own purse. He had a small pouch on his belt. He took the coin from there."

"Were there other coins in the pouch?"

"The pouch was full of them. I suppose he's been cheating people all across the territory. ...But the thing is, I don't think he's left here."

"What do you mean?"

"I'm almost certain I saw him in town a week or two back. He rode out with another man that I've seen before, but don't know. He was there that night too. Gambling with the others."

"What did that man look like?"

The woman shrugged. "There's not much to take note of there. He's average height. Not particularly handsome. Smells of cattle. Little heavier than most, probably from drinking. He didn't strike me as a particularly intelligent man, just obnoxious."

Cale grunted at that. He had a feeling this woman knew what she was talking about when it came to obnoxious men.

"Did you ever hear either of them called by name?"

"No, I never did. ...Why is this so important, Mr. Bennett?"

"Well, and you must not tell anyone this—"

"I don't have a soul to tell, Mr. Bennett."

"It might have something to do with the fire."

"The fire?" the woman gasped. "You mean he might have started it?"

"I don't know. Maybe him, or someone who beat him in a game of poker and won a gold coin."

The woman sat back in speechless silence. She stared at Cale for a long time before speaking. "Now I see why Mr. Jorgenson insisted I come."

"Yes. It's very important. ...Tell me, Miss Parker, how did you come to Grassdale? I don't think I've ever met you before. I can't believe we've lived in this tiny town together—for three years no less—and never crossed paths."

The woman looked down at her hands. For a moment, she played with the fingertips of her gloves. Then without looking up at him, she said, "It's not a very lovely story, Mr. Bennett. It's not lovely at all, but it's one I'm trying to change."

"Some of the loveliest stories I've ever heard started out unlovely, Miss Parker."

Cassandra sighed, glancing up at him for a brief moment and then away as she considered where to begin. "I grew up in a well-to-do family, Mr. Bennett. We were happy most of the time until...until my mother died. Then my father started drinking. By the time I was fourteen, he had drunk himself to death. My sisters and I had no way of supporting ourselves, so we began working wherever we could find work. My brother was apprenticing with a banker. It was an unpaid apprenticeship, and he couldn't support us. At first, we tried to stay together, but it became too difficult. So we went our separate ways.

"For a while, I survived by cleaning boarding houses, but that paid so little. One night, as I was dragging myself home from a long day of cleaning, a man met me in the street. He said he'd seen me several days in a row, walking home and looking underpaid and exhausted. He said he had better work for me. He gave me an address and told me to be there the following morning.

"Mr. Bennett, I wish with all my heart that I had never gone there. It was a saloon and hotel. That man was cruel. At first, he made me feel as though he had rescued me. But when I refused to do anything for the customers other than serving food and drinks, he changed. He treated me terribly. Finally, he said, 'You were a housemaid when I found you because that's all you're good for.' He set me to scrubbing floors, washing dishes, and scrubbing linens. It was hard work made harder by his abusive tongue, but I didn't care. I wasn't going to be what he wanted me to be. Then Scotch found me.

"It's true that he brought me to another saloon, and he can be quite the fool at times. But he's never treated me the way that man treated me. I told Scotch I would serve food and drinks and clean and work hard but I would never set foot in the brothel. He honored that.

"I don't like who I've become, Mr. Bennett. I want to be better, to work in a better place. I want to do good work. I don't want to be Sadie Rose for the rest of my life. I want people to know me as Cassandra Parker. That's why you've never seen me, Mr. Bennett. I don't leave the hotel much except to go to work. I keep to myself. I'm tired of living that way. I want to move away from this place and start over somewhere else."

Cale studied her for a moment. "I believe you, Miss Parker, and I believe you have the grit to do it." Cale reached into a drawer and pulled out five, one-dollar coins. "Will you allow me to buy this coin from you, Miss Parker?"

"Buy it?"

"Yes. It's evidence against a man whose actions almost killed one of my best friends. I'd like to buy it from you."

"But it's worthless."

"Not to me. I want to buy it from you." He held out his hand and waited until she held hers open beneath it. Then he dropped the coins into her palm. "Please, take it. Put it toward startin' that new life."

Tears pooled in the woman's eyes. "But, Mr. Bennett, it's too much."

"It's what you thought you'd been given. I want to make sure you receive it. Now, promise me that if you ever see that man—or his companion—in town again, you'll tell me."

"I promise. Thank you, Mr. Bennett, thank you."

The woman stood, wiping at her eyes. He extended a hand to her, but she was too moved to take it. She waved the gesture away and hurried from the building.

❋ ❋ ❋

Susan Bennett pulled her youngest son up further in her lap. She scooped a spoonful of mashed potatoes into the boy's mouth and turned her attention to her husband. His eyes were red with fatigue, but it was the tension in his jaw that bothered her.

"You're very quiet tonight," she began. "Are you all right, love?"

"Hmm?" he said, his gaze rising only slightly from his half-eaten plate of food.

"Cale."

The man looked up, his face full of confusion.

"Cale, is something wrong?"

The man groaned, running his hand over his forehead. "We live in a broken world, Susie, a very broken world."

The pretty redhead scooped up one last spoon of potatoes for her son and then set the boy on the floor to play. "What are you talking about, Cale? Did something happen at the bank? Is it the fire?"

"I met a woman today who has lived in this town for three years—"

"Wait. You met someone today who has lived here for three years? Cale, this town isn't that big. Who did you meet?"

"Her name is Cassandra Parker, but she said most know her as Sadie Rose."

"Sadie Rose! Is she still here? I had no idea."

"You know her?"

"Well, I met her once…at the General Store. She was very reserved, very… I don't know how to describe it."

"Beaten down?"

"Yes. That describes her perfectly. I tried to be friendly with her, tried to welcome her to town, but she would hardly speak. In fact, she set her shopping basket down and left the store. Later, Mrs. Lewis told me her name was Sadie Rose. She said Sadie worked at the saloon. Is that true, Cale? Has she worked in the saloon all these years, and no one even knew she was there? Where did you meet her?"

"It's true. I met her at the bank. Scotch told me a couple weeks ago that one of his girls had received a coin from someone passin' through. It was a gold coin like the fake we found at the fire. I told him I needed to talk with her, and he said he'd send her by the bank. I was beginnin' to think she'd never come, but today she did."

"And?"

Cale rubbed his tired, blue eyes, trying to hide the tears that threatened.

Susan took her husband's hand. "Cale, what is it?"

"All I could think of was Annabelle. I never want a life like that for Annie. Never."

"What do you mean?"

Cale sighed and then launched out in the story Cassandra Parker had told him earlier in the day. Susan listened, absorbing every detail, stopping him from time to time to ask a question. More often than not he couldn't answer. Finally, he stopped and sighed.

"It broke my heart to think any of our children could ever end up on such a path. I know it isn't what her parents wanted for her, no more than she wants it for herself. ...All I could do for her was change out the coin, but she needs so much more."

Susan studied her husband, thinking over the things he had shared with her, knowing the depth of love he held for his family. "Cale, one thing I know for sure. If anything ever happened to me, you wouldn't respond the way Miss Parker's father responded. And you wouldn't be dealing with things alone. The preacher and Wes and Dunn and the Tiedemanns — none of them would let you alone. You remember how things were for Jason when Emily died. That man could barely find a moment's peace. It would have been the same for Wes if — "

"If he hadn't been so completely broken by it."

"Yes. But look what the Lord has done for him. Look how He has turned that grief into compassion. Look how God used Wes to help Jess. Cale, don't let it trouble you so. You know as well as I do that if anything ever happens to me or you, God will care for the other. And if anything happens to either or even both of us, God will care for our children. We must walk in that hope — that confidence. To do otherwise will only weaken your walk now, let alone later if something ever should happen. To do otherwise is not to trust, love."

"I know." Cale sighed, studying his wife. "I'll be glad when this fire business is over. I'm tired of it draggin' on."

Susan considered her husband's statement. The search for whoever had started the fire had worn on all of them. She was just as ready for it to be over, but something had been bothering her for several weeks. "Cale, please don't think me impertinent when I ask you this, but... How much have you prayed about the fire? I don't mean a passing prayer, Cale. I mean how much time have you spent really praying over it?"

"I've prayed. I mean, well — " he paused, letting his eyes run over every line of her sincere face. "Not like I should. I've prayed in frustration."

"Do you think God has a bigger purpose in this than finding who started the fire. Maybe He allowed this so we would meet Miss Parker and help her. Maybe there are other things too. Things we haven't even seen yet."

"Like what? What are you sayin'?"

"I'm saying we need to pray. We need to ask the Lord for His guidance, and we need to ask Him if He wants us to help that girl. I agree with you. This whole thing seems to be taking much too long to resolve, but maybe that's our timing. Maybe *all* of this was for her."

"But what could we ever do to help her?"

"That's what we need to pray about, love. And notice I said *we*. It's not all on you. Maybe God wants us to be the family she hasn't had for so very long."

Cale found himself wiping away tears again, but this time the true charity he saw in his wife had brought them. What a beautiful woman he had married—beautiful from the inside out. He studied her face, the depth of her blue eyes, and the vibrancy of her red hair. He smiled, lifting her hand to his lips and kissing it.

Susan leaned forward and kissed his cheek. "The Lord will show us His plan, dear," she whispered. "Now finish your dinner, so we can put the children to bed."

Chapter 39

Jess listened as the wind ripped and roared about the house. She drew the folds of her quilt tight about her shoulders and forced her attention back to the book she'd been reading. Another gust of wind beat against the windowpanes, raking sharp bits of ice and snow across the glass.

"Oh, it's no use." She clapped the book shut, tossing it onto the bed. "Where are those men?"

Jess rose from her chair and went to the tiny window, still wearing the quilt about her shoulders. The night was dark. She could see nothing beyond the glass and the shards of ice that slammed into it. She turned away from the storm and sank onto the windowsill with a sigh.

One more day and Wes and Zane would be a full two weeks late. Dunn had reached his breaking point days earlier. He was tired of waiting. He'd decided to leave with Ronald Gray as soon as the weather cleared. They'd start in town with the hopes of finding a telegram or letter. If nothing had come, they'd set off for parts south and east. Maybe someone would have seen them. Maybe they would find them in some small settlement. Maybe they would be in Billings or Miles City. Dunn knew the maybes outweighed the certainties, but he was determined to find his brother.

Jess, on the other hand, hated the idea. How, she had asked him, could sending two more men out into that frozen wilderness make things any better? How could he justify risking more lives?

He'd sobered at that thought and agreed to wait until the end of the two weeks. That had come now, and still, there was no Wes, no Zane, and no word from either of them. Dunn and Gray would be leaving soon, and Jess was a ball of nerves. Dunn had promised to be careful, but so had Wes—and so had Joe.

She went to her bed, picking up the book once more as if to shun the thoughts racing through her mind. Then she was up again, pacing between the bed and the window. What could be done? Nothing would ensure the safety of Zane and Wes without risking the lives of others. They had already tried sending telegrams to men with whom Wes had done business in the past, but no one had heard anything from the two men. Tom had neither seen nor heard anything from them. In fact, the stagecoach had stopped running a week earlier because of the heavy snows.

Jess went to the window once more, but it didn't help. Pacing the floor didn't help. She sighed. Only one thing would help at a moment like this. She gathered up the long folds of the quilt and knelt beside the bed.

"Oh, Father," she whispered, "I don't even know where to begin. You know all that's in my heart. You know how afraid I am. Afraid something has happened to them. Afraid Anna will lose her son and afraid of the effect that would have on this family. Afraid for Zane. He's so young, Lord, and I don't think he knows you."

She hesitated a moment, feeling a knot tightening in her stomach at the confession she was about to make.

"I'm afraid for myself too, Lord. I'm afraid of losing another friend in the same way I lost Joe. Afraid of losing someone who has come to mean so much to me. I don't know when it happened, but it has. I doubt if he even knows it, and I don't know what to do about it. Please, Lord, protect them. Comfort our hearts. Help us trust You."

She sat in silence, aware of the storm still raging outside, the pounding in her chest, the tears streaming down her cheeks, and of the stillness in the rest of the house. She drew in a deep calming breath. In that moment a psalm whispered its way into her heart.

"What time I am afraid, I will trust in thee," it said softly.

A smile rose on her damp face and new tears — tears of joy — slid down her cheeks. "Oh, Lord, I am afraid, but I will trust. I put Wes and Zane into Your hands. I trust that if You allow anything to happen, then You will use it for good and for Your glory. Help us to rest in You. Help us to walk in Your grace and peace."

Jess leaned back on her heels and looked around her. The room appeared no different than it had before. But a peace had come over it. Her heart pounded wildly in her chest with new hope. She wiped away her tears and got to her feet. Then she scrunched up her face, a little surprised at herself.

"I think I want a cup of tea. Why, at this hour, anyone would drink a cup of tea? I don't know. But I want a cup of tea."

She discarded her quilt and donned a heavy robe. Then, taking up the lantern that sat next to her chair, she made her way downstairs.

The fire on the hearth had died long ago. In fact, the whole house was cold. With a shiver, she went to the kitchen and rebuilt the fire in the stove. A kettle of water already waited nearby. She topped it off and set it on the stove. Hoping not to wake Anna or Travis, she crept to the fireplace to build a fire while she waited for the kettle.

She stared into the tiny flame that licked up around the kindling and grew as it spread to the logs. She smiled at the thought of Travis and his daily trips in and out carrying wood to the box by the fireplace. He complained at times, but for the most part, he was a happy boy.

A sound at the front of the house broke into her thoughts. She listened for a moment but heard nothing more.

"The wind must've driven something into the house," she mused aloud, rising to go to the window.

Thud. Thud. Thud.

The tapping stopped her, a cold hand gripping her heart. That wasn't the sound of the wind. It was too methodical, too rhythmic. Her head told her to go to the window, but her fear told her nothing good could be out on a night like tonight.

"Foolish," she whispered to herself. "That's what you are, Jessica Bennett. It's nothing. If anything, it's one of the men. Probably been down at the barn with a new calf all night and needs some coffee."

She stepped forward with determination, but a new sound stopped her. The front steps groaned under the weight of someone ascending them. She heard the sound of tripping feet, and her heart sank. Surely, it wasn't that. Surely, Ronald Gray hadn't been drinking again.

Jess hurried to the window, but she couldn't see anything. She inched sideways, hoping to see further to the right, but still there was nothing. She heard shuffling and fumbling at the door. Horror gripped her heart as the memory of the day Gray had threatened her flashed through her mind. She considered rushing to the kitchen for the frying pan, but it was too late. The door swung open, and a snow-covered man stepped inside.

It wasn't Gray. Even in the dim light, Jess could see that the man's beard was darker and considerably shorter than Ronald's. He was several inches taller as well. Light from the fire glinted off a rifle as the man turned to close the door. Jess stared in fear. Then, as he reached for the saddlebag slung over his shoulder, something stirred recognition in her. She gasped.

"What are you doing out in weather like this!"

The man turned sharply toward the sound of her voice. Then he smiled.

"Oh, Wes, I've just built a fire, come sit." She hurried to his side, taking him by the arms and leading him toward the fireplace. "Where's Zane?"

"He's finishin' up in the barn. I promised him something to eat."

"I'll take care of that. You get warmed up. You two must be half frozen."

Wesley laughed through chattering teeth. "Maybe even three quarters."

"Well, I see your sense of humor hasn't frozen. Let me take your wraps, and then I'll get some coffee going—unless you want tea. I've already put the water on."

Wesley grinned as his friend helped him out of his coat and scarf. "Tonight, I'd drink just about anything so long as it's hot. Tea will be fine, but make it strong."

"I will." Jess stepped back, studying her friend. He sat down in the chair closest to the fireplace and began removing his boots. She saw fatigue in every movement. Tears pooled in her eyes, whether from heartache or relief she wasn't sure. She wiped them away before he could see them and hurried to hang his coat on its peg near the door.

"How have things gone here?" he asked, tugging on the second boot, "we've missed everyone."

"It's been quiet. Well, as quiet as it can be with fifteen children cooped up inside all day."

Wes set his boots aside. "Have they been good for you?"

"The children? Very. They're too afraid of your brother not to be good."

"Of Dunn? Why would they be afraid of Dunn? I've never met a child that was afraid of him. They come to him like he's got pockets full of candy."

Jess chuckled as she set a skillet out on the stove. "One of the older boys gave me some trouble one day. Dunn happened to be passing through the kitchen and heard the whole thing. He came to the schoolroom and made it clear that anyone who chose to disobey me would have to deal with him. Then he took the boy home and made sure his parents knew what was going on."

"Duncan?"

"Duncan. The children love him. They don't want to upset him. Who knows? Maybe he does slip them candy from time to time." Jess laughed at the thought. She'd never seen any such behavior from Dunn, but it would explain why the children flocked to him. "How was your trip?"

Wesley took a deep breath and let it out loudly, remembering his own candy slipping in Twin Pines. "Oh," he said, drawing the word out as if remembering it all required massive effort. "It was good. We just ran into so much weather. Spent a week in one spot because it was too snowy and cold to move on. At least the company was good. That's why we're late getting back. It wasn't the snow so much as the cold. It was so cold."

The man didn't miss the concern that washed over his friend's face. He smiled at her reassuringly. "God took care of us. We never had to sleep out in the cold, not once. He always brought us to shelter at the right time."

The teacher's eyes brightened. "We prayed He would."

The front door swung open, and Zane staggered inside. He closed the door and turned to see Wes seated at the fireplace. Disappointment registered on his face. He glanced toward the kitchen, hoping to see food on the stove.

"Miss Bennett! What are you doing up so late?"

Jess smiled at his obvious surprise and delight at seeing her. "I couldn't sleep. I'd just come down to make a cup of tea when Wes came in."

"Couldn't sleep, huh?" Zane said, casting a teasing grin in Wesley's direction. "Were you worryin' about us?"

"As a matter of fact, I was. Worryin' and prayin'. We'd about given up hope on you two. No one knew where you were. We'd even sent out telegrams. Dunn and Gray were going to head out looking for you as soon as the storm cleared."

Zane sobered. He glanced at Wesley, who looked shamefully back at Jess.

"We had almost given up hope on *you* two," she continued, "but we hadn't given up hope in the Lord. And you see, all is well. You are home and safe, and I am very happy—very thankful—and glad to see you. Let's get you out of those cold, wet wraps, Zane."

Jess dumped the remnants of supper into the skillet, which she'd been warming on the stove. She stirred the leftovers until they were properly distributed and then went to Zane's aid. "Come on, let's get that coat off of you."

Amazed at the woman's composure, Zane obeyed. As Jess spun him around to remove the coat, he glanced wonderingly at Wes. But Wes said nothing.

"Come to the table you two. It won't take long for your food to heat up. The night's more than half gone, and both of you look exhausted."

The men obeyed.

"Have the calves started comin'?" Wes asked as Jess placed a fork and knife in front of him.

Jess chuckled. "According to Carlson, they're droppin' like the spring rain."

"Ugh. I'm sure Dunn isn't happy about us being gone when that started."

"Dunn has been worried sick about *both* of you for two weeks. He'll just be glad you're home."

"I'm sorry we caused so much concern."

Jess shrugged. "You're home. That's what matters. ...I may not feel as gracious in the morning, but for now, I think everyone will just be relieved to see you home."

She set their plates out in front of them and brought the skillet of potatoes, onions, and sausage to the table. Both men leaned forward, smelling the wonderful aroma that rose from the sizzling food and leaning back with a satisfied, "Ahhh."

Jess laughed. "You'd better hurry and pray over that food, Wes, before your stomachs go after it without you."

The conversation that followed was lively though hushed. Zane was his usual talkative self, asking about the children and various people from town and the happenings around the ranch. Occasionally, Wes shot a warning glance in his direction, which Jess caught once or twice. She wasn't sure what it meant, but Zane seemed to know.

Wesley was content to listen for the most part. He savored every bite of the warm potatoes and sausage. He watched Jess as she worked and chatted with Zane. He was proud of her. He wished he could tell her so, but now wasn't the time. He could see his tardiness had caused her great concern and struggle, but He could also see she'd allowed the Lord to carry her through it. She caught him watching her once and blushed. His gaze dropped to his plate, and he smiled to himself. Maybe he had more of chance with her than he'd dared to hope.

Wes lingered longer than Jess expected. Zane had already made his way down to the bunkhouse, but Wes didn't seem inclined to move. At last, Jess felt she could wait no longer.

"I can't believe you're still up. I'm exhausted, and I haven't been out in that mess all day like you have," she said, starting toward the stairs.

He smiled a weary but contented smile. "I'm enjoyin' my own fireside. There's just something about comin' home."

"Yes, that's true. There's also something about one's bed." She laughed and began the climb to the loft, but then she stopped. "Wesley, thank you for letting your fireside be mine as well."

He nodded. "Goodnight, Jess."

"Goodnight."

When she had gone, Wes sighed and rose from his place on the sofa. He fixed a third cup of tea and gathered a few items from the writing desk in the corner. Returning to the sofa, he pulled the low coffee table close and set out an inkwell and pen. He spread out a clean sheet of paper, and began to write:

> *"Dear Mr. Bennett,*
>
> *"Zane and I have just returned to Grassdale. Not two hours have passed since the wind blew us up our front steps. It's very late, but I have been so blessed by what I have found in your daughter..."*

The letter was short but full of joy and boasting of the best sort. He reread it once, signed it, folded it neatly, and put it in the saddlebag, which he'd left by the fire. Then he leaned back in the crook of the sofa and sighed. It had taken sixteen days to make the three-day journey from Twin Pines. But now he was home. The fire was warm, the sofa so soft and dry. He closed his eyes to enjoy the moment for just a little longer. And that is where he was still to be found when Jess came down to start breakfast.

Chapter 40

As a doctor, Jon Bennett had long been amazed by the wonder and beauty of birth. He always felt a thrill of excitement run through him at the thought that *he* had the privilege of being the first to lay eyes on tiny little lives as they entered the world. It had always amazed him, but being there to deliver his own child — his own son — was indescribable. Happiness pulled a smile across his face and up into his eyes as he walked from the bank, past the livery, and toward his home. He all but bounced through the snow that lay thick in the streets.

"Dr. Bennett?"

The voice that called from behind him was unfamiliar. He cringed, closing his eyes for a moment and groaning. He didn't want to be called away from his family, not now. He'd only ventured out of the house so he could tell Jonah and Kate the good news. He wanted to go home and be with his wife and hold his new son and watch his firstborn begin to discover what it was to be an older brother. Today, he didn't want to be a doctor. He wanted to be a father.

"Dr. Bennett!" the voice came again, this time much louder but void of urgency. Maybe things weren't serious. He could just keep walking and duck behind the "Closed" sign hanging in his front window.

"Dr. Bennett, wait!"

This man wasn't going to give in. Jon bit his lower lip, sighed, and turned toward the voice. Behind him, at the door of the livery stood a young man. There was something familiar about him, but Jon didn't recognize him. The newcomer waved at Jon with excitement, grinning as if he'd found a long lost friend. Then he bounded into the snow, careening toward the big doctor.

"Jon!" the man said, sliding to a stop in front of him, "It's good to see you!"

Jon stared back at him quizzically, trying to place the face before him. He knew he'd seen it before, but where?

"I don't suppose you recognize me," the young man panted. "It's been a long time. I was just a kid. You were roommates with my brother, Freddie, while you were in medical school. I'm—"

"Jacob Voght! Of course! I knew you looked familiar. But you're grown up! You've grown a foot since I last saw you. You're nearly as tall as me! Last time I saw you, you hadn't reached my shoulders. What are you doing here? How are you?"

"I'm well. Happy to see you."

"How is your brother? I think of him often? Has he— I see by your face that he hasn't. We'll keep prayin'. Have you had anything to eat?"

"No. I just got to town."

"Well then, come home with me. We'll have to keep things quiet. My wife had a baby early yesterday morning. I promised her I'd do the cooking for the next few days. Which means you're stuck with my cuisine, but I know she'll be glad to see you."

"Congratulations! Boy or girl?"

Jon's grin broadened. "Boy. My mother was convinced it would be a girl, but I was right. He's a healthy little boy. Come on in." Jon led the way inside the house. "Hannah," he called. "I'm home."

"All right, dear."

"We have company."

"What? Who? Just a minute. I'll be right out."

A moment later, the pretty blonde stepped out of the hallway and into the sitting room. She stopped short of the sofa and stared at the young man.

"Is this…"

"It's Jake!"

"Jacob Voght. I never…I never thought we'd see you again. Come here!"

The two crossed the room, meeting halfway and embracing one another. Hannah stepped back and examined him. "You're no boy anymore."

"No ma'am, ten years has a way of turning a boy into a man."

"Ten years? Has it been that long?"

"Since we first met. Four or five since we last saw one another. I'm not eight anymore, that's for sure."

"No, you must be, what, eighteen?"

"Yes, ma'am."

"Jon, we're getting old."

Jon laughed. "Hardly, dear, he's just catchin' up with us. Are the little ones asleep?"

"Yes, both of them."

"Well, I suppose you'll have to meet them later then, Jake. Why don't both of you come to the kitchen, and we'll catch up. I've had soup simmerin' all afternoon. I'm sure it's ready by now. I don't know about the two of you, but I'm starvin'."

Hannah smiled, knowing that, like most of the Bennett men, Jon was always hungry. "That sounds wonderful. The smell has been tempting me for the last hour."

The trio made their way through the short hall that led from the sitting room to the kitchen at the back of the house. Jon motioned for the other two to be seated while he busied himself about the task of getting the meal to the table. In truth, Jon wasn't a bad cook. He'd managed on his own plenty of times while in medical school. The boarding house matron, though she prided herself on her fare, hadn't been especially talented in the kitchen. As a result, both Jon and his roommate had learned to fend for themselves. Now, he set out three bowls and three spoons. He brought the pot of soup to the table, foregoing the tureen his wife would have used in the presence of company. She glanced at him disapprovingly as he turned back to the counter in search of the ladle. But as he returned, she saw the expression of absolute joy on his face and couldn't chide him.

"Where are you stayin', Jake?" she asked.

"Haven't found a place yet. I'd just put my horse up at the livery when Mr. O'Leary spotted Jon."

"Then you'll stay with us. I can't promise it'll be peaceful with a newborn and his curious older brother around, but you're more than welcome."

Jake grinned, his blue eyes twinkling. "I'd love that, Mrs. Bennett."

Jon set out a basket of biscuits and then slid into his seat. He indicated they should pray and bowed his head.

"Lord," he began, "what a wonderful week! Thank you for bringing Jake this evenin'. What a blessing to see him. Thank you for bringin' our little Joseph safe into the world and for protecting Hannah. Thank you for the food you provide. Bless it, Lord, that we might serve You with the strength it gives. In Jesus name, amen."

Jon reached for the ladle and began dishing soup into the others' bowls, speaking excitedly as he did so. "So what brings you here, Jake?"

"Well, I was lookin' for you. I've been lookin' for you, trying to get here for two years. I needed a friend, and I knew I'd find one in you."

Jon set the ladle down. The joy in his face dissolved into concern. "Two years? You've been lookin' for me for two years? You must really need a friend."

Jake nodded, his own face darkening. He sighed. "I needed to start over, Jon. I was barely sixteen, and I already needed to start over. I have no one left back east. They're all done with me. I don't regret my decisions. I've made my choices, and they're the right choices. But I've always been the sort who needs family and friends around. So when I found myself with no one, I came lookin' for you. I knew I could trust you. If it weren't for you, I wouldn't have made the decisions I've made. I remembered all the stories you told 'bout your family, and I knew this was where I needed to be."

Jon stared, not sure what to make of what he was hearing. "You came lookin' for me? How did you know where to find me...us?"

"In theory, it wasn't hard. It just took me a while to get here. I knew you were from Montana, so that was my first goal. Before I left home, I came across some of Freddie's things. I found the letters from you. Some of them had never been opened. I also found the letters you had enclosed for me. Thank you for writing. I didn't receive them until that day but thank you for writing. Anyway, that was how I knew you were in Twin Pines. So I set out, and here I am — two years later."

"Well, we're glad to have you," Hannah said, beaming at him as an aunt upon a nephew of whom she is very proud.

"So you plan to stay in Twin Pines then?" Jon said, his voice void of emotion.

Jacob laughed. "If you'll have me. I don't want to be a burden. I'll find work and a place to live. I just want to be close to good people."

"What sort of work would you be wantin'?"

"For now, I'll do whatever's available. I grew up farmin', but I've done so many things trying to get here that I'm willing to try about anything these days."

Jon glanced at his wife who smiled in return, knowing what her husband was thinking. She nodded encouragingly.

"Jake," the doctor said, "I might have just the thing."

✿ ✿ ✿

Marc tossed yet another board across the room. It clamored down onto the pile he was making at the back of the barn. As it fell, he thought he heard someone call his name, but then decided that was wishful thinking. He was hungry and wishing for lunch, but it was still too early for lunch. He pulled two more boards from the pile of lumber in the stall and heaved them toward the back of the barn, missing the pile by several inches. Again, he thought he heard his name.

"Eat more for breakfast next time if you don't want to get hungry so early," he muttered to himself. He stooped and picked up another board, this one quite large, and swung his arms back to fling it across the room.

"Marcus!"

Marc jumped, nearly hitting himself in the face with the board. "Jon! Where did you come from?"

Jon laughed. "Where'd I come from? As if I suddenly appeared. I've called you four times, and you just now heard me. What are you doing?"

Marc dropped the board and then stepped down from the pile, pulling his gloves off as he did so. He looked down at the pile and then back at his brother and the man beside him, still trying to catch his breath from the exertion the task required.

"That cow over there is real close to her time, and I think she's going to need help. This stall's bigger than the one I've got her in, so I'm trying to get the lumber cleaned out of it. Wish I'd thought of that when we stacked it here this summer."

"I'm sure the racket you're makin' is helping her a lot."

Marc shrugged, grinning. "Maybe it'll get things over with quicker, and Danny and I won't have to be out here all night."

"Want some help?"

"Well, if you think we can do it without killin' each other."

Jon rolled his eyes. "We might have to carry it instead of tossin' it."

"Where's the fun in that? I'm savin' time by savin' steps."

Marc's eyes danced with mischief, something Jon hadn't seen for a long time. It encouraged the doctor.

The three men made quick work of moving the stack of lumber. Then they stepped back and surveyed their handiwork as all completed tasks require.

"Marc, I haven't introduced you to my friend yet. This is Jacob Voght. His brother Freddie was my roommate. Jake, this is my brother, Marcus."

The two men shook hands, exchanging sincere pleasantries.

"Thanks for your help, Mr. Voght. I don't usually put my company to work — well, that might not be true. I don't usually put people to work before I've been introduced to them. You two sure came at a good time though. Are you hungry? I am. Lunch must be soon."

"Marc, it can't be past ten-thirty! Didn't you eat breakfast?"

Marcus laughed, his eyes shining once more. "Apparently not enough. Let's go."

The men were soon seated at the table, enjoying a cup of coffee and Mary's fresh bread with butter and honey. For a moment, Jon thought Marc was so intent on his bread that he'd forgotten about their guest. But then, after devouring half of the first slice, he set it down and brushed the crumbs from his hands.

"So, Jake," he said around the chunk of bread in his cheek, "What brings you west?"

"It's your brother's fault, I suppose." Jake grinned at Jon and then took a long sip of coffee to set him up for his story. "When your brother and mine were roommates, your brother did all he could to help my brother see his need for Christ. I was there a few times when Jon was talkin' with him about it. As I got older, I realized that, whether Freddie was interested or not, what Jon was sayin' was true. I knew I needed Christ. So one day, when I knew Fred wouldn't be there, I went to the boardin' house.

"Jon and I talked for a while, but not long because I'd already heard enough to know I just needed to call on the Lord for salvation. I knew myself well enough to know I was a sinner in a need of a Savior.

"After that day, I went to church with Jon whenever I could get away from the house on Sundays. When he left to come back here, he made sure there were people in my life who'd help me stay in church. My family didn't care too much for my newfound 'religion.' It didn't matter what I said or did, they tried to find a way to get at me. If I tried to tell them about Christ, they did their best to chase me away. If I said nothin' and just went about my business, they still chased me away.

"Finally, two years ago, Father'd had enough. I came home from church and he told me to gather my things and be out of the house by mornin'. Said I wasn't to come back until I'd come to my senses. I knew

I'd never change, and while I hope they do, I knew it was time for me to move on. I had to start over somewhere else. I had a little money, but no work since I'd always worked for my father. While I was packin' things up, I found letters Jon had written to Freddie. I knew this was where I needed to be. I didn't know it would take me two years to get here, but I knew this was where I needed to be."

Marc, having completely forgotten about his bread, shook his head in amazement. "I'm sorry you had to leave your family behind, Jake. That— I can't even imagine how difficult that must've been. Takes courage and faithfulness to make a decision like that. Don't ever lose that."

Jake nodded and looked down, his cheeks coloring at the other man's praise.

"Marc," Jon said, "Jacob needs a job. I promised you a year ago that I'd find someone to help around here, and I have yet to do it. You've been lookin' for someone, and I've been lookin' for someone, but neither of us has found anyone who'd be a good fit for the family. Until now. Would you give Jake a chance? Just for a week or two. Or maybe through the calvin' season. Then you can make your decision about the long term."

Marc's gaze shifted from Jon to the young man next to him. He wasn't surprised by Jon's suggestion. In fact, when Jake had so readily pitched in with moving the lumber, he'd rather hoped that was why Jon had brought him. Now, having heard the man's story, he was the more excited.

"Have you ever worked on a farm, Jake?"

"Grew up farmin'."

"We're pretty crowded here, and with a new little one on the way, it'll be even more crowded. We've built a lean-to on the barn for whomever we found to work here. You'd have to stay there. It's not much, but you'll have a bed, and it'll be warm."

"I'm sure I've stayed in worse over the last two years."

"It won't be easy work, especially here in the beginnin'. We've got at least thirty cows to watch over the next few weeks. Then there'll be calves to keep watch over and, seems to me, it's going to be cold for a while longer."

Jacob shrugged. "Marc, I'm just glad to be here. I've spent two years trying to get here. I'll do whatever it takes to stay."

"Well then, I say we give it a try."

Jacob smiled, reaching across the table to shake Marc's hand. "Thank you, Marc."

"There's just one more thing," Jon said.

"What's that?" the other men questioned simultaneously.

Jon glanced around the room. He leaned in and whispered, "My sisters are off limits."

* * *

"Go on and get some sleep, Jake," Marc said, rubbing his tired eyes. "I'll have Danny do the morning chores. Never meant to work you this hard your first day, but I'm sure grateful you came when you did."

Jake smiled. "Me too, boss. I can't imagine how exhausted you'd be if you'd been out here alone."

Marc shrugged. "I suppose we would've managed. Mary would've helped, or Joy, and, of course, Danny. But having a grown man on board made things a lot easier."

Three more cows had started showing signs of labor by the time the men finished their conversation. Marc and Jon had move them to the barn. Then Jon headed back to town, leaving Marc and Jake with the task ahead of them. Now, four calves later, it was two o'clock in the morning, and both men were exhausted.

"You still wantin' to go out and check the herd in the mornin'?"

"There's no rush to get movin' in the morning." Marc continued. "I'll take the little ones to school if the weather's decent. Miss Nausbaum's not happy with the amount they've missed already. For now, we need to call it a night. Get some sleep."

"Thanks. You too." Jake smiled. "Thanks for giving me a chance."

"Jake, I'm pretty sure you're an answer to a lot of prayers, and so far, I'm very pleased with what I see."

Jake grinned. He waved goodnight and slipped out the side door of the barn to the lean-to.

Marc watched him go and then turned to leave the barn, grabbing a lantern as he went. He was exhausted, but his heart was full. His path led him away from the barn and the house and up the snowy slope to the top of the butte. The snow made the climb slower than usual, but even at this hour, it didn't lessen his joy. He crossed the flat of the butte to the boulder where he so often went to pray. Climbing up on the rock, and securing the lantern beside him, he peered out over the snowy landscape. For a moment, he stared at the world below him in complete contentment. Then a tear slid down his cheek.

"Lord," he said, "here I sat, doubtin', strugglin', prayin', and delayin' in my obedience. Wonderin' what I could ever do, wonderin' where help would come from. And all that time, for all those months, help was already on its way."

He shook his head in amazement. "Forgive me for doubtin'. Forgive me for not knowin' You as I should by now. You always provide for our needs. Always. Thank you. I never could've found a better match on my own. Thank You for Your timin' and for Your patience with me. Oh, Lord, my heart is overwhelmed, but it is in the best way. Thank You for showing me—in a way I never could've understood through my own devices—just how great Your plan and ways really are."

Marc sat in silence for a long time, completely in awe. His mind drifted over the concerns of the previous months. God had sent out help at the very time He'd placed the burden to preach in Marc's own heart. The help had come exactly when it was needed. A day earlier and Marc still could've handled things on his own. A few hours later and it would have been just a tad too late. The timing had been impeccable. It had been perfect.

Chapter 41

The days passed, but nothing was said about the purpose of Wesley's journey. Whenever asked about it, he only said it had gone well, and time would tell if anything would come of it. He seemed content to keep it to himself. Zane was no more enlightening than Wes, and people began to realize how little anyone actually knew about the young man. Though he rarely stopped talking, he was very good at keeping secrets.

Anna watched her son closely, wondering if Dunn and Gray's suspicions about his feelings for Jess were true. On more than one occasion, she caught her son watching the young woman, and she saw the girl blush under his gaze. She saw the way he teased, and the way she returned it. They each had become more aware of the other's needs and preferences. The development didn't surprise her, but the fact that she had missed it before baffled her.

Dunn's response was even more confusing. Anna saw him withdrawing and couldn't help but wonder if some part of him had been interested in the schoolteacher. Anna hadn't been privy to the conversation, but Wes had hinted that his brother had effectively expressed his frustrations over the timing of the trip. Anna loved both of her sons and Jess. She didn't want there to be any hurt or awkwardness between them.

Gray's response to Wesley's return had everyone curious. At first, they thought the man lingered after breakfast because he was hoping for some clue into the purpose of the journey. But as time passed, they realized he was listening to the family's Bible reading and prayer time. Near the end of the second week, as March was approaching, everything changed. As soon as Dunn finished their closing prayer, Gray was on his feet and out the front door. The others thought it was strange, but let it pass. A few minutes later, however, when Wes stepped out the front door and onto the porch, he found Gray pacing back and forth.

"What are you doing, Ron?"

"Boss, we need to talk. I-I mean, I need to talk. Private like." The man trembled with anxiety and nervousness. Wes had never seen him in such a state.

"Sure," he replied with a calm voice, hoping to soothe the man's nerves. "Is something botherin' you?"

Gray glanced around, checking to see if anyone was watching. He lowered his voice as he met Wesley's gaze. "I can't keep livin' like I been livin', boss. I can't."

"What do you mean?"

"I ain't been livin' at all. No, I've been breathin' in an' out. For nigh onto eighteen years, I've been doing nothin' but survivin'. I ain't been livin', and I know it's because I'm such a wreck inside. I done blamed God for every problem I ever had in my life. I turned my back on everything my parents taught me about the Good Lord. But I can't go on like that. I thought—"

The man turned away abruptly, running a hand through his wiry hair. "I'm so ashamed." He spun back around, his eyes intense with passion. "Boss, I thought when you were so late coming home— well, I thought Miss Bennett would go back to what she was before. She told me one day that when she come here she'd been runnin' from God. She told me about her fiancée who'd died in a blizzard. I thought... I thought when you was so late that she'd be angry at God. I was ready, waiting for the opportunity to laugh at the whole idea of trustin' God. I was ready to say, 'See, it didn't work for you either.' But she never changed. She was so peaceful. Sure she worried, but she never got angry. Never gave up hope on God."

Once more the ranch hand stepped away, still frustrated. He paced back and forth across the porch. Wesley waited, knowing the man needed to express whatever he was feeling on his own. Finally, Gray returned to him. The passion in his eyes had turned to desperation.

"Boss, I've been such a fool. I know I need what that girl has, what you and your brother and Mrs. Close have. I know I need God's forgiveness. I'm such a wreck. Do you s'pose He'll forgive me?"

Wesley smiled and took the man gently by the shoulders. "I know He will, Ron. I know He will. That's the whole reason Jesus died."

"I know. I've been listenin'. You said, that is, the Good Book said, that He saves whoever believes and whoever calls on Him. I heard you read that."

"So why not do it?"

"Now?"

"Sure. What holds you back?"

"It don't have to be in church?"

"No, Ron. God hears you wherever you are."

Gray searched his boss' face. Tears filled his eyes. Then, to Wesley's great surprise, the ranch hand dropped to his knees, closing his eyes, and clasping his hands together. Wes knelt beside him.

"Oh, God. I'm such a wicked man," the words rushed out with a torrent of tears close behind. "I've ruined this life You've given me. In the war, I killed men what never wronged me, and I stole food that weren't mine when rations run short. I hated You for takin' my sweet Phoebe and little Ava. Oh, God, I've done so many things since then that I can't recount them all. I don't even know most of 'em 'cause I was so drunk most of the time. I'm a wicked man. But, God, I heard Your words in the Good Book. I know You sent Your Son to die for us. I know You loved us...me...that much. I know I don't deserve it, God, but please, I'm askin' You to forgive me. I'm askin' You, God, please save me."

The man's voice trailed off, and Wesley put an arm across his friend's shoulders, beginning to pray.

"Dear Father, I thank You for the work You've done in Ron's heart. I thank You for makin' a way of salvation for each of us. Thank You for savin' Ron. I pray, Lord, that You would bless him as he follows You. Help me, help all of us, to be good friends to him and to help him grow closer to You. Bless him, Father. In Jesus name we pray, amen."

Wes opened his eyes to see the other man staring humbly at the floorboards beneath them. At last, Gray looked up, his cheeks wet, and a smile brightening his entire face.

"He done it, Boss. He took that weight I've carried all these years. It's gone."

Wes grinned and patted the man's back. "I knew He would. Come on, let's go in and tell the others."

Gray rose to his feet, still smiling. He turned to the house in time to see the others scurry away from the window. Then he laughed the truest laugh anyone at the ranch had ever heard him laugh. "I think they already know."

The day was one of the brightest the ranch had seen for months. The Closes, Jess, and Carlson, who'd had a similar moment three years earlier, were as happy if not happier than Gray himself. But Anna saw something that surprised her. She saw that for every glance of joy and excitement Wes gave Ronald Gray a similar glance darted in the direction of their young teacher. She wondered about those glances until it nearly drove her crazy.

Wes lingered in the house that night until Jess had gone on to bed. Then he slipped an envelope out of his pocket and went to the writing desk.

Anna could bear it no longer. She sent Travis to bed and marched to Wesley's side. "What are you doing?"

"Writing a letter."

"To whom?"

"A friend."

"What friend?"

"Does that matter?"

"I'm thinking it does. I'm thinking you've been keeping secrets long enough."

He turned toward her, intending to tease, but something in her face wouldn't allow it.

"You've fallen in love with that girl, haven't you?"

"What?"

"With Jess. You've fallen in love with her."

"Why would you say that?"

"Because I've been watching you, and Gray has been watching you, and Dunn."

"Dunn? What's Dunn —"

"He thinks you're in love with her."

"He told you that?"

"Yes. Well, he said he suspected it. Back when we were all wondering where you were. One afternoon, he came in to talk about where you might be. Jess overheard us from the schoolroom. It must have bothered her because she closed out the conversation by shutting the door. That's when he told me he thought you had fallen in love with her. He couldn't understand why you would leave when you did and cause her the worry you caused her."

Wes sighed. "He was pretty upset about that. I thought maybe he was overreacting. Do you think he was overreacting?"

"No, son, I don't. We had a terrible storm on the day of the anniversary. Dunn came in and found her standing at this window crying. She was afraid for you and Zane and she was mourning her Joe. Wes, she did well. Sometimes, I think she did better than Dunn and me. But you being gone when you were gone with the weather the way it was — Well, at the very least, I'd say it was a great test of her faith."

"One, which I'd say, she passed." Wesley took his mother's hand and peered up into her face lovingly. "I didn't mean to cause her such anxiety. I didn't mean to cause any of you such anxiety. But I had to go, Ma. I had to."

"But won't you tell me where you went? Must it be a secret?"

"I went to meet her family, to ask her father's permission to court and marry her." For all his secrecy, Wes now faced his mother with confidence. His voice did not waver. "I was afraid if I waited any longer I wouldn't have the chance. And that...that was important to me. I know from Abigail, who never had the chance to have Pa's approval, how very important that will be to Jess. I had to go, Ma."

Tears welled up in Anna's eyes. She tried to blink them away, but instead, the action forced one out onto her cheek. Wesley stood, he wiped the tear away and smiled down at his mother. "I do love her, Ma, and I am so very proud of her."

"Have you talked to her yet?"

"No. I wanted to wait until closer to the end of the school year. I don't want to jeopardize her reputation or her position. I also, well, I wanted to see if I have a chance with her. I don't know if she feels the same way about me."

"How was her father when you saw them?"

Wes shrugged. He motioned his mother to the sofa. "He's not well by any means. Marc said that over the weeks since Christmas he'd had more bad days than good. But, Ma, he's a happy man. Content. Having met him, I can understand why Marc is the man he is...why Jess is the woman she is."

"How was Marc? I know Jess has been worried about him."

"I don't think that worry is unfounded. He's a good man, a hard worker. His family will never have to worry about being cared for. He'll always make sure they're cared for—even if it kills him. That's the part that worried me. He's tryin' to be everything they need, and he's taken on so much in the process. There's little of himself left to give."

Anna smiled and patted her son's knee. "I remember someone else doing that once. We wouldn't have made it without that sacrifice, Wes, but I was so worried about you."

"Mrs. Bennett worries for him, and he for her. I talked with him, maybe more bluntly than I should have."

"What did you tell him?"

"I told him his family needed *him* not the things he was doing. I told him he needed to hire help before calvin' season began or everything was going to fall apart. I offered to do whatever we could while we were there."

Anna studied her son. He had been a good brother-in-law to Jason and had remained so since losing Emily. She could see that the relationship with Jessica's family would be no different, though the distance would make loving them in that way less practical.

"What did her pa say?"

"He didn't right away. He made me wait. They all did. I'm pretty sure Jonathan had Marc reporting back to him on a daily basis. But in the end, they all gave their approval. I was just getting ready to write to him and tell him about Gray. I have a letter already started, but I haven't mailed it yet. Haven't been to town since we came home. If the weather's good, I'll ride in tomorrow. I need to talk to Cale anyway."

"Well, don't risk it if the weather isn't clear."

"I won't."

"I'll let you get to your letter writing. I'm done for the day." The small, gray-haired woman stood, but before leaving she turned toward her son, looking deep into his brown eyes and laying a hand on his cheek. "If it means anything to you, Wes, you have my approval as well…and I think your father would agree with me."

Wes felt his chest tighten with happiness. "That means the world to me, Ma. It really does."

Chapter 42

Brandon Bishop sat in the lobby of the Grassdale Bank, waiting until Mitch was available to send Mr. Edelman's telegram. The ranch hand's gaze flicked lazily around the room, taking in the occasional picture or plaque that decorated the walls. The front door opened, and two men entered. He recognized them as the brothers from the Crescent Creek Ranch. Both men nodded in his direction and then passed through the lobby to Cale Bennett's office.

"Hey!" Cale all but shouted. "Wes! Glad to know you're still alive! What brings you to town?"

"I had a letter to mail, and I wanted to talk to you about something."

"Well, come on in. Have a seat. How was your trip?"

"It was good. Cold."

"I'm sure it was."

Bishop leaned forward in his seat, resting his elbows on his knees and straining to hear. He knew the three men had been investigating the fire. Things had been tense at the Edelman place for months. Now, he hoped the other men had news that would let them put it behind them. He let his gaze shift casually around the room, hoping no one would notice his listening.

"When did you get back, Wes?"

"Oh, about two weeks ago. I've wanted to get in here and talk to you, but the weather hasn't made it possible. After that trip, I wasn't eager to get back out in it."

"Don't blame you. ...I had an interesting conversation while you were gone."

"Oh?" the brothers chorused.

Bishop saw Cale lean forward, resting his elbows on the desk. The banker lowered his voice, but not as much as he thought he had.

"Someone here in town was given a coin like the one we found out by the fire. For now, I've decided it would be best to keep her name out of it, but she brought the coin to me. She also gave me a fairly good description of the man who gave it to her. He doesn't sound like anyone I know, but she said she's seen him in town once or twice since then."

Bishop's brow furrowed. Coins? Strangers? This was pointing to a much bigger web than he'd ever imagined. No wonder it was taking them so long to uncover who had started the fire. Unconsciously, he rubbed a bright scar that ran across the back of his hand from the thumb to the ring finger. His thoughts wandered to his own suspicions until Dunn interrupted the banker.

"Wait," the rancher said. "She was given a gold nickel?"

"Yes. It was given to her, in my opinion, by someone who wanted to mock her. She said he was a tall, yellow-haired man."

The ranch hand's gaze shot up again. He knew a man who fit that description. A man who had joked about giving fake coins to saloon girls on more than one occasion. But why would he start the fire? He had no reason to do such a thing.

"I told her if she ever sees him in town to let me know," Cale continued. "I have a feeling this could be a big part of finding whoever set that fire."

"Well, I'll tell you this," Wes interjected with a tone of confidence, "I don't think it was Scotch Jorgenson."

"What makes you say that?"

"Remember when I told you that something about the hoof prints and that piece of leather didn't make sense?"

"Yes."

"Well, I figured it out."

Bishop heard the sound of paper being unfolded. He glanced toward the office and saw Wes come around the desk to where Cale sat.

"Look at this," Wes continued. "While I was gone, Zane and I ended up stayin' with a trader named Fisher Smith. He's a tracker. We got to talkin' about things, and I told him I couldn't put my finger on the problem. So he asked me to draw it out for him. When I did, I noticed something. Here's where the piece of red leather was. This is the second set of tracks, the ones I didn't notice the first time I was out there. I thought I was losin' my mind, Cale. I couldn't figure out how I had missed both those tracks and that piece of leather. But look at the tracks in relation to the piece of leather."

Cale squinted down at the paper. "I don't—wait. Wait, it's the angle. That's the angle you'd have to come at to put that piece of leather there. Someone put it there on purpose."

"Exactly. Someone who wanted us to think Scotch had been there."

"But where would that leather have come from if it didn't come from Scotch's saddle?" Dunn asked.

"I don't know, but we need to start looking for another source," Cale replied.

"When I was in Twin Pines—"

"When you were *where*?" Dunn cut in indignantly.

"You were in Twin Pines?" Cale echoed.

"Yes. I was in Twin Pines."

"Does Jess know?" Dunn stared at his brother in shock.

"Not yet, but she will. And don't you go sayin' anything about it either. I've had to keep Zane on a tight leash as it is."

"I won't, but..." Dunn chuckled and then broke out in full laughter. "You were askin' permission to marry her, weren't you?"

Even from the lobby, Bishop saw Wesley's face go red. He stifled a laugh, hoping once more not to give himself away.

"You were!" Cale laughed. "You're red!"

"Don't say anything to anyone, you two. The time isn't right, not yet. School's still in session. Besides, I wasn't just askin' to marry her. I was askin' to court her, which hasn't happened yet and has to come before marriage."

Dunn grunted and waved the comment away. "You live on the same property. How much courtin' needs to be done? Just marry her."

"You two have completely gotten off track. Listen. While I was there, I spent a lot of time workin' alongside Marc. He has a respectable tack repair business goin'. I watched him work quite a bit. It's fascinating. I noticed that he keeps a selection of dyes on hand for his more ornamental jobs. He said most of them came from the mercantile in Twin Pines. If they don't have what he needs, they order it for him.

"After I drew up this map, I was thinkin' about that conversation. I remembered many times when I've seen dyes here at the General Store."

"So you're sayin' it could be anyone who had access to red dye," Cale said. "That could be anyone in town."

But Dunn was shaking his head. "No, Cale, that means it could be anyone in town who had dealings with this yellow-haired man, or maybe even the man himself."

Cale drummed his fingers on the desk. "If only we knew who he was, but I don't know anyone who fits that description."

Bishop groaned inwardly. He ran a hand through his hair as Mitch motioned for him to come to the counter. The further the conversation had gone the more convinced he'd become that he knew the yellow-haired man. If he was right, life was about to get very complicated.

Chapter 43

"Sixteen days," Marc said, shaking his head and folding up the letter from Wes. "I can't believe it took them sixteen days to get home."

"But think of the work God did through those sixteen days," Cynthia said.

"God is good, son, so good." Jonathan's voice was weak, but neither his son nor his wife missed the joy there.

"Yes, He is Papa. He is so faithful." Marc slid the letter back in its envelope. He glanced at his mother who sat on the other side of the room, wiping tears of joy from her eyes.

"Ma's crying again," he teased.

"Hush, Marc."

"Your mother a'ways cries when she's happy."

"I know. That's one of the reasons we all love her."

Marc sighed and stretched. At first, the others thought he was about to leave, but then he leaned forward in his seat and looked into his father's weary face.

"Jake's doing a good job, Pa."

"I like him. He's respectful. Good with the children too."

"He's a hard worker. Did I tell you it took him two years to get here, and yet he still kept going?"

"No. I don' believe you did."

"Do you realize, Pa, that I started prayin' about our town's need for a church two years ago, or thereabouts?"

Jonathan smiled. "God had a plan. Have you told Jonah about this?"

"No, sir. I haven't seen him yet."

"Well, be sure you do. You told me how he goaded you in the right direction along the way. It would bless him to know tha' detail. ...It's

260

been a long time since I've had a chat wi' Jonah. You should have him out soon."

"I will. The weather is nicer now. The stage will be runnin' again soon. Next time I go to town, I'll ask both him and Kate to come out. It's been weeks since I've had a good chat with him myself."

Jonathan smiled and then faced where he knew his wife to be sitting. "You're quiet tonight, love."

Cynthia's eyes lit up at his attention. "Oh, I'm just enjoyin' listenin' to the two of you. It's been such a lovely evening with the Nausbaums here for supper and Jake teachin' the children new games and Marc readin' to everyone. Now this letter from Wes. I'm just enjoyin' the moment, dear."

"It has been a lovely day. One to remember." The man took a deep, cleansing breath. "D'you know," he resumed, "God has blessed me wi' so many 'days to remember.' D'you remember, Cynth, the day we crossed tha' last river before arrivin' here? ...It was a hard day. We lost supplies in tha' river,...things we would need over the next weeks."

"But we all survived."

"And tha' night...tha' night we celebrated the crossin'. We sang and told stories and laughed."

"I remember," Marc said. "Just as we were startin' to get tired and about to call it a night that trapper stepped into the firelight."

"Your mother jus' 'bout jumped outta her skin, scared her so bad."

"I seem to remember you, Jonathan Bennett, scramblin' for your rifle."

Jonathan chuckled. "He turned ou' to be such a nice man. What fun he brought to that fire. Ah, so many days to remember. I am blessed. I've never lived in a palace, but my life...I think my life woul' be the envy of any king...because I've had you. ...All of you."

Cynthia wiped tears from her cheeks once more and bit her lip at her husband's words. She could not speak.

Marc took hold of his father's hand. "We're the ones who are blessed, Pa. ...We should let you rest. Or at least I should. I'll let Ma make up her own mind. Goodnight."

Marc left the room and stepped out into the common area of the house. His chest was tight with emotion. Everyone else had gone to bed, but he wasn't ready. It was nearly midnight, but he didn't care. He crossed the room and took up his coat and hat. He stepped outside, pulling the coat on as he went, and started the trek to the butte and his quiet place. He needed the air, needed time to think and pray.

His father had begun to speak more and more often as a man who knows his days are short. Marc regularly felt compelled to run from such conversations or to rebuke the man for saying such things. But he never followed through on the compulsion. He respected his father too much for that. He knew the man wouldn't have talked that way if he didn't truly feel the days were growing shorter.

Marc went to his usual place, seating himself on the boulder and gazing out over the landscape. At first, he fought back the emotion that raged within him. But as he relaxed and could breathe more easily, a strange peace fell over him. Papa was right. They had all been blessed, and whatever days remained would be as much a blessing as the days that had gone before.

He sat there for a long time, thinking, praying, thinking some more. He pulled out the letter from Wes. The moon hadn't risen yet so there was no light to read by, but he didn't need to read it. He knew the contents. He knew the joy it contained. He was as happy for Jess and as proud of her as Wes. They'd seen her go through so much anger and frustration and doubt. To hear of her walking in such faith made his heart soar.

He had just contemplated repositioning himself on the rock and sitting there to watch the moonrise when the sound of hurried footsteps startled him. He spun in his seat to see Mary rushing toward him. Her coat hung open over her long winter nightgown. She wore no hat, no gloves, not even a scarf.

"Mary, what are you doing?"

"Marcus," she panted, "I don't know why you're up here at three o'clock in the morning, but you need to come to the house. Ma's going to have the baby."

"What!" Marc scrambled down from the rock and rushed toward his sister. "But it's early!"

"Well, apparently, the baby doesn't think so."

Chapter 44

Cale sat on his parlor floor playing with his children. He had just pulled out a book and was about to begin reading to them when his wife rushed into the room.

"Cale, you'd better come out here. Someone's here to see you." Susan's eyes were wide with surprise. She pointed back through the house toward the front door.

Cale got to his knees, surprised that anyone would be looking for him so near the supper hour. "Who is it?"

"Just come," she said, jerking her head in the direction she had pointed.

Cale shrugged and sighed, getting to his feet. He stepped over Willy and followed his wife to the front door where he stopped abruptly.

"Miss Parker," he gasped. "What brings you here?"

"Hello, Mr. Bennett. I'm sure you're surprised to see me. I'm sorry for taking you away from your children, but...but I've seen him."

"Seen who?"

"The yellow-haired man. Just a moment ago. I was leaving the General Store when he walked inside. I didn't know what to do. I was sure the bank was closed for the day, so I asked someone nearby how to find your home. I hope you don't mind. They told me how to find you, and here I am. I think if you hurry, you might still catch him while he's there."

Cale, who was already donning his coat, smiled kindly at the woman. "I don't mind at all, Miss Parker. I'm glad you came. I'll head that way now. You stay here. It won't take long. I probably won't talk to him. I'll just see who it is. ...Why don't you join us for supper?"

Cassandra faltered, surprised by the invitation. "Me? Why would you want me to join you for supper?"

"Why not? It will give you a chance to meet my wife and children. I'll be back. You two enjoy yourselves."

263

Cale rushed from the house, forcing himself not to run, but willing himself to get there as fast as possible without drawing attention. He slowed his pace as he entered Main Street and came to a complete halt before going into the store. He took a moment to catch his breath and regain an appearance of calm. Then he pulled open the door and stepped inside.

The store wasn't crowded. A woman stood at the counter, paying for the items she had selected. A tall man stood with his back to the door near the counter. Cale could see movement among the shelves further back in the store, but couldn't see to whom those shadows belonged.

As the door closed behind Cale, the man near the counter turned to face him. In the same moment, his eyes lit up and a smile stretched across his face.

"Cale," he said, "good to see you."

Cale's gaze jerked up to the other man's face as the rancher stepped across the room with outstretched hand.

"Wes, what brings you to town so late in the day?"

"Oh, I've been here all day. I'm trying to finish up so I can get home. Wanted to pick up the mail first. What are you doing here? I'd expect you to be home."

Cale lowered his voice. "I was, but then someone told me they'd seen the yellow-haired man come in here."

Wes glanced over his shoulder, his eyes scanning the store. "Really?"

"Yes. I just want to catch a glimpse of him and figure out who he is."

"Well, let's have a look. Seems it'll be a few minutes before I can ask about my mail anyway." The tall rancher turned away, shoving a hand into his pocket and strolling toward the tall shelves behind him. "Ma always seems to need more baking powder. Guess we eat too many biscuits. Does Susan need anything?"

Realizing Wes had committed their path toward the shadows among the shelves, Cale picked up his step and fell in stride with the other man. "Now that you mention it, I think she said she was just about out of sugar. Or was it vinegar? I don't remember. I'll have to ask and come back tomorrow."

They stepped into the aisle where the baking powder resided, but the only other shopper was a woman and her small son. Wes grabbed up a can of baking powder and motioned for Cale to follow him to the next aisle.

"What about tea or coffee?" he asked as they went. "I think I heard Jess say we're just about out of tea. Maybe I'll pick some up for her. She'd be lost without it."

They rounded the corner to see a tall, blue-eyed, yellow-haired man standing in front of the shelves. He juggled a can of beans, a spool of black thread, and a bar of soap in one hand while reaching with the other hand for a small bag of coffee beans. Hearing them coming, he turned and nodded a greeting in their direction. Then he turned his attention to the coffee, which was slipping from his grasp. Managing to catch the coffee against his leg, he scooped up the bag, nodded at the men once more, and then walked away.

Wes and Cale followed the man, tiptoeing behind him as far as they could without leaving the shelter of the shelves. They watched as he made his way to the counter at the front of the store.

"Do you recognize him?" Cale whispered.

"I've seen him before."

"Who is he?"

"I can make a pretty good guess."

"Where did you see him?"

Wes groaned and stepped further behind the shelves. "The Edelman place."

"What?" Cale hissed, glancing at the yellow-haired man once more, then back at Wesley. "Are you sure?"

Wes nodded. "I saw him from a distance the day I went out there to warn them about Scotch. He was with Bishop."

"Then that means…"

"That means the yellow-haired man is Cantrell. The man who couldn't *possibly* have anything to do with the fire because he wasn't in the area yet. We've been had, Cale. I don't know how it all fits together, but we've been had."

Cale peered out again and watched as the man picked up his sack of goods and left the store. Then, stepping out into the open, he motioned for Wes to join him.

"We really don't know how he fits into the picture though, Wes. All we know is that he had the coins. That doesn't mean he was out there when the fire started. Even if he was, what motive would he have had for starting it? He hadn't been out there long enough to make any enemies yet, at least I wouldn't think so."

Wes gnawed at the corner of his mouth. "Maybe all we need is a connection. Maybe he didn't start it, but he and those coins are the link we've been missing. Think back over everything you've heard and seen, everyone you've talked to. Maybe now we'll see whatever we weren't seeing before. I've got to get home. ...And I guess now I need to go pay for this baking powder."

"Did you want tea?"

Wes laughed. "I probably should. Just in case. Listen, the weather has been so much nicer this week. If it's still nice on Sunday, come out to the church services and we can talk over lunch."

"The preacher won't be here for church on Sunday."

Wes stopped his intended grab for the tea container's lid. "Why not?"

Once more, Cale peeked around the shelves, this time to see if anyone was close enough to hear them. Satisfied that they were not, he returned his attention to his friend. "Last night, Jason and I bumped into one another as I was walkin' home. Jason noticed Scotch sneakin' out of an alley and down the road. Not Main Street, mind you. He was headed down *my* road, but he was definitely headed out of town.

"We jumped into my yard, and... I'm ashamed to admit this... We hid behind my fence and watched through the slats. He left town, pure and simple. And what is in that direction?"

"Maiden."

"Exactly. I was going to follow him, but Jason wouldn't hear of it. He reminded me that I have a family to consider. He asked me to have Susan pack up several days' worth of provisions, while he gathered his gear. Less than a half hour later, he was underway."

Wes stared. "You sent him out there by himself?"

"No, he went. I didn't send him. I intended to go. He'll be fine."

"But don't you think that could be dangerous?"

"Frankly, I think a preacher showin' up in a town like Maiden could be quite interesting. I kind of wish I could spy on him. He can take care of himself. Stop your worryin'. You sound like your ma and Jess when you were gone."

"I guess I probably do." Wesley scooped several ounces of black tea into a small sack and then turned back to his friend. "How is it that I had no intention of spendin' a nickel when I walked into this place, and then I meet you and end up leavin' with my hands full?"

"Just so you're not spendin' gold nickels. That's all I care about."

✿ ✿ ✿

Supper was a happy affair. Cassandra expected slighting comments about her work at the saloon or disparaging glances, but they never came. Cale asked questions about her sisters and her childhood. Susan followed suit. They asked about her future plans and goals, but those didn't expand beyond the hope of starting over somewhere safe. When the children had been dismissed and eventually put to bed, the threesome made their way to the parlor. They sat in its quiet comfort, each sipping at a cup of tea. After a long silence, Cassandra spoke.

"Mr. Bennett, why did you invite me to supper? It's been a lovely evening. I haven't had an evening like this in years, but why would you do that? Why would you expose your children to someone like me?"

Cale's brow furrowed. "Expose them to someone like you? What's wrong with you?"

Cassandra cast an embarrassed glance in Susan's direction. She tilted her head in a manner that said, "You know."

"You mean because you work at the saloon?"

"Well...yes."

"Miss Parker, you impressed me the other day. I sensed that you were genuine in your desire to start over on a new path. I'd like to be a part of that if you'd allow it. Susan and I both would. We've talked about it, more than once."

"You have?"

"Yes," Susan said. "Miss Parker, Cassandra, I know from what Cale told me of your story that it's been a long time since you had a family. I also know that, as of now, you intend to leave Grassdale. Until then, or if you decided to stay, we'd like to be your family. There's no reason anyone in this town should have no one. We want you to know that there's a place for you at our table whenever you wish to join us. No invitations are necessary. You simply come."

Cassandra stared in amazement. She looked from Susan to Cale and back again. "I-I don't know what to say. No one, *no one* has ever made such an offer to me. Why would you do that?"

"We feel it's what the Lord wants us to do," Cale said, "And if you're willing to give Grassdale another chance, I'll do whatever I can to help you get work."

"You would do that?"

"I'd give it my best. Just consider it."

"I will. Believe me, I will!" The pretty, young woman sat back in her seat smiling. She sipped her tea and then leaned forward once more. "Mr. Bennett, I've been thinking about something ever since I saw you that day at the bank."

"What's that?"

"Well, I know I caught you in the middle of inspecting your icy walls."

Cale laughed. "Indeed you did."

"Well, if your office is cold, then you need a rug to hang on the walls. It will keep out some of the drafts and hold in the heat."

"That's a good thought, but where would I find a rug big enough?"

Cassandra smiled. "At the hotel. They have a lovely rug in the lobby. They've had it on the floor, so it's a bit worn. But the housekeeper hates it. She's always threatening to roll it up and put it out of the way. Maybe Mr. Jorgenson would sell it to you, just to stop her complaining."

Cale's gaze darted to his wife and back to the young woman. Realizing this was, in part, Miss Parker's way of thanking them for their offer of friendship, he smiled. "I may just have to check into that. I'm tired of freezing all day."

"And I'm tired of listenin' to you complain about it all night," Susan said.

Cale rolled his eyes. He smiled in his wife's direction, happy to see the approval in her eyes. They had made the decision to invite Miss Parker into their family days earlier. The mysterious Cantrell had just provided the opportunity.

Chapter 45

Wesley strode out of the barn, his dog close at his heels as he whistled a tune into the late-March air. A chill still clung to the breeze, but it was much warmer than it had been even two weeks ago. The days were noticeably longer. The snow had disappeared, at least for now. Spring would be upon them soon. Another couple of months and they'd be well into the long warm days of summer. For that he was glad. He'd never minded winter, but this year winter seemed longer than usual. So caught up in the beauty of the evening was he, that he missed his own passage across the yard and up the front steps. The aroma of simmering soup drew him back to his surroundings as he stepped through the front door.

"Well, hello," Jess beamed up at him from the table. "When did you get back?"

"About a half hour ago. What happened? Why are you so excited?"

"I found the pile of mail you left on the table. Did you look through it?"

"No. I just put it there with the supplies. Did you find the tea?"

"Yes, thank you. But, Wes, the mail! Listen to this letter from my brother."

Jessica's words forced the color from Wesley's face. He looked down, giving his attention to a chair as he pulled it out from the foot of the table and hoped she hadn't seen him blanch. What if Marc said something about his visit? How would he explain himself? He took a deep breath and seated himself.

"Go on."

> "*Dearest Jess,*
>
> "*What wonderful news I have for you! In fact, this letter will probably contain more good news than any letter I have ever written. I'm sure of it.*

"You, my dear sister, are once again a sister. Your newest brother was born last night. He is beautiful. His name is Timothy Luke. He seems perfect in every way. Mama is doing well.

"Papa was thrilled to hold his new son. You know we all doubted he would have that joy, but God still gives the desires of the hearts that delight in him.

"If this weren't enough good news, you should also know that your newest nephew was born about two weeks ago. Jon is beside himself. Hannah is doing well. I haven't seen the baby yet, but I hope to be in town soon to catch at least a glimpse of Joseph Stephen. It's a good name, don't you think?

"Our house is absolutely bursting with joy, but there's more! God is so faithful to provide. You know we've been praying and searching for help around the farm, and we've come up empty handed month after month. The day after Joseph was born, a man stopped Jon in the street. He wasn't looking for work. He was looking for Jon. He'd been looking for Jon for two years!

"Jacob Voght, who I'm sure you'll remember, left Boston about the same time God started putting this burden on my heart to preach. Jon brought him to the farm, and he's been the perfect fit. He works hard. The day he arrived the first batch of calves arrived. God's timing couldn't have been better.

"I hope you're well. I love and miss you and pray for you often. Give our love and greetings to the Closes, and our gratitude for their care of you.

"Rejoicing with you, Marcus"

"Now *that* is a letter," Wes said. "Have you showed it to Ma?"

"No, you're the first. I'm not sure where she is actually. I had just come out of the classroom to check on the soup when I saw the letters on the table. This one was on the top. I'd just finished reading it when you came through the door."

"Well, I don't know when, if ever, I've heard a better letter. What else is in that stack?"

"Let's see. Here's something for Carlson, a letter for your Ma from Tabby. Oh, and another from Abigail. Here's one for Travis from Abigail. Here's an announcement of a cattle auction. Somehow, I don't think that came with the mail. Now, this is strange."

"What?"

"Well, it's addressed to you, but if I didn't know better I'd say— It is. It's from my brother.

"From your brother? Marc?"

"Yes. I wonder what that's all about."

Wes felt the warmth of embarrassment rising in his neck and crawling up into his cheeks. He wasn't sure he wanted to read that letter with her sitting across from him. He swallowed hard, trying to hide his nervousness.

"Let's see," he said, reaching for the letter. "Didn't you say he's wanting to expand his herd? Maybe it's about that."

"Could be."

He could still feel her gaze as he tore open the envelope and slid the letter out. Hoping to discourage the questions he knew must be churning in her mind, he read silently. He hadn't read far before realizing that, though written in Marc's hand, the letter wasn't from Marc.

> *"Dear Wesley,*
>
> *"I was pleased to receive your letter and the good report of my daughter. Your praise of her brought us joy. We also rejoice with you in the news of Mr. Gray's salvation. What a glorious thing.*
>
> *"I hope to hear soon of the progress you're making with Jess. You are much talked about and missed. Which is an especially good thing considering how short a time you were with us. Gretel, in particular, speaks of you often. She is always asking when Jess' Mr. Close is coming back. Please, make it soon, and bring my daughter with you.*
>
> *"Blessings, Jonathan Bennett."*

Wes glanced sidelong at Jess, and then read the letter again.

"Everything okay?" she asked.

"Hmm?"

"What does Marc say? Is everything all right?"

"Yes. It's a happy letter, nothing wrong. I'll have to think about how to respond."

"He can ask some tough questions, that brother of mine."

Wesley smiled and then looked away as he slid the letter back into its envelope. He studied it for a moment and then looked back at her.

"What are you doin' right now?"

"Besides distractin' myself with the mail? I'm in the process of fixin' supper."

"Oh."

"Why? Did you need something?"

"I was just thinkin'. It's a nice night out. There's something I want to show you that we've never shown you before. I think tonight would be the perfect night for it. It's too early right now anyway, but can I claim you as soon as supper is over?"

"I-I guess. Are you sure nothing's wrong?"

Compassion drew a smile across Wesley's face. He looked deep into her eyes, searching, hoping to see there what he longed to see. He was almost surprised that she did not flinch under his gaze. He felt embarrassment rising in his cheeks. He had butterflies in his stomach again. "Nothing's wrong, Jess. I just want to show you something."

"All right."

"How about if I help you until Ma comes back from wherever she's gone. Then you won't be behind from reading the mail."

A teasing light had come up in his eyes, and she couldn't help but return it.

"*You* want to help me with supper?"

"It's not like I've never cooked before," he defended.

"This is true. You just don't do it often."

He shrugged. "Why should I when you and Ma do it so much better? Maybe I'll learn something."

With that, the letter went into his pocket, and he was on his feet, ready to cook.

Chapter 46

Brandon Bishop flung his chaps up on the workbench and studied the holes where the buckle straps belonged. He'd always thought that whoever made the chaps had put the straps too close to the edge. Today, he'd proven it. Falling from the horse he was breaking had been bad enough, but getting drug across the prairie had proven to be too much for the garment. The straps had ripped through their small holes, and now the left pant leg gaped open.

He winced in pain as he reached for a drawer. Realizing his left arm wasn't going to cooperate, he stepped back to use his right. He was almost certain he'd seen one of the other men with an awl that would allow him to punch new holes in the soft leather. He was pretty sure the awl was in that drawer. Still feeling the frustration of losing his chaps to the untamed beast, he reached out with his right hand and jerked the drawer open. Then he groaned. His arm wasn't the only thing hurting. His entire body ached. He began searching the drawer. It always bothered him that the workbenches on this ranch were never kept in order. But it was worse in moments like this when a fella needed something quickly.

Finally finding the awl, he set to work, attempting to punch new holes where the old ones had torn. But it wasn't a task he could accomplish one-handed. If he could have at least steadied the leather with his left hand, maybe. But he couldn't seem to raise his arm. Giving up, he tossed the awl back into the drawer.

"What ya doin', kid?" Came a gruff voice from behind.

Turning stiffly to confirm that it was Banton, he greeted the man with a one-shouldered shrug. "Attemptin' to fix these before tomorrow comes."

"You're lookin' rough. Did Mrs. Edelman check out that cut to your face?"

"Nah. It bled good."

"I reckon you'll be sore tomorrow."

"I'm sore tonight. Just haven't paid it any mind 'cause I'm too riled about that critter gettin' the better of me."

If there was one thing Banton had learned about Bishop, it was that he was honest. Honest almost to a fault. Somehow, he had a feeling the younger man would be so honest that the rest of them would pay for it. He liked the young man's company. He was cheerful, loyal, hardworking, and could tell a good story around a campfire. But he was just a little too honest to be trusted.

That was why he'd spooked the horse. No one else had seen him snap the whip just behind the skittish animal's hindquarters, but he'd managed to pull it off. For all his character strengths, Bishop was young. Banton figured that enough run-ins with bad luck, and the boy would be blaming the ranch. Especially, if Banton took care to plant seeds of doubt.

The fire gave him a good starting point, and then there was the mess Scotch had made with the creek and the holding pen. A few weeks back, Banton had made sure Bishop's ladder would break under his weight as he crawled up into his bunk. The younger cowboy had ended up with a nasty gash across the back of his hand from that one. Now, this. Some cowboys, Banton knew, were just superstitious enough to blame all that bad on some evil curse hanging over the ranch. With any luck, Bishop would be gone in a week, maybe two.

"You an' this place sure have had a string of bad luck of late."

Bishop's eyes narrowed. He was more suspicious of Banton than of any strange string of luck.

"I suppose though," Banton went on, "we all get beat sooner or later. Keep movin'. That's the best thing to do. Have somebody look at that face when you're done there."

"I will."

Banton disappeared, and Bishop returned to his task. He was about to shove the drawer shut when something caught his eye. With a cautious glance around the barn, he pulled the drawer back out and leaned down. A sturdy piece of leather had curled up and was about to jam the drawer open. But it wasn't the scrap's position that caught his attention. It was the color. He pulled it out and spread it flat on the workbench. Red. Exactly the same red as Scotch's saddle. The leather was new, but it had been scored on one edge in a jagged manner and torn away from something.

Once again glancing around the barn, he leaned down and searched through the mess of tools and scraps in the drawer, not finding what he was looking for. Finally, he crouched down, his heart racing as he did so. Below the workbench, a set of shelves held items that wouldn't fit in the drawer.

The shelves were just as messy as the drawer. He moved several tins, a few tools, and scraps of leather, growing more and more frantic in his search. His gaze frequently darted over his shoulder, in the hope that no one was watching. After one such glance, he looked back at the shelves and froze. There it was. The tiny gleam of light reflecting off of a small glass bottle. He reached around a scrap of leather and took hold of the bottle, pulling it out. Dye. Red dye.

Whoever wanted those men to think Scotch Jorgenson had started that fire was right here on Edelman's ranch. In fact, they'd be sitting with him at the supper table in a matter of minutes.

The sound of footsteps behind him pulled him to his full height. He slid the red scrap of leather and the bottle of dye under his chaps and turned toward the sound. It was Edelman.

"Bish, I hear you came off that horse."

"Yes, sir. Guess it was too soon to take him out with the herd."

Edelman stepped closer, lifting the lantern that stood on the workbench to dispel the shadows of the poorly lit barn.

"That cut is pretty bad. I think you'd better come to the house and let us take care of it for you."

Bishop started to say he'd be all right, but then he remembered the dye under his chaps. Edelman himself could have hidden that dye.

"If it's all right with you, sir, I think I'll ride to town and have Doc take a look. My shoulder's stiffened up pretty good too. And I can't fix these chaps one-handed."

"That's fine with me. Take your time. If you're not up to the ride back tomorrow, just stay there until you are. We'll be fine. You headin' out now?"

"I think so. Better get going before I'm too stiff to ride."

Edelman grinned his agreement. "That's for sure. Your horse saddled?"

Bishop hesitated. "My saddle's still on that brute. Don't suppose he's calmed enough to make it all the way to town. I don't think I could lift my saddle if I tried."

"I'll switch it over to your gray. You'll be more comfortable on a friend. You need anything from the bunkhouse?"

"No, sir."

"All right. You sure you don't want me to bandage that up before you go?"

"I'll be all right."

"Suit yourself. We'll be here waitin' when you come back."

"Thank you, sir."

In truth, Bishop was beyond sore. The more time passed the worse he felt. He wasn't actually sure he'd make it all the way to town, but he would try.

* * *

Supper was over. The crew had gone on to their evening pastimes and chores. Jess and Anna worked diligently to clean up the supper mess. Wes, to Dunn's surprise, had joined them. The younger man watched from the table. He liked the way they interacted. Both came at each task with a clumsy nervousness, which they didn't even see in one another. Each in their own way complimented the other. It was as though they'd been made for one another. Perhaps they had. He noticed his mother watching as well. From time to time, she stepped back with a smile, rolled her eyes in Dunn's direction, and then went back to work.

As he saw their work coming to a close, he stood, pushed in his chair, and stretched. "I'm headed down to the barn to make sure everything's ready for tomorrow. You comin', Wes?"

"Actually, I want to show Jess something. I was going to take her up on the hill."

"Now?" Dunn raised an eyebrow at his brother and his voice cracked as he spoke.

"Well, I need to grab something from my bunk, and she'll probably need to find a coat, but yes, now."

Dunn's brow furrowed, but then understanding dawned on his face. "Oh, I know what you're going to show her. Yeah. Tonight will be a good night for that. Good moon for that."

"Good moon?" Jess said.

"You'll see. Enjoy it."

Dunn made his way outside, leaving the others to finish their cleaning. He had just latched the door and was turning to head down the stairs when he jumped back a step. A bloodied man sat a horse just beyond the reach of the porch. Dunn leaned forward, squinting through the dim light.

"Bishop? Is that you?"

Bishop nodded, urging his horse closer.

"What happened?"

"I came off a horse I was breaking. I was going to ride to town and have Doc take a look, but I think I've ridden as far as I can."

Dunn moved to the man's side and helped him dismount.

"Let's get you inside. We've got a medical box in the kitchen. We'll get you cleaned up and bunked down in no time."

"Thanks, Dunn. Grab my saddlebags, would ya? I brought something along that might have something to do with the fire. That's why I came here. I was going to take it to Cale, but I just can't."

"I've got it. Come on." The two men climbed the stairs and stepped into the bright cabin — shattering Wesley's plans.

Chapter 47

"What happened?" Anna gasped. "Jess is that kettle of water still warm?"

Jess stepped up to the stove and checked the pot. "Yes."

"Good. Pour it out into a basin, and put more on to boil."

"Yes, ma'am."

"Bish, what happened?" Wes asked, coming to the table and helping Bishop into a chair.

"Oh, it was dumb. I took a horse out with the herd. I thought he was ready, but I guess he wasn't. Got my foot caught in the stirrup when he bucked me off."

"Drug you, did he?" Anna said, stepping up and tipping the man's face back so she could better see the wound.

"Yes."

The small woman dipped a clean cloth into the basin of warm water and began cleaning away the dried blood.

"I suppose I should've stayed there and let Mrs. Edelman tend to this, but I needed to get out of there."

"Get out of there?" Wes questioned. "Why?"

"Hand me my saddlebag."

"No," Anna said, swatting the man's hand down and then noticing that it too was scraped and bloodied. "You're bleeding. Let me finish this up and then you can have your bag."

Bishop winced as the woman carefully tried to rinse debris from the cut. He sighed in frustration.

"Somebody at that ranch started that fire."

"What?" all four listeners chorused.

Wes sat down across from Bishop. "What makes you say that?"

"I overheard you talkin' to Cale Bennett at the bank."

278

"Oh?" Wes replied, glancing at Dunn and wondering how many others had overheard them. But Anna didn't give him long to wonder.

"Wes, come look at this. I think it's going to need sewing up. It'll heal better."

Wes rose and went around the table to examine the cut. He poked and prodded for a moment, then nodded his agreement.

"Yeah. I think it would be best. What do you want to do, Bishop? I can stitch you up. Or we can bind it up, see how it looks in the morning, and take you in to Doc if we need to."

"Just fix it. I don't want to go nowhere."

"All right, but it's going to hurt. I don't have anything to numb it. Let me get things together."

"Dunn," Bishop said, "empty my bag out on the table. You'll see what you need to see."

Dunn grabbed the bag and unfastened its buckles. He spilled out the contents and began spreading them across the table.

"What do we have here?" he said.

"What is it?" Wes asked, glancing over his shoulder towards his brother.

"A scrap of red leather and a bottle of dye. Just like you were talkin' about with Cale. Like you said— I mean, the dye you said could be picked up at any mercantile or general store."

Wes came to the table, needle in hand. "Where did you get those, Bish?"

"After I came off the horse, I was mad. It ripped up my chaps, so I drug 'em to the workbench in the barn. I was putting things away, and I found the scrap of leather. It's new, but somebody worked hard to make sure it looked like it had been through a battle to separate it from whatever was cut off of it. I found the dye hidden down below the bench on the shelves."

Wes, at his mother's bidding, turned back to his patient. "Hold still, Bish, this shouldn't take more than two, maybe three stitches."

The conversation lulled as Wesley worked. He stitched carefully, but he could see the doctor would have done a much neater job. He added a fourth stitch for good measure and then stepped back.

"Well, I'm sure it doesn't feel good, but that should do the job."

"Thanks." Bishop leaned forward with a groan.

"What else is hurting?"

The young cowboy laughed. "Everything. My shoulder's pretty rough, but it'll be all right, I reckon."

Dunn stepped up to the man and began checking the shoulder he'd indicated. "It's not broken, at least I don't think it is. But it's not where it belongs. It needs some serious attention, Bish. I think I can put it back in place for you, but I'm not sure that's something Ma and Jess will want to be around for. Wes, I know you were going to take Jess up to the hill, why don't you go on. Ma—"

"I'll be fine here with the two of you. I've never been squeamish."

"All right," Wes said, turning to Jess. "I need to get something from the bunkhouse. You get your coat, and I'll meet you on the porch in just a few minutes."

Jess nodded, but Bishop held up a hand to stop them.

"There's something else. I know about the gold nickels."

Wes turned to the man, wide-eyed. "You really did hear everything we were talkin' about, didn't you?"

Bishop glanced in Jessica's direction and then back at Wes with a grin. He chuckled. "Yes, I did."

Wesley's face went red, but Bishop hurried on and Jess never noticed.

"I heard you say something about a gold nickel given to someone by a yellow-haired man."

"We already know that was Cantrell," Wes interrupted.

"But just because he has the nickels and just because the dye was at the ranch, doesn't make it Cantrell who set the fire."

"True, but why do you say that?" Dunn said.

"Because I was thinking about it on the way here, and I think I know who did it. I just don't know how to prove it."

Chapter 48

"Do you suppose Mr. Bishop will be all right?" Jess asked as Wesley approached from the bunkhouse, burlap sack in hand.

"Sure. Nothin' a little rest won't cure. I have a feelin' he won't move far beyond his bunk tomorrow though—maybe not for a couple of days. We'll take good care of him. Are you ready?"

"I think so. Where are we going?"

"To the top of the hill behind the house. You can see the whole lower end of the ranch from there and up into the mountains—parts of the ranch you haven't seen yet. But I suppose it's too dark now to see all that. Speaking of which." The man darted into the house and returned with two lanterns, each burning brightly.

"Wes, I don't understand. If we won't be able to see, then why are we going?"

"You'll see. Come on."

Wesley led the way across the backyard to a steep trail that led up the high hill behind the house. He said nothing, but Jessica sensed excitement in his steps. It was odd, such excitement mingled with the apprehension she saw in his other movements.

"You're acting very strange, Wesley Close. You and Dunn both."

"It's one of those things, Jess. You have to see it. I can't explain it. Watch your step here. The path is rough."

Jess glanced down just in time to avoid twisting her ankle between two jagged rocks. Her mind fixed on the ground below her, and she almost missed Wesley's deep, satisfied intake of the evening air.

"I love the weeks between winter and spring," he mused. "The smell of thawin' earth, the warm sun in the daytime, and the damp night air. I love it all. ...Do you like it here, Jess?"

"Yes. I didn't at first, but you know that. Now, I can honestly say that I do. I love everything about Grassdale. I love the children, their families, and the others I've met from town. Even Scotch has grown on me."

Wes chuckled. "Somehow he manages to do that. ...Do you miss home?"

"Of course I do. It wouldn't be home if I didn't miss it. But I'm content here. A letter like that one tonight makes me want to hop on the next stage and get there as fast as I can, but I really am content here."

"And the ranch? Are you happy here with us?"

Jess could hear the nervousness in his voice again. She was tempted to remark on it but thought better of it. "Wes, sometimes I'm ashamed of how happy I am. I don't deserve it. I was runnin' from God when I came here. He turned everything around and changed my heart and gave me a second chance—and a second family. I feel so blessed."

As she finished, she could feel him smiling at her. She glanced up from the rocky path and met his gaze.

"I'm glad you like it here," he said. "We're all glad."

Wet grass slipped and shifted beneath their feet as they crested the rise. Wes led them across the flat of the hill to a place where two benches faced out over the vast world below them. He motioned for her to sit, and she slipped down on the smooth, pine seat. To her surprise, he slid down beside her. She'd expected him to sit on the other bench. She smiled, finding that she didn't mind. She enjoyed the closeness, the security of his presence. He took her lantern and set it next to his own on a stump.

The lamps cast their gentle, flickering light back on the pair. Now, Jess could see the nervousness she had sensed in her friend earlier. But then he sighed, and the anxiety melted away. He leaned back and looked at her matter-of-factly.

"Do you remember that trip I took?"

Jess laughed. "Do I remember? You *are* talkin' about the trip that had us all terrified, aren't you?"

He grinned sheepishly. "Yes. That's the one."

"What about it?"

"Jess, I'm sorry I caused you so much worry. I thought the anniversary had already passed. Dunn and Ma have both told me how upsettin' it was to you. I'm so sorry. Please—"

Jess stopped him, laying a hand on his arm and waiting for him to meet her gaze.

"Wes, how could you know? I never told you. Please, don't let it trouble you."

He looked away, fiddling with his fingers.

"I um— I didn't tell anyone where I was going because I was afraid I would be turned down when I got there. If that happened— Well, I didn't know how I would— I mean—" He stopped, anxiously rubbing his hands together. "Jess, I—"

"Wes, what's wrong? Why are you so nervous? Did something happen? I thought you said the trip went well."

"It did. It went very well. It's just that— Jess, I don't know how to say this. ...A few months ago, a beautiful woman stumbled into my life. She stole my heart. So...I went to meet her family."

Jessica drew in a sharp breath. Tears sprang to her eyes at the thought that he—her hero, the man she admired and respected, the man she had fallen in love with—loved someone else. And why shouldn't he? She had treated him horribly. Her mind reeled at the revelation. She wanted to be happy for him, to support him as he had supported her. But her heart wanted to flee and find a place to weep. She forced herself to focus, to hear what he was saying.

"I wanted to do things the right way. But I was afraid they wouldn't give their blessing. If that happened, I was afraid I wouldn't be able to face anyone. I didn't know how I would face *you*."

"Me! Why me? Wes, why should you worry about facin' me, regardless of what her family said?"

"Why?" He hesitated, blinking back confusion of his own. Then a kind smile lifted the corners of his mouth and pushed the confusion out of his eyes. He lowered his voice and took hold of her hand. "Because...it was *your* family I went to see. Don't you understand, Jess? *You* are that woman."

"Oh, Wesley," she gasped, covering her mouth and trembling with surprise and excitement.

Wes reached into the burlap sack that he'd carried with him. He pulled out an envelope and rolled it over in his hand as he spoke. "I went when I did because I wanted to talk to your pa. But I didn't want to rush you into something you weren't ready for. I know it's only been a year since you lost Joseph, and I— I didn't want to presume that you were ready. I didn't want to do anything that would hurt you further. But I couldn't wait any longer. I love you, Jess."

"But, Wesley, how could you love someone who treated you so miserably? Who not so long ago despised God and almost everything else in life, and would have included you on that list? ...Wes, I don't deserve to be loved by you."

"Jess, that's all in the past. If you had stayed as you were, we wouldn't be having this conversation. Even though I know I'd already begun to love you then, if you hadn't turned back to the Lord, our paths would have gone separate ways. But you didn't stay where you were. You let God change you as only He could."

He studied her for a moment, seeing her tears and confusion and humility mix in the dim light of the lanterns. He squeezed her hand and smiled, hoping to calm her heart and cheer her.

"You have a wonderful family, Jess, so gracious and loving. Well...Jon wasn't too fond of me at first, but he got over it."

Jess laughed, wiping the tears from her face as she did so. "Jon is a hard one, especially where his sisters are concerned. How long were you with them?"

"They gave me a week."

"A week? To meet their approval? Oh, Wes!"

Wes sat back, laughing at the horror in her voice. "Yep. A week. That's all I had really. We tried to get back in those two weeks, Jess. We tried as hard as we could. There was just so much cold and wind and snow." He paused, rolling the envelope over once more and then holding it out to her. "Your pa sent this."

Jess slipped the letter out of his hand, her fingers trembling. She stroked it lovingly. The handwriting was Marc's, but she knew the words inside would be Papa's.

"It's okay if you don't want to read it now. I understand if you're more comfortable readin' it when I'm not around."

"No, I'll read it now. I'm just so overwhelmed. Why would you go to all that trouble for me? You could have died out in that weather, both of you."

"But God protected us."

"If I had known—"

"You wouldn't have let me go. That's why I didn't tell you. I had to go, but I knew you wouldn't want me to. ...Thank you for trustin' me and for trustin' the Lord."

Jess couldn't speak. She blinked away new tears and turned her attention to the letter. She unfolded its pages, holding it up to the lantern and reading aloud:

"Dearest Jessica,

"When you came home in the fall and told us of how God had used Mr. Close to show you His love, your mother and I were convinced that if any man was made for you, it was probably Wesley Close. But we knew only time and God Himself could reveal that to the two of you. We have prayed for God's will ever since.

"When Wesley arrived, we weren't surprised by his purpose for coming. Although he may have told you that his path wasn't easy in the beginning. Still, as we told him, many things make a man who he is, and we wanted to see who your Mr. Close really is. So we gave him a week.

"A week isn't a long time, especially to come to know a stranger—although, in a house as full as ours, a week can be a very long time for the stranger. The week truly wasn't enough. Not because it was insufficient to get to know Wesley but rather because we all wanted to keep him longer. He is a fine man.

"The decision is yours, Jess. Only you and the Lord know your heart, whether you are ready for such a thing. Only you and the Lord know whether your heart may be given to Wesley. We're not looking for a quick answer. But if your heart is inclined toward Mr. Close, you have our fullest blessing. The Lord will guide you. I will pray for you to know what is right.

"Your mother and Marc are with me. They want you both to know they will be praying.

"Much love, Papa."

Jess stroked the pages down against her lap. Love swelled in her heart as she thought of the effort it must have taken Papa to dictate such a letter. Now, more than ever, it meant the world that he respected the man she loved. Somehow, Wesley had known that.

"I don't know what to say, Wes."

"Then don't say anything. I only wanted you to know how I feel. From there, you proceed as the Lord leads. I love you. I want the very best for you, whatever that is." He stopped, glancing down at the burlap sack and then back at her. "I saw someone else while I was in Twin Pines. ...You didn't tell me Joseph's last name was Phillips. I've done business with his father in the past. Remember when I told you I wanted to see Marc but couldn't remember his name to ask directions? I was there to buy cattle from Ethan Phillips. I realized who they were when I asked Marc about talkin' to Joe's family. They are fine people, Jess.

...Joe was a good man. I only met him once, but he impressed me as a good man."

"You knew him? You went and saw his family?"

"I felt it was only right. Marc said he thought they'd want to talk, so I went. I didn't want them to think I was askin' you to forget the memory of their son or to put him behind you. I would never do that. I wanted them to know that I love you. I want to protect you and give you a home and a family. They were so gracious. I spent an entire evening with them. I hope to do it again someday."

He reached down into the sack and pulled out a small package, wrapped in brown paper and twine. "Here, they sent this."

Jess lifted the package from his hands and laid it on top of the letter from her father. Loosening the twine, she slid out the folded sheet of paper that had been attached to the package and began once more to read aloud:

"Jess,

"When Wesley arrived this afternoon, we were ready and waiting for him. We'd heard he was with your family. After hearing your story this fall, it didn't take much for us to guess why he'd come.

"Ethan rode to town yesterday and talked with Jon about it. Jon told him of his own first reaction but also said that Wesley had proven to be an upright man with your best interest in mind. He spoke of him with great respect. Knowing how close Joe and Jon were, we knew if Jon trusted Wesley, then we could trust him.

"He has spent the entire afternoon and evening with us. He is a fine man, Jess. Don't let the past hold you back. Joseph would want you to love and be loved. I think he would approve of your Wesley.

"I've wanted to send this package for some time now. I asked Wesley if he minded my giving it to you. He said he would be honored to be the one to carry it to Grassdale. I think you should have it, dear, especially since I know you have nothing of Joe's left.

"We look forward to seeing you when your path brings you back this way.

"With much love from all, Laurel Phillips."

Jess passed the letter to Wesley and began peeling the brown paper back from its contents. Then she stopped, gasping at the sight that met her. "Oh, Wes. It's his Bible. I can't believe she would send such a precious gift. I— She— Oh, Wesley."

Jess buried her face in her hands. Great sobs shook her entire body. "Why do any of you love me? I don't deserve it."

Wes wrapped his arm around her shoulders, stirred by the unexpected display of raw emotion. He pulled her in tight as if hoping to pull her out of danger.

"Jess, don't. Of course, we love you. Oh, Jess. That's the beauty of love. None of us deserve it. But true, genuine love, loves regardless of faults and failings.

"Those things you hold over yourself, all those reasons why no one should love you, they've been forgiven. We've all put them behind us. Now, it's your turn. Please, Jess, let us love you. All of us."

His voice was soothing, full of kindness and love. His words and all that he had done in pursuit of her over the previous months broke some final link in the chain of guilt that had still clung to her heart. She wiped her tears, eager for the grace he was offering her and weary of carrying the past.

"Thank you," she whispered.

She felt him relax. An edge of his coat dropped over her lap. She reached out and fingered it, trying to absorb everything he had told her about his trip and comparing it with her own journey. She sighed.

"The day you came to the school and told me you'd take Travis out of the class if things didn't change, I thought I'd lost you all. That was when I realized how much you meant to me. At first, it was just the friendship that I'd found in your family, but then…you were so honest with me, even when it meant saying things I didn't want to hear. The only men who have ever done that are my father and brothers. Even Joe was rarely that open with me. But you…you cared more about my well-being and your family than about whatever pain the circumstance might inflict on you.

"I was ashamed at first. No, I was ashamed for a long time. I felt it was a betrayal of Joseph to feel such things toward you. But you kept loving me and showing me Christ's love. I tried to tell myself I was imagining it. I tried to push it all out of my heart, but the more I saw of you and your kindness, the harder it was. I didn't realize how deep it went until your trip."

Her gaze rose. She studied his face in the light of the moon that had risen above them. She reached for his hand and clung to it as if back in the frightful blizzard that had ushered him home.

"I was so afraid I would lose you. ...I don't have to think about it, Wes. I know where my heart stands. I love you ever so much. Now I just have to learn to let myself feel and express it."

Wes smiled down at her through tears of his own. He squeezed her hand and was pleased when she returned it. "You don't know how long I've waited to hear you say that."

His words brought a happy fluttering in her chest. She leaned her head against his shoulder. But then a new thought shadowed her joy. "Wes, what about the school? My position doesn't allow for suitors."

"That's why I went to town today. I talked to the members of the school board. The school year's almost over. They were very understanding, all of them. It's a unique situation as far as they're concerned. They gave me their blessing. They ask that we exercise discretion. I believe Mr. Vincent's exact words were, 'I don't want my daughter comin' home with reports of how romantic Miss Bennett and Mr. Close are. I prefer to hear about arithmetic.'

"I haven't talked with Jason yet. I'd prefer to talk to him before word spreads too far. That's...that's actually very important to me. I just haven't seen him for a while. ...It'll all work out." He squeezed her shoulders and then stood, offering his hand. "Come to the edge of the hill with me. You should be able to see it now."

"See what?"

"What I brought you here to see."

"There's more?"

He laughed. "Yes, after all that, there's still one more thing. Come on."

He led her to the very edge of the hill, pointing out over the wide valley below. "Isn't it pretty in the moonlight?"

"It's beautiful. The creek is so—luminous. Like a crescent moon."

"That's exactly what Ma thought. In the summer, when there's no ice in the creek, the contrast of the light against the darkness is even more spectacular. That's how the ranch got its name."

"It's breathtaking. Absolutely breathtaking."

Wesley wrapped his arm around her and heaved a contented sigh. It had been worth it all—the snow, the cold, losing his breakfast, the ice and the wind, all of it—for this moment. His deepest wish had come true. She loved him!

* * *

Not far below, the house nestled into the covert formed by the hills and mountains. On the back porch, stood a very quiet and very pleased Duncan Roe. From his vantage point, he could see the pair silhouetted in the lantern light. He was happy for them both.

As he watched, something changed within him, something he had never experienced, never expected. He didn't know why or how or when, but a strange stirring in his heart told him his time at the Crescent Creek was coming to an end. A pang of sadness shot through him, grief even. And yet he knew God wouldn't take him anywhere without a purpose. He sighed and watched as the couple made their way back to the house. They shared their joy with him and then with his mother and Travis, and soon the sadness was all but forgotten.

Chapter 49

Jason French slowed his horse and slipped into the shadows cast by the late evening sun. From this vantage point, he could see just beyond the bend that led into the bustling mining town. He pulled at his collar and the bandana knotted at his throat. It had been cold overnight, but now he was more than a little aware that spring was just around the corner. He'd give anything for a drink of cold water and a chance to ease out of his coat. But he didn't want to risk being seen, and a movement like that would catch someone's eye.

He squinted into the sunlight, watching the silhouette of the tall, lanky horse and its round rider. The trip had been arduous. Jason had always considered Scotch a man who indulged in the comforts of life. He'd always imagined him finding the most leisurely course in any endeavor. But such had not proven to be the case.

Jason had left Grassdale three-quarters of an hour after Scotch, but it had taken three hours to catch up with him. The preacher had set a safe distance between them, and expected Scotch to travel at a slow, easy pace. Scotch, however, had pushed his mount. He rode all night, only stopping at daybreak for a cold breakfast. Within an hour, they were underway again. In the mid-afternoon, Scotch had left the road, dismounted, and led his horse into a thicket of trees.

Jason followed suit, dismounting and tethering his horse behind a low rise. He climbed the hill, crawling on his belly until he came to a place where he could watch the thicket without being seen. To his surprise, smoke already filtered up through the trees. The rich aroma of brewing coffee and frying beans drifted across the breeze. For dinner to be ready so quickly, Scotch must have had a permanent campsite hidden in the trees.

Jason crawled back down the hill to his horse, pulled out his own provisions, and returned to keep watch. He'd almost finished his meal when Scotch and his horse emerged from the trees and made their way back to the road. Dropping the remnants of a dry biscuit, Jason sprang to his feet and ran to his horse. He tightened the saddle and mounted with such haste that he nearly went over the animal's back and onto the ground. Regaining his balance, he'd kicked the startled horse into a lope until Scotch was within sight.

Once again, they'd traveled all night, stopping only once. The second day followed the pattern of the first until finally, Maiden had come into sight.

Jason had never been so happy to see a place as he was to see the scrappy town nestled between the gentle slopes of the canyon. He watched Scotch ride through the bustle of miners and townspeople, nodding at some, waving at others.

"They certainly know you around here, Scotch Jorgenson," the preacher muttered. "Where are you going?" Jason moved forward, straining to see the name above the door of the building Scotch had just entered. "The livery. Makes sense."

A moment later, Scotch emerged from the building. Afraid the man would catch sight of him, Jason dismounted and then led his horse into the bustle of the street. Scotch passed a hotel and a boarding house. Two days earlier, this might have surprised Jason, but not now. Now, he was sure nothing would ever surprise him where Scotch was concerned. But he was wrong.

Scotch walked a short distance up Montana Street. He turned left onto a side street and climbed the front steps of the third house. Scotch had yet to cross the porch when the door swung open and a girl of about twelve rushed out to meet him. She threw her arms around his neck and shouted with excitement, "Papa!"

The door opened again and a tall, slender woman with a hint of gray running through her carefully groomed hair followed the girl outside. A beautiful smile brightened her face, and she greeted the man — Scotch Jorgenson — with a kiss.

Jason's mouth dropped open. He stared in complete and utter disbelief. Scotch Jorgenson with a *family*! How could such a thing be possible? Jason watched from his hiding place around the corner of a neighboring house until the family disappeared inside. Then he turned around and leaned against the building, his mind whirling.

"No wonder he never told us what was going on," he said. "No one would have believed him. And no wonder he's closin' everything down in Grassdale. Good for you, Scotch," he said with one more glance at the house. "Good for you."

* * *

Jason stepped into the livery, leading his weary horse behind him.

"Can I help you?" came a deep, gravelly voice from the far end of the room.

Jason strained to see through the dim light of the building's interior. A huge, dark-haired man stepped out into the open. Jason had no doubt but what the giant could challenge half the miners in Maiden at once and win. The preacher faltered. He stepped back a pace and then scolded himself inwardly for being so easily startled.

"Just lookin' for a place to stable my horse," he managed. "We've had a long ride. He could use some rest."

The man's boots clomped loudly as he stepped up to Jason, towering over him and extending an enormous hand. "You've come to the right place."

Jason shook the man's hand, the iron grip confirming his initial impression.

"How long you stayin'?"

"Not long. Tonight and tomorrow night, maybe the night after."

"You here on business?"

"You could say that."

"Well, we'll take care of your horse for you. No worries there. Looks pretty rode down. Let's get him situated, and then we'll settle everything else."

Jason followed the man to an empty stall and set to caring for the horse. He was as tired as the animal. His mind and body wanted to be finished with the day, but he knew this would be his best opportunity to gather information.

"You own this operation?" he asked casually.

"Sure do. Been here a while now."

"You've got a nice arrangement."

"We try to do things so they work 'round here."

"Someone told me about a saddle they sold here. I wondered if you might still have it."

"Oh? How long ago was it they sold it to us?"

"Not sure. Six months at most."

"That long. I doubt we've still got it. Lot of people in and out of here."

"Well, maybe you can tell me who bought it. It was an unusual saddle."

"Unusual? In what way?"

"It was circus red. Very ornate."

"Sure! I know that one. Nobody wants it!" the man's head tilted back as he rumbled out a deep, belly laugh. "You want it? I'll sell it to you for half what I paid—just to be rid of it." He laughed again.

Jason couldn't help but join in the jovial man's laughter. "No. I don't want it either! But I'd like to look at it."

"Look at it? Why?"

"I need to prove it had nothing to do with a fire that started last fall and burned a school, a home, and a lot of grazing land."

"Now, that's pretty serious. Scotch brought that saddle in here. Why would you think he had anything to do with it?"

"I don't. Not really. But I have to prove it before others decide he did and put a noose around his neck."

The giant stared in surprise for a moment. "Now look here, Scotch is my friend. He does good business here. That's his horse right over there waitin' to be shod. His family don't need no lies spread about 'em."

"I'm not here to spread lies. I'm here to disprove lies. I'm here to prove Scotch had nothin' to do with that fire."

The giant's eyes narrowed. He scrutinized the slender, blonde form before him. There was an honest appearance about the stranger. His intense, olive eyes never wavered. That was unusual. Most men found his size intimidating, but this man seemed unperturbed. "Well," he began, "if you're really here to help him…"

"I am."

The stable owner nodded, convinced by the determination in the open face before him. "What is it you need to see?"

"I need to make sure the saddle is intact."

"Oh, it's in fine shape. You done there with your horse?"

"I think so."

"All right, let's go have a look see."

Jason followed the tall man out of the barn area and into the office. The smell of well-worn leather, wool, and horse greeted them. Saddles, bridles, harnesses, and other tack lined the walls and sat in piles around the edges of the room. The giant stopped in the middle of the room. He looked around and then, with two long strides, was across the office and scooping up the red saddle.

"Here ya go," he said, swinging the saddle onto the counter with ease. "What do you need to see?"

"I need to make sure nothing has torn off of it."

"Oh, I can tell you right now it's in fine condition. But look for yourself anyway. Don't want no questions."

Jason stepped up to the counter. He inspected every inch of the saddle and then stepped back. "You're right. Not a single tear. Hardly even a scuff or scratch."

"So that proves he had nothin' to do with it?"

"In my mind it does."

"But maybe not in the minds of others?"

"Well, we'll see. What can you tell me about Scotch's family?"

"His family? Well, now, I'm not one to talk much about others' business."

"I'm not here to gossip. Truth is, I'm against gossip. I'm just here to find whatever I can to help me prove Scotch had nothing to do with that fire."

"Does he know you're here?"

"No. I followed him from Grassdale. Plan on tellin' him myself in the mornin'."

"So that's the fire. We heard about that. So whoever done that would be in big trouble with the law."

"Most likely."

"And you're here to prove Scotch had nothin' to do with it."

"Exactly."

The big man sighed. "Well, I suppose then, since he's my friend, I ought to do what I can to help. Scotch and his family came here, oh, eight or nine months ago. They come together, but Scotch seemed none too happy in those days. Drank a whole lot. Once they'd been here long enough to set up a house, it seemed the wife and daughter were the only ones around. He left and no one saw him for weeks at a time. We found out he had business in other places and was travelin' back and forth. That woman is a fine woman, but I reckon she's had a hard life. I think...well...I think you should ask him the rest. Seems he'd like to stay here. Told me the last time he was here that he'd sold his home in Grassdale."

Jason nodded. "He told me that too. ...How much do I owe you for the night?"

"If you're here to help my friend, you owe me nothin'. But if I find out otherwise, I'll find you and make sure we settle things proper like."

Jason considered the stable owner's conditions, noticing the man kneading one massive fist with the other hand. Jason wasn't exactly sure what he meant by 'settlin' things proper like,' but he was certain he didn't want to find out.

"Fair enough. But do me a favor. Don't tell Scotch I'm here, or anyone else for that matter."

The man smiled a big, toothy grin. "How can I tell him you're here? I don't even know who you are."

With a grin of his own, Jason extended a hand for one last knuckle-crushing shake. "Name's Jason French. I'm the preacher from Grassdale. I don't mean Scotch or anybody else any harm."

"A preacher, huh? Well, if you're here long enough, let me know. I'll direct you to a family what likes to read the Bible together Sundays."

"I'd appreciate that. Have a good night...mister?"

"Hamlin. Tobias Hamlin."

"Good to meet you, Mr. Hamlin. Have yourself a good evening." Jason tipped his hat and left the livery, still massaging his hand.

Chapter 50

Marc stepped back from the heavily laboring cow and gratefully received the towel Jake offered him. Wiping his forearms and hands, he took a moment to catch his breath. This should be their last calf of the season. It was also proving to be the most difficult to bring into the world. He wiped sweat from his brow and glanced from the cow to Jake.

"I think we're about there. She'll be fine, but that's one stubborn calf."

"Tell me what you want me to do, boss, and I'll do it."

"Just be ready to help me pull."

Jake nodded.

The men went back to work, trying to move the calf into position for a safe delivery. Marc had just flashed a grin in Jake's direction, letting him know they were almost there when a new sound sent terror ripping through his heart.

"Marcus! Marc! Are you in here!" It was Marianne. Her voice rang with panic.

Marc maneuvered the calf into position as Jake waved Mary toward them. Grabbing for the towel once more, Marc stepped out to meet his anxious sister. He smiled as she approached, attempting to calm her.

"What brings you down here? I thought you'd be fixin' lunch about now."

Mary stepped close, taking hold of his arm. She said nothing. Tears pooled in her blue eyes.

"What is it?" he whispered.

"Ma says you're to go to town and fetch Jon and-and wire for Jess to —" Mary stopped. She bit her bottom lip, letting her gaze drop to the scattered bits of straw on the floor.

"Mary, what's happened?"

Mary shook her head, the tears finally spilling down her cheeks. "I don't know, Marc. Papa's not responding. He won't wake up. He's still breathing, but he won't wake up. We've tried to wake him for the last fifteen minutes, but he won't wake up."

Marc glanced over his shoulder. Jake had already stepped into his place, doing all he could to help the struggling cow. "All right, I'll go as fast as I can, but I need your help. Saddle Ezra for me while I help Jake finish. If this calf isn't born by the time you're done, I'll need you to take my place so I can go. All right?"

Mary nodded, but she didn't move. Marc saw fear in his little sister's eyes. It tore at his heart. Taking gentle hold of her arm, he led her to the tack room. Before entering, however, he stepped away and out into the bright sunshine.

"Danny!" he yelled, louder than ever before. He waited a moment and yelled again. A second later, the boy's inquisitive face poked out the front door of the cabin. "Come down here. We need you."

Danny nodded and then disappeared, presumably going in search of his shoes and coat.

Marc returned to the barn and led Mary into the tack room. "Mary," he whispered, "someone has to help Jake. If we don't get that calf out soon, we're going to lose it—maybe lose the cow too. I need you and Danny to help. Please."

Again, Mary nodded without a word. Instead, she turned toward the rack where his saddle hung against the wall, picked it up, and hurried out to saddle Ezra. Marc rejoined Jake and a moment later Danny was standing at his side, his eyes wide with excitement. The three worked until Marc felt a hand on his shoulder and turned to see Mary standing behind him with his horse.

"He's ready to go, Marc."

Marc stepped away from the cow and took the horse's reins from his sister. He could see Mary's heart hadn't calmed. She was no less afraid now than she had been when she'd arrived a few minutes earlier. She was no less afraid than he was.

"Go back up to the house," he whispered. "They'll be okay here. The little guy is just about here."

"Are you sure?"

He nodded.

"I'm afraid, Marc. I know I shouldn't be, but I'm afraid."

"I know. But the Lord will take care of us. We're in His hands—just as Papa is. Just keep your eyes on the Lord."

"Whew!" came an exhausted but exuberant cry from the stall behind them. Marc turned to see Jake and Danny grinning back at him and the small calf blinking up from the floor.

"See," he said, turning back to Mary. "Everything's going to be all right down here. Now, go on up to the house. I love you."

Mary stepped away, sending a faint smile in his direction as he swung up into the saddle and urged Ezra into a run.

Chapter 51

Jason rarely slept late, but that morning he rolled out of bed at ten o'clock. His entire body ached with the fatigue of the previous days' ride. Breakfast had long ago finished by the time he made it to the hotel dining room. To his own shame, he'd gone back upstairs, struggled through the reading of a psalm, and slept until he heard the other guests making their way to lunch. Then he'd donned his boots and clumped down the stairs to join them.

As he ate, he noticed curious glances from those who staffed the establishment. He suspected Tobias Hamlin hadn't been as silent as he'd promised. Jason sighed at the realization. He needed to get to Scotch before word of his presence in Maiden went any further.

Not bothering to return to his room after lunch, the preacher dragged his weary self across town to the house where Scotch's journey had ended the night before. Jason groaned as his aching legs carried his stiff body up the stairs and across the porch. He'd just reached out to knock when a strange feeling told him someone was watching. He turned to see Scotch sitting comfortably at the far end of the porch.

"I wondered when you'd come knockin' at my door," Scotch said, showing no sign of surprise at the preacher's appearance. "Come have a seat. We'll chat a spell."

Jason studied the other man, surprised at the relaxed tone and calm demeanor. He'd never known Scotch to be congenial, never even suspected he knew how to be gregarious or polite. But he was seeing just that.

"Aw, what ya starin' at, Preacher? Come sit down. I ain't no different in Maiden than in Grassdale. Same man just a different place. Sit."

Jason obeyed, crossing the porch and sinking into a round-backed saloon chair. A soft cushion padded the seat, for which the preacher's saddle-sore body was grateful.

"How did you know I was here?"

Scotch shrugged, reaching for a cup of coffee on the small, round table that stood between them. "I heard there was a preacher in town. This place ain't got no preacher, so I figured it must be you. Funny, I would've expected Bennett to follow me all the way over here. How'd you get the job?"

A smile lifted one corner of Jason's mouth. "Cale and I saw you sneakin' out of town. I didn't think he should leave his family, so I told him I'd follow you. ...You ride hard, Scotch. I don't know how you do it. I'm so sore I can hardly walk."

Scotch grunted out a laugh. "I wasn't all tensed up wonderin' what the other guy was gonna do. Sure, I pushed hard, but I knew what I was up to. You didn't."

"The coffee you made at that stand of trees about drove me mad."

"Thirsty were ya?"

"You could say that."

"Have you had any this morning?"

"No. I slept too late. Missed breakfast."

"We'll fix you up. Alma!" he called toward the house.

"Alma?" Jason stared in surprise. "Alma your wife? Your first wife?"

Scotch grunted. "My only wife. Not too likely a man'd find two Almas, is it?"

"But, Scotch, all these years you've been alone in Grassdale. We all assumed she was dead, or...or that you'd abandoned her."

Scotch considered that for a moment. "I suppose there's a sense in which I did. I..." he paused, formulating his answer as much for his own sake as for the preacher's. "I left her behind so's I could find our dream, establish a life for us. Then I was gonna go back for her, but I was a mess without her—and I made a mess of my life without her."

The front door opened. The tall, pretty woman who had greeted Scotch with a kiss the night before emerged, her gaze full of questions.

"But now she's here," Scotch said, his eyes brightening, "and I'm finding myself nearly whole again."

The woman blushed, knowing the men had been talking about her. "Did you want something, Adam?"

Jason had never heard anyone pay Scotch the courtesy of addressing him by his given name. It both surprised and pleased him.

"Alma, this is, well, I hope in the future I'll be able to say he's my friend. This is Jason French. He's the preacher over at Grassdale."

The woman's eyes widened. "The one you nearly strangled last fall?" Realizing she might have said too much, the woman covered her mouth. Her cheeks turned crimson.

"Well," Scotch faltered, "yes. That's the one. I'm sorry, Preacher. My Alma gave me quite the lecture when she heard about that. It never should have happened. You were right on every count. And I *had* been drinkin', just like you said. There's no excuse for behavior like that. There's no excuse for — Alma, is there any coffee left? The preacher could use some. And while he's drinkin' it, I think it's high time I told someone what's been goin' on."

"It's nice to meet you, Preacher. I'll be right back with a cup of good, hot coffee, and we'll all talk things through. Have to make sure Adam gets the details right, you know?"

Jason chuckled. "Yes, I suppose you do."

* * *

Jason sipped at his coffee. He watched Alma Jorgenson seat herself in the sturdy rocking chair opposite his own seat. Catching him watching her, she smiled.

"So tell me," Jason said, turning to Scotch, "how did a man like you end up with such a fine wife to begin with?"

Fortunate for all their sakes, Scotch didn't miss the teasing gleam in the preacher's green eyes.

"Well now, I haven't always been the superb specimen you see before you today," he replied, running a hand over his large belly. "When we were younger — I wasn't any taller, mind you — but I was more slender and very fit. Not fit as a fiddle, but I could hold my own. ...And I had all of my hair then too. It may surprise you to find out that I met Alma at a church social. It *won't* surprise you to find out that I wasn't there to hear the preachin'. I was there to meet the girls. And I did! We fell in love and married a few months later."

"Adam was very charming." Alma had a soft, pleasant voice, and, unlike her husband, she carried herself with refinement and confidence. "In those days, he was reliable and a hard worker. But about the time we were expecting our daughter —"

"So she *is* your daughter!" Jason blurted out.

"Yes, Amanda is my daughter," Scotch said with a tone of forbearance.

"Sorry." Jason squirmed, realizing the many implications of the unchecked remark. "I apologize, Mrs. Jorgenson. Please go on."

"That's quite all right, Mr. French. As I was saying, about the time we were expecting Amanda everything changed. For all of us, not just our family, but for our entire town."

"What happened?"

"The mill where I worked burned to the ground. The owner was the father of a good friend of mine—both were trapped inside. Neither of them survived. I was out of work, but so were most of the men in town."

"That fire changed Adam. Although, I don't think it was the fire so much as the loss. The loss of work, the loss of his friend, the loss of security for his family."

Jason saw Alma glance at her husband, whom he expected to be squirming with embarrassment, but Scotch was still. The man's eyes were fixed on his wife, finding security in the serenity of her face. Jason smiled, genuinely happy for this man who had caused so much trouble over the previous months.

"Something broke in him one day," Alma continued. "He sent me to live with his parents until he could get better established somewhere else. He came home when Amanda was born, but he was never satisfied. He always wanted something more, something to fill the void, to make him good enough, fulfilled enough. I could see he was heading in a very bad direction, but he didn't see it."

"*Wouldn't* see it," Scotch interjected. "You know me well enough to know that, Preacher."

"One day, Adam came home to see us. I was happy to see him. Then he started talking all this nonsense about going west. I realized he'd been drinking. I told him I wouldn't consider it until he'd sobered up and could talk through it in his right mind."

"So I left. Dumb, dumb, dumb, I know. But that's what I done."

Alma nodded confirmation. "He disappeared. Completely. We didn't hear from him for months. Eventually, we started hearing a little here and there as he traveled west. When Amanda was four, he wrote that he'd settled in a place called Grassdale. He promised to send for us as soon as he'd earned enough money. I didn't know his way of earning money was swindling everyone he could out of the little bit they had."

"What do you mean? Scotch, I thought you ran a mercantile when you first came to Grassdale."

Scotch's face colored. "Well, I did. I ran it for three years. That don't mean I ran it fairly. Let's just say it didn't cost me near as much to get the goods to Grassdale as I let people think. I justified the high prices because they would get my family to me sooner. But being in Grassdale just about ruined me and a lot of other people."

"But it wasn't Grassdale that caused that damage," Alma chided.

"No. No it wasn't. It was my own fault."

"So," Jason ventured, "what happened? I mean, when I came to Grassdale you didn't own a mercantile. You had a saloon, a hotel, and were about to open a brothel. Most folks didn't exactly see you as a family-minded sort of man."

Scotch shook his head. "No. And most folks still don't. Just like they don't see those women as women they'd like to keep in their town. Except for Bennett. That man has got some notion in his head that he can help at least some of them. I'm not so sure."

"Really? He hasn't mentioned it to me."

"Probably afraid you'll think he's gone mad."

Jason laughed. "After the strain this fire business has put on his family, I just might."

Scotch grunted. "It's put a strain on a lot of people, people who didn't deserve any of it. Miss Bennett and the Closes at the top of that list."

"So what happened?"

"Oh, I was in Grassdale a couple years, always scraping up as much as I could to bring Alma and Amanda out to me. Then, just before I was ready to send for them, I got a letter. My father had died. My mother was gone already, so the estate had to be closed. I shut down the mercantile and headed east. Never told anyone why or where I was going.

"My father was well to do. I took my time settling his affairs but always wanted to get back here. On my way back east, I'd noticed the thriving towns had attractions that we didn't have in Grassdale. Hotels and saloons were two of them. They seemed to turn a good profit. I told Alma we'd go back, start a hotel, and be set for life."

"But," Alma interrupted, "I figured out what he was really thinking. He didn't want a hotel. He wanted the saloon. I didn't want any part of that. I told him I wouldn't come if that was his plan. That wasn't the life for which I'd been raising our daughter."

"So," Scotch said with an exaggerated sigh, "I left again. I came back here angry and hateful and spiteful. Instead of doin' the right thing, I did everything I knew Alma wanted me not to do. Just to spite her. Even though she wasn't here. Then last February, a year ago, Alma wrote and said they'd received notice to vacate the home they'd been leasing. They only had until spring. They had nowhere else to go, so they'd be coming to Grassdale."

"I'd been raising Amanda alone for eleven years, Mr. French. I didn't know what else to do or where else to go, and I was tired of carrying the burden by myself."

"I panicked. Alma was about to find out the truth about my life. People in town were fussin' because we didn't have a teacher in Grassdale. Some threatened to move the school off the property. I couldn't afford to lose the rent from the school. And, truth be told, even though nothin' else I had to offer my family was honorable, I wanted Amanda to have a good education.

"My chickens had come home to roost, and I felt doomed to break every egg they laid. I started searchin' harder than ever for a new teacher. I went over the notes from when the school first started and found the information on Miss Bennett. So I wrote to her. I lied in every way possible just hopin' to get her here. Then I panicked again. What was I going to do when Alma and Amanda and Miss Bennett arrived and discovered all my lies? I started drinkin' more to calm my nerves, but it just got me into more trouble."

"I'll say," Jason agreed. "Did he tell you he met Miss Bennett at the stagecoach so drunk that he couldn't stand up straight?"

Alma nodded. "Yes. He's told me a good many things, most of which I find deplorable. That's why we're working on making things different—working on making them right."

Scotch's cheeks were coloring again. "I didn't want Alma to know the truth about me. I couldn't fix it all in time before she came, so I bought her passage here—to Maiden—instead of Grassdale. I rented this house and met her here two weeks after the day I nearly strangled you in the schoolhouse.

"I was so happy to see them both, but I was ashamed of what had happened over the previous months—years—leading up to it. I felt unworthy of their love. After Amanda had gone to bed that first night, we sat here on this porch, and I told Alma the truth. We talked all night. By the time she'd heard it all, she handed me the cash I'd given her upon their arrival and told me to go to the hotel. We wouldn't be sleeping under the same roof until she'd sorted things through in her mind."

"It took me a few days, Preacher. I was so angry with him for the life he'd chosen for himself, and in particular, for the women in his employ. He may have no part in the goings on in that brothel, but he made it possible."

Even now, Jason could see a flush of indignation in the woman's cheeks. He tilted his head, his eyes narrowing with curiosity. "But you came around?"

She shook her head. "I'll never be in agreement with what he did. But I realized the scoldings you and others in Grassdale had given him, the scolding I had given him, and his fear of losing us again had brought him to a breaking point. We talked, and he agreed to start making changes. He wanted to make things right. He's been looking for work for the women, all but two have work in other towns now. The brothel hasn't been operating for months."

"But I've seen —"

"You've seen the girls around there, but since I got rid of Madam Beast, there haven't been any men allowed in."

"Adam, stop calling her that."

Scotch shrugged. "It fits her. Bennett said he'd consider hiring one of the girls from the saloon at the bank. We're still lookin' for work for the other."

Jason's eyes widened. "Cale said that?"

"I told you, you'd think he lost his mind. The saloon is next. I need to find someone who'll buy the building. Then it'll close or turn into whatever the new owner wants to use it for. The hotel we'll hold onto for a while. I can manage it from here until we have enough money set aside for whatever we're going to do next."

"I want us to go back east," Alma said. "We can start over there. We can go back to friends who will support us and help us. I haven't quite convinced Adam of the benefits of this yet, but there's a good preacher in our town. He'll help us very much."

"There's a good preacher sittin' right here, Alma. I don't know. I ain't sure any church is ready for me just yet."

Jason smiled. "It doesn't matter if a church is ready for you or not. What matters is that God is always ready. Ready and waiting. We don't have to get good to come to Him. All the good comes from Him."

Alma smiled at her husband as if to say, "See, I told you."

Scotch shrugged. "What would you do, Preacher, if you was us?"

Jason drew in a deep breath. He stretched his long legs out in front of him and lifted his clasped hands to his chin. "It's not an easy thing, Scotch. There's half a community over in Grassdale—the angry half, mind you—that thinks you had a part in that fire. Word has gotten around about what you did after Cale and I spoke with you about the fire that first time. People think that's clear evidence you're guilty."

Alma, her displeasure evident in the set of her gaze under her eyebrows, tilted her head. Scotch, understanding perfectly, turned red. He squirmed in his chair, fumbled about for something to say, and then mumbled. "I paid them all back."

"That isn't the problem, dear. There shouldn't have been anything to pay them back for in the first place."

"The ones you paid back aren't the problem. *I* was one of the ones you paid back. The problem comes from the ones who think it confirms your guilt. They've made life miserable for Cale. In fact, I'm pretty sure his wife is ready to pack up and move."

"But I had nothing to do with that fire."

"I believe you, but we have to prove it. Frankly, I don't know how."

"Mr. French, there's something you need to know about my husband. After the mill fire, he wouldn't come close to a stove or fireplace for months. Fire terrified him."

"That may be so, Mrs. Jorgenson, but that doesn't seem to stop him from lighting a cigar. I've seen him throw a lit match into the street more times than I can count."

"But there's nothin' in the street to burn, 'cept manure. Besides it don't stay around long enough to get to that point. Not in Grassdale. Folks clean it up too fast. Here, on the other hand, I never throw down a match in this place. With my luck, it'd land in a pile of playin' cards and burn the whole town down."

Jason laughed. Even as tired as he'd been the previous evening, he'd noticed the strange presence of playing cards scattered all over town, out in the streets, and tucked tight by the wind against the structures and walkways.

"Preacher," Alma said, the seriousness lingering in her gaze, "I've watched him for months now. He doesn't leave the house without checking every lamp, the stove, the fireplace. He checks it all. I imagine if you check with any of his employees, they'll tell you the same."

"That's all good, but that doesn't mean you don't still have to face your accusers." Jason paused, considering the information he'd gained since arriving in Maiden. "Thanks to Mr. Hamlin, I can confirm that piece of leather didn't come from your saddle. I can confirm you were here when the fire started. We know that matchbox didn't belong to your wife. We know that coin came from someone other than you."

"So how does he clear his name in the matter?"

"I think each of you should write a signed statement telling your whereabouts during the fire. Particularly on the day it started. Scotch you need to include when you were out at Edelman's that week. I'll see if Tobias Hamlin will verify your statements and if he has a way to verify when he purchased the saddle from you. If anyone else in town can verify your statements, let me know before I leave. We'll get written statements from all of them. The more witnesses we have from here, the better for you."

"Then what?" Scotch asked.

"Then I take everything back to Grassdale, and we submit it with the rest of the evidence when the judge comes through. He'll decide what to do with things from there."

"But, Mr. French, won't people want someone to be punished for the fire? If not Adam, then who?"

"We're working on finding who did it, Mrs. Jorgenson. Something Cale told me the night I left town, makes me think we're getting close. Scotch, I think you should stay here with your wife and daughter. There's no need for you to be back in Grassdale unless you have business that can't wait."

"I have a lot of business to tend to. I still need to sell that saloon. We'll still need to manage the hotel."

"Would you consider staying on to run the hotel after the judge leaves?"

Scotch was thoughtful. Finally, he shook his head. "No. If I could get some land west of town, I might consider puttin' in a mill like the one I worked in so long ago. There's enough forest in those mountains to keep it runnin' for a long time. But like I told you and Bennett the other day, I'm done living in that town, at least for a while."

"But you'd consider staying in the area?"

Scotch shrugged. "I'd consider it."

Jason could see the disappointment on Alma's face. He smiled at her kindly. "I only make the suggestion, Mrs. Jorgenson, because I know Grassdale. Some good people there might surprise you with their willingness to help you start over."

The woman looked doubtful. "We'll see."

"Scotch, what would you think about selling the saloon to the church and school?"

Surprise widened Scotch's eyes, but then a grin spread across his face. "I'd feel very good about that. I'd even give you a good price."

"I have some thoughts about the hotel as well, but I'll have to talk to Cale about it when I get back."

"What do you think we should do with the brothel?"

Jason shrugged. "I'm not sure. We'll put it in God's hands for now. Maybe someone will want to start a boarding house or something."

Scotch was thoughtful. "All right. Give me a couple of days to tend to business here. Then I'll ride back with you. And this time, you can come into my camp and have coffee with me. Instead of sufferin' in some damp hidin' place."

The preacher laughed and extended a hand to the other man. "Adam Jorgenson, I'd be glad to share a fire with you anytime."

Chapter 52

Night had long ago fallen when Jess finally sat down at the writing table in the sitting area. She smiled as she laid out the day's school papers and prepared to grade her students' work for the last time. Some of the students had already finished their work for the year. Their families needed them on farms and ranches. The other students were itching to follow suit. Part of her was ready for the last day. The rest of her would miss the children terribly over the summer. She lingered on that thought for a moment. Was it just over the summer?

Wes had talked with the school board again, but no decision had been made about the future. They supported the growing relationship between the pair. But as a rule, the school didn't allow their teachers the liberty of courtship and marriage. Most schools didn't. Jess was willing to continue teaching if Wes was in favor of it, but the school board would make the final decision.

In the two weeks since their walk to the hill, Wes had behaved himself very carefully around the children. He avoided the house during the day, often eating lunch after the others had finished and returned to their places. But as soon as the children were gone for the day, he appeared, asking questions about the day, helping Jess clean the classroom, working alongside her as she helped Anna with the supper preparations, or suggesting walks to explore parts of the ranch she had never seen. He usually drug Travis along when they went exploring and both Wes and Jessica found the boy to be good company. Tonight there had been no exploring.

"It's good to have a bit of rain," Anna said as she joined her sons in the sitting area.

"It sure is." Wes looked up from the book he'd been reading near the fire. "It'll green things up a bit. I'm sure ready for some color."

"It's only the beginning of April! Give things a chance." Dunn laughed.

"You're always ready for spring, Wes," Anna said. "Always itching to get out under the hot sun."

"I confess, I am. I love how fresh everything is, and new."

"And that won't happen without rain," Dunn added, flipping over the sheet of paper in his hand.

"What are you readin'?" Wes leaned forward, trying to see the title on the page.

"Oh, it's a pamphlet someone in town gave me about how things are expandin' to the west."

"Is it interesting?"

"It's not very well written. Can't make sense of half of it. I'm not even sure why I'm tryin'." He paused, his gaze rising to the ceiling. "Wow. Listen to that. It's pourin'. Makes me cold just listenin' to it." Dunn rose and went to the window, watching the rain stream from the roof over the porch. "Makes me even colder watchin' it. Anyone want something hot to drink?"

"I'd take some tea," Anna replied.

"Oh, me too," Jess chimed eagerly.

Neither Wes nor Travis responded so Dunn went on with his task. The room fell silent but for the rain on the roof, the clock on the mantel, and Dunn's clattering in the kitchen.

Bang! A crashing blow rattled the front door.

Everyone in the room jumped, Jess nearly spilling her inkwell.

Bang! Bang!

"I thought I heard something a minute ago. What's wrong with that dog. She's supposed to warn us when someone's coming." Wes hurried to the door and pulled it open. Then he stepped back in surprise. "Tom! What are you doing here? You're soaked. Get inside."

"No, Wes, come out here. I need to talk to you."

"What's going on? Did Cale send you? Is the preacher back?"

"Just come out here."

"Okay." Wes glanced over his shoulder at his mother and shrugged. Then he stepped out onto the porch, closing the door behind him.

"What's going on, Tom?"

"I don't even know where to start." The man rubbed his forehead, knocking his hat back on his head at a precarious angle. "I just came from Twin Pines. I saw Marc Bennett there. His Pa is real sick. Marc had just sent a wire, but he asked me to make sure you'd gotten it. I

checked and the telegram was still at the bank. Cale apologized profuse-
ly. He said he doesn't check the telegrams. Mitch should have taken note
of the urgency of the message and let him know. Cale would have come
out with it personally if he'd known. ...She needs to go home, Wes. You
need to take her. It's bad. Marc said the whole family is welcome if you
want to bring everyone. So Mr. Bennett can have a chance to meet
them...if—"

"If we make it in time."

"Exactly. I'm sorry to bring such news, Wes, but it had to be done."

Wes nodded, tension building in his eyes. "Thank you, Tom, especially for comin' in this rain. You aren't plannin' on going all the way
back to town tonight, are you? We've got plenty of room here and dry
clothes too."

Tom shook his head. "I'm spent. We'll have to leave early though.
The stage heads that way again in the mornin' and there won't be another until I get back next week. I'll head into town before the rest of you
do, but I won't leave without you. Just don't get there past eight-thirty
or nine. The roads won't be good."

"I'm sure they won't. Take your horse on down to the barn, and I'll
dig up some clothes and supper for you."

"Thanks, Wes."

"No, thank *you*."

Wesley watched the man step back out into the rain, wondering how
to break the news to Jess. He slipped inside, a knot forming in his gut as
he went. "Jess, didn't I see you takin' some clothes off the line this afternoon?"

"Yes. Did you need something?"

"Would something there fit Tom? He's soaked to the bone."

"Oh, I'm sure there's something. Let's go look."

Jess led the man down the hall to a basket of freshly folded laundry,
which sat just inside the back door. She stooped down to sort through
the items in the basket, but Wesley stopped her.

"Jess, I'll find it. I need to tell you something."

She smiled up at him in her usual happy manner, but one look at his
face drove her smile away.

"Wes, what is it?"

He hesitated, his silence pulling her up to her full height.

"Wes?"

"It's your pa. He's real sick. Marc wired, but Tom beat us to it. Marc wants you to come home as soon as you can."

The color drained from Jessica's face. She gasped and turned away, trying to get control of her emotions.

Wesley stepped around the basket, resting his hands on her shoulders and pulling her close. "I'll make sure you get there. You just be ready by mornin', okay?"

She nodded.

"Are you all right?"

Again she nodded.

"Go on upstairs and start packin'. I'll send Ma up to help."

Jess turned back to him, but she didn't meet his gaze. She bent over and retrieved the set of clothing she'd been searching for, handing them to him. "I think these will work for Tom. They're Carlson's. Please give Tom my thanks. What a horrible night to have to ride so far."

"I will. He's going to make sure we make the stage in the mornin'." She started to pass him, but he stopped her. "Jess, are you all right?"

At last, she met his gaze. "I will be."

"I'm not going to send you alone, Jess. Ma and I will go with you." He paused, his heart breaking as he took her hands and looked deep into her eyes. "I love you, Jess. I'll be right there. We'll do this together."

A single tear slipped down her cheek. "Thank you, Wes. I love you too. I'll be all right." She walked by him, gently squeezing his arm as she went. "I'll be all right."

Chapter 53

Marcus met them in the yard. He stood silently, watching the wagon with little more than a feeble wave as they approached. For a moment, Jess saw the sixteen-year-old boy, standing stoop-shouldered by the barn all those years ago. Instinctively, she reached for Anna's hand.

The woman responded with a squeeze. "It's okay," she soothed. "Don't be afraid."

Jess blinked back tears and watched as the figure on the lawn grew larger. Jonah had met them at the livery. His presence and the absence of both her brothers had driven home the reality of their situation. Now her chest tightened. For a brief moment, she feared she wouldn't be able to breathe, but as the wagon pulled to a stop Marc caught her eye. A warm smile touched his lips, and she relaxed.

The farmer stepped up to the back of the wagon and began unloading their bags as they climbed down. He greeted Jonah, telling him to take the team to the barn and then come in for supper. He greeted Wes with a hardy handshake and introduced himself to Anna. He kissed Jessica's cheek and took her hand without a word. Then he led them all inside.

"Mary," he said as they entered the tiny cabin.

The slender blonde turned toward them. "Oh, Jess!" Her whispered exclamation was as full of tears as of excitement. She discarded the spoon she'd been using at the stove and came to her older sister's side.

"I'm so glad you're here, so glad," she said, embracing her sister. "Now we're all together as it should be."

Jess forced back the tears she'd been shunning for days. She held her sister tight, both of them finding comfort in the other's presence. At last, Jess stepped back and looked into Mary's tired, blue eyes. "There's someone I want you to meet. You know Wes, but this is his mother, Anna. Anna, this is my sister, Marianne."

Mary extended a hand to greet the woman, but Anna stepped forward and took Mary into her arms. "It's good to finally meet you, dear girl. I've heard so much about you."

Mary stepped back from the embrace. "I'm glad to meet you too. Thank you for taking care of Jess for us."

Anna chuckled. "I think Jess takes care of me most of the time."

"Mama will be glad to see you both. Supper will be soon. Make yourselves at home. The Nausbaums will be here shortly. They'll take you home with them after we've eaten. It'll be crowded—very crowded—but they're our closest neighbors."

"That's fine, Mary," Wes said. "Whatever makes things easiest for your family."

"Thank you."

"Marc," Jess said, turning to her silent brother, "how is Papa?"

The young man sighed deeply, his somber eyes full of pain. He looked away for a moment. When he looked back, the hurt had been hidden—buried—and replaced with a strange emptiness. He plunked his hat back on his head and managed to meet her gaze.

"Papa's going home soon, Jess. That's all I can tell you." Then he left the house.

Jess turned back to Mary, but Mary was no longer beside her. The younger woman had returned to the food on the stove, and picked up the conversation with a nervous quake in her voice.

"Ma and Jon are with Papa right now, Jess. Perhaps you can go in to see him when they're done. He's weak, but still full of love. Hannah's in Marc's room with her little ones. Our little people are upstairs with Joy."

"Do you need help, Mary?"

Mary didn't turn to face the others. With trembling hands, she picked up a knife and began chopping potatoes into irregular shapes. "I have bread in the oven. It should be about ready if you want to check it. If Wesley doesn't mind hunting down Marc or Jake and helping them get the extra table set up, that would be helpful. Then we could put the dishes on and be ready to sit down when the Nausbaums get here."

Jess, hearing the pain in her sister's voice, crossed the room and stepped up to her side. She placed an arm around her and pulled her in tight. "Are you all right?"

Mary nodded and wiped at an escaping tear.

"Oh, Jess," she whispered. "Marc's givin' us all he's got and then some, but he's hurtin' something terrible inside. It's all I can do to watch. He was doing so well after Jake came, but the last week…" she shook her head sadly. "He just keeps going and going, night and day. He won't give himself a chance to stop and think. I think he's afraid to. Oh, Jess, I'm so glad you're home. And I'm so glad Anna and Wes came with you. We need you."

The evening passed quietly. Cynthia was glad to have her daughter home and equally as glad to have Anna and Wesley there. They didn't feel like strangers. In a short time, they had become family. Wesley brought needed strength. His quiet presence and willingness to help wherever possible carried them on a little better. Cynthia found comfort in Anna's joyful spirit. Knowing that Anna had already come through the valley they were entering gave Cynthia hope. They would survive the days of pain that lay ahead of them all.

"Where's Marc?"

"Hmm?" Cynthia said, looking up at Jon from her seat in the rocking chair near the fireplace.

"Were you sleepin'?"

"No, just thinking. Didn't even realize I'd closed my eyes."

He smiled at that. "You should try to get to bed earlier tonight, I think."

"I doubt your youngest brother will allow that. That child never sleeps."

Jon grinned. "Sounds very familiar. Do you know where Marc is?"

"No. I haven't seen him since the Nausbuams and Closes left. He could be down at the barn, closing things up. I doubt he's turned in for the night, but he might have. He looked awful tired at supper."

"He's looked awful most of the day. Although, I can't say I've seen that much of him."

"He's trying not to get underfoot. He's also trying to get the planting finished. Has to make sure we have food in the fall."

Jon didn't respond. He thought back to his conversations with his brother the previous fall when Jonathan had been so sick. He knew Marc was dealing with things in his own way. He didn't understand it, but his mother seemed to. Jon knew it would be best not to push Marc to be near, or even in, the house more often. Something told him Marc would come to see his father when no one else was around. That was just Marc.

The front door swung open just then, and Marc strode inside.

"Oh," Jon said. "We were just wonderin' where you were."

"Sorry. I guess I forgot to tell anyone where I was going. I rode home with the Nausbaums. I helped the preacher and Wes get settled in the barn while Anna and Millicent re-situated everything in the house. Then I walked home through the fields to see how things look. ...We need to have a good rock-pickin'."

Jon chuckled. "We always need to have a good rock-pickin' around here."

"Pretty much. Did you need something?"

"No. We were just wonderin' where you were."

"Oh. Well, now you know. Think I'll head down to the barn unless you need something, Ma."

"I'd take a hug."

A grin slid across the farmer's weary face. "I can handle that." He crossed the room, kissed her cheek and whispered his love as he embraced her. Then he straightened and slapped his brother's shoulder.

"Goodnight to you both," he said, and then he was gone.

Morning dawned gray and heavy, though there was no rain. The dreariness slowed them all. Breakfast was later than normal. The chores were later than normal. Devotions finished late as well. But no one seemed to mind. The Nausbaums brought Wes and Anna around ten and then returned to their own little corner of the prairie. Jess wished they had stayed. Their presence brought a calm that her heart longed for. Yet with that thought, she realized her heart needed something more than the peace found in a friend's presence. It needed the confidence she'd found in the Lord during the long days of waiting for Wesley's return. Perfect peace, she knew, would only come from keeping her mind on the Lord—from dwelling in His presence, in the shadow of the Almighty.

Shortly after the Nausbaums' departure, Jess slipped into her father's room, followed closely by Wesley and his mother.

"Papa," she said in a low voice.

The man turned his head ever so slightly in the direction of her voice.

"Jess?"

"Yes, Papa. It's me. Wesley did as you said and brought me home."

"Is he here with you?"

"Yes, and his mother too."

"Thank you, Wes." Jonathan's voice was weak and raspy, but his face showed the joy and gratitude he felt in his heart. "I'm glad you came. Both of you. I thought—I thought you might wait too long."

"I'm sorry we didn't come sooner, sir."

"No. Your timin' is good." He sighed. "I'm goin' home soon. ...I'm glad you're here. ...Don' let it hurt you, Jess...not like before. ...I'm ready to go. ...I'm glad to go. I'm...I'm tired, Jess."

Tears pooled in the young woman's eyes as she reached for her father's hand. "I know, Papa."

Jess felt Wesley's hand on her shoulder. A tear slipped before she could catch it, sliding down her cheek and splashing on her father's hand.

"Don't cry, love. I'm at peace."

She leaned forward, kissing his cheek. "Thank you for loving me in spite of everything, Papa," she whispered. "Thank you for never giving up on me and for being such a wonderful father to all of us." She squeezed his hand again, stepping back and wiping her tears. They were quiet for a long time. Then he spoke.

"Have you seen our new little one?"

"Yes, Papa. He's beautiful. He looks like you."

"Tha's wha' they tell me. Poor thing."

"Papa! Oh, Papa, that's a good thing. You're one of the most handsome men I know."

Jonathan chuckled softly. "I'm glad you think so. ...I don' know if he'll agree."

A few moments later, Jon watched as they left the room, all smiling. It made him happy. He was glad they had come. Still, he was concerned for the family as a whole. Marc had been in to see his father at lunch, but beyond that, he'd kept himself busy. Cynthia assured Jon that it was the younger man's way, but it didn't dissuade his concern. He caught himself watching his brother throughout the evening meal—every bit as close as he watched his parents.

Chapter 54

"What do you mean Wes is gone?" Jason said as he dropped onto a bench at Cale Bennett's kitchen table. "What's wrong with that man all of a sudden? Used to be you could hardly get him off the ranch. Now, he's disappeared twice in the last four months."

Cale raised an eyebrow at his friend.

"What? I don't get it."

"You really don't know?"

"What am I supposed to know?"

Cale cleared his throat. "Well, the easy answer, as Dunn would sum it up, is that Wes has fallen in love."

"Are you serious?"

Cale nodded. "That's where he was in January and February."

"Where?"

"Asking my Uncle Jonathan for permission to court Jess."

The preacher's eyes widened, delight dancing in them. He chuckled, then broke into full laughter. "I can't tell you how glad I am to hear that. I've been worried about him. I can't think of a better match. So where is he now? They didn't get married without me did they?"

Cale shook his head. "That's the hard answer. Tom brought news from Twin Pines. Uncle Jonathan isn't doing well. Wes took Jess and Anna home. They were just hoping to make it in time to see him."

The preacher sobered, and Cale thought for a brief moment that he saw tears in his eyes.

"That girl has been through a lot over the last year and a half, hasn't she?"

Cale nodded but said nothing.

"Are you going?"

"No. I thought about it. But their house will already be full. I'm hoping we can go later. ...Sometimes you need someone to be there later."

Jason nodded. "I agree. I'm sure you'd *like* to be there though."

Cale shrugged, his resignation obvious in the motion. "Yes, but I know this isn't the time. ...So what are you so fired up about that you need to talk with everyone?"

"I brought Scotch back from Maiden. Or maybe he brought me back. I'm not exactly sure. Anyway, you're all going to want to hear what he has to say. We may be able to solve several problems. Cale...he..." the man paused to lean forward and lower his voice as if afraid someone would hear some great secret. "Cale, he has a family."

"What?" Cale hissed, leaning forward and resting his forearms on the table. "Are you sure?"

"Yes. I spent two weeks with them."

"Did he get married? When?"

"It's the same family he's always had."

"Alma?"

"Yes. She's never given up on him. She's in Maiden with their daughter, and she is whipping him into shape. I also have signed statements from six people confirming that Scotch was in Maiden when the fire started. But more importantly, I think we can help his family get back to where they need to be, whether that's here or back east. We can help the women that still need jobs and help the church and school without having to build a new building."

"What? How can you do all that?"

"Well, it will take all of us, but I think it can be done. That's why I wanted to talk to everyone. Maybe we should get Tiedemann and Dunn in the morning, and go out to Edelman's. Talk it over. Scotch is going to be itchin' to get back to Maiden."

But Cale was shaking his head. "We can't go out to Edelman's place. We have to leave Edelman out of things for now."

"What? Why?"

"Because we're pretty sure someone on that ranch started the fire. Some things happened here while you were gone."

"Do you know who did it?" the preacher said, still whispering.

Cale nodded. "We think so. We've just got to figure out how to prove it and how to approach it."

"What are you two in here whispering about like a couple of schoolboys up to no good?" Susan said as she entered the kitchen.

The men sat back in their seats, attempting to take on an air of innocence.

"Look at you," she said. "You're up to something. Both of you."

Cale grinned. "Maybe. But according to the preacher, it might be something you'd approve of. Why don't you join us? Then you can be part of the conspiracy."

The woman laughed. "I'm not sure I want any part of your plotting."

"It might give us a better chance to help Miss Parker."

Susan hesitated. "You mean it?"

The preacher nodded.

Cautiously, Susan sat down on the end of a bench and slid in next to her husband. "What did you have in mind?"

Chapter 55

Marcus slipped into the dark house, wishing he could keep the door latch from clicking. He removed his boots at the door and tiptoed through the common area to the kitchen. To his surprise, the kettle of coffee at the back of the stove was still warm. He poured a cup and turned back to face the rest of the house. His eyes swept across the dark room. The only light came from the glowing embers in the fireplace. The doors to his bedroom and his father's room both stood open. An overwhelming sense of loss filled his heart at the sight. A great void would soon overtake every nook and cranny of the home his father had built.

Marc sighed, pushing the thought away and padding to his father's bedroom door. He stood there for a long time, sipping the coffee and watching the sleeping man through the darkness. When the coffee was gone, he went to his father's bedside, pulled up a chair, and sat down. A movement caught his eye, and for a moment hope filled his heart.

"Are you awake, Papa?" he whispered.

But there was no response. Marc set the empty cup on the floor and leaned back in his seat to study his father.

"I'm not ready for you to go yet, Papa. I know that's selfish. I know you're ready to go…but I don't want you to go yet."

He groaned. In his heart, Marc knew he must do now as he had done that night on the butte all those months ago. He must put his father in God's hands, just as he had done with Jessica. But he found this much more difficult.

"Oh, Lord," he whispered, "forgive me for being so selfish. I know he'll be better off with You." The tears came without warning. They streamed down his face, dampening his shirt and trousers as they fell unchecked. "Lord, please help me. I don't know how to do this—any of it. I need him still. Please—" His voice trailed off. He didn't know how to finish. He didn't know how to pray. He knew what he should say, but somehow he couldn't find the strength to say it.

Marc leaned forward on the bed. He buried his forehead in the blankets and cradled his father's hand against his cheek.

"Oh, Papa, I love you."

It was then that Jon, having heard his brother come into the house and all that had followed, stooped down beside Marc. He placed a hand on the younger man's back. The big doctor rested his cheek against his brother's shoulder and took hold of his arm.

Marc sighed a heavy, wobbly sigh.

"God won't forsake us, Marc. You know that. I know you do. ...It's not lovin' Pa any less to let him go, Marc. He needs to know you're okay. That you're as ready as he is."

"But I'm not. I'm not, Jon. I've never been without him, not since he was away with the railroads. That was so long ago. I don't know how to do it. I don't know how to help Ma and the other children without his help."

"You still have his principles to live by, and you still serve the same God who has guided him—and you through him. Marc, Papa just wants you to follow God as you always have."

Marc considered his brother's words, but he did not respond. He thought back to the first conversation he'd had with his father after the barn collapsed. Marc had felt as though he'd failed his pa and the entire family. But Papa had told him the same thing Jon had just said. He sighed, unable to process everything in his heart.

"He needs to be able to go, Marc. He needs to know that you're able to walk on without him. I know in yourself you're not ready, neither am I. But in the Lord—in the Lord, we'll make it. He'll carry you now just like He's carried you through everything else. Come on, let's get to bed. Why don't you lay down on the sofa, and I'll bring a blanket out for you?"

Marc shook his head. "I want to stay here. I just want to be with him. I'm fine now, Jon. Thank you, but I want to be with him."

"All right."

Jon squeezed his brother's shoulder. He stood and studied the pitiful scene before him. Marc still leaned upon the bed, his head resting against his father's side. He still clung to the man's hand. But the tension in Marc's frame had lessened. He seemed more at peace. Jon knew that, as uncomfortable as the position had to be, Marc would soon be sleeping.

"I love you, Marc."

Once again, Marc could only sigh, but Jon knew his brother's heart. He knew his love was returned. He knew his brother's grief wasn't only for their father, not only for his own loss but for every member of their family. Jon gnawed at his lip. He swallowed back his own tears and then tiptoed back to bed.

* * *

Jess awoke first. She crept out of the loft bedroom and made her way downstairs. Like Marc, she was surprised to see the two bedroom doors standing open. And like her brother, she went to her father's bedroom.

"Marcus!" she gasped, immediately covering her mouth and hoping she hadn't woken anyone. Only a faint light crept in at the eastern windows, but it was enough to see her father and her brother. Tears climbed in her eyes as she stared into the room, unsure of what to do. "Oh, Marc."

"Is everything all right?" Jon asked, stepping bleary-eyed into the common area as he spoke.

Jess motioned for him to come near. When he had, she pointed toward Marc.

"He's been there most of the night. Just like that. Came in around eleven or twelve. Guess he must've been workin' on something late and just finally made it to the house."

"Should I wake him?"

"No. Jake and Danny and I can take care of the chores. If he's slept like that all night, he must be exhausted."

"It'll be a wonder if he can even move, sittin' all hunched over like that. I don't think I'd even be able to get out of the chair."

Jon smiled. "My back's aching just thinkin' about it. Let's close the door. He'll be embarrassed if the others see him like that."

The two left their younger brother, closing the door softly and dreading what the day might hold.

An hour later, Cynthia slipped into the room. Her intent had been to call her son to breakfast. But seeing him as he was, she couldn't simply wake him. She wasn't as surprised as Jess had been. She knew her son well. She had expected this or something like it.

She set an old, rickety chair next to her son and seated herself. Cautiously laying a hand on his back, she sat in silence. For a moment, she considered the pair beside her. The two men were so much alike, and yet each different in their own unique way. Together they had been her support year after year. Now, before the week was out, one of them would be gone, and the other would feel as though the earth had shattered beneath him.

The woman sighed. She liked to think she would be as strong for her son as he would attempt to be for her, but she doubted her ability to do so. She wondered, in fact, how she would even survive. She had to survive. She had eight children unmarried. One was still an infant. Jess would most likely be married before the end of the year. There would be a wedding to plan. She would have to go on. But the thought of all those weddings, all those courtships, all those growing-up days without her Jonathan brought emptiness to her heart. This was not how they had dreamed of their story ending. They would grow old together. That had been the plan. But plans...plans and dreams are not reality.

Tears trickled down her cheeks. She didn't wipe them away. She let them fall as she studied every line of her husband's face. It had changed so much over the previous months. But he had not changed. He had remained faithful to the Lord, faithful to their family, faithful to pray, faithful to love her. She saw the pain on his face, the weariness. She wouldn't hold him back from heaven. But, oh, how the thought of letting him go ripped at her heart.

"He's Yours, Lord," she whispered. "I know he'll obey You. I know when You call him, he'll go. I only ask that You comfort, strengthen, and help us when he's gone. For while he'll be so much better, our hearts will be breaking."

The sound of the children coming to the breakfast table broke into her prayer. She wiped her tears and shook her sleeping son.

"Marcus, son, you need to wake up. It's time to get up."

Marc groaned. His body ached. His back and shoulders were stiff, and his head swam with exhaustion.

"Son, breakfast is ready. Come on, sit up."

He tried to obey, nearly falling from the chair in the process. Startled and confused, he grabbed the seat and stared at her wild-eyed.

"It's okay, Marc. You're all right. Just a little off balance."

He shot a quick glance in his father's direction, but the movement was a mistake. He groaned again. "That wasn't a good way to sleep."

Cynthia smiled and pulled him into a motherly embrace.

"I'm sure it wasn't. It'll be a wonder if you can stand. Jon and the boys already took care of the morning chores. Why don't you come out and get some breakfast? Then you can lie down on your own bed for an hour or so. I'm sure you'll feel better."

She saw him glance hesitantly at his father.

"It'll be all right, Marc. He'll be fine if you leave for a while. It'll give Jon and me a chance to care for some of his needs. Come on, let's go get breakfast. The others will be waitin'."

"I'll be there in a minute. I need to wake up a little more before facin' a whole table full of conversation."

Cynthia chuckled. "You do look like you're still half asleep."

"I am."

"Come when you're ready, but don't be too long."

"I won't."

Marc watched his mother go and then turned toward his father. "Are you awake, Pa?"

There was no answer. Marc sighed. His father's face held pain, and yet it was full of peace.

"I know you're ready to go, Papa. I don't want to be the one holding you back. Can we...can we just have one more day together, now that everyone is here? Just one more time together around God's Word. Can we do that, Pa? Maybe we can't, but I would so much love to just have one more day. I'm going to get some breakfast. I'll be back in a bit. I love you."

The young man unfolded his stiff body and leaned over to kiss his father's forehead. Then he staggered out into the common area of the house, still rubbing his eyes.

✿ ✿ ✿

Cynthia did everything in her power to slow the day. She didn't want it to be gone. She wanted to cherish every moment, to savor it, to cling to it. As she had predicted, Marc had gone to his room after breakfast, shut the door, and slept for two hours. The Nausbaums and Closes arrived while he was still sleeping. Throughout the day, each member of the family took his or her turn sitting with Papa. The man said little but seemed to enjoy listening very much.

As supper was approaching, Cynthia sat with her husband, allowing the other women to prepare the meal. As the women worked, their quiet conversation and occasional laughter drifted into the bedroom.

"I'm glad to hear them happy," Jonathan said. "It gives me joy."

She smiled. "They'll be glad to know it."

"Cynthia. You...you know how much I love you, don' you? ...I haven't neglected to show you, have I?"

The woman choked back tears. When she spoke, her voice was soft and trembling. "You have shown me your love in a thousand ways, day after day. Even when we disagreed, you still found a way to show me. I've never doubted your love, Jonathan. Never. Not every woman can say that, but I can. And I love you so. You know that, don't you?"

The man reached for her hand. "Never doubted it."

A knock at the doorframe caught their attention. Cynthia looked up to see Joy standing nervously in the doorway.

"Supper's ready, Ma."

"Thank you, Joy. I'll be right there." Cynthia watched the girl go and then turned back to her husband, squeezing his hand.

"Watch out fo' her, love," the man said. "She concerns me...more than any...of the other children. ...I'm sure she'll be fine...with the Lord's help, ...but she is so quiet. ...It's hard...to know wha' she's thinking."

"I promise, Jonathan. We'll all look out for one another. Do you need anything before I go to supper?"

"No. I'll be fine."

"You're sure?"

"Yes. Go on. I'll listen from here."

Cynthia smiled, kissed her husband, and went to the table.

Chapter 56

Jonathan listened as his family gathered in the common area. There were too many of them, he knew, to fit around the table. They'd be using the makeshift table Marc kept stored in the barn.

Jonathan was content to hear their chatter. Puss and her funny questions caught his attention. Then there was Danny and his squeaky, changing voice. Elizabeth with her quiet politeness, always seeking a way to help someone else, passing this, getting that. Joy spoke little, except to ask for food or to answer questions directed at her. Marianne's voice seemed almost musical at times, full of love and joy, just as her mother's had always been.

The gentleness that had nearly disappeared from Jessica's life a year earlier now permeated every word. He heard no trace of the anger that had followed Joe's death. For that, he was relieved. Wesley too had a certain calmness of spirit about him that complimented Jessica's manners. He never could have found a better match for his eldest daughter. How grateful he was for God's working in their lives.

Anna spoke little, but when she did Jonathan heard joy, vivacity, and wisdom in her words. Jon and Hannah kept the conversation moving with questions for everyone. The Nausbaums and Jacob were also at the meal. They seemed such a part of the family that he'd almost forgotten they weren't.

When Cynthia spoke, Jonathan heard the love in her voice. He knew she must be weary. He knew she must be anxious, though she hid it well. How he loved her. How grateful he was that she had been given to him of all men. So many others could have had her, but God had given her to him.

"Papa." Marc's voice broke into his reverie, and he realized he'd heard nothing from his son throughout the meal.

"Yes?"

"We're almost done eatin', and we'll be readin' soon. Do you want us to come in here with you, so you can listen?"

A weary, lopsided smile crept across the man's face. "I've been waitin' for tha' all day."

Fear gripped Marc's heart. Maybe it was just the way Jonathan had said it. Maybe it was just his father eagerly awaiting time with his family. But he couldn't help wondering if the other man had heard him. The thought made his stomach churn.

"I'll have everyone come in when we're finished. It'll just be a few minutes."

"Marcus," Jonathan said, hoping to stop his son before he turned back to the rest of the house.

"Yes?"

The older man hesitated, knowing his question might seem strange.

"Did you need something, Papa?"

"I was wonderin'…have the roses started to bloom?"

Marc smiled at the question. Tears crept into his eyes. He glanced over his shoulder toward his mother and then back at his father. "I've seen a few. I'll bring some in and put them by your bed. When the sun sets, they'll be there for her."

Again the lopsided smile came, but this time it seemed weaker. "Thank you, son."

Marc sneaked out of the house while the others were finishing their meal. He went to a place along the lane where he had seen several small bushes of roses. He cut several short stems of the delicate, pink roses then headed home. He removed his hat, hiding the roses in its crown as he snuck them to his father's bedside. He put them in a glass of water and set them on the crate they used as a table next to the bed. Then he returned to the common area.

"All right, everyone," he said, "there's still chorin' and the like to be done tonight. Once everyone's finished eatin' and the tables have been cleared, we'll go in with Pa and read our psalm. Let's hurry. Puss, you've been gnawin' at that same piece of bread for a quarter-hour. It's time to finish."

One by one, the members of the family trickled into Jonathan's room. Each of them took a moment to greet the man with a kiss or an embrace, or a simple, "Hello, Papa, we've come to read the Bible together." Twenty people crowded into the tiny space, but somehow it didn't seem crowded. It seemed just right. They all belonged there, every one of them.

"Who remembers which psalm we're supposed to read tonight?" Marc asked as usual.

"I do," came a small, cheerful voice from the floor.

"All right, Puss, which one?"

"Psalm one hundred twenty-seven."

"Very good. You've been paying attention. This is a special psalm. It's a good psalm for us tonight because our whole family—our whole house—is here together. Listen closely and consider why it's so important for us.

> "Except the Lord build the house, they labor in vain that build it: except the Lord keep the city, the watchman waketh but in vain. It is vain for you to rise up early, to sit up late, to eat the bread of sorrows: for so he giveth his beloved sleep. Lo, children are an heritage of the Lord: and the fruit of the womb is His reward. As arrows are in the hand of a mighty man; so are children of the youth. Happy is the man that hath his quiver full of them: they shall not be ashamed, but they shall speak with the enemies in the gate."

Marc paused to gather his thoughts, but before he could say anything his father spoke, his voice weak and his words slurring together.

"Children, I'm so happy. ...My quiver's full. ...The Lord...has built our house... He's built it...and I am so happy."

Marc couldn't have chosen a better psalm for the evening if he had tried. He felt Marianne slip her arm through his and glanced down at her with a smile, not surprised to see tears in her eyes. He let his gaze drift around the room as he picked up where his father had left off.

"We need to let the Lord continue to build our house. Many things cause us to worry, but we're not to take those things upon ourselves. I'm guilty of doin' that more often than I'd like to think. But we're to let God lead and let Him build. Sittin' up late won't help." He stopped, chuckling to himself. "It just makes you tired the next day."

Jon sent a meaningful smile in Marc's direction. He knew it took courage for his brother to admit his own weakness in front of everyone. He knew the passage was hitting very close to home, and yet he could see Marc was receiving it with grace.

"We're simply to trust," Marc continued, "to rest in the Lord. That's how the Lord gives His beloved sleep." As his eyes traveled the room,

Marc could see he wasn't the only one who sensed the significance of the psalm for their family. Soon, God would be giving one of His beloved sons sleep from which they would never see him get up again. Marc also saw that the others realized they must continue on as they had before. He saw this recognition in Jessica's face, in his mother's eyes, in Jon and Hannah and Mary. He smiled at each of them, knowing he need say nothing more. They would all walk on together.

"Who would like to pray for us tonight?"

"I would, son."

"All right, Papa."

The room grew still.

"Dear Father," Jonathan began, "thank You...fo' my family...fo' their love. Bless them. Guide them. Love them. Strengthen them. Please, continue...to build our house. Help us...to trus' You...to trus' Your plan. To let You...give us sleep. In Jesus name, we ask, amen."

A gentle wave of whispered amens floated through the room. Marc and Cynthia watched as the others slowly, one by one, kissed Papa goodnight and went to some other part of the house. At last, Marc stood and leaned over his father. Embracing him, he whispered, "Thank you, Papa. I brought the roses. They're on the table. I love you. Goodnight. Sleep well."

"Thank you, Marc. I love you, son."

Cynthia waited until Marc had gone, grateful that he pulled the door shut. She took her husband's hand and lay down on the bed next to him. She cuddled her cheek against his and held his fragile frame as best she could.

"I love you so much, Jonathan. Thank you—" but she couldn't say what she wanted to say without breaking into sobs. She swallowed back her tears and kissed his cheek. "Thank you for your prayer."

She stayed with him a few moments more until she felt she must go. Then she kissed him gently. "I love you, dear. Rest."

Cynthia joined Jess and Mary in the kitchen. The three women set about washing the dishes and storing the leftover food. She worked as diligently as ever, but a nervous, sick feeling had risen in her stomach. She couldn't keep her eyes from wandering to her husband's room.

An hour passed. The women had almost finished in the kitchen when Elizabeth called out from Jonathan's bedroom. "Mama! Come see the sunset! It's beautiful!"

Cynthia laid aside her towel and went to answer her daughter's call. As she reached the room, she stopped short. Jonathan's face was so peaceful, so full of joy—but he was no longer there.

"Look, Mama, it's as if heaven opened a window, so we could have a glimpse."

Blinking back tears, the woman came to her daughter's side and wrapped an arm around her shoulders. The sun had sunk to the bottom of the sky. It painted the empyrean expanse a rich, vibrant purple, etching every line of every tree and cloud and ridge with golden light. The child was right. Heaven had certainly opened its windows.

"You're right, sweet one. I think it has."

The woman kissed her daughter's head and then turned back toward her husband. For the first time, she noticed the small glass of pink roses, their petals illuminated by the golden sunlight. She bit her lip, covering her mouth in an effort to hold back her emotion. Tears trickled down her cheeks as she stepped closer. She stroked the delicate petals, her sweet husband's last gift to her. She ran her fingers through his graying hair and down his cheek. Her chest tightened as she leaned over to kiss his forehead. God had given His beloved sleep. Jonathan would suffer no more. He had gone home.

Chapter 57

The door clicked shut behind Marcus, but he didn't hear it. He only faintly heard his brother's voice behind it. He knew Jon was offering to help with the chores. He'd intentionally shut the door before the offer had been made. He didn't want help, not now.

The wind tossed a spray of mist into his face. He pulled at the collar of his unbuttoned coat and shrugged against the unexpected spring rain. The day had been beautiful until sunset. Then the whole world had come to a crashing halt. Black clouds had rolled in, and the rain had begun.

Marc's chest tightened at the thought. His breath caught in his throat, and he hastened his pace toward the barn, hoping to escape the anguish that dogged his heels. He gasped as he opened the large door and strode into the dark, familiar building. But the breath did not release the pain. Instead, he felt it spread from his chest to his neck and across his shoulders.

Tears burned his eyes, but he held them back. Someone would see them, someone who needed him to be strong. He stepped into the tack room and grabbed a lantern from the worktable. He fumbled about, fingers trembling, until at last he had the lamp lit. Shirley was waiting. Today was no different for her than any other day. She must be milked. She must be fed — like all the other livestock.

The lantern cast eerie shadows as he crossed the large building to the stall where the cow stood waiting. He hung the light on a nail inside the stall and then crossed the room again. This time he went to another lantern, which was securely mounted on the opposing wall. He lit it, followed by another further down the row of stalls. The animals began to stir, sensing their supper wasn't far off.

Marc stood silent, his gaze panning around the high ceilinged room. They had built it together — he and Jon and Papa. They had worked day and night. Pa had designed it. Planned every inch. Marc's lip quivered, and he bit down hard to stop it. He had to be strong for the others. They were depending on him.

He scooped up the milking stool and bucket and then returned to the cow. She snorted as he pushed past her, his gentle shove causing her to sidestep. The bucket clanked against the floor as he positioned it. He warmed his hands, rubbing them together, rubbing them against his pants legs—just as his pa had taught him.

The tears were there again. His chest was tightening further still. It was going to explode, he was sure of it. He had to keep going, just like he always had. He *would* keep going and then...and then there would be no Papa to talk things over with.

Shring. Shring. The milk hit the side of the bucket, faster and faster. Tears streamed down the farmer's face, dropping into the bucket and mixing with the milk. He had to get control of himself. Someone would hear him, someone would see...but it hurt. Holding it in hurt. He would explode.

But what about Gretel? What if she saw? It would frighten her. She had never seen him weep. He couldn't let that happen. He drew in a sharp, rattling breath and forced the tears back.

Shring. Shring. Shring.

The others needed him. They all needed him...but, oh, how he needed Papa.

"Oh, Lord, I know he's better off with You. Forgive me for wantin' him back...but, oh, how I want him back!" The words didn't merely fall from his lips. They were torn from his shredded heart and flung at the walls around him. They bounced back empty and unanswerable. Papa wasn't coming back. Papa was never coming back. Never. It was over. This was how his story would end.

The young man's body shook. He gasped again and cried out in the pain that coursed through him. He leaned forward, resting his head against Shirley's flank, and wept.

He had known this day would come, had done everything in his power to prevent it, had somehow hoped that his efforts would ease the pain—but they hadn't. Papa was still gone. All these years, he had managed to carry the load, but now, how would he do it? How would he carry the others when he couldn't carry his own pain?

The cow bawled, and Marc lifted a gentle hand to her side to quiet her. It was a natural instinct, a gesture he had made a thousand times. *That* was how he would survive. He would just do what had to be done. He would make sure they had food, make sure they were clothed, make sure the buildings were kept in repair. He would do it. He had to do it. Papa would want him to. He had promised...he had promised Papa.

The pain was back, ripping through every muscle. He wanted to hit something. That would help. Like when he'd stubbed his toe in the past and had the inexplicable desire to pound the table or bite his knuckle. If he could just hit something. Afraid of the overwhelming urge that had come over him, Marc stepped away from the cow. He stared at the animal, and she blinked back at him. He grabbed his hair, pulling for all he was worth, but it didn't help. He wasn't ready for this. He still wanted to do so much with Papa. There was so much he needed to learn.

Papa had urged him to marry, but Papa would never see any of his children marry, including Marc. He would never see Timothy walk or hear him speak, and Timothy would never know his Papa. Instead, Marc would be his pa. This wasn't the way it was supposed to work. This wasn't the way things were supposed to go. It was wrong, wasn't it? It had to be. How could this be right? They needed Pa. They all needed him.

The pain was too great. He could contain it no longer. With one explosive movement, the young farmer grabbed hold of the milk pail and flung it with all his might to the end of the barn. A loud cry of effort and pain filled the room. The bucket slammed against the far wall, spraying milk in every direction, unsettling the livestock, and clattering to the floor. Marc's heart trembled. The bucket lay empty, just as his heart—his tattered heart—was empty. Papa was gone.

"Seems I remember doing that once."

Marc, unaware that anyone had been watching, spun around at the sound of the calm voice behind him.

"Hurt so bad that it was either put my fist through a wall or throw the closest thing to hand as hard as I could."

Marc stared at Wes, not sure whether to be embarrassed or relieved at the other man's presence. Not sure he cared what the other man had to say, and yet afraid not to hear it.

"Milk cow wouldn't have a thing to do with me for days after that."

Marc's brow furrowed, questions filling his grey eyes.

"The closest thing to hand was a hatchet. ...Hurled it right past her. ...*Thwap*. ...stuck it right in the wall next to her head. She kicked at me every time I tried to milk her for the next week."

Despite himself, a laugh escaped the younger man. He wiped moisture from his face on the back of his sleeve. "Can't say I blame her," he managed as he searched for a handkerchief.

Wesley watched his friend without a word. He could see the agony in every movement.

"How long have you been standin' there?" Marc questioned, his embarrassment evident in his voice.

Wes shrugged. "Doesn't really matter. ...I knew you didn't want your brother's help, and I knew why. Ma wants us to stay here tonight. I thought I could sneak in here when your back was turned, go to the guest room, and just let your brother think you had help. I knew you didn't want any, but once I got down here, I thought maybe you needed it anyway."

Marc's gaze dropped to the floor. He could feel his neck and cheeks coloring with shame and embarrassment.

"Marcus, you do what you need to do. Do it down here or out in the field if you must, but don't hold it inside. It'll rip you up if you do."

"I don't think I can do this, Wes. I feel like my legs are gonna go out from under me just supportin' my own weight. How am I going to help everyone else? I need to be strong for them, and I've got nothin'."

Wes considered the question. He'd felt the same way once, but he'd been proven wrong. "That isn't true. If you take a deep breath and think about it for a moment, you'll see it isn't true. You're not alone in this. They aren't yours to carry, Marc. You still have a Father. It took me a long time to realize that, but it's true. You and I both still have a Father."

Marc blinked back at him, tears forming once again. He nodded. "I know."

"Jess tells me there's a place you folks like to go to think and pray."

"The butte."

"I thought as much. Why don't you head that way, and I'll take care of things here. I reckon you'll end up a bit wet, but the time with the Lord will be worth it. ...Ma and I will stay as long as your family needs us to. But, Marc, once we're gone, it's going to be on you and the Lord. Take advantage of us being here. Get your heart and your head where they need to be."

"Yes, sir." The words tumbled out as if from a little boy.

The corner of Wes' mouth twitched with an amused grin. "I'm sorry. I sound like a bossy older brother."

Marc smiled but didn't respond. He closed his eyes for a brief moment. His shoulders rose and fell with a deep sigh.

"Go on, Marc. I'll take care of things here."

"Thank you, Wes."

The rancher nodded. He'd done what needed to be done. That was all. But then, as the other man started to pass, he did something more. He reached out and wrapped his arms around his friend.

"God will carry you through this. I know because it's the only way I survived."

Marcus nodded again and stepped away. He tried to respond, but the words couldn't get past the horrendous lump in his throat. His chest was tight again. He blinked back tears, waved his gratitude to Wes, and hurried out of the building.

Chapter 58

The tiny loft room was silent. As ever, it's mattresses filled the floor, marshmallowing over one another. Someone stirred in the darkness, but no one said anything. No one slept. No one spoke. Five hearts lay weeping. Jessica, Marianne, Joy, Elizabeth, and Gretel—Jonathan Bennett's daughters—all stared into the night.

Jess blinked back shame. A year ago, she would have done anything, had done everything, to get away from her father. Now, she would have done anything to have his strong arms around her and to feel his gentle kiss on her forehead. She was glad they had reconciled, but how she regretted the time they had lost.

Joy, like Marc, felt the agony of bottled emotions. She mustn't cry. The others might be sleeping. She couldn't wake them. They were all so tired. She was exhausted, but sleep wouldn't come. Her mind and body wouldn't let it. Her eyes fixed on the ceiling. Her heart screamed. Her papa couldn't be gone, he couldn't. Not her Papa. She loved him. She needed him. He was hers—and she was his. He was the only one who had ever understood her. Now, she would be alone.

Elizabeth chewed at her nails. Tears trickled down her cheeks. How could the others sleep? She couldn't even close her eyes. When she did, she saw him—lifeless, cold, gone. He had left them. She would never be ready for him to go. She tasted blood and pulled her fingers back from her lips. Papa wouldn't like her chewing her nails. He always told her not to do it. She would stop. For Papa. She sighed. He would never know. Or would he? It had seemed heaven had opened its windows to send them a glimpse of its beauty at the very moment Papa had entered in. Perhaps he would see after all. She would never forget that sunset. She would never forget that moment. She would never forget him.

Mary listened. She could hear her sisters stirring. None of them were sleeping. She knew them well enough to know that. But that wasn't why she was listening. Marc had yet to come in. She listened for the front door to click into place and for him to cross the room to the kitchen, to fix a cup of tea or coffee, and find a seat in one of the rockers. But he hadn't come. Maybe he wouldn't. Maybe he would go straight to bed on one of the cots in the barn.

She wondered how he would handle this. She'd been wondering that for months now. Papa was the dearest person in the entire world to Marcus. How would he...He *would*. She knew he would. He would take it to the Lord and let God take him through it. He had to. It was the only way any of them would survive. If Marcus didn't let God do the work, none of them would make it. But, how could she put it all on Marc? She would need to bear up under the load as well. Her mother would need her. The ache in her heart would have to be put away. But how could she do that? It overwhelmed her. It suffocated her every time she dared consider it. *She would*. She would do it lovingly and as cheerfully as possible for all their sakes. She bit her lip, and prayed silently, "Oh, Lord, you will have to help me. I can't do it on my own. It hurts too deeply. I need Your strength."

Something stirred at her feet. She lifted her head but could see nothing in the darkness. Again, she felt the movement.

"Mary," a tiny voice summoned, "may I sleep with you?"

"Yes, Gretel. Come ahead."

There was little difference between where Gretel had been and the place into which she was now crawling. The two sisters had been separated only by Elizabeth and the break between two of the mattresses. But, Mary knew the girl's pain, and somehow the thought of the tiny child curling up next to her was a comfort.

Gretel struggled through the blankets, sat down on Mary's pillow, and squirmed in between the sheets. She slid close to her sister and pulled the young woman's arm around her.

"Markey isn't home yet," she whispered.

"I know. I've been listening too, Puss."

"Is he going to be okay? He looked sick when he went outside. Or angry. Was he angry?"

"No, Gretel, he wasn't angry. He was sad. Just like you."

"I'm going to miss Papa very much. Did he really go to heaven?"

"Yes, he went to heaven."

"Is he with Joe?"

A lump formed in Mary's throat. She heard her older sister gasp beside them. Mary reached for Jessica's hand and gave it a squeeze.

"Yes, Papa is with Joe."

The girl was quiet. "I want them to come back, Mary. I know Marc said Joe wouldn't come back, but I want them to."

"I know, Little Bit. We all do. But they are with God, and that is so much better than it is here. Papa isn't sick anymore. He isn't suffering. He can see again and walk again. He could dance if he wanted to."

"But can he see us?"

"I think so. I know God can see us, and He is going to take care of us, just like He always has." She kissed the girl's temple. "Go to sleep, little one. It will be morning soon."

But despite her advice to the child, Mary did not sleep. She lay quietly, cuddling Gretel, holding Jessica's hand, and listening, always listening.

✿ ✿ ✿

"Ma, it's well past midnight. Won't you go lay down?"

Cynthia tore her gaze away from her husband's face. She turned in her seat as her eldest son came to her side. He crouched down beside her, placing one hand on her arm and the other on her knee. He gazed up at her with imploring eyes.

"Please, Ma. You're exhausted."

"I can't leave him, Jon. I'll never see him again. Never. It's our last night together. I can't leave him."

Jon wiped tears from her cheek. "I know, but I don't think Papa would want you to make yourself sick. At least let me pull up his chair. It's more comfortable than that old, hard-backed thing you're sittin' in. Maybe you could at least doze for a while."

Helpless eyes looked back at him. She wanted him to tell her what to do. Was she so broken that she couldn't discern her own need for rest?

He rose. "Stand up, Ma." He watched as she stood, and reached for her as she swayed. She was trembling. He brought her into an embrace, and, not for the first time, she wept.

"Oh, Jon, I knew it would be today. I knew it, but no matter how prepared I tried to be…"

"Ma, we're never prepared. It's okay. We're going to be okay."

As he held her, he pulled the wooden chair out of the area beside the bed and set it behind him. His father's chair was too heavy to move that way, but he wanted to be ready when his hands were free.

"Come on," he said at last, "let me pull the chair up for you, and you can sleep here. I'll find an extra blanket or two."

Cynthia stepped aside and allowed her son to move her husband's soft armchair close to the bed. She let him help her into the seat.

"Has your brother come back yet?"

"Marc? No. I'm about to go lookin' for him."

"He's been gone since we put the little ones to bed. I'm worried about him, Jon. Is it still rainin'?"

"It's hard to tell. The mist is so fine. It falls gently without any sound on the roof or windowpanes. I'll go find him as soon as I get you settled."

The man's words cut at Cynthia's heart. Jon was her son, just as Marc was. He had cared for his father every moment of the last two weeks. The doctor had done everything he could to give the man just a few more days. She didn't want to burden him further. Not with her own needs, and not with Marc's.

"Jon, are you all right?"

The man stopped fidgeting with the blankets he had found on a footstool near the door and stared at his mother.

"What?"

"You've been so strong for the rest of us. I've hardly seen you wipe your eyes, let alone cry. I know you must feel just as broken as we do."

Jon looked away almost ashamed. He didn't feel broken. Not yet. "I'm numb, Ma. I've spent so long bracing myself against this that, now that we're here, my head knows what's going on, but my heart hasn't caught up. ...Like when you run hard into something, but the bruise shows up a week later. Let me be strong for you now, Ma, while I can...before I break." He winked at her, procuring the smile he'd hoped for. He spread the blankets over her and stooped to kiss her cheek.

"Goodnight, Ma."

Jon knew the butte well, but the night was dark. Even with a lantern, he found it difficult to distinguish the features of the world around him.

"Marcus, are you up here?" He called as he stepped out on the broad plateau. He waited, but no answer came. The butte was only a half-mile wide, which was enough if you were looking for someone in the dark. But it was a full mile long, and Marc had been known to walk its entire length if he were frustrated enough. That wasn't a happy prospect.

"Marcus!" Again, his call was met by silence. "Guess I'd better start walkin'." Jon moaned, but as he turned, a slight movement caught his eye. He stared toward a large boulder, the one to which most of them resorted when they needed to think. He'd heard something from that general area. He stepped closer, then closer still, but he couldn't see anything. It was too dark. A faint moan reached his ears, and he realized the sound wasn't coming from atop the boulder. It had come from its base. His gaze dropped to the ground to see the slumped form of his brother, resting against the rock, knees drawn up to chest, hat bent toward the rain. Jon made his way through the sandstone and tall grass. He dropped to his knees next to his brother.

"Marc, what are you doing out here?"

Marc stirred but said nothing.

"Asleep? How can you possibly be asleep in this mess? Marcus, wake up!"

The younger man's eyes opened and made contact with his brother's gaze.

"Are you mad?" Jon scolded. "What are you doing up here in the rain, sound asleep. No blankets. No fire. You'll make yourself sick."

"Did I fall asleep?"

"Yes! Now come on, get up."

The doctor stretched out a hand to his brother. Marc clasped on and pulled himself to his feet.

"I'm sorry. What time is it?"

"I have no idea. It's after midnight. Let's go get you some dry clothes. Ma's worried about you."

"I'm sorry, Jon. I didn't mean to—"

"I know. I'm just glad you're safe." Jon stepped back, stumbling slightly over a long wooden object. He stooped down, surprised to find a shovel at his feet. He lifted both the shovel and the lantern toward his brother. "What have you been doin'?"

"What needed to be done."

The lifeless, gray gaze that stared back at Jon through the lantern light sent a chill down his spine. He tossed the shovel aside and took his brother by the arm. "Come on. Let's get out of this rain."

"Jon, I— Thank you. Thank you for being here."

Jon stopped his persistent tugging at his brother's arm and stared at him through the darkness. "Did you ever think I wouldn't be? How could you think that, Marc?"

"I didn't think it. I feared it. I was afraid we wouldn't get to you in time, or that we'd get to town and find you'd gone out to help another patient. I was afraid it would just be Ma and the kids and Jake and me when it happened, and I wasn't sure I could handle that. Thank you."

Jon put an arm around his brother's shoulders. "I was afraid of that too, Marc, but God took care of it. Let's get back to the house. You can get some dry clothes, and then call it a night."

* * *

Hannah heard her husband and Marcus rummaging through drawers in the dark, but she didn't open her eyes. She listened to their hushed conversation, but caught only a word here or phrase there. She heard Marc leave the room and then bid his mother goodnight. She listened for the click of the latch as he retreated to the barn. She must have drifted off before hearing it because she found herself waking a few minutes later as her husband crawled into bed beside her.

She said nothing, not sure if he wanted to talk. He sighed but did not speak. He lay on his side, facing away from her. She was sure that was by design. He lay very still, much more so than normal. She sensed the tension in his body. He was fighting hard, but his emotions were about to win. She wrapped her arm around his middle and felt him slip his fingers between hers.

"It's okay to hurt, Jon. He was your papa too."

His answer was slow in coming. "It doesn't seem real," he whispered. "But I know it is. He's gone. Just like that. And we'll never see him again, never talk with him over coffee, never laugh together, or cry together."

"That's not true. You'll see him again someday."

Jon sighed. "I know, but not soon enough. Oh, Hannah, not soon enough."

The anguish he had defeated all evening swept over him. He felt his chest swell and his body temperature rise, and then the tears flooded down his cheeks. He hadn't followed in his Papa's shoes the way Marcus had. He hadn't stayed around the farm the way Marc had, but the hurt, the loss, the heartache went just as deep. The man he admired more than any other, loved and respected more than even he could fathom was gone, and the world would never be the same.

❖ ❖ ❖

Marcus sat on the floor of the stall where Shirley happily chomped away at her breakfast. He'd fed and milked her earlier than normal, but she didn't seem to mind. He'd encouraged Jon to get some rest, but he hadn't managed it himself. He'd tossed and turned for two hours and then given up. Now, he waited for the others to begin waking. He pulled his knees up toward his chest and went back to flipping through the little black New Testament the preacher had given him to keep in his workbench. He'd been flipping through it for at least an hour.

As he turned the pages, a word caught his eye. *Comforted.* Questions filled his mind. "Who," he wondered aloud, "in the early chapters of Matthew was being comforted?" He straightened in his seat and leaned over the book intently. Then he drew a sharp breath. Reading the verse over and over.

"Blessed are they that mourn, for they shall be comforted."

"Blessed!" he said almost indignantly. His mind reeled with the thought that the pain of the previous moments and hours could be the marks of a blessed man. "How does mourning equate to blessing? How —" but then he stopped. It wasn't the mourning that was blessed it was the mourner. And it wasn't because he was mourning. It was because he would be comforted — comforted by God. Another verse crept into the empty spaces of his heart. *"I will not leave you comfortless: I will come to you."* The thoughts settled around him like the warmth of a woolen blanket. For the first time since Papa had gone home through that beautiful sky, Marcus could breathe.

He knelt, burying his folded hands and his face in the straw. With tears of gratitude streaming down his cheeks, he whispered, "Thank You. I know You make no mistakes. Thank You that Papa's suffering is over and that he is safe with You. Thank You that *'death is swallowed up in victory'*. Thank You for Your promises and Your unfailing comfort and love."

Chapter 59

Wesley stared out the window of the stage, watching the countryside roll by. They weren't far from home now. Another two hours at the most should have them back in Grassdale. His mother slept in the seat opposite him, but he'd hardly slept since they'd left Twin Pines. His heart was with the Bennetts. He'd hated to leave them, but Jess had insisted they would be fine. He sighed, his thoughts traveling once more over the events of the previous two weeks.

Jonathan had been buried on the butte in an area the man had long ago marked out as the family cemetery. In the days that followed, the home had been the quietest Wes had ever seen such a crowded house. He and his mother had stayed on to help as long as the family needed them. To his surprise, Jess had brought up the subject of their departure one night after supper. She'd expressed concern that Wes needed to get back to the ranch. He'd insisted they were okay, but Jess knew his mother needed to get home to plant their own garden if they were to have any harvest later.

Wes had watched them all. He'd seen struggles from every corner of the house, but he'd also seen Jess be incredibly strong for her family. He was proud of her, but his heart ached at the thought of leaving her behind. He'd insisted they talk things over with their mothers and Jon and Marc. He smiled now at the thought of the conversation.

They'd waited until the younger children had gone to bed. Marianne and Hannah had joined them at Marc's request. They'd all settled around the fireplace with tea and coffee for everyone. The conversation had focused entirely on the practical—planting, plowing, spring round-ups. Wesley had fidgeted in his seat the entire time. What concerned him most seemed furthest from their minds. At last, he left his place on the floor near the fireplace and stepped up in front of Jess who sat on the sofa. With more passion than he'd intended, he'd blurted out, "There's only one way I'm leaving here, Jessica Bennett."

He'd realized later that he'd interrupted at least two other conversations, but even now he didn't care. He grinned to himself, remembering

344

the shock on the faces of the others as he'd rushed on. "Jess, the only way I'm leavin' is if you'll promise to marry me when I return."

Jon had nearly choked on his coffee, but he said nothing, so Wes had gone on.

"Jess," he'd said, "I know everyone has assumed it since the very beginnin'. We've talked about it. I've even talked about it with the school board, but I've never actually asked you. I don't want to leave without knowing. Will you, Jess, please be my wife?"

Jess blushed slightly, but her smile outshined the color in her cheeks. He'd seen tears in her eyes as she took his hand. "Yes, Wesley. Of course I will. I've just been waiting for you to say the word."

Marcus laughed heartily. "Finally! So...planting, roundup, wedding. I think that will work."

Jess had blushed again at her brother's teasing, but she didn't let it sway her confidence. She squeezed Wesley's hand and blinked the tears back. "I think that's what Papa would want. I don't think he'd want us to put it off any longer than that."

Even Wes had to admit that it was the least romantic proposal he'd ever heard of. Passionate? Yes. But not romantic. Still, he was glad for the way it had happened. He would never forget the smile it had brought to Cynthia's face. She'd needed that moment as much as he had.

Now, he and his mother were nearly home. They would plant the garden, round up and move the herd, and then head back to Twin Pines with the whole family. Just a few more weeks.

❀ ❀ ❀

Two and a half hours later, Dunn and Wesley sat alone in the Bennett's parlor, waiting for Cale and Jason to join them.

"Tell me again why we're stayin' here tonight, and not going home to our own beds?" Wes said, not bothering to hide the confusion and annoyance in his voice.

"Didn't you see the pile of ashes where the brothel used to be? We've got business to tend to, and I'd rather leave Ma and Travis here with Susan while we're tendin' to it. A group of us from town will head out before light. Carlson will have the men ready to ride by the time we get home."

Wes raised an eyebrow. He *had* noticed the burned-out building, but Cale had refused to discuss it with the women around. Something was afoot. Just the same, Wes had always been of the opinion that nothing was as good for any day's business as a good night's sleep—in one's own bed.

"Just give it a minute," Dunn said. "You'll understand once we get to talkin' things over. You're not going to believe what's been going on since you left."

"If it involves Scotch Jorgenson, I just might."

Dunn chuckled. "Even Scotch might surprise you. ...Listen, before the others come, there's something I want to talk with you about. I suppose it could wait, but I need to get it off my chest."

Concern shadowed Wesley's eyes. "Is something wrong?"

"No. It's just..." Dunn sighed, not wanting to say the words out loud. He'd thought them over in his head a hundred times, but saying them was another matter. "Wes, after the weddin', I'll come back here and take care of things until you and Jess get home. Take as much time as you want gettin' here."

"Thank you. I appreciate that—"

Dunn held up a hand to stop his brother. "When you come back...I'll be leavin'."

"What?" Confusion drew Wes forward in his seat. "Leavin'? Where are you goin'? Why? Why are you leavin'?"

"I don't know where yet. West, I suppose. I have no desire to go east, that's for sure. There's nothin' but dry grass that way."

"But why?"

"I feel this is what the Lord wants me to do. I've been prayin' about it for weeks. I never...I never had any thought of leaving. It never entered my mind until the night you told Jess about your trip. I saw the two of you up there on the hill, and as I watched, I just knew. The Lord made it very clear. He just said, 'Dunn, it's time for you to move on.' I don't know where or to what or why, but I intend to follow. He'll show the rest when the time comes." Dunn stopped, wincing at the pained expression in his brother's eyes.

"But, Dunn, we need you. You...you're...Are you sure about this?"

"Were you sure when you took that trip to Twin Pines in January?"

Wes nodded, knowing the simple act validated his brother's decision.

"I have to go, Wes. I don't know the details yet, but I have to go."

Wes leaned back in his seat. He let his elbow rest on the arm of the chair and chewed at the tip of his fingernail. He stared across the room, avoiding his brother's gaze. He blinked back tears. This wasn't what he'd expected to come home to. They were on the verge of truly putting their family together as it should be, and now Dunn was leaving?

"Don't tell Ma yet. I'll tell her when the time is right."

Wes nodded, still not looking at his brother. There had to be a way around this.

"Wes, I can see what you're thinkin'. Don't. I've prayed through every possible option. This is what God wants me to do, and you know as well as I do that means I need to do it."

Wes took a deep breath and leaned forward, rubbing his face with both hands and meeting his brother's gaze. "I don't like it. Not at all. But if you think that's what God wants you to do, I'll stand behind you. Just like you've stood behind me so many times."

Dunn sighed with relief. "Thank you, Wes. Thank you."

The door swung open and Cale strode into the room with the preacher close behind.

"Well, boys," the banker said. "Tomorrow we catch us an arsonist."

Chapter 60

"Everyone know where they're supposed to be?" Cale asked, looking up from his rough map. Fifteen men surrounded the Closes' table, most having ridden through the early morning darkness to gather at the ranch. The men nodded, but Ronald Gray's eyes revealed concern.

"Something troublin' you, Ron?"

"Well, it's just that...I'd like to know there's someone goin' with you boys what knows a little 'bout fightin' if it comes down to it. I didn't come all this way and finally get in a good place only to have these two shot down." He waved a hand at Wes and Dunn. "I wanna ride with you boys. These other fellas can handle the rest."

"All right. I'd be glad to have you along. Everyone else okay with that?"

Again, everyone nodded.

The preacher removed his hat and bowed his head. The room quieted. "Father," he prayed, "we don't want anyone to get hurt in all this. We ask for your protection and for sane heads. We pray that you would bring things to a peaceful end. In Jesus name, amen."

"Well, let's go," Cale resumed. "We should get there just as they're finishin' breakfast."

The men filed out of the ranch house to the row of horses waiting in front of the porch. They swung up into their saddles and broke off into three groups, each group slipping off into the early morning fog a few minutes apart. Wes, Dunn, Cale, Jason, and Gray made up the third group. They rode at a quick pace. No one spoke until they reached the end of Edelman's lane.

"Are we ready?" Cale asked.

The four men responded with sober nods.

"Then let's get this over with," he said.

They rode forward, five abreast. Cale pushed his horse ahead of the others as they approached the section of the lane that broadened out across the farmyard. He motioned for the men to spread out, hoping to block the entire width of the lane. He took a deep breath and was about to call to the house when the front door swung open.

Francis Edelman stepped out into the morning air, wiping crumbs from his face. He stopped at the sight of the men in his lane.

"Bennett? What brings you boys out here so early?"

"Morning, Frank. We need to talk to you and your men."

"I assume this is about the fire."

Cale nodded.

"Banton's already left the house. Might be in the barn. I'll call the others out." The man stepped back inside. A moment later he returned, followed by Bishop, Cantrell, and two other men. They stepped toward Cale and his men, but Cale raised a hand to stop them.

"You think Banton is in the barn? Why don't you call him out here? We need to talk to everyone."

"Banton!" Edelman waited, but no response came. "Banton! Get out here!""

"I'll be out in just a second, boss," came a muffled reply from the barn.

"What's this about, Bennett? We've got work to do."

Cale eyed the man with disapproval. "Frank, we've spent the last eight months tryin' to find out what happened here. I think you owe us a few minutes."

Edelman dropped his gaze. "Didn't mean to seem unappreciative."

"We've learned a lot about the fire over the last few weeks. As a result, we thought we should come out and talk it over with everyone."

"You think someone here started it?"

"Up to now, all the evidence has pointed to one person. Everyone here knew you owed Scotch money. A couple of your men suggested he did it, so you wouldn't have a place to graze your stock over the winter. Come spring, you wouldn't be able to make your payment again, and he could take your land."

"I've heard them talkin' that way, but that never made much sense to me. Well, not until the day he broke the water trench. That made me think he does whatever comes to mind to get even with people he don't like."

Cale shrugged. "That was dumb. I'll admit that. But don't forget he paid you back for the repairs. That seems odd for a man who's out to destroy you. Just the same, we found a few items where the fire started that made us stop and think. You already know about the wax from the candle that burned down into the kerosene."

Cale didn't miss the flinch from the yellow-haired Cantrell. He paused, his eyes narrowing as he scrutinized the man. "We also found a matchbox, a pretty little bronze box, that had the initials ABJ on the back. Now, all of us know that a long time ago Scotch used to talk about his wife Alma. With the A and the J there we all figured that pointed to Scotch. But when we talked to him about it, he told us his wife's middle name was Gene."

"Sure, but his wife's not around to verify that. He could make that up on the spot and nobody'd be the wiser."

"You're right. He could. But he didn't."

"How do you know?"

"We'll get to that. We found something else that pointed to Scotch, a piece of red leather. It was the same color as that ridiculous saddle of his. But when we asked him about it, Scotch told us he'd sold the saddle."

"Yes, and that seems like the thing to do if you're tryin' to hide something."

"Seems like it. But Scotch told us the saddle was in perfect condition when he sold it, and he told us who to see in Maiden about it. ...But the saddle wasn't the only thing he sold. He also sold his house, and he's in the process of gettin' the saloon off his hands. He was tryin' to decide what to do with the brothel, but someone set it on fire two nights ago."

"What?" Edelman and all four of his men stepped forward, staring back at Cale in surprise.

"The same man who started your fire started this one."

"How can you tell?"

"Because he was dumb enough to go about it the same way. Fortunately, no one was inside. The building is destroyed but no one was hurt. If there'd been any wind and if Mitch hadn't spotted it on his way home from the bank, the whole town might be gone. ...But I kept thinking why would a man who's so obviously fixin' to leave Grassdale want your property enough to burn part of it? He wouldn't be able to sell it with it damaged like that. So why would he want to harm it?"

Edelman, who'd listened with his arms crossed over his chest, let his hands fall to his hips. "You're right. That don't make much sense." He scrutinized his line of men for a moment and then turned back to Cale. "Go on."

"We found a gold coin out by the fire, but it wasn't a real gold coin. It was a new nickel, covered with a thin layer of gold."

"What?"

"It was a fake," Dunn said.

"Where'd it come from?"

Cale was once again eying the nervous Cantrell. "We couldn't seem to find a link to anyone. Then a gal who used to serve food at the saloon told us about a yellow-haired man that left her a gold coin—a gold nickel. A fake."

Every eye was on Cantrell. The young cowboy shrank back several steps into the shadows cast by the house. He waved his hands frantically. "I didn't have nothin' to do with no fire."

"Maybe. Maybe not, but I'll bet you've got a stash of gold nickels in your bunk. And that's enough to hold you until the judge comes, or until we can take you to a judge. Bishop, you'd best grab hold of him there to make sure he doesn't run while we're finishing things up here."

Bishop obeyed, stepping up beside the other man and taking a firm hold on his arm.

"So you're tellin' me I've got a counterfeiter on my ranch, who had nothing to do with the fire, and you're still not sure who started the fire?"

"Well now, not exactly. The preacher here went to Maiden. He found and inspected the saddle. It was in perfect condition. He also found Scotch's wife—whose middle name is Gene. Here's the thing. Someone found a red scrap of leather in the workbench in your barn. They also found a bottle of red dye. We matched the piece of leather to the one found at the fire. More to the point, however, the clerk at the Grassdale General Store sold a bottle of red leather dye—to Cantrell."

"What!" Edelman turned his full attention on Cantrell, his face growing red with anger.

"I'm tellin' you, boss," Cantrell defended, "I had nothin' to do with that fire."

"You bought the dye. You had the coins. If it wasn't you, then who was it?"

Wes cleared his throat. "You know, Frank, not to change the subject, but I've wondered for a while now how you go about hirin' your men. It made me wonder about this kid here. How'd you come to work here, Cantrell?"

Cantrell shrugged, not understanding how this could have any bearing on the issue at hand. "Banton hired me."

"And how did you meet him?"

"I met him in town at the saloon...playing poker."

"And what was in the pot?"

Cantrell's eyes grew wide with understanding. The fear in his gaze changed to hope as he spoke. "A gold nickel...Banton won! There was a fancy matchbox too. *And* it was Banton who sent me to town with a list right after I started working here."

"And what was on that list?" Wes continued.

"Red dye, candles, and thread. He had a hole in his pocket, and he made a point of telling me he'd just run out of candles and needed more. ...But why? Why would he?"

"That's what I was hoping, Mr. Edelman could tell us. Why would Banton want to get even with you, Frank?"

Edelman's face went red, the arteries in his neck bulged. "Because I'd had enough of his laziness. I told him as soon as we got the cattle moved to the winter pasture he was done. ...So I guess his answer was to destroy the winter pasture, create more work for us. Work he knew I'd need help doin'." The muscles in Edelman's jaw rippled with rage. He turned, stomping angrily toward the barn.

But Banton had been listening. A flash of motion and the thunder of hooves stopped Edelman. Banton and his horse flew out of the barn. The foreman yelled, whirling a rope above his head to startle the other horses as he spurred his own horse into a run.

Gray was the first to follow after the renegade. He urged his horse forward, reaching a gallop as they came to the end of the lane and turned east down the road, away from town. He could hear the other horses behind him, but he dared not look back. They would manage their own riding and progress. He must focus on Banton.

They rounded a bend and came to a straightaway. Banton discarded the rope, hurling it into the grass along the road. His next movement sent chills down Gray's spine.

"He's got a pistol!" Gray yelled, instinctively ducking as the first shot split the air. He heard the bullet whiz by and ricochet off a rock.

Gray straightened in his saddle, but Banton had turned toward them to shoot again. The pistol came up. Then Banton's horse stumbled, breaking stride and forcing the man to save his balance.

A blind curve lay less than fifty feet away. They had to make that curve, Gray knew. He saw the pistol coming up again, but this time he didn't duck. Instead, his own pistol came up. He shot, aiming high above Banton's head.

Banton, seeing Gray draw the gun, hunkered down around his horse's neck. He turned to see the road ahead of him. Just beyond that bend was a stream. A few feet beyond the point where the stream intersected with the road, an animal trail led off into the wooded mountain slopes. If he could make that trail, he'd be a free man.

He spurred his horse, hoping to get a little more from the animal. Just thirty more feet. He glanced back. Gray was closing in. Twenty more feet. If he could just get there before Gray caught him. Ten more feet. He was safe. The other man was too far back to catch him now.

Banton's horse rounded the corner and then skidded to a stop, rearing on his hind legs. He sidestepped, screaming in terror as a volley of gunshots exploded above them. The animal danced backward, then sideways, then forwards, then sideways again, terrified at the unexpected noise and the emotion he sensed from his master.

"Don't move, Banton!" Henry Tiedemann growled. "You've gone far enough. You've done enough damage. Throw your gun down. You're outnumbered, and we're all armed."

Banton stared, wild-eyed and panting. Before him, Tiedemann, Zane, the redheaded Amos from the Crescent Creek, and two men from Tiedemann's ranch sat their horses, each with a rifle leveled at him. He'd barely taken stock of the men before him when his pursuers thundered around the corner and pulled their mounts to a stop behind him.

Dust and tension hung thick in the humid morning air. The horses huffed and snorted, pawing anxiously at the ground. Banton's head jerked around as his gaze shot from one line of men to the other. He pointed his pistol first to one side then the other. His mind raced, drowning out the silence of the ten men surrounding him.

Ronald Gray nudged his horse in closer, pistol still drawn and trained on the man before him. "I've already shot at you once," he growled. "I intended to miss. Next time, it'll be your horse. If that doesn't get it, it'll have to be you. Now throw your gun down."

Banton obeyed, watching as Zane dismounted and went to retrieve the pistol.

"Get off your horse," Gray continued, his eyes narrowing into an intense glower.

Banton didn't move. He gawked at Gray, terrified by what the man might do at even the slightest movement.

"Banton." Gray's voice was low and dangerous. "You just about killed one of the best men I've ever known. It's your fault this town lost its church and its school and that Anna Close lost her home. I don't think it's time for you to start makin' up your own rules in this game. Get. Off. Your. Horse."

The hammer came back on the pistol, and Banton raised his hands.

"I'm gettin' down," he insisted fretfully. He swung his leg over the horse and slid to the ground, growling and cursing under his breath. "Bishop. Shoulda made sure that horse —"

"What's that?" Gray said with a scowl.

"Nothin'."

But Gray had heard every word. He glared at the miserable coward before him. "You tried to kill that boy, didn't you? You spooked that horse."

"Didn't try to kill nobody. Weren't nobody s'posed to get hurt."

"But you *did* spook the horse," Wes demanded.

Banton glared back, unwilling to confess.

"Zane," Wes continued. "Grab that rope Tiedemann's got for you, and tie him up. Amos, you get hold of his horse before he runs off."

"What are you gonna do with me?" Banton whined.

"We ought to hang ya on the nearest tree," Gray muttered.

Cale nudged his horse closer. "There's a shack behind the hotel. Maybe you've seen it. It's just large enough for a straw tick. Scotch is in town with some of the men right now turning it into quite the little jail. You'll stay there until the judge comes, or until we can get you over to Fort Maginnis. Don't worry. We'll feed you."

"But..."

"But what?" Gray said, with an impatient roll of the eyes.

"But it's still cold at night. That shack don't have no stove."

Gray shrugged. "That's your problem."

Cale shook his head, rolling his eyes at Gray's disagreeable comportment. "You'll have blankets," the banker said. "But don't expect any special attention. You brought this on yourself. And don't get any bright ideas either. You'll be guarded round the clock. Any trouble and we'll make sure Mr. Gray is your escort to Fort Maginnis."

A wry smile slid across Gray's face. A hint of a pleasure crept into his eyes. "I think I'd like that. Zane, get back on your horse, and hold onto that rope."

Confusion crossed Banton's face. "But, I don't understand. How am I supposed to get back on my horse if he don't help me up?"

"Now, why would I tell you to get off your horse only to put you back on it? That don't make sense. We've all seen you can ride. There's no sense in takin' chances. Start walkin'. The way I figure it, we should be to town by lunchtime...our lunchtime...and maybe yours."

Chapter 61

Cassandra Parker sat at the table in the large dining room. She stared at the group of people around her. Cale and Susan Bennett, Wesley Close, Duncan Roe, Anna Close, and the Preacher were all there.

"But..." she faltered, her mind reeling from everything they had just told her. "But I know nothing of running a hotel, the kitchen maybe, but an entire hotel?"

Cale chuckled. "That's why we want to help you. Miss Parker, you've overcome amazing odds in your life. We, all of us, believe this might be the second chance you've been lookin' for. The bank bought the hotel outright from Scotch, but the goal is to see it become fully yours. In the process, we'll be here to help, and we'll probably be learning just as much as you. Scotch is even willing to help for a time. We'll help you get accustomed to hirin' good help, takin' care of the finances, whatever needs to be done. That's something you won't have if you try to start over somewhere else."

He paused, weighing his words. "Originally, there were to be two of you. But the other woman wanted nothing to do with changin' the course her life was takin'. She left on yesterday's stagecoach. That means you have this entire group of people here to stand behind you. We don't want to force you into it, and if you say no, we'll understand. We just want to help."

"But...no one has ever wanted to help me before. Why would you want to?"

"Miss Parker, after we talked at the bank that day, all I could think of was my own daughter. What would happen to her if my wife and I were suddenly gone? Would someone take care of her, or would she be left alone? When you told me of your refusal to do anything in the saloons but cook and clean, I was skeptical. But Scotch confirmed it.

"You show a determination to be who you were raised to be, to be who you ought to be despite your circumstances. But there's more than that. I knew if it was my daughter in your place, I'd want someone to help. If they didn't, I'd be angry. I realized I'd be angry because I knew that would be what God expected them to do. It would be, as they say, the Christian thing to do because of the love God has poured out on all of us. I just want to obey Him, Miss Parker. The offer stands for however long you need to think about it, no strings attached."

Cassandra looked around the table. Tears rose in her eyes. She felt the motherly touch of Anna's hand going around her own. No one had touched her in that way for years. No one had cared for her, and now here they were, all of them, offering themselves as her own new family. She smiled and a tear rolled down her cheek.

"I don't have to think about it, Mr. Bennett. I already know. If you and Grassdale are willing to have me, then I am more than willing to stay. I don't promise that I'll get things right the first time, but I'll do my best to make it work."

Everyone around her smiled. The banker leaned back in his seat, satisfied with where the whole undesired brouhaha surrounding the fire had led them. If it had all been for this one moment, he'd do it again and again.

Chapter 62

Marc laughed as Wes picked up his coffee and swallowed back the last of it. "Sounds like Gray had that man scared half out of his skin."

"Oh, he was scared all right. I think he really thought we were going to make him freeze in that shack."

"So how did it all turn out?"

Wes leaned forward, resting his arms on the Bennett's table and turning his cup in his hands. He was relieved at the curiosity and light in Marc's eyes. Over the previous two days, that light had been rare. "The marshal and the circuit judge came through about three weeks ago. The trials went fast. We had so much evidence against both Banton and Cantrell that the juries came to a quick decision. Banton finally confessed to the marshal that he set the fire in the brothel."

"Why? That part makes no sense to me."

"Seems he figured out Scotch was closing it. He knew someone had found the dye and the leather. He'd done everything he could to point things either to Scotch or Cantrell, but he was still afraid we'd see it was him. So he wagered if the brothel caught fire, everyone's attention would be back on Scotch. It didn't make sense really, but he was desperate. Both men were taken to Fort Maginnis. They'll go on to prison from there. I think it's worked out as it should." He paused for a moment, but then a smile shot across his face. "Edelman has a new foreman."

"Oh? Who?"

"Brandon Bishop. Couldn't have made a better choice."

Marcus laughed once more, scooting his chair back from the table. "I'd say things really did work out the way they should have. ...Well, I've got work to do. Care to join me?"

"Sure. What did you have in mind?"

"I've got a field at the base of the butte out behind the barn a ways that just isn't producin'. It needs some attention."

"All right. I'll do whatever you want me to do."

Marc grinned. "Are you sure about that?"

A shadow of suspicion came over Wesley's eyes. "I was until you said that."

Marc stood from his usual seat at the foot of the table and reached to take his hat down from the peg near the door. "I'm just messin' with you."

"Would one of you mind hangin' around for a minute?" Cynthia said from the kitchen.

Wesley turned to face her. "Did you need something?"

"I'm almost done with this washin'. It's dreadful. Timothy was a mess when he woke up this mornin'. There's no way I can use this water again. Would you mind takin' the tub out and dumpin' it when I'm done?"

"Of course, I'll do that. Do you need me to haul more water in to re-place it?"

"No. No, I need a break for a while. It's about time to start workin' on other things anyway."

Marcus watched the interaction between his mother and Wesley. It pleased him. Wes fit in with the rest of the family as if he'd always been a part of it. Dunn, Anna, and Travis were proving to be good additions as well.

He had to admit that he envied, even if just the tiniest bit, the happi-ness he saw in his brother-in-law to be. For years, Papa had been en-couraging Marc to find a wife and settle down. But Marc never saw a need to hurry. Jon and Hannah had married while still in the east. There had been no courtship or engagement to observe. Joe had died before Jess and her parents had settled the matter of the engagement. But now, he saw his sister's happiness and the sheer joy that followed Wes around everywhere he went. It made Marcus think that maybe, someday, he might be more interested in marrying than he'd thought. Now was simp-ly not the time.

"I'll let you two take care of that. I'm going to head down to the barn and grab a few things that we'll need out there."

"All right. I'll come down as soon as we're finished."

Wesley stepped out the back door and headed for the patch of dry earth where Cynthia had told him to empty the washtub. As he went, he could hear voices coming from around the front of the house. He lis-tened.

"What are you up to, Marc?" Jess asked.

"Oh, Wes and I are going to see what we can do with that field by the butte."

"Is something wrong with it?" Millicent asked.

"Can't seem to get anything to grow. I think the ground needs to be broken up a bit more. I've noticed water standin' after the rains. I don't think it's able to soak down in. If that's the case, the roots probably aren't gettin' in deep enough either. So they're either fryin' under the sun or drownin' in the rain. Got all that land, but as long as it's in that shape this garden will produce a hundred times more than that field."

"So you're going to break it?" Gretel asked. "How do you break it?"

Marc chuckled. "We're going to break up the dirt. We'll probably plow it and mix some good things into it that will make the soil better."

"Are you going to put stuff in there from the stinky pile?"

This time, even Wesley was laughing.

"No," Marc replied, "I'm going to let Wes do that."

"Oh, Marcus, you're terrible." But Wes could hear the laughter in Jessica's voice. She was enjoying being with her family, as was he, and that made him ever so happy.

"May I come with you?" Gretel asked.

"No. We'll be a long ways from the house. It'll be better for you to stay here."

"You can help us," Millicent suggested.

"What are you doing?"

"We're gathering rocks to edge your Mama's garden."

"Where are you gettin' them?" Marc said.

"I noticed you'd picked quite a few large rocks out of the field," Jess said, pointing toward the west field. "I thought we'd start with those."

"I'll tell you what. If you put what you want in a stack, I'll have Jake wheel them up to the garden for you."

"That would be wonderful. Thank you."

"Well, I'd better get goin'. Send Wes down to the barn when Ma's done with him."

Wes dumped the water as the conversation lulled. He'd just started back across the lawn to the back of the house when he heard Millicent's voice once more.

"Jess, is anything the matter?"

"Hmm? Oh, I was just thinkin' about something Marc said."

"What?"

"About that field, how big it is and how little it's producing. I was thinkin' about how the field and the garden are like people. Like me and Marc for instance."

"What do you mean?"

"Well, think about it. Like that field, I've had so much opportunity for growth. I've had an education, experience, so many people have poured themselves into my life. But when it came to being fruitful and living my life for God...I let my field lay barren.

"Marc, on the other hand, has never finished school. He hasn't traveled any further than he has to go for a cattle auction for I don't know how many years. And yet every day, he takes that little plot of land that God has given him and he tends it. He weeds out the things that shouldn't be there. He adds stuff from the stinky pile until his modest garden produces a hundred times more fruit than my field."

She sighed. "Millie, I want that in my life. I don't ever want to go back to being that barren field, but I have so much cultivating to do."

Wes considered her words. He saw things differently, quite differently. He heard the sound of soft footsteps on the grass and knew that Millicent had gone to Jessica's side.

"Jess, as long as you're letting God work in your heart, you have nothing to worry about. It's His work. He knows how to tend the soil. We just have to be willing—surrendered—to let Him do it, and to let Him show us our part through His Word. That's what He means when He says, *'I am the vine, ye are the branches: he that abideth in me, and I in him, the same bringeth forth much fruit: for without me ye can do nothing.'*...God has something special in mind for you, my friend. I think it has to do with helping men like Ronald Gray and women like Miss Parker. Your field has already begun to spring up, and it's beginning to bear fruit."

Wesley smiled. Now *there* was something he could agree with.

* * *

The week passed quickly. Soon, Jessica found herself standing at the front of the church, hanging a braid of flowers and prairie grass across the teacher's desk. She couldn't help but think of all that had transpired here: her classes with her students, her brother sneaking in and scaring her half to death. Joe had proposed here. Marc had argued with her here, as had Jon. But that had all been put behind them. They had gone to church here together. They had found strength here after Papa died.

As the sun was beginning to sink low in the sky, Jess heard footsteps at the back of the room. She turned to see Wesley striding toward her, a small bouquet of pink roses in his hand. She smiled as he reached her.

"What are you doing here?" she asked.

"They say it's bad luck to see the bride before the wedding on the wedding day, so I came today."

Jessica laughed. "Somehow, I don't think there's any way we'll avoid seeing one another before the wedding. The church service comes first, remember?"

"Yes. ...I'm ashamed to admit that I hope it's a short sermon. I brought you something." He held out the roses and allowed her to take them gently from his hand.

"They're beautiful. Where did you get them?"

"They were growin' along the road. They made me think of you. Jess, I need to confess something to you."

"You do?"

"Yes. I did some eavesdroppin' the other day. Your ma sent me on an errand, and I overheard a conversation you had with Millicent about a garden and a field."

Jess blushed.

"I wanted you to see a different perspective, Jess, I mean... Everything you said, it's a wonderful lesson for all of us. Something we should always keep in mind, but that's not the way I see you. I don't see you as that barren field. Millie was right. There's fruit in your field. ...I once met an old man. I believe he was Cheyenne. We were talkin' about the land and the things that grow well. He told me something I've never forgotten. Did you know, Jess, that sagebrush is almost impossible to kill?"

She laughed. "That would explain why it's everywhere."

"Yes! Exactly. That man told me that fire is just about the only thing that will kill it. But even after a fire, silver sagebrush will grow back. It may even grow back stronger. It grows back, and it will bloom again.

"That's what I see when I look at you, Jess. Maybe your field did sit barren for a while, but you let God's chastening fire do the work that needed to be done—so you could bloom again. And with you, there was no waitin'. The blossoms have already come."

Jessica smiled, but she could not speak. A tear slipped down her cheek, and he caught it with his finger, wiping it away.

"I love you," he whispered.

❊ ❊ ❊

Marc waited at the foot of the stairs leading into the church. He tugged at the hem of his suit jacket and straightened the ridiculous ribbon under his collar.

"Suits you better than pink flowers."

Marc looked up to see his older brother striding toward him across the barren churchyard. Marc was beginning to realize he would never live down the pink calico bandages Jon had used after the barn accident the previous year. Or maybe it was his own response to the pink roses dancing around his head that he wouldn't live down. Marc rolled his eyes and groaned.

"Well, I didn't have any more choice in this than I did in that."

Jon laughed and slapped his brother's shoulder. "Mary says they're just about ready."

"It's about time. If I were Wes, I'd be — " But whatever Marc would have been was never to be learned for, at that moment, Jess stepped out of the tent that had been arranged for the ladies' dressing needs. She was beautiful. He'd always thought all of his sisters were beautiful, but today, Jess was especially beautiful. He couldn't help the grin that spread from one ear to the other. He felt a little swelling of pride in his chest as she returned his smile and moved toward them.

"How do I look?" she said as she reached them.

Jon stooped to kiss her cheek and Marc followed suit.

"You look wonderful, Jess," Jon replied. "Papa would be so proud of you today. So proud."

Marc's chest tightened. Papa. He would be proud. He would have looped his arm through hers and marched her into that church with as much gusto as his feeble frame could muster. He would have given her away with a tremble of sadness in his voice, a glint of joy in his eyes, and a tear on his cheek. He would have kissed his daughter's hand, placed it into the hand of her groom, and whispered, "Take care of my little girl." Papa would've been proud.

But Papa wasn't there. Marc forced back the emotions that threatened to overwhelm him, realizing the others were doing the same. He was glad Jon was there. They would fill Papa's shoes together. He wasn't sure he could've done it on his own. He was proud for the honor

363

to stand in Papa's place, but the hole in his heart throbbed with every breath.

Marc realized Jess was speaking and forced his attention back to the moment.

"Papa would be proud of both of you," she said. "Not just would be, but was. He was so proud of both of you. Thank you for being here."

"Ha, you think we'd miss it?" Jon scoffed. "Not only would we never miss it ourselves but if we tried Ma would have our hides."

Jessica laughed. "Not to mention Anna. I've seen a whole new side of her this week. I always knew she was feisty, but I don't think I've ever seen so much energy out of one tiny woman. Except perhaps Mrs. Vass. Is she here?"

"Mrs. Vass? Of course she is!" Jon replied. "She wouldn't have missed it. She'll want to have a first-hand account to share with everyone who comes for tea and cake."

Jessica laughed again, knowing there was more than a measure of truth to her brother's jesting.

Marc smiled dully and a moment later felt his brother's strong hand come to rest on his shoulder. At the same time, he saw the big doctor take Jessica's hand.

"There's one thing I'm certain Papa would do right now," Jon said. "He'd pray. I think we should do the same."

Marc nodded, reaching for his sister's bouquet with one hand and taking her hand with the other. His foggy brain ran most of Jon's words together. Still, a sense of peace fell over him so that, as they turned toward the church a moment later, he could draw a deep breath and smile.

Wesley stood at the front of the church. Preacher Nausbaum stood to his right and Dunn to his left. His gaze dropped from the back of the church to his mother who sat on the front row. Cynthia sat quietly beside her. Anna smiled at him with joy. Cynthia did the same, though her smile was weak. She was missing her husband. He could see it in her eyes. And why wouldn't she? Of all days, this was a day when his absence would be felt keenly.

On an impulse, he stepped forward and embraced Cynthia. He kissed her cheek and embraced her again. "Thank you," he whispered, "thank you for being willing to do this now. I know it isn't easy."

He felt her grip tighten on his arms as she whispered back, "Thank you for lovin' my daughter the way you do."

He stepped back, smiling at both women again. A sound at the back of the room caught his attention, and he looked up to see Jessica standing between her two eldest brothers. There was no fanfare. No elaborate gown. But she was beautiful. She wore a simple light green dress with delicate white lace around the neckline. She had never worn it before, but she would wear it again. Her auburn hair was pulled softly away from her face, revealing the happy glow that had come into her cheeks and brilliant eyes. She smiled at him as her brothers looped their arms through hers and led her toward the front of the room.

He noticed the small bouquet she carried. His roses. And to them, she had added just a few sprigs of silver sage. He smiled and let his gaze drift back up to hers. He had waited for this moment for months. But now he realized this wasn't the moment he had been waiting for, it was all the moments that waited beyond this.

The service droned in Wesley's head. He spoke when he was told to speak. He listened when he was supposed to listen. But he was happiest when everyone had left the building and begun making their way across the prairie to the Bennett's home, where the evening would be spent with games, food and as much fellowship as any of them could handle.

As the last person stepped out of the church and into the spring air, Wesley stopped his bride from following. He took her gently by the shoulders and studied her happy face once more. He fingered the sage in the bouquet she still carried, pleased that his words had touched her heart. His eyes returned to her face, finding peace there. She was beautiful, perhaps more so today than any day he had known her so far. And best of all she loved him. She loved him as much as he loved her. He kissed her. Then he took her by the hand and led her out of the church into their new life together.

Author's Note

Roses at Sunset is, by far, the most difficult book I have ever written. The original drafts, created more than twenty years ago, contained only the storylines of the Bennett and Close families. The mystery of who started the wildfire wasn't a part of the plot. As the published series developed, the material remaining after *Field of Ashes* was too little to stand alone. The original story had to merge seamlessly with the new wildfire storyline and characters to create a complete book.

But this wasn't the most difficult aspect. From the very beginning, Jonathan's story would always end here. Two years before publishing *Winter's Prey*, I learned what it is to lose a father. The story took on new meaning and depth. Chapters fifty-seven and fifty-eight of *Roses at Sunset* were not part of the original drafts. They were written in the dark of night with tears streaming down my cheeks as I sorted my own grief. They flowed from the experiences surrounding the loss of my father. What you read there is almost word for word what was written that night.

I never expected Jonathan's story to so mirror our own as far as dates and seasons. Nor was it my intention to release the book on the anniversary of Dad's home going. But, if our schedule holds, it appears that will happen. I know this is not a coincidence but has been allowed by the hand of my Savior—not for my hurt but for my healing. Perhaps this is the best way to express my gratitude to the God of Comfort and to honor the man whose humble life left such an impact on so many.

Scripture Used in Roses at Sunset

Chapter 16

"Take therefore no thought for the morrow: for the morrow shall take thought for the things of itself. Sufficient unto the day *is* the evil thereof." Matthew 6:34

Chapter 29

"Thou wilt keep *him* in perfect peace, *whose* mind *is* stayed *on thee*: because he trusteth in thee. Trust ye in the LORD for ever: for in the LORD JEHOVAH *is* everlasting strength:" Isaiah 26:3,4

Chapter 39

"What time I am afraid, I will trust in thee." Psalm 56:3

Chapter 56

"Except the LORD build the house, they labour in vain that build it: except the LORD keep the city, the watchman waketh *but* in vain. *It is* vain for you to rise up early, to sit up late, to eat the bread of sorrows: *for* so he giveth his beloved sleep. Lo, children *are* an heritage of the LORD: *and* the fruit of the womb *is his* reward. As arrows *are* in the hand of a mighty man; so *are* children of the youth. Happy *is* the man that hath his quiver full of them: they shall not be ashamed, but they shall speak with the enemies in the gate." Psalm 127

Chapter 58

"Blessed *are* they that mourn: for they shall be comforted." Matthew 5:4

"I will not leave you comfortless: I will come to you." John 14:18

"So when this corruptible shall have put on incorruption, and this mortal shall have put on immortality, then shall be brought to pass the saying that is written, Death is swallowed up in victory." 1 Corinthians 15:54

Chapter 62

"I am the vine, ye *are* the branches: He that abideth in me, and I in him, the same bringeth forth much fruit: for without me ye can do nothing." John 15:5

About The Author

Rachel Miller has been involved in children's and ladies' ministries for two decades, and has had the joy of serving both in her hometown of Billings, MT as well as in various countries around the world. She is the executive director of Forbid Them Not Ministries, which works with orphans, single moms, and those walking alongside of them. Rachel is also the proud aunt of 10 nieces and nephews and slightly addicted to life in Montana. Connect with Rachel, her books, and ministry at the links below:

Books and Blogs:

Facebook: https://www.facebook.com/rmillerwriter/

https://www.facebook.com/TheKingsDaughterBook/

Blogs: http://www.rachelmillerwriter.com/

https://barrenfieldsfruitfulgardens.wordpress.com/

Forbid Them Not Ministries:

Website: http://www.forbidthemnot.com/

Blog: https://forbidthemnot.wordpress.com/

Facebook:

https://www.facebook.com/forbidthemnot/

Twitter: @forbidthemnot

Other Books By Rachel Miller:

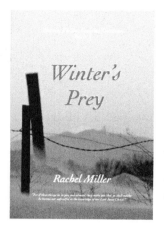

Winter's Prey (Barren Fields, Fruitful Gardens, Book 1) - When the cruel elements of the Montana Territory inflict tragedy on the Bennett family, life is forever changed. Jess is certain the answer to her pain lies in starting over. Her brother Marc is determined to stay true to what he has always known.

Amidst the constant battle for survival and the conflict in their hearts, both siblings stand at the threshold of surrender to God. What will they choose?

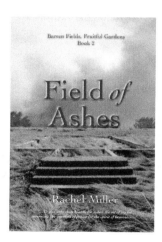

Field of Ashes (Barren Fields, Fruitful Gardens, Book 2) - After losing her fiancé to the wild elements of the Montana Territory, Jessica Bennett is sure the key to her happiness is in leaving Twin Pines. But from the moment she steps foot in the untamed, cowtown of Grassdale, Jess discovers a whole new world of challenges: An unruly superintendent, a ramshackle school, drunken cowboys, and a letter from home that changes everything. When the hidden wounds of her heart are discovered, will one man's secret past hold the key to her healing?

Easy has never been the path Marcus Bennett sought, but as summer unfolds he comes face to face with the one struggle he has avoided for years. When life takes an unexpected turn, he finds himself torn between his responsibilities, his love for his family, and the promptings of his heart. Would God really ask him to abandon his home and family?

This sequel to *Winter's Prey* explores the beauty of God's amazing grace and astounding love, the freedom of surrender, and the hope of experience, though faith be tried by fire.

The King's Daughter: A Story of Redemption (Bible Study) - Abandoned. Left to die. Rescued. Redeemed. …Adoption. Betrayal. Unfailing love… *The King's Daughter: A Story of Redemption* traces one of the most beautiful love stories of all time. This collection of short Bible studies searches out the life of the King's Daughter, a familiar figure of Psalm 45. Though often lifted up as an example to Christian women, her full story is rarely told. Has she always been the most beautiful ornament in the King's throne room? Will she remain so? Will she turn her back on the One who loved her more than any other, or will she let Him be as a bundle of myrrh about her neck? From a field to a palace, from disgrace to glory, from shame to restoration: her story reveals not only the magnitude of our redemption but also the chastening hand of a loving Father and the beauty of His everlasting covenant.

In All Thy Ways (Devotional Journal) - Some journals will feed you, find verses for you, and even pray for you — What's left for you to do? God wants us to dig into His Word for ourselves. *"In All Thy Ways"* offers eight weeks of journaling pages, each designed to help you dig deeper into Scripture. It asks simple questions that bring depth to your daily Bible reading and application to life. It also provides room for word studies, prayer, praise, and for recording God's working in and through you. Don't let someone else chew your food for you. Dig in, and dig deep!

In All Thy Ways: Walking in His Promises (Devotional Journal) - Has your world spun out of control? Are you looking for something to grab onto — something that never moves, never changes? Are you looking for hope as you seek direction, or the strength simply to survive? God's promises offer unfading light in the darkness. The *Walking In His Promises Journal* presents the opportunity to step out of the storm and into the safety of His presence. Like its predecessor, the journal provides eight weeks of journaling pages — 56 verses of promise and assurance. Enter the world into which those promises were spoken through contextual readings, cross-referencing, prayer, praise, and simple questions designed to bring depth to your study and application to your life. Don't remain unanchored in a world spinning out of control. Take hold of His promises and rejoice as you record His unfolding plans for you.

Made in the USA
Middletown, DE
14 October 2021